...vrence lives on a farm in Anglesey with ...sity lecturer husband, assorted pets who ...s strays and never left, and sometimes one or ...er boomerang sons. When she's not writing ...es to be outdoors gardening, or walking on ... the beaches for which the island is famous— ...ng with being the place where Prince William and ...atherine made their first home!

...hantelle Shaw lives on the Kent coast and thinks up ...r stories while walking on the beach. She has been ...rried for over thirty years and has six children. Her ...ve affair with reading and writing Mills & Boon ...ories began as a teenager, and her first book was ...blished in 2006. She likes strong-willed, slightly ...usual characters. Chantelle also loves gardening, ...lking and wine!

CLAIMING HIS UNKNOWN SON

KIM LAWRENCE

HER WEDDING NIGHT NEGOTIATION

CHANTELLE SHAW

MILLS & BOON

CLAIMING HIS UNKNOWN SON

KIM LAWRENCE

CHAPTER ONE

'No!'

The Madrigal Hotel's assistant manager was a consummate professional accustomed to the idiosyncrasies of the rich and famous so his practised smile stayed painted in place, despite the sudden outburst from the woman in front of him. He was rarely surprised, but at that moment, as he braced himself for a diva meltdown, he was.

He prided himself on being able to tell at first glance which of their VIP guests were going to be hard work, but he hadn't had this beautiful guest down as one of the awkward ones.

First impressions had certainly not given him any clues, as up to this point she had lived up to her public image. Her arrival had been low-key, as befitting the rarity she was said to be, someone not in the business of promoting *herself*, just good causes. People spoke about how freely she gave of her time and energy and her dedication in continuing to support the charities that she said were her late husband's legacy.

The rare unfriendly pieces that appeared in the media he had always attributed to the hack's frustration in not being able to find a story. You could see it from their point of view—they were used to being invited into the homes of the rich and famous, and Marisa Rayner never even gave them a glimpse behind closed doors.

There was still no meltdown forthcoming, but what was happening was even more alarming than a hissy fit. She hadn't moved a muscle; she was just standing there like a pale frozen statue. What if she was ill?

He experienced a sudden flurry of panic as the question entered his thoughts, realising that would also explain the other-worldly, almost unfocused expression in her wide amber eyes when she'd removed her fashionable shades earlier, as he'd walked beside her through the hotel's famous art deco doors. At the time he had put her pallor down to the lights from the glittering chandeliers overhead.

An ill guest was never good, but then he reasoned nobody who felt really ill would make such an effort to smile at all the staff she had encountered. At least, she had up until now.

The friendly, genuinely warm smile that charmed everyone it was aimed at was now totally absent as she stood on the threshold of one of their premiere suites looking as if she had seen a ghost.

He gave a philosophical shrug and waited. The Madrigal's reputation had been built in part on the hotel's ability to satisfy the most difficult of guests, especially when they had the money to pay the exorbitant prices the Madrigal charged for their premier luxury suites, and the lovely Marisa Rayner was one guest who could certainly afford it.

The fact she had been the sole beneficiary of her husband's considerable estate after his death made her a natural target of envy. The story of the rich older man married to a very much younger woman was a magnet for the scandal-loving red tops. She could have gone through her life with a 'gold-digger' label attached to her, but the forensic dirt-digging exercises had come up empty-handed and she was considered a scandal-free zone—aside from a little guilt by association. But even her dead father, with his colourful history of affairs and a taste for high-stakes gambling, was nothing in this day and age.

No young lovers pre-or post-marriage—just a few malicious suggestions, which was par for the course, but they had faded away too after she had not morphed as predicted into a 'merry widow', but had remained a dedicated, hard-working one devoted to charitable works.

The adjective mostly attached to her name was *classy* and for once, he decided, the press had it right.

If she had any skeletons in her closet they were deeply hidden.

'Do you have another room?' Marisa heard the quiver in her voice that stopped *just* the right side of hysteria, and bit down on her full lower lip while buying time to regain her composure by making a meal of smoothing back non-existent loose strands of shiny silver-blonde hair that was safely secured in a smooth simple knot on the nape of her swanlike neck.

She knew she had to pull herself together, but unfortunately *knowing* that was no help right now.

'Another room? This is one of our—'

'Sorry, yes, this is marvellous,' she gushed. 'But… something…on a lower floor, perhaps? I… I don't have a very good head for heights.'

'Of course, if you'll just bear with me for a moment.' The man pulled out a slim tablet and began to scroll through it.

Get a grip, Marisa, she told herself fiercely, if for no other reason than this poor man who was only doing his job looked as if he wanted to run for the hills—and who could blame him? *Scared of heights?* She was beyond feeling embarrassed, no doubt that would come later when she revisited this moment—*in her nightmares!*

The gut-freezing panic had hit her the moment the taxi drew up outside the hotel. The signage on the well-known art deco frontage was ultra-discreet—it didn't need to be flashy; everyone knew the iconic façade of the Madrigal—but to Marisa those letters had seemed to be written in neon and came accompanied by a loud soundtrack of guilt and shame. She still couldn't remember how she had got out of the taxi, as the sheer horror of the moment had blanked her brain completely.

Of course it ought not to have been a shock, *wouldn't* have if she'd been paying attention. Her delicate dark blonde brows drew together in a straight line above her heavily lashed amber eyes. Even distracted, she had managed to hide her disappointment when her assistant, Jennie, had triumphantly announced that she'd managed the impossible and secured an alternative last-minute venue after their original booking at a country-house hotel had fallen through.

She could remember Jennie mentioning the prestige of the alternative venue, she *had* to have mentioned the name, but Marisa's mind had been elsewhere and she hadn't registered it. No, because she'd been too busy torturing herself with every possible, and highly improbable, disaster that could occur in her absence.

Her glance darted around the room, reached the slightly open bedroom door and retracted hastily, focusing instead on her feet clad in leg-elongating nude court shoes that added four inches to her willowy five feet ten inches.

She brought her lashes down in a protective sweep over eyes that continued to be drawn to that open door, her mouth twisted in frustration as she acknowledged all the missed opportunities that would have at least given her time, if not to avoid this moment, then to at the very least prepare herself for it.

Even as late as getting in the taxi would have been something, she thought, considering another missed opportunity. Jennie had waited until she was in the cab before they'd parted company, her PA heading towards the Tube to spend some well-deserved time off with her family. Jennie *had* to have given the driver the address of the hotel, but again Marisa's thoughts had been elsewhere.

Where was a convenient icy shiver of premonition when a girl needed one?

Up to the point the taxi had pulled in, she hadn't even glanced out of the window. Instead, she had spent the journey from the station scrolling through some emails and checking in with Jamie's nanny, Ashley, who had responded to her anxious questions with cheery positivity and a series of soothing photos of Marisa's four-and-a-half-year-old clearly having the time of his life at junior soccer practice.

It wasn't that she doubted Ashley's competence, but this was the first time she had left Jamie since he'd been given the all-clear by the doctors.

Up to this point, any trip away from home had deliberately *not* included an overnight stay, or if it had, she had taken Jamie with her. This was a big step for her, though less so, it seemed, for Jamie, who had been too busy playing with a new computer game to do more than give her a casual wave before he got back to his screen.

On one level she knew that he was fine, he was safe, and she knew her fear had no basis in logic but, as she had already discovered, it wasn't always about logic. When you had lived with fear this long it was something that

was hard to let go of. For so long she had been afraid of
losing her precious son and— She took a deep breath and
deliberately dampened the panic she could feel rising. No,
she told herself, repeating the phrase like a mantra, she
was *not* going to lose him, because he was healthy now.

Her son was a survivor, one of the lucky ones, and he
had made a complete recovery. Despite the fact he was
noticeably smaller and more delicate-looking than his
contemporaries, Jamie was, so the medics told her, as
fit and robust as any other four-year-old and would soon
catch up developmentally.

The assistant manager cleared his throat and lowered
his tablet. 'We do have an alternative room although it
is not as—'

'That's tremendous, thank you so much. I'll take it.'

Reaching for her sunglasses, she slid them on her
small straight nose, hiding behind the tinted glass as
she dredged deep to produce a faint smile.

'Right then, if you can give me a few moments I will
make the necessary arrangements. The room is on the
second floor—will that do?'

'That's fine. It's just the balcony up here that bothers
me.' She stopped, well aware that the balcony she spoke
of was not actually visible from where they stood.

'I understand totally.'

Luckily for her he didn't.

'I will be back momentarily.' He held out a straight-
backed chair situated by a small table and after a pause
she took it.

'Can I get you anything?'

She made an inarticulate sound in her throat and
vaguely registered the sound of the door closing, the
images floating in her head exerting a tug she couldn't
resist.

She was standing on the balcony that she knew existed behind the heavy curtains in the bedroom. It was night, as dark outside as a city ever got, and she was staring down at the shining lights, the glistening moisture on the rain-soaked pavements, when she felt the quivering downy hair rise on her skin a second before the back of her neck started to tingle—she was no longer alone.

Her breath left her lungs as his big strong hands came to rest on her shoulders. As if connected by an invisible thread to his body, she leaned back against his chest, drawn to the hard warmth of his maleness, breathing in the clean unique fragrance of him. For a few moments they stayed that way, her heart beating heavy and slow in anticipation for a long while before he twisted her around to face him, and, like a parched flower turning to the sun, her face had tilted as she had strained upwards to meet his cool, firm lips with her own.

The languid heat that had spread through her body like a flash fire had made her bones dissolve and she would have slid to the floor had a muscular arm not banded her narrow ribcage before he'd picked her up and…!

Behind the smoky lenses of her sunglasses her pupils dilated as she swallowed hard, pushing the memory kicking and screaming back into its box. She glanced at the bedroom door again and felt her insides tighten.

With a cry she shot to her feet, opened the suite door a crack and positioned herself within reaching distance of the door handle for a quick escape should she need it, before pressing her rigid shoulder blades against the wall and closing her eyes…

What were the odds of finding herself in the exact same suite?

Fighting to keep her thoughts in the here and now, which, no matter how uncomfortable, was infinitely pref-

erable to obsessing about the past, she took another deep
mind-clearing breath.

She was winning and then she just *had to* sabotage her
own progress and peek through the open bedroom door
and see that bed. With no warning the past collided painfully with the present again with a concussive impact.

'No!' Teeth clenched, she ran across the room and
closed the door with a decisive click before leaning her
back against it, even though she knew a couple of inches
of wood was no defence against the memories that had
been playing in a loop ever since she'd got out of the taxi
and found herself standing in the exact spot where it had
all begun more than five years earlier.

Suddenly, she was feeling the rain from that day over
five years ago beating down from a leaden sky, plaster-
ing her water-darkened hair to her head, much longer
then than the shoulder-blade length she favoured now.

The soaked strands kept getting in her eyes, though
with her head down against the driving force of the cloud-
burst all she could see were people's feet and the standing water on the pavement increasing in depth with each
passing moment.

It had taken seconds for the thin linen jacket she was
wearing to become totally saturated, her bare legs below
the denim skirt she was wearing were slick with rain and
her feet in wedge sandals squelched as she avoided another lethal umbrella that was being wielded like a shield.
Any trace of make-up was a mere memory, and she gave
up brushing away the droplets trembling on the ends of
her long curling eyelashes before falling into her eyes.

It had seemed like such a good idea when she'd been
sitting waiting for Rupert to come out of his weekly appointment with his oncologist, less so now. But when
the page of the glossy magazine she had picked up had

opened on an advert for the opening of the new London branch of the famous Parisian chocolatier that Rupert, with his sweet tooth, adored, it had seemed like something nice to do for the man to whom she owed so much.

Rupert, the man who legally at least she was married to, had called their arrangement *symbiotic* when he had offered her an escape route from the seemingly endless nightmare she had fallen into after her father's death, but to her it often seemed more like a one-sided deal.

She wasn't even sure that this mysterious debt Rupert had claimed he owed her father existed, though the men's friendship certainly had. Her father had been a man with a lot of friends; he'd been funny, articulate, generous to a fault and he'd thrown legendary parties—of course he'd had friends. Only for the most part, they'd turned out to be the variety that had disappeared when it had become public knowledge after his death that, despite his lifestyle, there had been no money left, just debts.

His death was the only thing that had kept the bailiffs temporarily away from the door of the lovely home she was living in that was mortgaged up to the hilt. The staff had not been paid for two months, though selling her jewellery had dealt with that issue, and everything else would have to be sold too: the fleet of cars in the garage; her father's share in the racehorse that never won anything but cost a bomb in trainers, stables and veterinary bills.

She'd been poor before, that was not a problem for Marisa, but what had been a nightmare was the money that the lawyers said her father owed, and not all the debts, she'd soon learnt, were owed to legitimate sources. Some, the ones whose sinister representatives Marisa had come home from the funeral to find sitting uninvited in her living room, were not inclined to stand in line to be paid a fraction of what they were owed.

They'd wanted their money right then, all of it, and the dark consequences they'd hinted at should she not come up with the goods had been chilling enough, though not as much as the stomach-curdling suggestion that she could reduce the debt by being *nice* to important friends of their clients.

She had still been shaking with reaction to the crude suggestion when Rupert had arrived. He'd sat her down, poured her a stiff brandy and had teased the story out of her. It was then that he'd shared his own shocking news, explaining not just his medical diagnosis, but that his disease was terminal. He considered it a private matter, he didn't want her sympathy, and wasn't afraid to die— he was ready.

What he didn't want, he'd told her, was to die alone, and he'd been alone ever since the death of the love of his life, a man whose funeral Rupert hadn't even been able to attend because his long-time lover had had a wife and family who didn't know, or didn't want to know, that he had been gay.

Marriage to Marisa, he'd said, would make everything so much easier legally after he died—*she'd* actually be helping *him*. And, for some reason he'd refused to disclose, he'd owed it to her father to ensure she was safe. Marisa, ignoring the voice of conscience in the back of her mind, had let herself believe him. Grief-stricken, desperate and so very alone, she'd agreed.

They had married in a civil ceremony a week later. There had been no honeymoon but they'd shared a bottle of champagne, and that had been the first time Rupert had told her upfront, to her acute embarrassment, that it would be fine with him if she wanted a life outside their marriage. If she had friends, *male* friends, he'd added, in case she hadn't got his drift.

She had got it, but, as she had informed him there and then, that wouldn't be an issue for her and she had meant it. She had never been a particularly *physical* person and she had always avoided intimacy of that nature. What she'd been looking for in a relationship was what she had always craved: safety and stability.

School friends had always envied Marisa her adventurous lifestyle, not knowing about the unpaid bills that her father had cheerfully binned whenever the drawer he'd shoved them into had got full, never dreaming that their friend, who got to mingle with famous people and order her dinner from room service in five-star hotels, instead longed for the security of their boring lives.

Ironically she now had the dreamt-of security, although this had never been the way she had visualised it coming about, and up to a point it had worked. But to her, at least, it was becoming more obvious with each passing day that there was nothing *equal* about her and Rupert's deal, and there was a certain irony in the fact that her attempt to assuage her guilt in a small way had set in motion a sequence of events that would lead to her act of betrayal. And no matter that Rupert had virtually given his blessing to her taking lovers, for Marisa, what she had done remained a betrayal.

Waiting until Rupert was taking his afternoon nap she had set off to purchase his surprise treat, taking the shortcut through the park because it was such a lovely afternoon—or at least it had been, until the heavens opened and the rain came pelting down!

She was just wondering whether there was any point getting a taxi when she sidestepped a puddle and walked full pelt into a person—or it could have been a steel wall; the amount of *give* was about the same—the impact driving the air from her lungs in a sharp gasp as she bounced off him, very nearly losing her balance.

Grappling with the distracting sensation of hardness and warmth left by the moment of contact while trying to keep her balance, she was saved the embarrassment and pain of landing on her bottom in a puddle by a pair of large hands that shot out, spanning her waist and quite literally putting her back on her feet.

'I'm so, so sorry...' She began tilting her chin to look up...a long way, as it turned out, but as she finally made it to the face of the man who still had his hands on her waist she promptly forgot what she was going to say, the clutching sensation in the pit of her stomach giving way to a shallow gasp of shock.

She now knew why it had felt as though she were walking into a wall. Everything about the stranger was hard. He was lean, broad-shouldered and several inches over six feet; the long drovers raincoat he wore open over a suit and tie did not disguise the muscular athleticism of his body.

If the physical impact had snatched her breath away, the impact as her gaze collided with the dark heavy-lidded eyes of the stranger made her heart almost stop beating, the raw masculinity he projected like nothing she had ever encountered before in her twenty-one years. Strange, scary sensations were zigzagging through her body, as though her nervous system had just received a million-volt hit.

It was the weirdest sensation. The noise of other people, the busy traffic, the storm raging overhead were all still there but they receded into the background. Instead, her world had contracted into the space, the air molecules between her and this man... There was just this extraordinary man, and he really was the most beautiful thing she had ever seen in her life!

She knew she was staring at him but she couldn't stop. His strong-jawed oval face was all sculpted cheekbones, carved planes and intriguing angles, and the skin stretched over bones of perfect striking symmetry was a deep vibrant bronzed gold. Looking at his firm, sensually moulded mouth sent her core temperature up several painful degrees—it was a sinful miracle.

The thick brows above his eyes lifted and she couldn't help noticing that they were as black as the curling lashes that framed his deep-set dark, quizzical eyes.

'Are you all right?'

He had an *almost* accent—it was there somewhere in the perfect diction and the deep, smooth drawl. There was a smile and something else in his eyes that was as lushly velvet as his voice.

It was the something else that intensified the violent quivering in the pit of her stomach.

She lifted a hand to push the hair from her cheek, the rain-soaked strands tangling in her slim fingers while beneath the film of moisture her face felt hot.

'Fine, fine… I'm fine.' And surprisingly she was, for someone who had quite clearly lost her mind and couldn't stop shaking.

She just hoped the internal tremors did not show on the outside, but she realised that on the plus side she would no longer need to pretend to have a clue what people were talking about when they mentioned lust at first sight.

On the minus side, she knew in a distant corner of her mind that she was making a total fool of herself because she didn't have the skill or the experience to hide what she was feeling.

His incredible cynical eyes said he knew *exactly* what was happening between them.

'You're wet,' he said, dragging a hand across his own hair, removing the excess moisture from the jet-black strands, then he reversed the gesture, causing his hair to stand up in sexy damp spikes. As he stood there just staring at her, Marisa had the oddest feeling he could see the thoughts swirling in her head, so maybe that was why he suddenly said abruptly, 'Would you like to come inside?'

'Inside...?' she echoed stupidly.

Without taking his eyes from her face, he gestured with a tip of his head towards the entrance of the Madrigal Hotel.

She paused long enough so that he had to know she'd considered it before she began to babble, hating the breathy sound of her own panicked voice as she took refuge in good manners.

'No, no, I'm fine. I'm sorry I got you wet and thank you for...' She stopped short, figuring she had already made herself look as ridiculous as it was humanly possible to. She shook her head but didn't move, her soggy feet feeling as glued to the ground as her eyes were to the face of this tall, imposing stranger.

He arched a dark brow. 'Well, if you change your mind I'm here all week.'

His offer, if that was what it was, broke her free of the paralysis that had gripped her, and with another shake of her head, this time with her eyes safely on the pavement in front of her, she turned around and in seconds was lost amongst the body of people surging along the wet pavement. Her heart was pounding so loudly it felt like a sonar locator as she rushed on, welcoming the cooling caress of the rain as it hit her hot face.

After the initial surge of relief that she'd escaped—

from exactly what was not a question she wanted to explore—she found herself wondering what would have happened if she had accepted the stranger's invitation.

Really, Marisa, you're not that naïve, are you? mocked the voice in her head as she squelched along, the rain numbing the heat of embarrassment in her cheeks. Or was that *excitement*?

That would have been the end of it, and *should* have been the end of it had fate and her school friend Cressy's domestic emergency not intervened.

'It would be good,' Cressy had said when they'd bumped into one another the previous week, 'to catch up.'

It was the sort of vague, socially polite thing that people said without actually meaning it and Marisa had responded in the same vein, never for a second expecting to be asked to follow through.

But Cressy had invited her out for a meal, and in the end it had been Rupert, so cheered at the prospect of her getting out, who had made her agree.

That evening she left him with his chocolates and a video of his favourite film and went out, and it was actually quite nice to dress up and get out of her comfortable clothes for once.

That was the funny thing about clothes—especially when you added some bold red lipstick—and she left the house looking everything she knew she wasn't: sexy and confident.

Cressy, who was still struggling, she said, with her post-baby body, pronounced herself envious, but when Marisa watched her face as she scrolled proudly through the photos of her husband and baby twin boys on her phone Marisa knew her old friend was lying. Cressy wouldn't swap what she had for a size-eight figure and a few glamorous outfits!

They had not even selected their food when Cressy received the phone call from home.

'Yes, give him one spoonful if his temperature is up. It's in the bathroom cabinet in the boys' room, top shelf. Yes, I know you'll be fine and I will have fun… Love you…' Cressy slid the phone back in her clutch bag but she gave Marisa a rueful look and sighed. 'Sorry, Marisa, but…'

'Rain check. Don't worry, I get it. You go home… make sure your boys are all right.'

Cressy's relief was obvious.

Marisa finished her own cocktail and the one Cressy had not touched, and it was still only nine p.m. She was left all dressed up with nowhere to go but home again, where Rupert, who always retired early, would already be in bed, helped by the live-in nurse who had been with them for a few weeks now. Marisa decided to walk back as it was a lovely evening, and somehow she found herself standing outside the Madrigal, which was *almost* on her way home.

The stranger wouldn't be there, she reasoned, shivering as she thought of him. It was still so early…why not go in for a nightcap? She'd always wanted to see what the Madrigal was like inside and she was certainly dressed for it.

A combination of self-delusion and the cocktails that were not as innocuous as they'd looked got her through the doors and into the expensive-smelling wood-panelled foyer when the reality of what she was doing hit her, shame and mind-clearing horror following close behind.

She turned and would have headed back through the door had a voice not suddenly nailed her feet to the Aubusson carpet.

'Would you like a drink?'

Shocked recognition and stomach-tightening excitement grabbed her as, her breath coming faster, she spun back slowly on her heels.

With her heart trying to batter its way through her ribcage, her eyes travelled in an upward sweep over the long, lean length of his body, clad this evening in a beautifully cut dark grey suit, underneath which was a pale blue shirt open at the neck to reveal the tanned brown skin of his throat, and fine enough to suggest the musculature of his chest and torso. The expensive tailoring didn't do anything to lessen the aura of raw, head-spinning masculinity he projected.

'No, I didn't come here for—' She blinked and stopped. What had she come here for?

Exactly what he thinks you did, the voice in her head responded.

He took a step forward and held out his hand. 'I'm Roman Bardales.'

After the faintest hesitation she reached out, a shock of electricity of a lethal voltage running through her body as his warm brown fingers closed around her hand and didn't move, and she saw his polished brown eyes widen as though he too had felt the same stinging shock.

'Marisa Rayner.' She pulled her hand away.

'I'm glad you came.'

'I... I didn't...' One darkly delineated brow lifted to a sardonic angle and she rushed on. 'Well, I am here.'

'So I see.' The comprehensive sweep of his brown eyes as they slid over her body made her shiver. 'And now?'

'Now?' She had to force the word past the ache in her dry throat.

'Are you coming up?' The slight jerk of his head was directed at the lift behind him.

He didn't say for a coffee, or a nightcap, because they both knew that wasn't why she was there.

'I… I don't do things like this.'

'OK,' he said slowly in acknowledgment, and then he did nothing else to influence her decision besides standing there looking gorgeous enough to melt her bones.

Marisa had known deep down that she was just going through the motions pretending to delay. The decision had already been made as soon as she had made her way to the hotel this evening. Her struggle now was for appearances—her own, not his.

His impressive shoulders lifted in the faintest of shrugs. 'We could go for a walk instead?'

She shook her head. 'No, I'll…' She expelled a deep breath and started to move towards the lifts.

CHAPTER TWO

THE YOUNGEST ADDITION to the Bardales company was anxious to make a good impression, having checked and double-checked everything on board the private jet was as it should be. Instead of joining the other staff, who were chatting and drinking coffee while they waited for their passenger to arrive, Alex made his way down the steps looking for the chief steward to ask if there was anything else he could do.

He was a shiny foot off the tarmac of the private landing strip when he spotted the man he was looking for in conversation with the plane's pilot. Probably not the best idea to disturb them, he decided. Besides, there was such a thing as being *too* keen.

Alex was about to turn and retrace his steps when he spotted the cloud of dust in the distance on the road that snaked its way across the red earth with the mountains as a stunning backdrop.

He paused, watching the cloud of dust getting nearer, feeling a pang of envy as the sleek outline of the designer car emerged, barely slowing its breakneck speed as it passed through the tall security gates that magically opened as it approached.

The car drew to a halt on the tarmac and a tall, dark-haired figure emerged. He slammed the door hard enough to take it off its hinges and removed a pair of dark shades, tucking them into a pocket before sweeping the area with eyes that, even at this distance, appeared arctic cold to the new recruit. Alex took an involuntary step backwards, experiencing a stab of relief when a member of the security team, a fellow newcomer, moved forward to intercept the stranger, albeit without a lot of enthusiasm, and who could blame him? The broad-shouldered figure was emanating an aura of danger that enveloped his frame as visibly as the dust had enveloped his supercar.

Alex looked on curiously as the security guard moved back again…everyone present on the landing strip was stepping back to allow the unimpeded progress of the tall man, who looked capable of demolishing anything that got in his way.

Initially confused, Alex began to make more sense of the scene as the figure got close enough for him to recognise the carved contours of his face—some sense at least, but now the confusion remained for another reason.

Did his employer lead a double life?

True, Alex had never met the man in person, but he'd seen him in a photo when he'd pored over the company website before his interview, until he'd felt he knew everything about the Bardales brand that stood, so the logo proclaimed, for ethical quality.

In the photos the head of the company had looked sharply tailored and pristine; today he was wearing faded jeans that possessed more than a few frayed holes that had certainly not been placed there by any designer, and a dark tee shirt that clung to the well-developed contours of his powerful chest and bagged around his washboard-flat belly, giving a glimpse of the muscle ridges there, his dusty boots kicking up little flurries of earth as he walked.

In every photo Alex had ever seen, his employer's black hair had been fashionably cropped, but the man approaching now wore it long enough to curl on his neck with enough length on top to cause it to cover his strongly delineated dark brows. At regular intervals he swept it back with an impatient long-fingered brown hand.

The aquiline features looked to have the same carved symmetry of the internet version, though it was hard to tell as the previously clean-shaven lines were heavily dusted with facial hair that stopped just short of being a beard and gave its owner a look that could only be called menacing.

Looks, his mother always said, could be deceptive. Alex really hoped so because this man's appearance alone would have made any person with an ounce of common sense cross the street to avoid him, and he considered himself very sensible.

'Roman…!'

Alex registered the genuine warmth in the pilot's voice as the older man stepped briskly forward, skirting the plane and moving towards the new arrival, and comprehension finally dawned.

So this man was actually Rio Bardales's *brother*, the identical twin who, the carefully worded website blurb had explained, did not at this point take an active part in company operations. It had gone on to list the several innovations and successful financial ventures that this currently absent Bardales twin *had* been responsible for, before briefly mentioning his new career as a bestselling author.

Well, it wasn't exactly a secret. Alex had still been at school when Roman Bardales had been outed as the author of the bestselling thriller series that had taken the popular literature world by storm. Since then Hollywood had expanded the audience for the exploits of the enigmatic flawed hero of his books—Danilo, a man of few words with a taste for fast cars, extreme sports and beautiful brainy women, though the only permanent fixture in his life was his Czech wolf-dog, who was the canine version of his enigmatic lone-wolf master.

The publicity machine claimed Roman Bardales cared deeply about realism and that he never had his hero perform a feat he hadn't already mastered himself. Shots of him clinging, not a rope in sight, to the sheer rock face of a mountain with a dizzying drop below suggested this might not be all hype.

Alex had not read any of the books but he was a massive fan of the films—his friends were going to be so jealous when he told them. Maybe he would get to shake his hand? Or even—

'No, don't ask for his autograph.'

The youngster spun around. 'I wasn't—' he began, his voice fading and his blush blooming as the senior steward gave him a knowing look and then suggested, not unkindly, that he might like to do some work.

It took a few moments for the sound of the familiar voice to penetrate the zone Roman had occupied for the entirety of his drive. It was a technique he used when he climbed. You didn't think ahead, you just lived in the moment and focused on the next move, because if your mind wandered, if you allowed yourself to be distracted, the consequences could be life-threatening or, at the very least, life altering.

Today the danger was not an unforgiving two-hundred-foot drop below his dangling feet, and it was not a rock face he was clinging to by his fingernails, it was his rage. The moment he started thinking more than one move ahead the red mist threatened to consume him all over again and he had to stop thinking again… His eyes slid to his clenched right fist and the broken skin on his knuckles.

He flexed his hand, and rubbed it against his thigh. He and his twin had had any number of arguments before, some more heated than others. It was inevitable when two strong-minded individuals were involved—the clash of the alphas, their mother called it.

The thought of their remaining parent lifted one corner of his mouth, softening his expression for a second or two before it flattened again. This time, his and Rio's argument had been different; it had been…*visceral*.

It wasn't just the punch he had landed on his brother, it was the fact he had not wanted to stop hitting him, but Rio, *damn him*, wouldn't defend himself and he… Roman took a deep breath and let it out slowly, his thoughts drifting back to their recent encounter, a memory that would take a lot more than time to heal.

When his twin had begged him to hear him out, Roman had acquiesced, sprawling in one of the chairs, trying to hide his smile as he'd resisted the temptation to tease his twin a little. At that point he'd still been assuming his brother's confession had something to do with the cosy domestic scenario he had walked in on. It seemed Rio had a kid he'd not known about…and the kid's mother appeared to be in his dedicated bachelor brother's life too. Roman could see why that story might necessitate the deep breath his brother took before he'd started to speak.

He had allowed his brother to get to the end of his story. As it turned out, it wasn't a story about Rio's own domestic arrangements, but there was a secret child involved. Only it wasn't Rio's daughter, it was *Roman's* son.

Roman's smile was long gone when he'd got to his

feet, and it had been replaced by a ferocious scowl as he'd moved across the room until he'd stood toe to toe, shoulder to shoulder, with his identical twin.

'Marisa...' *His* Marisa, except of course she wasn't his, she was someone else's Marisa and she always had been, even while she'd been in his bed, while she was making him feel... Roman shook his head fiercely. It had all been a lie; even his own feelings, feelings that had felt real at the time, had been only an illusion, but the child was definitely real. 'She came to *you*?'

'It wasn't easy for her.'

The sympathy in his brother's eyes had only added insult to injury, and the feral sound that had escaped his compressed white-edged lips had risen up from some deep place inside his belly as he'd stood there clenching every muscle and sinew.

'But she was desperate. There was nowhere else for her to go.'

'How about me? If she'd needed a bone-marrow donor for her son, preferably a *"related"* compatible donor—' his lips curled as he drew mocking quotation marks in the air before his voice dropped to a base boom of fury '—then why not come to me if I'm the child's father?'

His stabbing finger stopped just short of his brother's chest, but Rio hadn't flinched an inch, he had just stood there looking as guilty as hell. *A bit late for that, brother!*

'Because you—' Rio had visibly bitten down on what he'd been about to say and finished flatly. 'We've got the same DNA. The child urgently needed a bone-marrow transplant from a...yes...preferably related donor. Should I have refused her request?'

'You *should* have told me...and because *what*? What were you going to say about why she hadn't come to me instead of you?'

'Because,' his brother had finally flung at him, 'you were all over the tabloids with that blonde flashing her ample cleavage in your face while coyly saying in a totally unconvincing way that your relationship was strictly professional. I had no reason to disbelieve the rumours that you were about to get engaged—and you certainly didn't deny it.'

'It *was* purely professional,' Roman had gritted back, dismissing the irrelevance with a wave of his hand. 'Petra was an agent for the film distribution company liaising with the publisher.' And a great loss to the acting profession.

The first time she had displayed her stage skills, Roman hadn't seen the cameras, so he hadn't had a clue what was going on when she had whipped off her glasses, unfastened several buttons of her blouse and plastered herself against him, her myopic blue eyes sending him a warning dagger look as she'd muttered an instruction to *'play along'*, snuggling up to him before displaying a very realistic shock when a series of camera flashes had exploded in their faces.

She had earnestly backed up his stony declarations of 'No comment' with a fluttering display of denials guaranteed to look suspect.

Roman didn't like this reminder of poor judgement on his part. Initially Petra's machinations had amused him and it hadn't seemed important then, so he had allowed the situation to go on longer than he should have. By the end, though, Petra had been in danger of forgetting she was acting—or that might have been an act too, for all he knew.

'Professional?'

He'd scowled at his brother's scepticism. 'A trade-off, then. The film company execs were throwing fits because I had refused to participate in a promotional tour of the latest movie and I don't give interviews, so they figured that, because everyone loves the idea of a romance, the occasional photo op with Petra would keep me and, more importantly, the film, on the front pages, without me having to say a word. I really don't see what that has to do with anything.'

'Then you really are stupid as well as forgetful.'

'So because I am stupid *you* decided that you would ride to the rescue and save *my* child while taking it upon yourself to conceal the fact I even had a child from me— and now you thought you'd ease your conscience by confessing all. Tell me, Rio, whose idea was it not to tell me in the first place? Yours or Marisa's? Did you offer her a shoulder to cry on? Yes, I can just see it now...' And he had, so vividly, been able to see Marisa's blonde head on his brother's shoulder, her soft body pressed against Rio's hard one... The taunting images had flashed in front of his eyes, and he'd furiously shrugged off Rio's placatory hand on his shoulder.

'I don't expect you to forgive me, Roman, but I truly meant it for the best—'

Playing the scene over and over again in his head, Roman was sure that Rio had seen the fist coming but he'd made no attempt to avoid it, he'd just stood there waiting for the punch to land.

Roman had left his brother lying on the floor, rubbing his jaw and staunching the nose bleed he'd acquired from hitting the coffee table on his way down, and had walked away, or at least had driven away at high speed. It had been thirty minutes later that he had realised he didn't have a clue where he was driving to, as for once his legendary sense of direction had deserted him.

As he'd drawn over to the side of the empty road he'd

remembered his twin's penultimate words… *'The jet will be waiting for you when you need it.'*

Roman had rejected the offer out of hand. 'You think I'm going to chase after her?'

'I thought you might like to see your son. If I were you, I would. They are in England.'

'You're not me, though, are you? And you can keep your nose the hell out of my business! I'm finished with you!'

Now the red mist had cleared, the fact there was a jet ready and willing to take him where he needed to go was not so inconvenient.

'Santiago.' Drawing his attention back to the here and now, Roman tipped his head in acknowledgment to the man who had been responsible for both him and his twin getting their pilot's licences, as the older man walked over, his hand extended.

The handshake morphed into a manly clap on the shoulder before the pilot stepped away, searching his face.

Something in his calm steady gaze lowered Roman's tension a couple of notches. 'It's been a long time, Santiago.'

'Two years, but who's counting? Oh, and thanks for the tip—still keeping your hand in, then?'

Roman looked blank for a moment, then a grin flashed momentarily, lightening the sombre set of his carved features. 'You invested in Raoul's start-up, then, like I recommended?'

The older man nodded. 'I'd still be kicking myself if I hadn't. Your friend wouldn't have any problem raising money these days, would he? They say the simplest ideas are the best, and I'm glad they're right. I have a nice pension fund for when I'm too old to fly these things any more.' He glanced towards the fuelled and waiting plane then turned his attention back to the man who co-owned it. 'You really can't *help* making money, can you?'

A cloud passed across Roman's face, cancelling out the half-smile and darkening his eyes. 'I get it from my father.' Unfortunately the ability to make money was not the only thing he had inherited from his father. It seemed he'd also acquired the rage and the jealousy that had dogged his parents' marriage.

'I don't remember him having your way with words, though. I read your last book.' Santiago's bushy brows lifted as his glance slid up from Roman's dusty boots to his windswept head, taking in everything in between. 'You been doing a photoshoot for your next cover? Channelling the inner lean and mean?'

Roman's uncomfortable grimace made Santiago's grin deepen, though underneath the laconic amusement he was relieved to see another slight lessening in the taut-tripwire level of tension that coiled the younger man's body tighter than an overwound steel spring on the point of snapping.

'I hear that you never write any hero stunt you haven't done yourself?'

'Don't believe everything you read. How is Meg?' Roman felt ashamed that his own self-centred concerns meant it had taken this long for him to ask.

'She's still in remission, and we're both enjoying it. You should try it.'

'What?' Roman said as he walked alongside the other man towards the plane.

'Marriage.'

'I'm not the marrying kind.'

But then again, you weren't the fathering kind, were you? And just look what happened.

'Neither was I until I met Meg.'

'The Megs of this world are rare.' The Marisas were rare too, but in a very different way.

The Marisas of this world lied their way into a man's head, made him think that she was as necessary as oxygen to him, and then went back to another man. Her *husband*. He had spent his life building up walls and she had knocked them down with one glance of those golden glowing, *hungry* eyes.

He let out another breath when the emotional shields he had constructed withstood the memory, as well as the image of a face of cut-glass delicate beauty. His nostrils flared; he'd been played and it had hit him where it hurt most—in his pride—but he had moved on.

It had taken some time for him to appreciate the fact that she had actually done him a favour in refusing to leave her husband; his *collision* with Marisa had been the spur he'd needed to shake him out of the rut he'd been in and into an entirely new life. He'd cut ties he'd no longer needed, been liberated from responsibilities he'd no longer wanted. He relied on no one but himself and no one relied on him; wasn't that the very definition of freedom…?

The unacknowledged question mark that accompanied the thought twitched his dark brows into a frown that deepened as his thoughts took the next logical leap forward. Now he had a son, and that was a responsibility he couldn't walk away from.

It was a responsibility he was running towards.

Maybe someone should warn the kid, mocked the sardonic voice in his head.

He tensed, unwilling even to acknowledge the deep-seated fear in his belly; it was an old fear that he'd always lived with. It was this fear and not a whim that had influenced his decision not to become a father. It was the responsible thing to do when you realised there was too much of your own father in you. Roman had intended to break the cycle because he didn't want his legacy to be an emotionally damaged child. *Dios*, this wasn't meant to be happening—there shouldn't *be* a child.

He'd taken precautions, but everyone except an idiot knew the only foolproof form of contraception was total abstinence, and that option had been off the table from the moment he'd seen her standing in the lobby balanced on crazy heels that made her incredible legs look endless and wearing a mere sliver of silk that had clung to her sleek curves like a lover's caress.

'You joining me?' Santiago nodded towards the cockpit.

Roman moved his head as if to dislodge the circling mesh of thoughts. 'Not this time,' he replied.

There were some familiar staff members on the flight and others less so, but he felt too drained to make the effort to even acknowledge the nods of recognition.

Fighting impatience, he took a seat and belted up. The effort of maintaining even an illusion of normality was beyond him at that moment, and he found it hard to imagine there would be any moments of normality in his life ever again.

He had a child!

When would it seem real to him? Hands clenched, knuckles bone white, he pressed his head into the backrest and allowed his eyes to close, the sweep of his dark lashes casting an extra shadow that highlighted the jutting carved contours of his high cheekbones. Inside his head the rapid thoughts and questions, the *anger*, carried on swirling, and, yes, even though he had pushed it right to the back of his mind, there was still the fear lurking, fear that he would do to his child what his father had done to him.

You're so like your father!

How old had he been the first time he had heard those words? Far too young—and he'd heard them far too many times since.

High too was the number of times he had watched his father bully, berate and belittle his mother, or seen the signs of an imminent meltdown as his father's face had become suffused with anger and his eyes had gone cold before he'd flown into a rage.

Roman had always used the same silent mantra on these occasions—*I am not like him. I won't be that man.*

The childish determination had morphed into an adult resolution that had made him the man he was today, the man who was aware of the need to keep his emotions under control, to never want anything or anyone so much that it became a dangerous obsession.

If that made him someone who was considered to be remote and emotionless he could live with that, and being called heartless by ex-lovers was not a high price to pay in his eyes.

No female had ever accessed the wild, dark inner depths of him until Marisa had walked into his life, and, to his horror, all the dormant suppressed emotions he'd always sensed were there had roared into life, his response to her primal and uncontrolled.

His jaw clenched as he tried to silence the memories. What he needed was…what?

He needed to *do* something—inactivity was not something he had ever mastered, and his usual ability to sleep anywhere any time had deserted him. There was too much time for thinking, for the frustration curdling in his gut to expand until he felt as if he'd explode!

Deaf to the polite question of the attendant standing at his elbow, he pressed his hands on the armrests and vaulted to his feet in one smooth motion, causing the attendant to take an involuntary step back.

He dragged his hair back from his forehead. The combined effects of the shock revelation and lack of sleep were beginning to kick in hard, but control was his bedrock, his strength, and although he had to dig deep he was able to stretch his mouth into something approaching a smile.

'No…no, thank you,' he said with a shake of his head. 'I'm just going to—' Gesturing in the direction of the adjoining compartment, he swiftly headed for the privacy of the bedroom suite.

Any personal items his twin might have left in there had been stowed away except for a snapshot of him and his brother tucked into the frame of the full-length mirror. He strode across, focusing on the snapshot rather than his own reflection, and two identical faces stared back at him. He felt something shift in his chest but before he could put a name to the emotion, he looked away quickly, directing his stare at his mirrored reflection.

Turning away again to avoid the accusation in the bleak dark eyes staring back at him, he retrieved his phone from the pocket where he had shoved it after he'd glanced at the replies to the stream of texts he'd sent once he'd rung ahead to commandeer the jet.

Scan reading was a useful skill but he wanted to be sure he had not missed any detail, though it was the missing details that were harder to deal with, or at least one in particular. It seemed unlikely that there was not a single photo of his son, James Alexander, in the public domain, but the investigative firm he was dealing with had always been efficient in the past.

He scrolled through the email and it didn't take long— it was short and to the point. The more in-depth report would land in his inbox in the next twenty-four hours as he'd been promised. There were a few extras, like Marisa's date of birth and her marital status, which he already knew… His thumb paused over the screen, his heart pounding as he discovered a detail he had not picked up first time around. Marisa Rayner was now a widow.

His mouth twisted into a cynical smile. At least his son would not be calling another man Father; other than that the detail was not relevant to him.

His glance returned to the stand-out detail that had drawn a smile of the blackest kind from him. The irony of it was darker than night. Marisa was to be found, with or without his son—that piece of information was apparently not available—in the five-star luxury of the Madrigal Hotel—the very same place where his son had been conceived.

His son!

He made a supreme effort and closed the lid on his rage. He would save it until he could vent it on the appropriate person. He made himself read the limited information once more, slowly and carefully.

No, he had it all memorised now; Marisa was a guest speaker at a fundraising international event being held at the Madrigal.

It didn't say if she was combining business with pleasure.

Not that he gave a damn who she slept with, he told himself. Marisa was not his business, but his son was.

It was perfectly legitimate for him to feel anger at the prospect of her introducing another man he had not vetted into his child's life, but she could take who she liked to her bed.

He could not imagine a woman with her sexual appetites being alone for long. Maybe she was a creature of habit and the Madrigal was her hunting ground.

It was a place to which he had never intended to return, as it was the scene of his complete humiliation. For months afterwards, what had happened had played on an unceasing loop in his head.

He remembered every word of his proposal, the ones he had got out anyway. Before he had got halfway through his prepared speech or even opened the box containing the ring he'd so carefully picked out, she'd begged him to stop.

'Roman, please don't say anything more. I came here today to tell you I can't go on seeing you.'

'You love me.' He could still hear the certainty in his voice, his utter unshakeable conviction.

The memory of Marisa's soft husky voice cracking as she had begged him not to say that still had the power to fill him with gut-tightening self-disgust.

'Please, Roman, don't do this. I don't… I can't…you don't understand. I can't marry you because I already have a husband.'

'That can't be true!'

Initially he had thought her confession was an invention. The discovery after the first night they'd spent together that she was a virgin had shaken him. Part of him had been angry that she had given him this gift with no warning, but another part of him had been totally aroused that he had been her first lover.

'It is a marriage of…of convenience. There is no…

We are not…' Crazy, considering what they had shared, she'd blushed before adding with husky self-consciousness '…intimate.'

'Then what the hell are you?'

'We are just friends,' she'd said softly. 'And I respect him more than any other person I know. I owe him so much and I won't leave him…'

Roman had done a quick translation.

'You mean you married him for his money! Well, sweetheart, you should have waited, because if that is what attracts you to men, I've got a lot more.'

She'd flinched but then continued quietly, 'I've hurt you and I'm so very sorry… I shouldn't have done any of this. It's all my fault and I know I wish I could go back and undo it…'

Roman caught another glimpse of his face in the mirror, seeing something in the eyes that looked back at him that he hadn't seen in a long time. It belonged to the days, weeks and months when he had been chained to the memories of being with her. He had finally escaped those memories, although it had meant reinventing himself, and he would not be going back except to claim his son.

What are you going to do with him when you've got him, Roman, or doesn't it matter so long as she doesn't have him?

Tuning out the sardonic voice in his head, he lifted a hand to his jaw, grimacing as he dragged it down over the rough three-day growth.

The self-mocking grin that tugged up the corners of his mouth only served to increase the look of bad-boy smouldering menace. It was a look that would open more than a few doors, but it wasn't bedrooms Roman was interested in right now.

Beneath the thick mat of stubble the slight cleft in

his square chin deepened as he imagined the reaction if he strode into the foyer of the hotel where Marisa was staying.

He narrowed his eyes and leaned in closer, touching his hair-roughened cheek and jaw again. The bottom line was, he looked like a hardened bastard with trouble written all over him, which was an effective look most of the time considering the sort of action-man hero with emotional issues that he wrote about.

It was less good when you wanted doors to open in the world in which Marisa moved, when you wanted people to look at you and see responsible *good* father material.

A good father... Would he be one? Was he capable of it?

His brother had a child and he did not seem to be afraid of fatherhood or of repeating the mistakes of their own father. Then again, his twin was not like their father at all. Not like Roman was.

Had there been a particular moment when he had realised that the things he hated about his father were actually there inside himself? Roman wasn't sure; he just knew that having a child was a risk he had not been willing to take.

Jaw clenched, he forcibly silenced the voices of doubt in his head that were alien to his nature. True, there were times when he could have reeled off a list of reasons why fatherhood was not a path he intended to take, but he knew that there was no point doing that now. Events had moved on and this was no a longer a choice that was his to make.

Hands flat on the tiled vanity surface, he surveyed his face carefully before reaching into a drawer and pulling out a cellophane-wrapped disposable razor. He needed to get into role because although in a perfect world appearances didn't count, in the real world they counted big-time.

After viewing his jaw from several angles he set to work. It took two razors but five minutes later he was moderately pleased with the close shave he had achieved. No way was he tackling his own hair; instead he would rely on the products he had no doubt his brother kept on board to tame it after he showered.

He walked through to the bedroom, opening one of the built-in wardrobes, not surprised when he discovered that conveniently his twin was still in the habit of keeping several changes of clothes on board.

He ignored the section devoted to casual wear, his long fingers flicking through the suits and shirts section before finally selecting a pale shirt still with the discreet designer tag attached, and a grey suit. He looked at the ties, lifting a hand to his neck with a grimace, imagining the confining tightness.

'Thank you, brother,' he said, a grim smile flashing as he threw the selection on the freshly made-up bed. The underwear in the drawers were all still in their wrappings and a moment later boxers and socks joined the suit, shirt and tie.

Compact but luxuriously appointed, the bathroom had a decent-sized shower that ran the entire width of one side of the compartment. Stripping off the clothes he'd been wearing for thirty-six hours straight, he let them fall in a crumpled heap on the floor.

He might not hit the gym the way he used to when he was working in an office, but his life for the past few years had involved enough physical activity to compensate for this lack.

Both brothers had always been competitive but, while Rio used to excel at team sports, Roman, not a natural team player, had gravitated in the direction of solo extreme sports where he was competing against himself, pushing his body to the limit, solo sailing, running, gymnastics and his lasting passion—rock climbing.

He'd discovered that solo climbing complemented his lifestyle as a writer; when his head was crowded with imaginary characters and convoluted plots he found climbing was the perfect way to switch off—and it had the added benefit of keeping him extremely fit too.

Fifteen minutes later he stood suited and booted before the mirror once again. It was amazing what a shave could achieve, he decided, and the slicked-back hair created a transformation so complete that it would have bewildered even the most sophisticated facial-recognition technology.

The suit, which was probably a perfect fit, felt tight and constricting across his shoulders though it hung perfectly. Roman ignored the feeling, glancing down at the only incongruity—his worn and dusty desert boots. But he wasn't willing to sacrifice comfort for appearances—his feet were a half-size bigger than his twin's.

When he eventually emerged from the plane onto the tarmac, nobody was looking at his boots. They were looking at him though. Many eyes followed the tall, dynamic figure with the perfect profile and the powerful aura, yet Roman remained oblivious to them all, his mind set only on his goal.

CHAPTER THREE

'OH, I'M SO SORRY, sir, but that suite is occupied,' the person behind the desk at the Madrigal told him.

Before Roman could react to the news that suite number one-four-four was not vacant, and in retrospect he could see there was something quite masochistic in requesting to revisit the scene of his humiliation, the assistant manager appeared at his elbow.

'Actually it is unexpectedly vacant.'

The suited figure produced a key card from his pocket like a magician and handed it to Roman.

A maid was emerging from the door to the suite as he approached. Roman smiled at her and watched her flush. He had already pulled the key card from his pocket when the thought came to him.

'Excuse me, miss…?' The girl swung back, her smile eager. 'I have a friend staying here, a Marisa Rayner…? I don't suppose you could tell me her room number.'

Her face fell. 'I'm sorry, sir, but that is not allowed.'

He sighed. 'I understand; it's just that it's her birthday and I wanted to surprise her…'

'Well, if you don't tell anyone it was me who told you…?'

'My lips are sealed,' he promised.

* * *

The screen went black and Marisa sighed and closed the laptop. She pressed her head back into the cushion, her neck feeling stiff with tension. The only question in her mind was did she take a shower before or after she read through her notes for tomorrow before she fell into bed?

She was definitely not going to think about that room somewhere above her head; she was already ashamed of her meltdown. It wasn't as if a room could hurt you, after all.

But memories could hurt and they did, even now. As did the sense of shame when she thought of those ten days when she had spent every moment she could in that room, in that bed, with Roman. It still felt like the actions of a stranger; she didn't know that person who had surrendered without a fight to the raw passion he had awoken inside her.

At least she felt a lot calmer now, especially after her reassuring report from Ashley and her chat with Jamie. Of course she was missing him but he didn't seem to be missing her at all, which was as it should be.

Her head lifted reluctantly in response to the knock on the door.

She huffed a breath and heaved herself tiredly to her feet. Stepping over her discarded shoes, she smoothed down her hair. If it was *another* fruit basket or chocolates she had no idea where they'd put it. Perhaps she ought to just tell the hotel staff she wasn't going to complain or give them any less than a five-star review because they had done nothing wrong.

She opened the door with a smile.

The rushing sensation of the floor coming up to meet her was so strong that she was surprised to find she was still standing upright.

Her skin bleached milk-pale as the electric surge reached her hands and feet and remained there in her tingling extremities. Her brain closed down for a split second, but when it kicked back in she stammered out a shocked but firm, 'No, this isn't actually happening.'

Roman would have taken more pleasure from her shocked reaction if he hadn't been experiencing a similar reaction himself.

He had been channelling pure rage and retribution as he'd waited for the hotel-room door to open, but it wasn't until it did that he realised it wasn't *pure* anything. What was superficially anger was actually far more complicated and multi-layered. When the door opened the combined force of his convoluted emotions hit him with such ferocity that it felled him, not literally, although he wouldn't have been at all surprised to discover he was lying at her feet.

He focused on the anger and not the empty ache inside him, though its existence made him mad as hell too, angry that the woman had made a fool of him, yet the sight of her had not just paralyzed him with lust, it had made him conscious of the emptiness inside him that he normally refused to acknowledge.

'Roman?'

His identity was not in question. What she ought to be asking instead was, *Why the hell are you standing outside my door?* A tiny choking sound left Marisa's lips as her eyes moved in a helpless sweep from his feet to the top of his dark head.

The lean, hungry look was more pronounced than it had been five years ago. He was harder; she looked into his eyes and saw blackness and nothing else. He might look the same but he wasn't, she realised as an icy chill slid down her spine.

'I am flattered that you remember me.' The mocking smile faded from his face and his words were terse and to the point. 'We need to talk.'

'Really?' She managed to inject a note of realistic surprise into her voice. 'Well, as much as I'd love to catch up,' she added with a smile of dazzling insincerity, 'right now is really not a good moment. I have a speaking engagement—' she gestured past him, hoping that he'd get the message she was not still the silly young woman desperately in love with him, so in love that she had sacrificed every principle she had lived by just to be with him '—and I need to speak with my PA rather urgently.'

'I think you want to make time for me.' There was nothing covert about the threat in his words. 'Are you alone?'

She stiffened, sure that guilt was written all over her face as an image of her son's face covered in chocolate cake flashed into her head.

He couldn't know about him, but then, if he didn't, why was he here?

'My speaking engagement—'

'Your speaking engagement is tomorrow.'

Her long lashes flickered as she veiled her glance and her chin lifted another few notches in cool defiance, which she clung to with single-minded determination. It was the only thing standing between her and outright gibbering panic.

'I like to be prepared.' *This* was something she couldn't have prepared for if she'd had a year; it was something that was not meant to happen—ever. How could anyone have prepared her for opening the door and finding six feet four inches of Roman Bardales standing there…in *this* hotel of all places?

Her thoughts continued to race in panicky ever-decreasing circles.

Could this be a coincidence?

Him—here in this place—now?

Or was it something more…? It was just her guilty conscience talking, suggested the voice in her head. She ignored it. Guilt was something she lived with every day; it was the price she'd paid, and it was something you were meant to feel when you made the conscious decision to conceal your child's existence from his father, irrespective of the reasoning behind that choice.

Seeing Roman again made her certain that, from a purely selfish point of view, she had made the right decision. Having this man dipping in and out of her and Jamie's lives would have made it impossible for her to build any sort of existence without him—he was such an incredible force of nature.

It was a decision she had made for her unborn child, yet robbing a child of his father was not something you did lightly, and her eventual decision had come with the knowledge that she would never stop feeling guilty. But better surely to have no father than one who rejected you or, at best, acknowledged you with reluctance.

She wasn't sure which would be worse, but Marisa knew from personal experience that a child who had been deserted by a parent grew up thinking that it was somehow their fault, even when logic and a loving father in her case had told her otherwise. Not that her dad had ever bad-mouthed her mother; he had just said that motherhood was something she was not equipped to cope with.

She'd had the advantage of knowing that one parent could be enough. Her dad had been enough for her; sure, he wasn't perfect, but whatever his faults she had always known he loved her and that was what mattered.

Her baby would never doubt her love or be made to feel that he was not good enough so she had never faltered in the belief that, morality aside, she had done the right thing... All right, perhaps she'd faltered a little...more a stumble, really, and that had only been her hormones. After Jamie had been born, in the post-birth euphoria she had nearly changed her mind about telling Roman.

She'd been so blown away by Jamie, she'd thought he was so perfect how could anyone *not* want to be part of his life? She had wanted so much to share this feeling with Roman, it had seemed selfish not to, and when she'd fallen asleep staring at the life she had brought into the world it had all seemed so simple.

When she'd awoken the memories had resurfaced, bringing with them a deep sense of sadness. Roman was only going to be happy about the news he was a father in her dreams. He would not share her joy. How could he when he had felt strongly enough on the subject to make it a condition of his marriage proposal?

Marriage to him, he had warned her, would not involve children...and this was not something he was ever going to change his mind about. A *deal-breaker*, he had called it.

So she had made her decision and lived with it.

'I'm sorry but, no, I'm not going to invite you in. I prefer to leave the past in the past,' she said quietly, wondering if it would actually stay there.

'I just bet you do.'

Trying not to look worried, she didn't ask him what he meant by that because he might just tell her, and though she knew that some fights were inevitable, you could at least choose your own time and place to have them.

Can we have a rain check on this conversation? How does thirty years' time sound to you?

He arched a sardonic brow. 'Fine, then we can discuss this out here if you prefer?'

She folded her arms across her chest in an unconsciously protective gesture. 'I don't want to talk to you at all.'

'Oh, by the way, my brother sends his love, or he would have if he'd been in any condition to talk when I last saw him.'

Marisa pressed one hand to her stomach and the other shaking hand went to her mouth. 'He told you.'

It wasn't a question but Roman responded anyway.

'Rio came over with a sudden attack of conscience,' he remarked dryly, before adding in a voice that was as hard as his eyes were cold, 'though it was a bit late in the day to matter.'

Without a word she turned around and went back into her suite, expecting him to follow her.

When the door closed behind him, she turned back to face him. She could tell he wasn't quite sure what to expect as she fixed him with a direct amber stare. 'Sit down.' She gestured towards the brocade-covered sofa and heard herself ask with stiff formality, 'Can I get you anything to drink...tea?'

If there was a single thing she could have said that would have sounded more ludicrous in the circumstances she couldn't think of it.

His explosive expletive and the glare of incredulity did not come as a massive surprise. She pressed a hand to her throat where she could feel the ferocious beating of the pulse at the base of her neck.

'I think you're taking this lady of the manor stuff a bit too seriously.'

Marisa ignored his sneer and shrugged. 'Suit yourself.' She glanced at his bruised knuckles.

'You fought with your brother over this?' She watched him place his uninjured hand over his bruised knuckles and her heart sank. 'You do know,' she began, her forehead creased with consternation, 'that your brother badly wanted to tell you.'

She had never wanted to come between the brothers but she had seen no other way. It wasn't until much later when Jamie had been given the all-clear that she had thought through the implications of putting Rio in that terrible position of keeping such a huge secret from his twin, but she had thought that so long as Roman never discovered what had happened it would be all right.

'But he didn't.'

'He wanted to tell you!' Marisa protested again.

Her defence of his twin only fed his anger. 'A conspiracy takes two at the very least.'

'It was my decision. We only had a casual relationship, after all, and not even a relationship in the real sense of the word, really—'

'I proposed to you! I wanted to get married! Admittedly I didn't know at that point you already had a husband, but proposing to you seems to suggest more than *casual* on my part, wouldn't you say?'

It was Marisa's turn to be angry. 'Why didn't I tell you about our baby? Oh, I don't know, Roman—how about the small print in your proposal?'

'What the hell are you talking about?'

Her fists clenched in reaction to his response, she shot to her feet, her anger energising her. 'You made it quite clear to me that if I did marry you there would be no children under *any* circumstances and you were not ever going to change your mind.'

A blank look spread across his face. 'I might have said something like that—'

'No, you said *exactly* that, so what would you have said if I'd come to you and told you I was pregnant, Roman? You'd have said, "Great, let's be a family," would you? Do me a favour, of course you wouldn't. You'd have told me to get rid of it.'

The accusation wiped all the colour from his face but, ignoring all the danger signs, she pushed on, the long-suppressed emotions spilling out of her.

'Jamie is only here because of me...you never even wanted him to exist.' Her flashing eyes dared him to contradict her, not that she allowed him the opportunity. There was a breathless passionate sincerity in her concluding words. 'But from the moment I knew he existed I *wanted* my baby.'

Her words rang with a truth that for a moment silenced him.

'We will never know what I'd have said or done, will we? Because you didn't tell me. You let the world and presumably your poor sucker of a husband believe that the child was his.'

'Rupert never knew. I didn't realise that I was pregnant until after he...after he died.' She had put the tiredness down to the upheaval of Rupert's death, always expected, but in the end it had all happened very quickly, leaving her feeling dazed and alone. Theirs might not have been a marriage in the conventional sense but while Rupert was alive she had always known there was someone who cared about her. His support had not just been financial, but emotional. For a short time, probably the only time in her life, she'd had a security that she had always lacked, that she had secretly longed for.

Her first suspicion had come when she was sitting in the lawyer's office feeling nauseous. She had got so tired of sitting there nodding in response to statements couched in dry, technical legal terms and had asked wearily, 'But what does all that *mean*?'

'It means, Mrs Rayner, that you are a very wealthy woman.'

'But if he had you'd have passed my child off as his, though I suppose that would have involved you sleeping with him first,' Roman jeered.

She felt her anger flare. 'You have no right to speak about Rupert like that. We had no secrets from one another, and if things had been different he would have made a fantastic father.'

'So you told him all about me, then?'

Her eyes slid from his for the first time. 'It wasn't the right time.' When she'd arrived back the evening of Roman's proposal the butler had greeted her at the door with the news that Rupert had had a very bad turn.

Rushing up the stairs to her husband's bedroom, she'd taken in at a glance his grey face and had immediately called an ambulance. How could she have offloaded her problems onto Rupert when he was so ill?

'Where is the child now?' Something flashed in his eyes. 'What do you call him? James or Alexander?'

'Jamie, and he is at home.' She hadn't even known the country estate in Sussex had existed until she'd inherited it after Rupert's death. Then it had seemed like the perfect place to bring up a child.

'So how often do you leave him?'

Resenting that he made her sound like some sort of absentee mother, she began to retort hotly and then stopped herself, realising she had been on the brink of explaining herself to him. 'Do you have a problem with working mothers?'

He blinked at finding she had neatly turned the tables on him. 'Of course I don't,' he retorted irritably.

'Actually, he has a very excellent nanny.'

'So where is home, exactly?'

'Sussex.'

'I want to see him.'

'Why?'

His brows met in a straight line above his dark eyes and he looked at her as though she had just asked the most ridiculous question on earth. 'Isn't it obvious? He is my son!'

'Biologically, yes, he is your son,' she agreed. 'But you're not his *father*—it takes more than DNA to be that. What do you want, Roman? To hear him call you Daddy or do you want him to appear in front of you on his best behaviour once or twice a year?'

'I want—' He paused and then went on slowly, 'You have robbed me of nearly five years of his life so I think you owe me this.'

'And if I say no?' She already knew the answer to that, and if she hadn't, the expression in his liquid dark eyes and the ruthless smile on his face would have been confirmation.

'I will not permit you to say no. You owe me, Marisa.'

She pressed her fingers to her temple where needles of pain were telling her that a migraine was inevitable at this stage.

Another inevitability was that if she refused Roman access to Jamie he would only find another way. At least if she agreed to a meeting, she could control the situation. A quick glance at his profile made her realise that she was being overly optimistic.

'I owe *Jamie*, but I can see how you might feel that. So how about Friday?'

The offer made, she held her breath and waited…

'Tomorrow.'

'But I—'

'Your event is in the morning. Sussex is not Outer Mongolia, is it? I'll be there at two.'

CHAPTER FOUR

RUPERT HAD BOUGHT the Carolean manor and the surrounding acres as an investment. But to Marisa it was her home, maybe her first real one. She had never known where she was going to spend her holidays: a hotel suite in the South of France, a luxury penthouse in London or, when her father was down on his luck, not that she had realised it at the time, as a guest in one of her dad's friends' homes. She had slept on a lot of floors in her time.

She'd had some pretty bedrooms too over the years but she had learnt not to get too attached to them. She kept her important possessions, the ones that mattered to her, in an easily transportable tin for convenience, kept under whatever bed she was sleeping in.

She wanted Jamie's childhood to have the feeling of permanence she had always longed for, have the pets she could never have and the lasting friendships.

She'd moved into Rozens Manor when she was pregnant so this was the longest she had ever lived anywhere. The previous owner had renovated the house and outbuildings and Rupert hadn't touched them, not interested in putting his stamp on the place into which he had just installed a skeleton staff to maintain it.

After opening it up Marisa had put her own stamp on it instead, enjoying the process of refurbishment, but she had seen no reason to increase the number of staff already employed. The place was, in estate-agent speak, a small manageable estate, in as much as anywhere that had eight bedrooms, a dower house and converted stables could be termed *small*.

The only new member of staff was the nanny, who even in this enlightened age had raised a few eyebrows, and he was with Jamie in the garden now as she waited for Roman's arrival with the sort of enthusiasm normally reserved for the flu.

She had given everyone else a day off. The local tongues had wagged enough when she'd employed a male nanny, but while gossip was inevitable, and would probably not be confined to the local community when Roman appeared, there was no point inviting it, especially this early.

Roman was obviously keen to stake his claim but, given that children had never been part of his plan, who knew how he would react when faced with the reality of parenthood, a reality that he had been so deadly determined to avoid? Marisa had no idea what his reasons were for not wanting children, and though she was ready to accept that people *could* change, this situation wasn't the same as discovering you liked broccoli after a lifetime of avoidance—this was *fundamental*.

Roman *said* he wanted to be part of his son's life but could she trust this knee-jerk reaction? She could wear contact lenses and have blue eyes, but they wouldn't *really* be blue. Roman said he wanted to be a father...hell, he *demanded* it, and he might even think he meant it, but would he really once reality hit?

There wasn't a single conclusion to the incessant questions that had kept her up into the small hours and none of the scenarios Marisa had dreamt up were ones that made her happy. She didn't want Roman in their lives, but for Jamie's sake she didn't want him to reject his son either.

One hand pressed to the coat of arms above the fireplace of the long-dead people who had built this place, she was staring deep into the bowl of hydrangeas that filled the carved stone recess when she heard a car door slamming.

Marisa swallowed and tugged nervously at the roll-collar neckline of the fine-sleeved navy cashmere top she had teamed with a pair of pale blue linen cut-off trousers and soft leather ballerina slip-ons, because she hadn't wanted to give the impression she was trying *too* hard.

She was going to be cool, casual but in control, and they were going to play by her rules because this was about Jamie.

She closed her eyes for the count of ten before squaring her shoulders at the distinctive sound of gravel crunching under a purposeful rapid stride. The sound spurred her into action because for some reason at that moment it felt important that she open the door, not respond to his knock demanding entry.

The soles of her shoes made no noise on the flagged floor as she made a dash to the door that was flanked by two carved stone lions and, rather more practically, a wellington rack. The massive metal-banded door complete with the original seventeenth-century key was heavy to open so she was glad she'd left it slightly ajar.

A last-minute smoothing down of her hair and a conscious effort to iron out the frown lines of tension on her brow and she pushed the door further open, her smile of welcome fighting with the wariness in her eyes.

Roman paused as the door swung open revealing the slim figure who presumably had been standing behind it. He took a deep breath and held it because she looked so...

His thoughts tailed off. He had no word for it or for the reaction her physical presence had on his nervous system.

He settled for *elegant*, ignoring the voice inside his head that scorned this cop-out. It was true, even drenched to the skin in mud-splattered clothes and with her hair plastered to her skull that first time they'd met, she had still radiated an elegance that was simply innate and no more contrived than being left-handed was. Combined with her earthy sexuality, it was a devastating combination.

He liked things of beauty—who didn't?—and even if there was more sex than aesthetics involved in the heat that streaked through him, settling in his groin, he knew there was no danger of him mistaking this reaction for anything more significant.

He had moved on.

Which did not mean he could deny the mind-sapping effect her physical presence had on him. He could enjoy the way she moved, though *enjoy*, he conceded, was perhaps the wrong word for the fascination her most mundane actions exerted and the inevitable gut-punch of raw hunger that followed—but there was absolutely no question of him doing anything about it. And, more importantly, no question of him mistaking what had been excellent, actually *exceptional*, sex for some sort of deeper bond between them.

They were going to have contact, it was inevitable, so in the meantime he was just going to have to suck it up, until this thing burnt itself out. He had never known it not to, so he was confident that in time this would too.

Cool, casual and controlled, Marisa felt none of the above, but then it had never been an exactly realistic expectation. Maybe there would come a time when she could, if not relax, at least feel less...exposed around

Roman, but that day was a long way off yet, so she decided to settle for guarded.

Employing her lashes to conceal the compulsive sweep of her gaze as it moved up his lean body, she noted he had opted for his version of casual today, wearing the black jeans that emphasised the length of his own legs and the power of his muscular thighs, his leather jacket open to reveal a summer-weight fine-wool tailored sweater.

His chiselled jaw was clean-shaven and his dark hair was shorter than it had been the previous day, the sharp, close cut emphasising the stark perfection of his bone structure, the overall effect one of *maleness*, effortless power and exclusivity.

Fragments of their conversation the previous day had been floating through her head ever since, all unresolved issues, question marks and guilt carried over to today, the weight of it all making it feel as if she were walking around in a heavy overcoat.

The couple of painkillers she had swallowed earlier had done nothing to relieve the headache; like the guilt, it was probably permanent, she decided dully.

Pushing through the negativity, she forced another smile. 'Hello, you found us.'

'You are not exactly hidden.'

Before she could follow up with an invitation for him to come in or work out the edge in his words he stepped past her into the hallway. Many first-time visitors stepping over the threshold were charmed by the light interior, commenting on the original flagged floor, the flowers set in the inglenook or the massive age-blackened beam above it.

Roman didn't look charmed, but then he was a Bardales and his horses probably lived somewhere grander than this.

'So nice to see you,' she drawled sardonically as he walked into the middle of the hallway and turned around to face her. Her nervous system was struggling to adjust to his presence—actually, she was just struggling, full stop.

He either ignored the sarcasm or he didn't notice it. 'I just drove straight in here.' Hands held out in front of him, palms facing upwards, he gave an incredulous shrug and waited for her explanation.

Not sure what sort of response he clearly wanted, instead she watched the muscles in his jaw quiver. She had no idea why he was angry...very angry, so she limited her reply to a cautious little—

'Oh?'

'Do you actually have *any* security?' He reached out and touched the door key, original and solid, seeming to imply her entire attitude to modern security was lacking.

Whatever she had imagined he was so wound up over it was not this—*security*? Had he expected to pass a guard checkpoint with metal detectors? To see guard dogs patrolling the perimeter of the small estate set in a leafy backwater where the crime figures probably skewed the national statistics?

'Security as in...?' His expression made her rush on before he exploded. 'Well, nothing beyond the basic, but we have a very good alarm system. It's only five years old.'

'A ten-year-old could break in here.'

His scorn made her lips tighten. 'Well, the insurance firm were more than satisfied.' When they'd given her their quote their only stipulation was that she keep all her jewellery in a bank vault, and that was no problem because Marisa couldn't imagine herself wearing any of the elaborate, mostly Victorian stuff she'd inherited from Rupert. She'd have given it to a surviving family member had there been one. 'There isn't really anything of enormous value here.' Not since she had lent Rupert's collection of modern paintings to a grateful gallery. They were not really to her taste and the artwork that had replaced them was an eclectic mix of mostly local artists, and certainly not valuable.

'How about our son?'

Her eyes widened as the colour seeped with dramatic speed from her face, leaving two bands of angry stain along the curves of her cheekbones.

She was shaking with fury…just… Well, how dared he walk in here and start implying she couldn't care for her own son? She inhaled sharply, then fixed him with a molten gold glare and folded her arms across her chest as if to contain the emotions she was struggling to control.

'So you think the best way to work out an amicable arrangement between us is to walk in here and start throwing around accusations? You are here as a guest. I do not answer to you. I have been taking care of Jamie for four and a half years…' Unconsciously her hands went to her stomach as she pulled in a tense breath. 'Actually, even longer than that. He is everything to me and has been ever since the moment I knew I'd conceived and I would—' She suddenly stopped. 'Why on earth am I defending myself to you?' she muttered half to herself.

She didn't add the words, *To someone who hasn't been here and didn't even want a child*, but she really wanted to. He clearly read the sentiment shining in the contempt of her glare, because he spread his hands, his long fingers extended in a pacifying gesture.

'I might have overreacted somewhat.'

Partly mollified by his unexpected climbdown, even if it had come across as reluctant rather than humble, she gave a slightly hysterical laugh from her dry throat, which she covered with a fake cough that quickly turned into a genuine one.

'Are you contagious?'

'You can't control a cough…' she retorted, reading irritation in his stiff expression. An image floated unbidden into her head of Roman, his face a mask of carnal need, curved over her, his knees between her thighs and his hands curled around her wrists. It was so real she could have sworn in the split second before she banished it that she could feel his warm breath on her face.

'Shall we start again?' he suggested.

Her fingernails inscribing crescent moons into the soft palms of her hands, she nodded and made an effort to unclench, everywhere.

'I know this must be hard for you—' she began, only to be spoken over immediately.

'I do not require your sympathy.'

She sucked in a breath and glared at him standing there, hauteur and disdain stamped all over his patrician face. 'Fine, then assume you don't have it,' she countered, her eyes flashing gold fire before she pulled her protective cloak of coolness around her once more. 'For the record, it's a very quiet area.' She made sure there was nothing whatever placatory about her statement. 'Jamie is never alone; if I'm not there, his nanny is.'

She could tell he was thinking that a nanny did not seem adequate protection against an individual intent on kidnap or whatever it was he was imagining would happen, but he clamped his lips over this observation instead.

'We really do have a good security system and the estate wall is several feet of solid granite,' she continued, 'but I want Jamie to have as normal a childhood as possible and he is perfectly safe here.'

She could almost see him fighting back another retort but she was too stressed to see the funny side of this—*was* there even a funny side to see?

'I never intended to imply—' he began.

She cut across him in a flat voice and dug her hands into the pockets of the trousers that were tailored enough to show off the narrowness of her waist and the shapely length of her thighs and slim calves.

'But you did.'

It was a relief when his intense gaze left her face and she took the opportunity to breathe, *really* breathe. She could only hope that this would get easier because the effort of maintaining the illusion that she was in charge of this situation… No, she *was* in charge, she told herself, but it was still exhausting.

Yet it was essential. If she lowered her guard she was convinced Roman would bulldoze through her to get to Jamie, and this, she reminded herself, ashamed that she even needed to, was all about Jamie and what was best for him.

If Roman got the idea that she was a doormat, he would keep trying to walk all over her. She unconsciously lifted her chin; in her defence it was easy to forget who was in charge when you were in a room with a man who dominated this and any other space he happened to be in.

'Can I get you anything…tea, coffee?'

The polite question brought his wandering gaze back to her face as he slung her an incredulous *Are you joking?* look.

'You can get me my son.'

It wasn't just the possessive inflection but the underlying hungry need in his voice that sent a fresh trickle of unease down her stiff spine. As the tension climbed back into her shoulders, she watched his eyes search the space behind her as though he expected to see Jamie suddenly appear.

'Jamie is outside in the garden,' she explained with a sense of calm she was certainly not feeling. 'I want to get a few ground rules sorted first.'

Astonishment flashed across his face. 'You...?' She could almost see the quivering line as he reeled in the rest of his response and stood there directing his fierce black stare at her, presumably waiting for her to fall apart or maybe at his feet begging forgiveness. He might have stepped out of the boardroom in recent years but he had lost none of the arrogance she remembered...if she had ever needed a reminder that he was no laid-back thriller writer. Roman was a maverick, the man who made the rules, not the man who followed them.

She moistened her lips with the tip of her tongue and waited as long as she could bear before she blurted out, 'So are you all right with that?' The tiny flash of something close to admiration in his dark eyes before he dropped his gimlet gaze might only have existed in her imagination, but her sense of triumph was real as she silently chalked up an invisible line in the air.

Her tiny burst of optimism vanished as she contemplated her immediate future stretching out in front of her like a winding road with no end in sight.

God, it was depressing! *Somehow* she would have to slot Roman into their lives, but as she regarded his tall, imposing person through the shade of her lashes, she felt her heart sink even lower. He really wasn't a person who slotted into any neat space; he dominated every environment. She repressed a sigh and thought wistfully of her life a few short days ago. It had been neat and ordered and her stomach *hadn't*... She hadn't *felt*... Her fluttering gaze lingered tremblingly for a split second too long on the sculpted firm contours of his overtly sensual mouth and her insides dissolved hotly as lust suddenly paralysed her ability to think *anything*.

'So what are *your* ground rules?' His voice was low and disconcertingly expressionless as he pushed the words past his even, clenched white teeth, but at least it gave her the impetus to drag herself free of the sensual vortex that had held her immobile for a few shaming moments.

This was what she had been trying not to think about: the fact, inescapable and shameful, that after all that had happened she was still disastrously attracted to Roman... No, *attracted* was an insipid word to describe her physical response to him, which in the past she had thought of as a form of temporary insanity.

Except it wasn't temporary!

She had been avoiding it by focusing on the practicalities involved with bringing him into Jamie's life. The irony of this scenario was wedged like a lead weight against her breastbone. He clearly resented her being in control when in actuality she had not felt less in control... at least of her own body for...well, actually ever since she had left his hotel room more than five years ago.

As the pounding in her head stepped up its painful tempo her aggravation and seething frustration exploded into speech. 'I really wish you wouldn't take everything so personally, Roman! I'm not trying to make a point, but actually, if you want to look at it that way, they *are* my rules.

'If you want to be *any* part of Jamie's life...' She paused, wondering if he actually knew what he wanted in practical terms, but not sure she actually wanted to know. 'I'm genuinely not trying to be awkward. *I'm—*' Her waving hand gesture and helpless shoulder shrug begged his understanding. When there was no crack in his stony façade she shook her head. 'I'm trying to avoid a difficult situation. He is only four and I don't want him confused, so you can't rush him. He needs to get to know you before we tell him who you are.'

Roman's head reared back as though she'd struck him. 'You're protecting him from me?'

The same way his mother had tried to protect him and Rio from their father.

'You need to be patient, Roman.' She sighed. 'You can't expect him to just…'

'Love me.'

A short, strained silence followed this interruption.

'That wasn't what I was about to say,' she said quietly. She gnawed gently on her full lower lip, the action causing his eyes to drift in that direction, pausing on the lush plumpness that bore the imprint of her teeth. 'I just wanted to warn…' He stiffened and she held up both hands. 'Oh, for heaven's sake, this is like walking on eggshells! This is hard enough without you being so damned touchy. I'm just trying to say—if you'll let me?'

Their eyes connected and after a short pause one corner of his mouth lifted. 'Go ahead…' He opened his hand in invitation.

'I'm just trying to warn you not to expect too much too soon. We haven't really discussed just how we're going to do this, but I don't want you to have unrealistic expectations.'

'You're trying to warn me not to expect him to love me on sight. I'm not an idiot, Marisa.'

'I think we should take things slowly.'

A nerve clenched in his lean cheek. He'd waited five years, he told himself; a few more days would not matter.

'In a few months when—'

'Months!'

Marisa lowered her gaze, seeing no point in pushing things any further. 'Let's just play it by ear, shall we?' His silence was better than an argument and she decided to interpret his grim expression as a yes. 'He's playing outside—this way.' She gestured to the open door to their left.

For a split second she thought he was not going to react to her invitation, and she allowed herself a little sigh of relief when he did.

Conscious of his towering presence, in every sense of the word, she led the way through the doorway to the rear of the house past what had once been a dairy and was now a boot room. She unlatched the closed portion of the stable door that led out to the kitchen garden, where gravel paths wove their way through a geometric arrangement of raised beds bursting with a variety of leafy green vegetables, herbs and soft fruit, each bordered by neatly trimmed box hedging.

'That one is Jamie's garden,' she said with a proud smile as they passed one of the raised beds that stood out from the other well-tended beds with their straight lines and leafy growth because there were no straight lines in sight, just patches of seedlings poking their way through the ground in artistic swirls, and seed packets tied to sticks fluttering in the breeze.

She turned her head to explain to Roman how much Jamie loved to watch things grow and his fascination with creepy-crawlies, and caught a look on his lean face as he followed her gaze and registered the swirls of green, that brought a lump to her throat and an ache of unexpected empathy to her heart. She looked away quickly but was left with a feeling that she had suddenly intruded on a very private moment.

When she turned back, the mixture of longing and loss was gone as he righted a wooden marker that said *trees*, the wobbly letters in green marker pen sloping, the *s* back to front.

'He calls broccoli *trees*,' she explained as he straightened up and dusted his hands on the seat of his immaculate jeans, causing a stab of longing to vibrate through her body, illustrating the danger of allowing empathy for him to breach her defences.

She had built a life that was stable and secure, for her and for Jamie, who'd had enough trauma in his short life to last several lifetimes. There had to be a way of allowing Roman access to him without disrupting what they had, and that wouldn't happen if she couldn't get her hormones under control.

She looked away and felt a fleeting stab of nostalgia for the days when she had imagined she was not someone who was particularly interested in sex. All it had taken was for Roman to appear on her horizon to blow that comforting theory completely out of the water.

'When he was…ill I promised him a garden. I thought he'd forget but—' she gave a rueful laugh '—he didn't, so don't go making any promises you can't keep because he'll hold you to them.'

Roman frowned. 'Very subtle.'

The sardonic rejoinder brought a sting of colour to her cheeks.

'Next you'll be telling me a child is for life, not just for Christmas. So is telling him lies prohibited or is lying by omission allowed?'

Roman watched her flush again as the jibe hit home, but it didn't make him feel particularly good.

She sighed.

'I'll tell Jamie you're a friend.'

He hid his reaction beneath his heavy half-lowered lids.

'So you'll lie to him again.' His head tilted to a mocking quizzical angle. 'Or are we friends?'

The mockery stung. Marisa knew they could never be friends...and she hated that the acknowledgment, quite illogically, made her sad.

People who had been lovers did stay friends but she assumed those people had things in common besides sex. The only thing they had in common besides sleeping together was Jamie. Without Jamie, Roman would not be here and she would not be... She took a deep breath and dragged her hand across the smooth hair that was moulded to her head like a shiny cap. She was skirting around the real elephant in the room, which was the complicated confusion of her feelings, the buzz in her bloodstream. She didn't want Roman here, so why did she feel more alive than she had in a long time?

'So you're all right with that?' she threw back with more than a hint of challenge.

The tightening of his jaw was a lot less casual than his shrug. 'Do I have a choice?'

She said nothing as she turned away, pointing to a gate in the low stone wall that ran down the length of the kitchen garden. 'This way.'

CHAPTER FIVE

THE STRIP OF WOODLAND was carpeted with snowdrops in spring and later bluebells but now in midsummer the undergrowth was tall and thick enough to scratch the legs of a little boy wearing shorts.

Jamie's yell of 'Not fair' drifted across the intervening space. He was fifty yards away on the other side of the small paddock where a goalpost had been erected, but Marisa could see that the blood oozing from a cut on Jamie's knee was not a scratch, at least in her head.

She took a deep breath and talked herself away from what she visualised as the panic ledge in her head. There had been a time in the not so distant past when she would have reacted to the sight of a grazed knee with full-blown drama; it was always a fight to repress her maternal protective instincts but she was getting there.

Wrapping Jamie up in cotton wool would have made her life a lot easier but she had recognised it wouldn't be good for him so she made an effort to allow him the rough and tumble that any little boy enjoyed.

Her own fight to control her instincts had distracted her for a split second from the man who was walking a few steps behind her.

The sound of his muffled exclamation brought her head around just as he released a low rush of words in his native Spanish. She had no idea what they meant but it was hard to hear the painfully raw intonation without feeling a stab of empathy for his shocked reaction.

Looking at the expression stamped on his lean features, an expression as raw as his words and filled with a kind of painful longing, made her throat ache; swallowing, she looked away.

The father of her child might be a virtual stranger to her outside the bedroom but every instinct she had told her that he would hate for anyone to witness anything that he would consider a weakness.

'Apparently he has excellent hand-eye coordination,' she said to fill the growing screaming silence and give him time to recover himself.

When he did speak it was clear that she wasn't going to be getting any appreciation for her sensitivity.

'So who the hell is *that*?'

Marisa's head turned in response to his snarled question, the verbal equivalent of what she imagined a wolf's growl would sound like.

Her sense of impending doom deepened as she took in the rigid lines on his scowling face, but now it was mingled with exasperation.

'Your son,' she said, delivering a tight fake smile in response to his accusing glare.

'Do not be cute with me, Marisa.'

Her lips tightened. He might not like being on the receiving end of warnings but he appeared to have zero problem issuing them. Her indignation soared. Here was she, bending over backwards to make this as painless as possible for everyone, and all he could do was—

She heaved a deep restorative breath before tossing her head, causing several strands of shiny flaxen hair to escape the ponytail on the nape of her slim neck.

'I am never cute.' You could not be *cute* when you were a whisper short of five foot eleven. 'I assume you're referring to—' But then she paused as he wasn't just referring, he was positively glaring! 'That's Ashley.'

'And just who is Ashley?' Roman growled back, his eyes fixed on the rear view of the tall male who was kicking a ball back to his son...*his son*! The emotion swelled in his chest as his gaze transferred once more to the child with stick-thin legs who squealed with laughter as he kicked the ball past the man and then punched the air.

'Not fair, I wasn't ready!' the young blond man yelled back.

'Do you often leave our son in the care of your boyfriends?'

She blinked, her astonishment genuine, but it swiftly turned to annoyance. Eyes flaring, she folded her arms tightly across her chest. 'Ashley is Jamie's nanny.' Her chin lifted a defiant notch as she fixed him with a narrow-eyed glare. 'And what business of yours would it be if he was my boyfriend?' she challenged, thinking this was rich coming from someone who had a partiality for scantily clad blondes.

Roman spun around. *'Nanny?'* he echoed, fixing on the relevant part of her retort before his eyes and his brain got snagged on the sight of silky strands of pale hair shining against her dark jumper. The image was the catalyst that took him straight back to a time and place when that hair was longer and tangled, drifting across his chest as she sat astride him, the feathery light contact sending electrical surges along his nerve endings, before the caress was replaced by the touch of her lips.

The effort of escaping the erotic images before he was sucked back into the past brought a sheen of sweat to his brow, and his fingers clenched as he dragged in a mind-clearing lungful of oxygen.

*Focus, man, think...*he ordered himself.

The problem was, the thoughts in question involved another man playing with his son, his son looking up trustingly into another man's face and laughing.

Roman realised he seriously hated the thought of that man being more than Marisa's employee. From a mental file in his head of similar incidents came the memory of a scene, of his father driving them home after dinner, cross-examining his mother just because she had smiled at a waiter. She had flirted with the man, he'd accused, and he was sure she had given him her phone number.

They had sat there, he and Rio, and listened as their father had called their mother names that no man should call a woman. As children all they could do was kick the back of their father's seat in protest to try to make him stop. No longer a child, he would do so much more if he heard similar abuse now.

He would not be that man.

'I didn't realise there were any male nannies.' It was a rational observation, and he could have added that in his opinion nannies did not look as though they hit the gym on a daily basis before they ran out into the morning surf.

Marisa resisted the childish impulse to stamp her feet. It wasn't even what he'd said, it was the *way* he'd said it, his attitude of teeth-grating certainty that by simply saying something it made it so.

'Have you never heard of equality?' she enquired sweetly and earned herself another glare. 'Or do you think women have the exclusive rights on *caring* for children?' she said with blighting scorn, seeing no reason to admit that it hadn't exactly been her own enlightened thinking that had made her shortlist Ashley, because until he had walked through the door and her PA had leaned across and breathed, *'Wow, can he be my nanny?'* she hadn't even realised that Ashley was a man.

He had been the last interviewee, she remembered, and she'd been ready to give up, as none of the other well-qualified candidates had seemed a good fit. Probably because she hadn't really wanted them to be, she thought wryly. She hadn't wanted a mother substitute; *she* was Jamie's mum.

She'd been the problem, not them, or at least the fact that she didn't want a nanny, she *needed* a nanny. The bad case of flu that had meant she literally couldn't get out of bed for a week—and, worse, had to keep away from Jamie because she couldn't risk exposing him to the virulent bug—had proved that.

It was times like that it really hit home to her what it meant to be a single parent with no husband to step into the breach. She had no family ready to rush to help out in emergencies either… At least she was one of the lucky ones who had enough money to pay for staff to help her, who had gone way beyond the call of duty, so Jamie was being well cared for, but it meant that she was imposing on people who she was sure would have preferred to be spending time with their own families.

Had she taken to Ashley so quickly because he wasn't a threat to her relationship with Jamie—he was not a mother substitute? She couldn't swear hand on heart that it hadn't been a factor but he was a good fit regardless, at least until Jamie started school full-time, or, to be more precise, the month before school started, which was when Ash was due to go travelling for a year before he started his university course next autumn, debt-free.

She really admired the young man's practicality, the

fact he had put his ambition to be an architect on hold and got a childcare qualification first so he could earn some money before taking up a university place and also had a way of earning his keep while he was there.

'You kept very quiet about him,' Roman observed tautly, interrupting her thoughts.

She shook her head in genuine bewilderment. 'Was I quiet?' He made it sound as if she'd deliberately not told him. 'I'm pretty sure I mentioned him.'

'That Jamie had a nanny, yes, but not that he was a *he*.'

Her lips tightened. 'I didn't think it was relevant, because it isn't.'

'So no one ever comments on it?'

Her eyes slid from his. 'Oh, for God's sake, what is your problem?'

'I don't have a problem,' Roman denied, knowing he was lying.

Her delicate brows lifted. 'Yes, it really shows.'

Her laugh brought Roman's teeth together so hard he could feel them grate. It wasn't caring men that Roman had a problem with, it was the strong possibility, no, more like the *probability* that he was not one of them, that this quality was something you couldn't learn. You either had it, like the guy currently playing with his son, or you didn't.

Did Marisa admire this guy's *caring* qualities or was it his muscles she was interested in? Recognising that this less than charitable thought yet again came straight out of his own father's playbook did not improve his mood one little bit.

'I don't have a problem with male nannies.' He had no problems with male *anything*, he just had a problem with this particular guy, who was quite obviously being a great role model for *his* son, but he was not—absolutely *not*—jealous.

He was not that man; he was not his father.

His jaw clamped, the white line around his lips standing out stark against his tan. *Dios*, yes, he was!

This reaction was the reason he had spent his life avoiding caring enough to become a monster like his father. Only twice in his life had he allowed himself to care and each time—

He closed his eyes momentarily to cut out the sight of his child listening attentively to something the blond guy was saying to him. In fact, he was hanging on every syllable.

He wanted his son to look at him the way he was looking at his nanny.

The shock of that vibrated though him, jarring like a discordant off-key note. He had accepted that he had a son, accepted that the child was his responsibility, but he had not anticipated having these feelings for him, or that they would be instantaneous.

He hadn't even registered the young guy who was the focus of his envy initially, because his focus had been so completely on the child running across the grass on his skinny little legs.

Knowing he had a child, he'd discovered, was an entirely different thing from actually seeing him, no longer a theoretical son, but a real flesh and blood kid. One with tangled hair, a shiny sweat-slicked face and blood from a graze on his knee staining one sock.

The impact was almost physical. Roman felt as if someone had just landed an unprotected direct hit on his solar plexus, the invisible blow causing the breath to leave his chest in a gasp as a nameless aching feeling rushed to fill the vacuum that was left.

It was not hard to recognise a game-changing moment when it hit you in the face, and this was it. Duty had brought him here but this totally unanticipated feeling was going to keep him here, was going to keep him in his son's life.

'Mum!'

Roman watched the child's face light up as he spotted his mother, who began waving back.

'Watch what I can do—it's really cool skills!' he yelled as he balanced the football on his knee for at least two seconds before picking it up and waiting for the applause.

It came right on cue, and the sight of Marisa's smiling face, her enthusiastic clapping, her cheery thumbs up, shook loose some fresh nameless emotion deep inside Roman that he didn't want to acknowledge.

'Excellent skills!' she approved.

He turned his head sharply, remembering again his brother's expression as his twin had held his own small daughter close to his chest. It had been a faint echo compared to what Roman felt now. *Envy, loss, regret...* None of them were legitimate responses for a man who had never wanted children.

He still believed in the reasoning behind his decision not to have children. The facts had not changed, and it was a decision he would make again if he had been able to. Why run the risk of passing on the tainted genes, replicate painful history, inflict the sort of emotional damage on his child his own father had on him and Rio?

But that option was gone; it was firmly in the past. In the present he had a son, that was the reality he was dealing with now, and it came with an unaccustomed sense of inadequacy he was struggling to deal with.

So far he had succeeded in not acknowledging the fear he knew was lurking underneath the anger, but it had been much easier to focus on confronting Marisa about her actions than acknowledging it.

If it gets tough, you can always fall back on blaming her for everything, sneered the contemptuous voice in his head,

Roman knew about this *visceral* connection, this blood calling to blood... He glanced down and saw that his white-knuckled fist was clenched against his chest, and self-consciously he allowed it to fall back to his side. Now he knew why his brother had finally decided to break his silence about Jamie's existence, break his promise to Marisa. Because of this *feeling* that was tearing Roman apart right now—Rio knew what it felt like to be a father.

To banish the surge of empathy, because he really didn't want to stop being angry with his twin, and he definitely didn't want to be *grateful* to him, Roman replaced his brother's face with a mental image of their own father, who had rarely noticed his sons were alive unless he'd wanted to use them to get to their mother. They'd only ever been a useful tool or an inconvenience to him.

The voice in his head urging caution was almost drowned out by the overwhelming surge of paternal feeling that had just materialised out of nowhere.

There were still very good reasons why this child would be so much better off without Roman in his life, but he knew he was not selfless enough to keep a safe distance from him.

'He is a big soccer fan.'

Roman didn't respond to Marisa, but she could feel the emotions emanating from him across the distance between them. She slid a glance up at him. His profile was as rigid as his body language; everything about him was *clenched*.

No wonder he looked tense—this had to be his nightmare scenario. His apparently ingrained sense of duty was probably the only thing stopping him from heading for the nearest exit at high speed.

Would it be a problem if he did?

Not for her, she told herself. Her life would be a lot easier without Roman in it, a lot more vanilla and safe, which obviously would be a good thing. She could live without drama; she could live without sex.

Always good to wait to be asked before refusing it, Marisa.

Feeling the heat climb into her cheeks, she retracted her gaze, retreating under the shade of her lashes. Any sympathy she might feel for Roman—the man whose antipathy for children was presumably strong enough to make not having them a condition of a marriage proposal, and who had then found himself a father—was tempered by her main concern for Jamie and the effect the sudden appearance of a father in his life would have on him.

Roman was here now, but who was to say that he wouldn't want to opt out at some future point, a point when Jamie would know he had been rejected? Having something and losing it was a lot different from not missing what you'd never had. A feeling she knew all too well, she mused grimly, reflecting on her blissful ignorance before Roman had taught her how to enjoy her own body and his!

This is about Jamie, Marisa.

'So is he any good at what he does?' Roman asked, resenting the ease with which Ashley was making his son laugh as he watched the interaction, the easy rapport between man and boy.

He made it look easy, and Rio had made it look easy too. To Roman it did not seem easy, it seemed—

He didn't even know what the thing he lacked was, he concluded with a burst of self-contempt for his sheer cluelessness.

Could you learn how to be a good father? Just the basics—or if you couldn't learn to be a good father, then at the very least one that did no harm.

Roman had achieved much that people would envy in his life, but it had all come so easily to him. At that moment he would have exchanged every single thing he had achieved for the nanny's ability to be so relaxed with a child, or rather this particular child...*his* child.

It was her little artificial laugh that broke the downward spiral of his depressing internal dialogue. His glance slewed her way; there was no amusement on her face to match the laugh.

She was standing there ramrod stiff, her chin lifted to a militant angle as she fixed him with a narrow-eyed glare of icy challenge.

'What exactly is *that* meant to mean?'

In the past Marisa had taken the teasing comments about Ashley and the inevitable double entendres when friends and other mothers had met the handsome young addition to her household in good part. None of it was malicious, although it got a bit tiresome at times, but nothing she couldn't handle. If laughter didn't close down the subject she had a whole list of comical comebacks at her disposal.

Somehow she didn't feel like laughing now.

Roman's brows tugged together as he studied her hot, antagonistic face.

'I mean...' he began, then stopped, comprehension spreading across his face as his gaze flashed between the young man and Marisa, something kicking hard in his gut as he joined the dots and watched a picture form that explained her defensive attitude.

Was it possible he had jumped to the *right* conclusion after all? Had she given herself to this youth with as much passion as she had him? Had Ashley watched the concentration on her face as she fought to reach her climax? Had he felt…? Damping the sweat he could feel beading on his upper lip with a slightly shaking hand, he clamped down on the feverish speculation that would only feed the ever-present ache of wanting something he couldn't have, something that, even after everything that had happened between them, he still had zero control over.

Zero control was a hard thing to admit for a man who prided himself on his, be it on the rock face, delivering a daily word count or picking apart an argument that had stupidity written all over it without losing his temper.

But what she made him feel was beyond his powers of self-deception. Far better to own a weakness than run away from it or get too hung up over it.

No point overcomplicating the situation. He was feeling something he didn't want to feel; wanting her and not being able to have her was a kind of torture, but, he told himself grimly, he could live with it, treat it like any other chemical imbalance in his brain.

'Interesting reaction,' he drawled. 'Have I touched a nerve?'

His sarcasm freed her from the embarrassment. 'Ashley lives in the flat over the stables. He is only a boy.' The moment Marisa said it she wanted to take it back, furious with herself for bothering to explain. Roman could think what he liked.

'I was a boy once too and a few years' age gap never seemed like an obstacle to me.'

'I just bet it didn't!' she snapped back. 'But before you start getting nostalgic about all the notches on your bedpost—' she diverted her gaze to the game of football '—for the record and because you clearly judge others by your very low standards, I am not *sleeping* with Ashley.' She shrugged and added, 'Yet.'

'Is that meant to make me jealous?'

'I thought you already were.'

When he didn't reply, she turned and lifted her gaze to Roman's face, catching the tail end of a puzzling expression that vanished so quickly she decided she had imagined it. 'Shall I call Jamie over?'

'That's what I'm here for.'

Marisa waved and called out, and with obvious reluctance Jamie came trotting over, his tall nanny following behind, the football in his hands.

'Jamie, this is someone I want you to meet. His name is Mr—'

'Roman.'

'This is Roman and he has come to have tea with us.'

'Tea…' The lower lip came out. 'I don't want tea. I wanna play football with Ash and afterwards—'

'Enough football for one day, mate. It's my afternoon off,' the nanny interjected.

Hands clenched at his sides, the little boy aimed a kick at the football that Ashley had placed on the ground. It went sailing away before he swung back to the trio of adults, looking mutinous, though most of his ire seemed aimed at Roman. 'But that's not fair…'

'Not fair is expecting someone else to pick up your toys…' Ashley nodded towards the ball that had sailed into a bed of flowers. 'Go get it, and I'll see you on Monday.'

Roman watched, the empty space in his chest aching,

as the child gave a deep sigh and trotted off across the expanse of green grass.

'He has quite a kick.'

Roman turned towards the nanny. Somehow the word did not fit a six-foot-three man with a tattoo on his neck, even one as innocuous as a rose with fallen petals.

He said nothing, seeing that the younger man was standing beside Marisa now. Clearly they'd been talking but he'd been too focused on his son to register the conversation. His eyes narrowed as he noticed how close the two were standing together, their posture, their body language revealing how comfortable they were with one another. He inhaled sharply. *Jealous*, she had said.

He made himself exhale again. She might not be sleeping with this particular man but it would be naïve of him to imagine that a woman of her sexuality had spent the last few years living the life of a nun.

Ashley made his goodbyes and turned to Roman with a polite, 'Nice to meet you.'

Roman could only manage a nod in response, his glacial stare still in place, and he could see Marisa heave a sigh of exasperation before she added, 'Enjoy your long weekend, Ash.'

'I will.'

Roman watched as the nanny jogged off and out of view.

'That was rude.'

One dark brow lifted. 'If that was rude, what would you call not telling a man he is the father of your child?' In his head the retort had not sounded quite so brutal but the result was the same.

All the animation went out of her face, and she stiffened, seeming to almost physically shrink back from him.

He should have felt satisfied at her reaction but her discomfort afforded him surprisingly little pleasure.

With clenched hands set on her hips, she turned to face him, her luminous eyes calm but determined in her pale face.

'If you imagine you can close down any conversation by playing the victim card, I think you should go for another strategy,' she advised him tartly.

And he had started to feel a glimmer of sympathy for her. Stung, he snapped back, *'Victim?'*

On another occasion Roman's expression of outraged incredulity would have made Marisa laugh but at that moment laughter was beyond her. This was an impossible situation, which she couldn't see getting better any time soon, but for Jamie's sake she had to try.

'If you're always going to resent me, fine, that is your choice, but if you actually do want to form any sort of relationship with our son—'

'A child should know who his father is.'

Her brow creased. 'That wasn't what I asked,' she threw back, annoyed by his politician's response.

Was he saying that he didn't want a relationship with Jamie, that he didn't want to be part of Jamie's life after all? She shouldn't be surprised and she definitely shouldn't be disappointed…after all, it would make her life a hell of a lot easier.

As Jamie breathlessly trotted back with his beloved football, she flashed Roman a warning glance and dropped into a crouch. 'That knee looks sore.'

'I didn't cry.'

'Well, I would have,' Marisa retorted.

'You're a girl.'

'Boys cry too.'

Her son looked doubtful. 'Do you cry?' he asked Roman.

She held her breath, fully anticipating a tough male macho response, only to release it when he replied.

'Everyone cries.'

'Come on, let's get that knee sorted and have some cake,' she said.

CHAPTER SIX

ROMAN WAS STANDING by the window when the door was flung open and Jamie bounced into the room displaying a boundless energy that made it hard to imagine him as a child who had had a life-threatening illness, his knee sporting a sticking plaster and his hands now clean.

Marisa followed close behind carrying a tray, which she set carefully down on the table between the two big comfy sofas, then she took a place on one and motioned Roman to sit opposite her.

He considered ignoring the invitation and sitting beside her but practicality won out over perversity. Even across the room the scent of her perfume—or was it just the scent of her skin?—brought back too many distracting memories, and hunger clawed in his belly.

'Do you want a biscuit, Jamie?'

'Can I have two?'

'No.' The child responded with a small shrug and grinned. 'Tea?' Her eyes brushed Roman's face.

He would have much preferred brandy but he nodded, unable to take his eyes off the little boy who was busy cramming his biscuit in his mouth. The son he had imagined in his head had been a blank canvas but he was discovering the reality was very different. Jamie was already a personality.

'Are you my mum's boyfriend?'

Roman's eyes flew wide as the four-year-old did what few others ever had—threw him totally.

Marisa choked on her first sip of tea. 'Jamie, you can't say something like that!'

'Why?' The child's mystification was genuine.

'Indeed, why?' There was nothing genuine about the puzzled look on Roman's face, but the taunting gleam in his eyes spoke volumes as he glanced at a pink-faced Marisa.

As the child exchanged a look with his father, oblivious to his identity, Marisa was suddenly struck by the striking similarity in their body language. Her throat aching, she jerked her eyes downwards, feeling something she didn't want to feel as she swallowed against the ache in her chest.

'Sam at nursery, his mum has a boyfriend and Libby Smith says her mummy has two, but I don't believe her. She shows off and she fibs. She says she can swim but I know she can't.'

'Can you swim?' Roman asked curiously.

'Y...' His eyes slid to his mother's face. 'Well, I can with arm bands on and I can kick harder than anything. Can I have another biscuit now, please?' His hand hovered over the plate. 'Chocolate?'

Marisa responded to the opportunistic request with a distracted, 'Yes.' Glad of the distraction as her son snatched one before she changed her mind, she watched him pull a toy car out of his pocket before he bounded across the room making the appropriate noises.

'You can be my mum's boyfriend if you like.'

Marisa could feel Roman's eyes on her face, but she refused to return his gaze, knowing full well she'd see mockery there and maybe something else... Besides, she would only end up staring at his mouth again and thinking about it sliding across her lips… The self-admission came with a tidal wave of heat that rose through her body until every inch of her skin tingled with embarrassment.

Or was that excitement?

'I'd prefer Ashley, but Mummy is too old for him.'

'Yes, she is much too old for him,' Roman agreed gravely.

'How old are you?'

'Thirty-one,' said Roman, feeling a lot older as he listened to the flow of childish confidences.

'I'm five next time, and I can already count to ten in French and I know *two* people who went to heaven. How many do you know?'

'Jamie, there are some bricks under the chair. Please will you go and put them back in the box?' Marisa instructed.

Roman, reeling and pale under his tan, directed his question in a low choked voice to Marisa. 'Does he mean…?'

Marisa, understanding shining in her eyes, tipped her head in confirmation, causing the cold knot in his belly to harden to an iron fist.

Shock bypassed his normal close-mouthed caution when it came to revealing anything about himself. 'And I thought *my* childhood was traumatic!' Caught up in his own thoughts, Roman didn't register the expression on Marisa's face. 'He sounds so casual about knowing people who have died.' He found that almost as disturbing as the brutal facts themselves.

'Children who have been through what Jamie has, they grow up quickly in some ways, but they are remarkably resilient. More so sometimes than the adults.'

She spoke quietly, her soft voice carrying virtually

no inflection but he could see the shadows in her eyes. For the first time he let himself think about what the nightmare experience must have felt like, wondering if her child was going to die. She had faced more than he had done in his life, and he felt humbled by the strength she had shown.

'Jamie knew how ill he was?' he asked.

'They don't lie to the children.'

'Even when the truth is—' He shook his head, appalled. 'I cannot imagine how hard it must have been for both of you.'

He had known his child literally for five minutes and already he was positive that if it were required he would lay down his life to spare him a moment's suffering. The absolute shock of this fresh discovery widened his eyes.

She would have done the same, he realised as he watched her throw out a word of encouragement and a smile to the child who was adding a final brick to the lopsided creation that looked in imminent danger of toppling.

But it hadn't been an option for her; instead, she'd had to sit there, day in and day out, watching her child suffering and feeling totally helpless. *Dios*, he could not even imagine the sheer horror of what she and Jamie had been through.

'I'm sorry.' The words emerged almost against his will, the deepening furrow in his broad brow an instinctive response to the inadequacy of the words he had never expected to hear himself voice.

She was desperate—wasn't that what Rio had said? Not that Roman had been listening, because he'd had no space in his head right then for reasons or excuses. Just anger, resentment and a strong sense of betrayal that still hadn't gone away, but he could see past it now, although

he didn't want to, and it made him mad as hell to acknowledge even in the privacy of his own mind that Rio
had only spoken the simple facts; Marisa had been desperate but not desperate enough to come to *him*.

And maybe she had been right?

He paused that chain of thought before it could get too
uncomfortable, her soft voice providing the escape route
that he grabbed hold of.

'It wasn't your fault that Jamie was ill.'

Her generosity was genuine enough to send a slug of
shame through him. 'I should have been there for both
of you.'

She had bent over to scoop up a couple of the stray toy
building blocks from under a table, and as she straightened, her ponytail landed with a gentle thud between her
narrow shoulder blades.

Face gently flushed from the exertion, she flashed a
glance to the corner of the room where Jamie was now
playing with his toy car again, before responding to his
statement.

'You didn't know. I should have told you, I see that
now, but at the time I was—' She turned her head but
not before he had seen the sheen of unshed tears bright
in her eyes.

Rio's words came back to him again. *Desperate*. She
had been *desperate*.

Clearing her throat, she turned back to face him.
'When you're in a situation like that, the only people
who actually understand, *really* understand, are those
who are living through it too. They become in some ways
your support network. You're all living in a bubble, and,
although the world carries on as normal, for you nothing is normal even though you try your—' She stopped,
a self-conscious expression seeping across her face as

their eyes connected and she gave a tiny jerky motion of her head, looking confused, as though she'd never actually articulated those feelings before.

'So do you keep in touch with the other parents?'

'A few.' Her eyes filled with tears again and he saw her try to rapidly blink them away.

Roman considered himself immune to female tears and the soul-baring and accusations they frequently preceded. He generally pretended not to notice them and made himself scarce; he certainly never had to fight an urge to hold someone and tell them it was going to be all right. Even Marisa's prosaic sniff before she launched into husky speech again located an unexpected vulnerable spot inside him, awaking a tenderness he didn't know he possessed.

'Amy, she…' She glanced towards Jamie and Roman noticed with a touch of amused pride that his son had appropriated yet another biscuit while they'd been distracted in conversation. 'We were both single parents; everyone else was part of a couple.' She saw him flinch. 'I wasn't trying to…you know…make you feel guilty.'

'I know you weren't.' It was becoming more than clear to him that Marisa did not play the blame game.

'Actually I think Amy and I were lucky.' Marisa saw his eyes narrowed with scepticism and she hastily explained.

'From what I saw an ill child often puts a relationship under a lot of strain. At least two couples I met while Jamie was being treated are in the middle of a bitter divorce now and another couple are giving it another go, so who knows?'

'Maybe the cracks were already there in those relationships,' he suggested, threading his long fingers together as he looked at where Jamie had crawled under a table and was happily building a tower out of bricks. 'Or maybe most marriages, once you look beneath the surface, are pretty toxic.'

The cynicism in his voice drew a wince from Marisa—he really didn't seem to have a high view of marriage, which begged the question why had he once proposed to her?

'Why—' She stopped and pushed away the question that felt as though it belonged in another life now; the person she had been then no longer existed, the things she had felt, *longed* for, all gone, like smoke on the wind. She had completely changed so maybe he had changed too. Maybe he was sitting there congratulating himself on his own lucky escape from marrying her.

It turned out it wasn't his own escape he had been thinking of.

'My mother only started living again when she escaped her marriage.' Distracted for a moment from the shocking developments that were dominating his own personal life, it was almost relief for Roman to turn his inner anger and frustration to another situation that he had even less control over.

His mother had freed herself from her marriage to a man who wanted to control every aspect of her life, a man whose warped idea of love was to cut the object of his affections off from everyone else who cared for her, who was jealous of anyone who took her attention away from him—including his sons.

And here she was getting involved with a man with one failed marriage already behind him. The thought of the theatre director his mother had been with for the last two years etched a frown into his brow.

He didn't give a damn that the man was twelve years younger than her; he didn't care that he was successful enough not to be after her money. His mother was a happy, confident woman now but Roman couldn't get rid of the image of her as the woman she'd been before, afraid to make any decision for herself, while seeming happy and content to the outside world.

What if history repeated itself with this other man and Roman couldn't see past the happiness and contentment so he couldn't protect her just as he hadn't been able to protect her as a child?

'Why did you ask me to marry you?' Marisa asked, sounding as though she simply had to know.

His gaze slowly moved to her face.

'Do you expect me to say I was in love with you?'

He had thought it back then, but he wasn't about to admit to her something that even now he struggled to admit to himself.

His lip curled in self-contempt as he remembered thinking he had finally found his soulmate and the idea of losing her, of not spending every possible minute of the rest of his life with her, had seemed like an insanity.

She had had him at a golden glance, and he had run with reckless haste to claim the very thing he had spent his life avoiding, with consequences that only proved how right he had always been to avoid it.

'No, I...'

'Love can, I have heard tell, survive the cruel light of day. But what we shared was not love, it was likely just a...temporary insanity brought about by our seething hormones. We wanted to get naked a lot, so it's perfectly understandable.'

Why it should hurt so much to hear him reduce what they had shared to a basic animal lust, Marisa didn't know, but it did.

'People get married all the time when they know they

shouldn't… How many people have you heard say, "I wish I'd never married you"?'

'We didn't get married,' she said quietly.

'Then you could call us lucky.'

A whoop of delight as Jamie's tower toppled, scattering bricks across the wooden floor, broke the spell of Roman's brooding stare, and she smiled at her little boy.

'He seems to take some delight in destruction,' Roman commented with amusement.

'Yes, he is your average little boy, but so kind, as well. Last week his nursery visited a petting zoo and he was so gentle with the chicks and…' She stopped, her reminiscent smile fading as she felt a self-conscious flush run up under her skin. 'Sorry.'

'What for?'

'I can get a bit boring when I talk about Jamie.'

'Mothers are meant to think their children are perfect and I am not bored.'

'Does your mother know about—' She glanced at Jamie.

Roman shook his head. 'I haven't told her.' He supposed it was possible that Rio had told her as his twin seemed to have been taking a lot onto himself of late. 'I'll wait until she's out of hospital again.' Always supposing the damned boyfriend ever left her side, he brooded, thinking of the tender hand-holding scene he had walked in on when he'd last seen her.

'She must have been glad to see you,' Marisa said.

'Not so that you'd notice,' he admitted, his lips twitching into a wry smile as he recalled her exasperated, *I do not need a guard dog, Roman.*

He saw Marisa's startled expression and tacked on, 'She is not the world's best patient, because she isn't— *patient*, that is. And you can't really blame her as this thing has dragged on long enough already. She had the initial surgery in Switzerland after a skiing accident, where she broke her leg.'

Marisa winced at the explanation.

'It was a bad break. They pinned it, but there was a problem with the pin, so she's needed further surgery.'

Marisa made a soft sound of sympathy before her features suddenly froze in an expression of dawning surprise. 'Jamie has a grandmother.'

'Jamie has a father too,' he countered grimly.

Marisa sighed. She was getting tired of ducking the guilt and she really hadn't seen that one coming.

'I'll tell her about us when she is discharged.'

Marisa's chin went up. 'There is no us,' she said and immediately wished she hadn't; it sounded so petty and she knew he hadn't meant that sort of us.

'We are connected through Jamie whether you like it or not—and on that subject, I have a proposition.'

Marisa lowered her eyes, hearing the word *proposition* and remembering his proposal. She took a deep breath and cleared her mind and her expression. 'Well, let's hear it, then.'

'Beyond me being his father, Jamie has a Spanish heritage that he knows nothing about and he should have access to that heritage.'

'Jamie is British.'

'He can be both; he can have two parents. He *has* two parents.'

Marisa sat there tensely waiting, wondering where this was going.

'I would like him to come to Spain.' She immediately recoiled and he tacked on sardonically, 'I am not about to snatch him from you—obviously you will come too.'

'Obviously,' she said coolly, not willing to own up to

her moment of panic. 'Look, I can't just drop everything.' Her lips tightened at his assumption that she could rearrange her life at a moment's notice for his convenience. 'I have a very busy schedule, and I think it would be far better if you visited him here to begin with. I don't think that's unreasonable. You could take him out or—' She was running out of alternative suggestions when he cut across her.

'You do realise that this situation won't stay just between us for long?'

She looked at him blankly and shook her head as if she didn't understand what he meant, but she did—she just didn't want to think about it.

'It will not stay a secret, Marisa. My face and name are well known, and if I walk down the street with a child who looks like me—'

She shook her head, holding up her hand to silence him and thought, *Too much detail!* It was too late, though, her imagination was already conjuring up the tabloid headlines, and the effect of those on her own and, more importantly, Jamie's life.

'All right, I get it, but is it actually so inevitable? If we—'

'It's inevitable,' he bit back, scorn edging his softly spoken words. 'Unless you want me to visit my son under the cover of darkness?'

His sarcasm sailed over her head as dread congealed in an icy cold lump inside her stomach.

'Of course not!' she exclaimed.

'It will be easier if we manage the story ourselves.'

The words brought her eyes back to his face, to see that his eyes were narrowed in concentration. He sounded as if he were discussing a hostile takeover rather than their son... Her eyes widened. *Their* son, she registered, shaken to her core. It was only one word but it represented a massive mental shift in her way of thinking, a shift that she had not been conscious of.

'*Manage!*' she echoed. 'How do you manage something like this?'

'We control the flow of information,' he explained, sounding a lot more boardroom than bestselling author. It made her wonder if he'd ever go back to work at the family company, and what had happened that had made him change direction so drastically.

'Which will be difficult if we are outed by some enterprising paparazzo with a long lens or a passer-by with a phone snaps me wheeling a pushchair.'

'He's four and a half. His push chair is an absolute last resort. He hates it.'

He arched a brow. 'I think you know what I'm saying, but it's true I know zero about children and even less about being a father, so it's just as well I have you to guide me, isn't it?'

'There's no need to be sarcastic,' she said, in no mood for some sort of conversational ping-pong match. 'There is no parenting handbook. It's more an on-the-job learning experience. I'm still learning too.' Her eyes brushed the figure of their child engrossed in his game. 'And making mistakes,' she finished wearily.

She fought against the sense of helplessness she felt tightening its grip. The picture he painted of their immediate future was not one that gave her a lot to look forward to.

Roman frowned as she lifted a hand to her head, but as if she felt his scrutiny her eyes lifted. As their glances met the pulse of sexual tension that connected them seemed to flare like a streak of flame.

Marisa broke the connection and sat back in her seat,

avoiding his eyes as she picked up a china teacup and lifted it to her lips, not seeming to notice it was empty.

'So this managing of the flow of information,' she said in a flat little voice. 'Do you have anything specific in mind or are you still working out the details?'

'I have something very specific in mind.'

Her enquiring golden gaze fluttered to his face.

'Well, I think it would be perfect if we had access to somewhere which is totally secure, where privacy is guaranteed and there are no prying eyes, like say a Spanish estate?'

'Or a prison?' she suggested bitterly, not hiding her displeasure at being played.

Something flashed across his face. 'I have heard it called that before, but there are no locks.'

'So much for security,' she muttered darkly.

His lips twitched appreciatively. 'I did not mean it literally. Look, why don't we call it a holiday? Let me get to know my son away from prying eyes, allow me to introduce him to his roots. We all need to know where we come from.'

She looked at him, the internal conflict she was fighting shining in her amber eyes.

'I think under the circumstances you owe me that much,' he said, with no qualms about pressing home an advantage when he sensed it looming on the horizon.

Her slender shoulders drooped as if she were carrying something too heavy to bear, and he watched as she ran the tip of her tongue across her dry lips. 'Three weeks.'

'I'll take that.' His eyes narrowed and it was clear to Marisa that he'd gone up a mental gear. He had already moved on, his sharp mind turning to the next sequence of events.

'I'll arrange the flight and let you know the details. I have a few things I need to sort out, but if you could be ready for around...ten a.m. tomorrow, I'll send a car—'

'No.'

His eyes landed on her face with an almost physical sensation. She smiled back with determined serenity and was rewarded by his frustrated frown.

'Don't bother with the car. I'll make my own way there and let you know what flight we get and when we land. If someone could get us from the airport that would be good.'

'Someone?'

She watched his features rearrange themselves, moving in a cycle that took mere seconds from astonishment to clenched-jawed annoyance, finally settling into cynical amusement.

The latter bothered Marisa the most and brought her chin up to a defiant, some might have suggested childish, angle.

'Are you sure about this, Marisa? You could land at a private airport, with no crowds, queues, delays...?'

It was her turn to channel superior amusement as he dangled that carrot in front of her nose. 'Sounds lovely but I prefer not to be tied down to someone else's schedule.'

He tipped his head in acknowledgment and slowly, elegantly unfolded his long frame from the sofa. 'Jamie is a good flier, then?'

Anxious to reduce the extra height advantage he held over her, she sprang to her feet, dusting invisible specks from her sleeve as she dodged his gaze. 'Excellent,' she said smoothly, thinking wryly that there was a fifty-fifty chance she was right.

Their eyes moved in unison to the area where Jamie

was playing, only to discover he was now curled up in a ball, thumb in his mouth, fast asleep.

'I've only ever seen a puppy do that,' Roman whispered.

'You don't have to whisper. He won't wake up.' She moved across the room and, despite her assurance, lowered her own voice as she posed over her shoulder, 'Do you mind seeing yourself out? I'll just take him to his room.'

She missed the flicker of expression on his face as he watched her scoop up the sleeping child into her arms with a smoothness that spoke of practice, the slender back she presented to him as much as her actions effectively shutting him out.

He slanted a last look at them before he turned and moved silently towards the door, struggling to combat a feeling that was utterly alien to him. It was such a weird reversal; he had spent his life avoiding women who were needy and now he found himself in a moment of weakness wanting a woman, a stiff-necked woman full of stubborn pride, to need him.

His hand was on the handle when a soft voice halted him.

He turned around, his breath catching in his throat. She was oblivious, he knew, to the image she presented standing there, the sleeping child cradled tightly against her body, his head tucked on her shoulder. Her face-framing silvery hair blazed with the sunshine that shone in through the window, and his hungry gaze roamed across her delicate features that didn't need anything cosmetic added to enhance their delicate cut-crystal beauty.

The sheer loveliness of her tentative smile hit him like a kick in the belly, releasing a flood of hot longing that he couldn't suppress.

For a long moment they stood there staring at one another, unspoken emotions zinging between them, until Roman found himself speaking, the words falling from his lips involuntarily, coming as much of a surprise to him as they seemed to be to her.

'I have a son.' He stared at Jamie's flushed sleeping face before shifting back to Marisa's. 'I cannot say yet if I will be a good father, but perhaps the best any of us can do is simply hope we do no harm.'

'You know, Roman, if I thought for *one micro moment* that you would be bad for Jamie,' she told him fiercely, 'in any way whatsoever, I would fight you tooth and nail to keep you out of his life.'

As her flashing amber eyes locked on his Roman felt a spark of unwilling admiration.

'So you don't think I would be bad for him?' He wished that he shared her confidence. He found himself fervently hoping that his son had inherited his mother's generosity of spirit.

'The jury is still out at the moment.' Her beautiful smile took the sting out of the warning and the defensive stiffness from his spine. 'Don't overthink it; just love him—that should be enough.'

If only he shared her belief in the power of love, but Roman knew all about its destructive power. His father's love for his mother had definitely not been enough; it had been far too much!

'I will send a car.'

Still wondering if she had imagined the shadow moving across his face, Marisa gave a sigh. Did he think if she conceded on one point she was ready to devolve all her decisions to him?

'I already said that I prefer to make my own way to Spain.' She stood still, hugging Jamie's warm body to her, enduring the forensic searching scrutiny of Roman's dark stare.

'Are you trying to make a point?'

'No, I'm just not comfortable being organised.'

He lifted his hands in an acquiescent gesture and took a step back. 'Fair enough.'

CHAPTER SEVEN

How many times had he visited the Bardales family estate in Spain since he and Rio had inherited it from their father? Three or four occasions and on only one of those had he extended his stay overnight. This might have explained the shock displayed by the staff on his unexpected arrival. Even the undemonstrative estate manager who had walked in as Roman was giving instructions concerning the guests they were to expect had looked shaken. In fact, the other man had been so thrown by Roman's presence that his handshake had turned into an affectionate bear hug for the man he had known since he was a boy.

He wasn't the only member of staff to seem pleased to see him, but Roman felt it wasn't an affection he deserved considering how long he had avoided the place that came burdened with too many memories.

Roman rarely slept late, but he had finally fallen asleep around five a.m. and by the time he clawed his way out of his restless slumber he glanced at his phone, saw the time and groaned.

He fell out of bed and into the car, the heavy traffic he had to negotiate on his way to the airport not improving the tension that had climbed into his shoulders. He was reluctant to admit even to himself that he was nervous, but this was definitely not your average day at the office. Even clinging to a rock face by a fingertip above a drop of several thousand feet would have been infinitely more relaxing.

He wasn't late, but he wasn't early either, and his efforts to check out the situation were frustrated by the arrivals board, which seemed to have gone totally blank.

He was making his way through the crowded concourse to the information desk when an overheard snippet of conversation made him stop. He tapped the man who had been speaking on his shoulder.

'London plane? You said they had lost contact with the London plane?'

The man nodded. 'You have someone on it?'

'My family.' Roman felt as if an icy fist had reached into his chest and grasped his heart. Then he shook his head, stubbornly refusing to accept that they could have...

'Which flight are they on...the one from Heathrow or Gatwick?'

Roman just stared at him blankly. His brain had stopped working and the suffocating black coldness was pressing in on him.

'Here you are. I've been looking for you everywhere!'

Roman spun around. Marisa was standing there looking tired, cranky and quite incredibly beautiful as she expertly jiggled a pushchair in which Jamie lay fast asleep.

She didn't have a clue what was about to happen as he reached out for her, one hand curving around the nape of her neck the other one framing her face. Her eyes flew wide in comprehension a second before his mouth came down hard on hers in a long plundering, sensually explosive kiss that went on and on.

When it ended she was leaning into him, her knees

shaking as she gasped for breath. He set her back on her feet a little way away from him.

Jamie, she saw, had not stirred.

'Why on earth did you do that?' She struggled to inject righteous indignation into her voice but she didn't quite get there, probably because she couldn't stop looking at his mouth, remembering that glorious kiss.

She had wanted it to go on for ever.

Roman dug his hands into his pockets. 'A London flight has lost radio contact with air traffic control and I thought you were on it.' Just one simple sentence and yet it covered a whole range of emotions that he had never felt before, and never wanted to feel ever again.

'Oh...so...*that* was why—'

'I was just glad to see you were alive.'

'Right, well... OK, then.'

In an action that had all the hallmarks of compulsion he was unable to control, he extended his hand back towards her face.

As Marisa's voice had earlier, her chain of thought broke, dilated pupils eating up the gold of her eyes. The quiver deep inside her expanded as he extended his reach, his square-tipped fingers brushing a stray strand of silvery-blonde hair from her cheek, the pad of his thumb trailing along the angle of her delicate jaw while he performed his task.

It was almost nothing, a whisper touch, but the nothing had the breath leaving her parted lips in a sharp sibilant hiss. The tenderness of his unexpected action made her throat tighten and she felt the heat of unshed tears stinging the backs of her eyelids.

Obeying an instinct too strong to resist, she turned her face until her cheek was nestled into his cupped palm and

she was vaguely conscious of a foreign-sounding expletive too soft for her to catch.

Jamie's sleepy murmur brought her to her senses and,
appalled by her weakness but with her skin still being
bombarded with needle-sharp prickles of attraction, she
laid a soothing protective hand on her son's head.

'Last resort?'

She looked up and nodded to the hand luggage balanced on the handles of the pushchair. 'I couldn't manage everything.' She paused and took a deep breath. 'I
really wish I'd come with you now.'

'Yes, you should have.' Those few awful minutes when
he'd thought he might have lost them for ever had taken
several years off his life. 'Let me take it.'

'Thanks.' Their eyes locked and she immediately
looked away.

The pushchair was easier to manoeuvre without the
hand luggage, so she was able to keep up with his long-
legged stride until she felt obliged to breathlessly point
out the signs for the luggage collection they had just
walked past.

'That's all been taken care of. This way.' He glanced
down at a now wide-awake Jamie and winked, and the
smaller version of his own eyes widened and, after a
pause, delivered a blink back. Then a small hand came
up and covered one eye before he blinked again as they
passed under an archway that took them out of sight of the
cameras and into a brightly lit underground parking area.

Marisa took in the empty parking spaces with reserved
signs on them, the occupied ones filled with an assort-
ment of top-of-the-range vehicles, which explained the
visible security presence and numerous CCTV cameras.

A man in uniform wearing a headset acknowledged them with a tip of his head as they walked past.

'Can I have a biscuit?' came a small voice.

'How long have you been awake?' Marisa exclaimed. She'd been nervous of Jamie's reaction if he woke in a strange place and found Roman there too but he seemed remarkably relaxed, looking around with interest.

'I wasn't asleep.' He gave her a cheeky grin from his pushchair and added, 'I was just resting my eyes.'

Marisa laughed, the soft musical sound bouncing off the low ceiling and walls.

Listening to the interchange, Roman found himself feeling like an intruder; they had a relationship that he was not part of.

Was he really envying the thing that he had spent his whole adult life avoiding?

He heard Marisa say, 'Say hello to Roman, sweetie...'

Roman dropped into a crouch beside the pushchair but, instead of responding to his own hello, Jamie reached out and touched Roman's cheek, startling an expression from him that made Marisa look away. 'Are you growing a beard?'

'Not deliberately.'

Marisa could hear the smile in his voice and a deep quiver shimmered through her body as from the forbidden depths of her brain a memory surfaced. They had been lying amid a tumble of sheets, their sweat-soaked bodies cooling, her nostrils quivering as she'd inhaled the warm, musky male scent of his body.

Her chest had lifted in a sigh as she'd lain there experiencing a cell-deep contentment that had been entirely new to her. In some ways, the aftermath of sex had felt even more intimate to her than the act itself.

'I need a shave,' he'd murmured.

Her eyes had opened at the touch of his fingers on her breast. Despite the aftershocks of the climax still rippling through her body she'd felt her insides tighten as she'd watched his fingers massaging the sensitised, still-tingling pink skin of her breast.

He'd stopped then, self-reproach in his face, and had lifted a hand to his face, drawing it down across the abrasive dark growth on his jaw.

She'd put her hand over his, drawing her own fingers down the stubble. *I like it,* she'd whispered.

'I will have a beard when I grow to be a man and I'll be tall too.'

Her son's confident pronouncement dragged Marisa back to the present with a disorientating abruptness. She felt a tide of guilty colour wash over her skin and she struggled to share the amusement with Roman as they exchanged glances above their son's head.

'That sounds like a plan,' Roman said.

Marisa was glad for the distraction when Jamie demanded her attention then. 'So can I?'

'Can you what?'

'Have two biscuits?'

'Later,' Marisa said, before adopting a diversionary tactic. 'Which car do you think is Roman's?'

'The one with our cases and the policeman standing by it.'

Her son, it turned out, was more observant than she was. The car in question was a big four-wheel drive with blacked-out windows standing about fifty feet away, and there was a security guard, not a policeman, standing beside the luggage she had last seen in London.

'I want to walk,' Jamie said, pulling at his safety harness.

Roman glanced at Marisa, who nodded before he carefully unfastened the strap and put the wriggling child on his feet.

'I want my case.'

'Fine, but you must hold my hand because of the traffic.'

Jamie's childish features settled into a mulish expression she knew all too well as he tucked his hand behind his back. 'But there isn't any—'

Before Marisa could respond Roman stepped forward. 'I need some help to put the cases in the car,' he said casually.

Jamie looked at the hand extended to him for a moment before his mulish expression became a sunny smile. 'OK…' He glanced at his mother. 'Can I?'

'Off you go.'

Watching them walk away hand in hand, Marisa experienced a rush of emotions at the poignant picture of father and son. She felt recede some of the doubts she'd struggled with over her decision to make this trip. It was an effort to hold her emotions back as she followed them, very conscious of the ache in her chest. For someone who'd said he had no experience of children, Roman was doing a pretty good job.

CHAPTER EIGHT

THE FOUR-WHEEL DRIVE they were eventually installed in was roomy, and the 'nice smell' that Jamie mentioned, ensconced in a booster seat in the back, was that of soft leather and newness.

It was not the only thing that Jamie commented on as they left the city lights behind them. He seemed to be enjoying a second wind, although finally the flow of questions petered out and his head began to droop once again.

Roman turned up the air conditioning on his side of the car, and a welcome blast of fresh air removed some of the distracting scent of Marisa's perfume from his nostrils.

After silence had reigned for five minutes Roman risked a quiet question.

'Is he asleep?'

He felt Marisa glance his way and saw her head nod in the periphery of his vision.

'So he's a good traveller?'

'Not always,' Marisa replied honestly, hoping that Jamie's best-behaviour mode hadn't raised false expectations in Roman. He was being a model child, so far only asking once if they were there yet, and happily accepting Roman's response that he would tell him when they were.

Jamie hadn't even requested a toilet break and the

chocolate biscuit she had finally allowed him—because sometimes it was just not worth the fight—had gone mostly in his mouth.

At least when he was awake she had been able to focus on him and the distractions his multitude of questions had afforded.

Now he was asleep, looking cute in his booster seat, cuddling the dog-eared giraffe that had been his companion and comfort all through his illness, and she was left with no option but to make polite conversation with Roman, polite conversation that did not involve mentioning that searing kiss at the airport.

She just wished she could stop thinking about it.

Roman's gaze kept repeatedly flashing to the reflection of his sleeping son in the rear-view mirror.

'Does he always ask so many questions?' He was here to ask the questions, and Marisa—his glance flickered to her profile—was here to drive him to distraction.

The kiss had not been a good thing. It had just made him realise what he was missing and had provided even more fuel for the ever-present ache inside him.

'Yes, but he doesn't always sleep like this, but it was his first flight and he bounced the entire way, he was so excited. Oh, is this—'

She strained her neck to look out of the window and Roman knew what she'd be seeing. They were passing through a massive ornate wrought-iron gate. The gatehouse beside it was lit up but although there wasn't anyone in it, there were security cameras mounted there. The road they were now driving along had fewer ruts for Roman to negotiate and it was less winding than the one they'd been on previously.

'Yes, we're on the estate now,' he confirmed, his thoughts travelling back to that moment in the airport when he'd thought the very worst had happened. Maybe you had to face having something snatched away before you realised how much you wanted it?

With the gut-freezing fear had come clarity. In that moment the idea of being a distant but supportive figure in his son's life, never realistic, had become a complete non-starter. Marisa had asked him what he wanted and he had dodged the issue because he hadn't known then. He had still been in denial and avoiding owning the fact that being a father absolutely terrified him.

Now he had shrugged off the uncertainty, he knew the answer he would give her. He wanted to be a father to Jamie, the best father he could be. He might not be very good, but if he messed up, no, he amended with a flash of uncharacteristic humility, *when* he messed up, as he no doubt would, he was sure that Marisa would put him right. His glance slid sideways long enough to register the delicacy of her profile as she gazed out of the window.

Long enough to disintegrate his determination to not want her as his body clenched in hungry desire. It was a complication that he would need to deal with at some point soon but his ability to effortlessly multitask appeared to have deserted him.

He thought of the glazed passion burning in her eyes after he had kissed her at the airport. Stopping so abruptly had just about killed him, so maybe he'd just let nature take its course?

Aware that his thoughts had taken a dangerous direction, he blocked them, but not before he realised that despite all the danger he had courted, all the extreme sports he had thrown himself into, this was the most alive he had felt in over five years.

His expression one of fake ferocious concentration, he turned his attention back to the road that he knew like the back of his hand from the days when he had learnt to drive in the gardener's Jeep. Until Rio, taking his turn in the driver's seat, had swerved to avoid a wild boar and they'd ended up upside down in a ditch. Roman had an interesting scar to show for it and Rio had climbed out without a scratch.

His father had banned them from driving after that, and grounded them for a month, but the real punishment had been his sacking of the gardener whose car they had totalled, making sure that his sons knew the man's fate was on their heads.

That ex-gardener was now his mother's personal driver but at the time it had felt like something they would never recover from.

How his mind took the seemingly seamless leap from the man who was now his mother's personal driver to the burning question of whether he and Marisa could live under the same roof and not end up sharing a bed would remain for ever one of life's mysteries, but it was there now, in his head, and it showed remarkable staying power.

'Are you all right?' Marisa sat on her own hands while her eyes kept straying to his. Roman's long brown fingers curled around the steering wheel were exerting a strange fascination for her, but it turned to concern when his light grip tightened until his knuckles turned an almost bloodless white.

He shot her a frowning look. 'I'd be better if you stopped asking stupid questions.'

As she hadn't said a word for a good five minutes the implication that she had been bombarding him with chit-chat struck her as deeply unfair. Lips twisted, she debated with herself whether to challenge him, but decided against it as she conceded, at least in the privacy of her own head, that he was allowed to be irritated after being forced to drive so far to collect them. Also she didn't want to distract him as the road they were travelling along had some pretty scary hairpin bends and a few dramatic drops.

It was ten minutes later, and Marisa had maintained her silence, if you discounted the couple of gasps when a bend had revealed a particularly awesome vista. She was starting to get an idea of the scale of the estate when they hit an avenue of tall trees lining what she assumed must be the last part of the drive. They were up-lit by spaced floodlights that gave the impression they were driving through a tunnel of light. As they crested a hill to see the *castillo* come into view Marisa caught her breath. The same floodlit effect gave the aged stone walls of the imposing façade a silvered tinge, while the lights shining out from the windows glowed a warm gold that matched the last fading rays of a magnificent sunset.

Marisa had not been anticipating anything on this scale. She was accustomed to a home that many considered grand, but this building eclipsed anything she had seen.

It was a castle in every sense of the word.

A possibility that ought to have occurred to her on the journey here now popped into her head, and she wondered if there would be family members on hand to judge her.

This had all happened so quickly, the pace that everything had moved at was a million miles from her normal controlled, cautious approach where there were normally no surprises, unpleasant or otherwise.

She slid a covert glance at Roman's patrician profile, the carved angles emphasised by the reflection from the outside lighting. It was hard to think of life around

Roman as not containing surprises—admittedly not quite the sort that her dad had used to spring on her. She really couldn't imagine Roman announcing that it would be fun to sell his Rolls-Royce so they could travel on public transport—but it was another reason she told herself to be glad that this visit was not a prequel to spending her whole life with him. She wasn't interested in living a life of surprises any more.

This was about what was best for Jamie, who had a right to know his father so long as that father was good for him.

Transferring her gaze to the façade of the looming building that looked grander and more ancient the nearer they got, she was conscious of the heavy nervous thud of her heartbeat. The darkness didn't help—it probably exaggerated the imposing vibe. Not that she was holding out much hope of it appearing any more cosy in daylight, but she would settle for less daunting.

She was starting to realise that there were a lot of other questions she ought to have been asking instead of simply allowing Roman to call the shots and rush her.

'Will any of your family be here?' It wasn't as if there wasn't room—a dozen families could have shared the place and not bumped into one another.

He turned his head briefly, his expression impossible to read in the fading light, his proud profile a dark silhouette. 'Unlikely. I assume my brother will be avoiding me for the considerable future.'

She took the sardonic comment as a reminder that she was responsible for a falling-out between the twins and squirmed uneasily in her soft leather seat, but then a noise from the back seat made her turn her head to look at her son.

Jamie was still sleeping, one hand thrown above his

head, his face flushed. When he had been ill she had only ever thought a day ahead, and the only thing she had dreamt of was him being well. It had certainly never crossed her mind that she was in some way depriving him because he was an only child. She had been an only child and she hadn't felt deprived, but last week when she had picked him up for a play date and seen him watching on as his little friend dropped a sloppy kiss on his chubby baby sister's forehead it had made her wonder.

Jamie's expression had brought a lump to her throat, despite the fact the children's mother had admitted ruefully that for the first six months big brother had been jealous of his new sister.

She hadn't missed out as a child, but *twins*, she thought, had a particularly special bond that shouldn't be broken. She settled back into her seat, silently vowing that if there was some way she could repair the damage she'd wrought, she would, though at that moment, reading Roman's grim profile, she couldn't summon much optimism on the subject of her influence over him. He was probably still thinking about the last few hours that he'd never have back again.

Looking at him was a mistake, because once she'd started it was hard to stop. There was something about his features that just pulled her in... Her eyelids half closed as her thoughts drifted back to the airport again, to the moment when his fingers had cupped her cheek. The gesture connected in her mind to the ache she felt deep inside.

Confusion pressed down on her; she had never needed a male shoulder to lean on. Sure, Rupert had been there for her in her hour of need, but his condition had meant that for most of their relationship he had been the one doing the leaning and that had felt normal to her. Her dad had been like a kid pretending to be an adult sometimes, and from early on it had been up to her to look out for him.

She comforted herself with the knowledge that the airport situation had been the result of a combination of factors—all high stress—and it didn't mean she had turned needy. She dragged her gaze free from his face, turning a deaf ear to the voice in her head that pointed out the multitude of flaws in her argument.

As the car crunched over the gravel, the purr of the powerful engine that had been imperceptible became more noticeable by its absence as they drew to a halt. The sudden silence made her aware of every sound inside the intimate space of the interior, the soft hiss of their intermingled breathing, the squeak of fabric on leather and, more distant, the eerie sound of an owl's call as Roman opened his door, allowing the fresh night air to flood the car.

She turned her questioning gaze to him and found her eyes snared yet again. Something in his steady unblinking stare and the impression the air was being sucked out of the space around her left her breathless, making her rush into speech. She said the first thing that came into her head, wincing slightly that the tone was all wrong; her voice sounded too breathless, too desperate.

'I can't imagine looking at someone and seeing the face I look at every day in the mirror.'

She watched one dark brow lift before the motion-detection lights on the gravel-covered forecourt that had illuminated the interior of the car chose to go out, adding another layer of darkness to the enclosed space.

It wasn't just the lines of his face that the darkness blurred, it blurred her resolve and it lowered her resistance… *to what, exactly?* she asked herself.

She shivered. She didn't really want to know the answer. It was bad enough she was unable to pretend that it was Roman she was fighting. The battle was with herself and the forbidden emotions, the *hunger* he awoke inside her.

She gave her head a tiny shake as if to dislodge the thought. She didn't want to think about it; she *wouldn't*.

She tensed as his deep gravelly textured voice broke the silence. 'We might look alike, but we are very different people.'

Marisa tore her eyes from his shadowed face, too spooked by the fascination it held for her to ponder the odd inflection in his flat statement.

She turned back and found that Roman was looking at her, making no attempt to leave the car. Her stomach muscles quivered with a combination of fear and something she refused to identify as excitement as she resisted the pull of the invisible silken thread that in her imagination joined them.

'How so different?' she asked, though she thought she already knew part of the answer. She had looked at his brother and her nerve endings had not tingled, there had been no silent thread connecting them and she had not wanted to breathe in the scent of Rio. She brought her thoughts to an abrupt halt, realising to her horror that she had begun to lean in towards Roman.

'From Rio?' he said, sounding as though he had forgotten what he had been talking about.

'Yes.' She straightened up in her seat, pushing her hair behind her ears as the outside lights, perhaps activated by some night creature, clicked on again.

'People say I am more like my father than Rio.' The bleak comment was delivered with a twist of his lips.

She felt pinned to her seat like a suicidal moth drawn to a flame by his dark complex stare.

'Is that a bad thing?' she wondered huskily.

The question seemed to jolt him, leaving Marisa with the impression that he regretted saying anything at all. She felt a surge of frustration; she had met clams that revealed more about themselves than him. *Or maybe that's just with me*, she mused. *Maybe he shares his innermost thoughts with other people...other women...?*

Unbidden, an image of the blonde with the impressive chest that he'd been glued to during the rash of publicity shots for one of his films a few years ago flashed into her mind. Maybe that woman brought out a different side to Roman? Maybe he showed his vulnerable side to her...?

She pushed the thought away, dodging the accusing voice in her head that was yelling, *You're jealous!* The idea was simply ridiculous. The last thing she wanted was to know what made Roman tick. The man was too intense for words, and just breathing the same air as him gave her a headache. As for him having a vulnerable side, it would be her first mistake to imagine he even had one.

No, Marisa, your first mistake was to walk into that hotel over five years ago.

A furrow formed between his sable brows. 'What's wrong?' he barked.

She shrugged at the accusing question. 'What do you mean? Why should anything be wrong?'

'You squeaked.'

Her chin went up. 'I did not—' she began and then broke off. This, she decided, could get very childish very quickly. 'I have a headache.' To her relief he appeared to accept the half-lie, as actually she did have the beginning of a headache. 'It's been a long day.' She glanced up at the building and thought, *It doesn't look like it'll be get-*

ting better any time soon. 'I still think it would have been simpler if you'd got to know Jamie at home.'

One dark brow elevated. 'So you were inviting me to be your guest?'

'God, no!' The words were out before she could stop them. 'I mean—'

'Yes?' he pressed when she halted, looking interested in her answer.

She compressed her lips and flung him an angry look. She was too tired for a conversational battle of attrition. 'You could have picked him up, gone for trips—' *And I could have observed from a safe distance, and there would have been no kisses.*

'Trips?'

'He likes the zoo.' He didn't seem too impressed by her hasty improvisation.

'So your expert advice is that a few day trips to the zoo is the best way to get to know my son? That it would make up for the last four and a half years.'

'He happens to like the zoo,' she gritted back.

'So you said.'

'I hadn't given much thought to alternatives because you were so obviously not going to accept the idea.' No, he'd wanted everything to be all on his terms, and because she felt so guilty she had agreed to it all in a moment of weakness. He'd claimed she owed him and he was right.

'Look, I'm aware that this isn't ideal.' His eyes flickered to the shadow of his ancestral home. 'It's not exactly warm and intimate, I know,' he admitted. 'But it is away from prying eyes.'

Marisa lowered her gaze, musing ruefully that could only be a good thing. Even thinking of the words *warm* and *intimate* in connection with Roman was dangerous.

'Don't you have somewhere else that is less—'

'I keep hotel suites in a few city locations,' Roman said, anticipating a surprised if not disapproving reaction to a lifestyle choice that had not won universal approval.

What was to his mind a practical option, his mother saw as some sort of inability to put down roots. Everyone, she claimed, needed a home. When he pointed out that he owned a tropical beach house and a mountain cabin, she pointed out that, no matter how picturesque it was, a place without road access and a half-day trek to reach it, or one that involved stilts and was only accessible by boat, could only be called homes by someone who was running away.

She didn't specify from what, and she was, as he had told her, over-exaggerating the situation. His choice not to buy a more traditional property was a purely practical solution. Why buy somewhere that would be empty most of the year when you could keep luxury suites where all your needs were catered for in several cities without the bother of maintenance or staff?

'You live in hotels?'

He'd encountered reactions to his lifestyle before, but not like the sympathy he saw in her face.

'It gets a bit boring, doesn't it?'

'You have lived in *hotels*?'

Marisa nodded. 'I've lived in lots of different places. My dad travelled and I travelled with him. There was one time when he had his credit card refused at the—' She caught sight of Roman's concerned expression and stopped. 'Sometimes we travelled first class and sometimes... Well, Dad was always generous even when he had no money and he had friends who were equally generous with their sofas and floors.'

'That must have been...worrying for you.'

'Not for him.' He'd always said he didn't need to worry because she did it for him. 'He always saw the bright side of life.'

'And you?'

'I didn't mind not having money sometimes. The posh hotels were nice but the novelty of on-tap room service and every whim catered for fades.' Instead, she had longed for the familiarity of a room and belongings that were all her own. 'It must have been fun for you and your brother growing up here.' Unaware of the wistful envy in her voice, she imagined two boys having a ball exploring a place that likely as not boasted secret rooms and, on first appearances, dungeons.

'It had its moments.'

A rather cryptic non-answer, she thought.

The information he'd offered about his parents' marriage and the heavy hints that his relationship with his father had not been very healthy would explain the conflicting emotions she saw on his face before his mask slid back into place.

'I think a home is people, not a place,' she mused half to herself. Jamie was her home and she was his.

'Are you offering to be my home? A roof over my head, my harbour in a storm…?'

His pointed sarcasm brought a flush to her cheeks and an unexpected knife thrust of pain to the region where her heart lived. 'No, of course not. I just meant—' A flustered hand pressed to her chest as though she expected to see blood seeping through her fingers and she stopped babbling; she had no idea what she meant.

The sardonic glitter faded from his eyes. 'I don't like to stay in one place for too long.'

Was he talking about a place or people? she wondered. Had the hinted-at bad memories from his childhood prevented him from putting down roots? Or was his comment shorthand for his preference for one-night stands and temporary affairs? Just the idea added nausea to her physical symptoms.

'We could not be more different, then,' she said quietly. 'But then I'm a mother and a child needs stability, routine—' She stopped, realising she'd started out talking about Jamie but what she actually meant was herself. They were the things that she craved.

'I'm a father,' he cut in harshly.

Unable to react to his brusque interruption or protest his interpretation of her comment, because he had virtually thrown himself out of the car door in his haste to get away from her, she opened the passenger door. Exiting the car with less fluid grace than Roman, she turned and found herself thigh to thigh, shoulder to shoulder with him.

She took an involuntary step backwards and mumbled, 'S-sorry,' to his chest. She would have taken a second distancing step back but with no warning his hand shot out, his fingers curling around her upper arm.

Heart pounding, her face lifted slowly to his, and she heard the breath snag in his throat as desire and longing twisted and expanded inside her chest.

Trapped as much by the desire coursing in a hot stream through her body as the hypnotic pull of his obsidian stare, she stood there quivering—*aching*. She had never reacted to any man this way, any man but Roman. He seemed to have direct access to a part of her that scared her.

A part of her that didn't recognise common sense or self-preservation, a part of her that didn't care about consequences.

The combination of passion and fear reflected in the

golden pools of her eyes should have made Roman step back but he found himself stepping closer instead, pushing his body into hers as his hand slid to the small of her back, pulling her against him until their bodies were sealed hip to hip.

He saw the moment she felt the carnal imprint of his erection, her pupils dilated and he heard the throaty little gasp that left her parted lips.

He could feel a growl in his throat as he bent his head lower towards her plump, trembling lips, his blood heating as he thought of plunging his tongue past them and tasting the moist warmth of her mouth.

'Oh, my God, what was that?'

Startled, he dropped his hand from her waist as she turned around, her wide fearful eyes scanning the darkness above their heads where moments before a ghostly apparition, a flash of white, and the beating of wings had disturbed the silence.

'An owl hunting.'

A predator, Marisa thought, looking straight at another predator, all six feet four inches of him standing there, his chest heaving as he dragged air into his lungs like a drowning man.

What am I doing?

'I thought it was a ghost.'

'There are no ghosts here. The past is dead and gone and it would be a mistake to try to resurrect it.'

Well, that didn't sound as if he was talking about nocturnal birdlife, but it did sound as if he was talking about their almost kiss. She was grateful the half-light hid her shamed blush.

She got the message loud and clear. Once he had wanted more than she was able to give, now it seemed that all he wanted from her was sex—and then only on his terms.

'I'm not trying to resurrect anything. I just want to get Jamie indoors and settled for the night,' she explained quietly. 'So what are we waiting for—the reception committee?'

'Don't worry, there won't be anyone around at this hour.'

He had reasoned that it would be less stressful for a child to arrive at a new place if there weren't lots of new people to cope with, as well, though he had to admit Jamie seemed a remarkably resilient child.

The swell of pride that tightened his chest as he turned to look at his sleeping son took him by surprise.

'So how do we do this?' Finding it hard to be the person asking for instructions, he directed his question to Marisa, aware as he looked at her of a fresh flare in the hunger that was still thrumming through his body. He'd told her he didn't want to resurrect the past, but that was because he had enough to deal with in the present without going around opening old wounds. He just hoped the logic would filter down at some point to his rampant hormones.

The things this woman did to him remained stronger than anything he had ever experienced; nothing had changed over the years they'd spent apart, and that was the problem. There was no volume control on the hunger she aroused in him; there was no halfway house. It was full on, and *it* controlled *him*.

He shouldn't have to remind himself that acting on it was a bad idea considering what had happened the last time.

Circumstances had brought her back into his life but Roman had moved on. Marisa was still his weakness but he told himself he had strengthened his defences. He lifted his avid gaze from the cushiony softness of her lips and swallowed.

'Will he wake up if we move him?' he asked huskily.

'That's really doubtful. He's flat out.' Despite her claim, as she scooped Jamie up, she closed her car door quietly and saw that Roman was following suit. As her eyes brushed his she hastily stepped back to put some distance between them, in the process backing into a low hedge. Immediately the warm night air was filled with the heavy summery scent of lavender.

'This way.' He gestured for her to walk ahead of him and tried not to notice the lush tautness of her bottom and the gorgeous length of her slim legs.

CHAPTER NINE

THOUGH THE PREDICTABLY massive space of the hallway was empty it was flooded with light. Marisa blinked and looked around with genuine pleasure.

The heavy dark wood panelling and stone walls could have been oppressive but somehow they weren't. The darkness was alleviated by the brilliant glowing threads of the antique rugs underfoot and the series of framed photographic landscapes on the walls.

'Did your mother plan the decor?'

'My mother hasn't been here since the divorce.' His lips quirked into a fleeting ironic half-smile as he added, 'As I said, other than a staff of thirty or so we will have our privacy.'

She couldn't return his smile; privacy of any sort was the last thing she needed. What she needed was space.

So why are you just standing there?

The question could have just as easily been directed at Roman, who continued to stare at her over Jamie's curly head.

'It's a lot to take in,' she said quietly.

'I'll show you to your rooms.'

He led her up the curved stone staircase to the galleried landing above.

'There a small salon just down there.' He nodded to the right-hand side of a long corridor with an ornately stuccoed barrelled ceiling. 'Your rooms are this way.' He took a right turn, this corridor a twin of the other.

'Here they are.' The door opened into a sitting room, but she didn't waste much time looking around as Jamie had woken up and started crying.

Correctly assessing her priorities, he pointed her to an open door. 'His bedroom is through there at the end.'

It took her hardly any time at all to settle Jamie, who'd fallen straight back to sleep before she had even pulled down the covers on his bed.

Checking the baby monitor, which was standing on a low table in the room, was working, she explored the other rooms in this guest suite before she returned to the sitting room.

She paused in the doorway. Roman was standing with his shoulder wedged against the wall, staring out of the stone mullioned window. He levered himself away and half turned.

'Did he go back to sleep?'

Lingering in the doorway, fighting a reluctance to enter, she nodded. *You're acting as if he's about to leap on you*, mocked the voice in her head.

It was the mortifying possibility she might be the one to do the leaping that continued to hold her back.

'He was so exhausted he barely stirred at all, not even when I put him in his pyjamas. He's totally out.'

'I asked for some supper to be left for us.'

It wasn't the idea of sitting in some dauntingly enormous room at a table laden with candelabra and antique crystal that made her stomach flip, it was the knowledge of the person who would inevitably be sitting opposite her, which was ridiculous. It was something she was going to have to learn to cope with—but not today, she decided, pushing this hill to climb into the future with a mental sigh as the almost-kiss outside by the car still weighed guiltily on her conscience.

'That's thoughtful.' Marisa, who had been hiding behind the heavy strands of hair that had escaped the knot on her nape, pushed them back before carefully closing the baby gate between the nursery and the sitting room, but left the door ajar. She'd been pleased to see there was a similar arrangement between the anteroom with the useful compact little kitchen, which connected to her own bedroom, and the nursery, so at night she could leave the doors ajar.

'But I'm not really hungry.' Her stomach chose that moment to growl so loudly to reveal her lie that his lips twitched.

Her lips stretched into a rueful smile that reached her amber eyes and immediately lit up her face, dissolving some of the tension.

'All right, I am starving actually,' she admitted, pressing a hand to her stomach. 'But I'll be fine.' There seemed to be plenty of tea and coffee in the kitchen area. 'I really don't want Jamie to wake up alone in a strange place.' This place was so enormous that even if she was alerted by the baby intercom it would take her far too long to reach him.

'I assumed you wouldn't,' he replied calmly. 'I'll bring up a tray for you.'

'*You* will?'

Her astonishment seemed to amuse him. 'On occasion I have been known to tie my own shoelaces. Make yourself comfortable and I'll be back shortly.' The advice was slung over his shoulder as he exited through the door.

What she would *really* have liked was to take advan-

tage of that spectacular en suite bathroom with its copper
tub massive enough that you could swim or at least float
in it. It was really calling to her and she could almost hear
it as she lifted a lid on first one and then another of the
glass flagons. Each sweet-smelling oil had an even more
gorgeously heady scent than the one before it.

She reached out and experimentally pressed a button
set into the marble tiled wall, jumping when the room
was filled with music. Hastily depressing it again, she
stood statue-still, listening intently, her eyes wide above
the hand pressed to her mouth, but after a minute she relaxed; the noise had not woken Jamie.

Resisting the bath, she stripped off her clothes and left
them where they fell, suddenly too weary to care about
the crumpled heap.

The fabric of the building might be ancient but it was
clear that it boasted the latest technology. She ran a finger around the edge of the bath tub and allowed herself
an indulgent moment to fantasise wistfully about floating in the foamy sweet-smelling suds, just to wash away
the day's grime and ease the ache of tension in her limbs,
before regretfully turning her back on it.

Grabbing a towel from the pile that was neatly stacked
on a chest, she headed for the shower, very conscious
that she had no idea how long she had before Roman appeared with her food, and as she didn't want to be drifting around in a towel when he did she allowed herself
the minimum time under the reviving spray.

Still damp and swathed in a towel, her skin pink and
tingling from the arrows of water, she tipped out her
carefully packed overnight bag onto the silk cover of the
four-poster bed. Rifling through the spilled contents, she
extracted the clean underclothes and the jeans and tee
shirt she always packed in her hand luggage after the last

time her hold cases had ended up on another continent, leaving her without even a toothbrush.

At least this time her luggage was not too far away, just in the car outside, but in some ways it was equally inaccessible. She had no intention of risking getting lost or setting off some sort of alarm trying to find it.

She had the basics, but not the time; in a feverish haste she had reached the stage of dragging a comb through her hair when she heard a sound which, unless she was being visited by one of the resident ghosts the place probably boasted, was Roman.

It offended her innately neat nature but she ignored the accusing pile of clothes she could see through the open bathroom door and glanced in the mirror, wishing she had time to disguise the violet smudges beneath her eyes, before she dashed for the door, arriving in the sitting room breathless and barefoot. The latter didn't register with her until his interest in her pink-painted toenails brought her own attention downwards.

At least it was an excuse not to look at him and it gave her heart a chance to slow to a bearable canter.

'I was in a hurry,' she said, her voice indistinct as she shook her wet head, sending drops of moisture flying, and wondering why on earth she sounded so defensive.

Roman wrenched his eyes clear of her denim-covered thighs, trying hard not to notice that she possessed the sort of legs that seemed to go on for ever. Her black tee shirt was emblazoned with a daisy logo and was tucked neatly into her narrow waist.

Catching the direction of his gaze and misinterpreting it, she touched the daisy with a not quite steady finger. 'Jamie was shopping with me and he loved this one. I'm afraid the rest of my bags are still in the car.'

'He has excellent taste.' Roman nodded towards the

door. 'The rest of your things are there. I'll take them through into your room.'

Her eyes flew to the stack of cases by the door that led out to the corridor, then back to his face. 'How?'

'I waved my magic…' He paused, because she didn't look in the mood to appreciate his laboured humour. 'I brought them up for you before I collected the supper tray.'

He had been in her room, just a wall separating him from her naked in the shower… She gulped. 'I didn't hear you come in.'

'Relax, I left them outside the door until I came back. I waited to be invited in.'

She felt her stomach muscles tremble in response to the predatory gleam in his dark eyes. 'Just like a vampire.' It didn't seem such a bad analogy at all; weren't vampires these days all sexy as hell and equally dangerous?

'Except with no blood involved.' Just a hell of a lot of self-control. What Roman hadn't said was that he had opened the door, heard the shower and closed it again, because he didn't trust himself not to go to her.

She reacted to the comment with a weak smile flashing out before she worked up the courage to meet his disconcertingly intense stare.

Dios, she looked as if stubbornness was the only thing keeping her upright. 'Sit down,' he said, his abrupt delivery hiding his concern.

His lip curled in self-disgust as she walked towards one of the sofas. He'd been too busy noticing how great her lush body looked in jeans to notice until now the cell-deep weariness in her body language.

She looked as though it was an effort to lift up her feet as she walked across to the sofa.

'You're tired.'

Her head lifted at the accusation.

'When did you last sleep?'

'What is this, twenty questions?'

Arms folded across his chest, he stood there waiting for her answer, and finally Marisa gave a sigh of defeat. 'All right,' she fired back. 'I'm tired but I've had a lot on my mind. Just don't fuss.' She knew from experience that even when you felt you couldn't go on for another minute—and there had been more days like that than she wanted to recall when Jamie had been ill—there were always reserves to call on.

The water-darkened ends of her hair brushed her neck as she sat down before carefully tucking the offending strands behind her ears.

'I have not exactly dressed for dinner,' he said abruptly as he bent forward to lay down the tray he was carrying on the coffee table between the two sofas.

She tucked her legs under her, thinking that he didn't need to dress for anything; he looked gorgeous whatever he was wearing—or not wearing. She veiled her gaze guiltily as the thought slipped past her tired defences. After a few hours' sleep this situation was going to be so much easier to cope with.

Want to bet?

'I'm not really hungry.'

He rolled his eyes. 'Not that again. You will eat,' he remarked pleasantly. 'Or I will feed you myself,' he promised with a steely smile that left his eyes grimly determined.

She snorted to show how unimpressed she was but, despite her claim, she felt her empty stomach rumble once more when he whipped off the dome cover with a magician's flourish to reveal a plate containing a selection of delicious-looking, artfully arranged sandwiches.

'I'd say I made them with my own fair hands but I didn't. The tea and coffee are, however, all my own work.' He nodded to the pots he had balanced either end of the tray as, instead of taking a seat on the other sofa or, and this was the preferred option for Marisa, heading for the door, he sat down beside her.

Marisa directed her gaze at the safer option, another plate, this one containing beautifully decorated small cakes that would have graced the window of any high-class patisserie.

Not looking at him didn't make her any less skin-tinglingly conscious of his closeness.

'Eat!'

Eyes slitted, she slung him a recalcitrant look, but reached for a sandwich. One bite of the layers of smoked salmon and cream cheese sandwiched between moist rye bread and she forgot her reluctance.

She sampled two more before sitting back with her arms folded. 'Well,' she challenged. 'Do I pass?'

He gave a concessionary grunt.

'So what happens now? Oh, not now as in we go to bed—' He snorted as an expression of comical horror spread across her face while she issued a hot-faced correction. 'That is go to bed, but not together— I mean—'

'I know what you mean and the answer is it's up to you what happens next. I'm assuming that Jamie might be tired tomorrow and a little off his game after the journey?'

'Cranky as hell probably. I usually try to keep to his routine as much as possible.'

'And his routine is?'

'When he is not in nursery I allow him to watch one

of his cartoons after breakfast.' She supposed that wasn't an option here. 'Ash or I usually take him for a walk later.' Turning over a piece of rotting wood on the ground and discovering all the creeping life beneath could keep Jamie fascinated for hours. She found herself suddenly wondering what Roman had been like as a child. Had he approached life with curiosity and enthusiasm as Jamie did? Then she stopped wondering because the price was an ache in her chest. 'In the afternoon it depends.'

'He mentioned enjoying swimming. We have an indoor pool and a gym complex.'

'Of course you do,' she muttered, trying to ignore the arm he had thrown across the back of the sofa.

'The outdoor pool is heated if you think that would be better for him.'

'Doesn't it seem a waste to you? Having all this here and no one to enjoy it?' Aside from the invisible staff of dozens, which she would no doubt encounter tomorrow.

'Rio and I never expected to inherit it.' His eyes flashed her way before he turned back to the contemplation of his threaded fingers. 'Disinheriting us from this place was always his threat of first resort and we both assumed he'd gone through with it, but he ended up leaving us the lot. I think he expected us to fail, but then he had never made any attempt to include us, or teach us anything about his empire. He was a total bastard, but at least he was a bastard with a golden touch. It wouldn't have mattered a jot to him that our failure would have a knock-on effect that would deprive so many families of their livelihoods too.'

'He sounds like—' Words failed her as indignation for Roman and his twin swelled in her chest, well, mostly for Roman, if she was honest. It was beyond her comprehension that a parent could harm their child like that, toying with their emotions.

'If you're into labels, he ticked all the boxes of a narcissist, a malignant narcissist.' He offered up the information in a curiously emotionless voice. 'He was an expert at manipulation. He became incredibly vindictive whenever he felt threatened by literally any decision my mother made without him. He took it as a personal affront and he responded by belittling her, and undermining her confidence until she was utterly dependent on him. His jealousy was totally toxic—'

'Coercive control,' she said, remembering an article she had read about the subject.

His dark brows lifted. 'I believe that is the term, yes.'

'But your mother escaped.'

'Yes, she escaped love, but she is a remarkably strong woman and not everyone would have been so lucky.'

Did he even realise what he had said? she wondered. Did he know how revealing his choice of words was? For Roman love was clearly something you escaped from, a trap. That seemed very sad to her, as did the suspicion that her own deception had probably played some part in setting this view of his in concrete.

As she struggled against a fresh wave of guilt she became belatedly aware that while he spoke she had turned towards him until she now faced him, her legs still tucked underneath her, the arm she placed along the back of the sofa stretched out so that her position mirrored his, their fingertips almost touching.

As surreptitiously as she could manage she slowly retracted her arm at the same time as she unfolded her legs and placed her bare feet on the floor, and she swivelled around so that she sat shoulder to shoulder against him.

'A pity that there is no DNA test for being a bad father. Some men should not have children.'

His pronouncement had a hard uncompromising note in it that made her twist back towards him. His earlier comments about being more like his father than his brother floated to the surface in her memory and she realised that he was really talking about himself, that it was Roman's inner fear that he would hurt those he loved as his father had.

A hundred images flashed through her mind before she accepted the truth—he *did* love Jamie. He might be the most aggravating, stubborn, difficult man she had ever met but Roman was no monster.

'You are *nothing* like the man you have described to me.' She caught the flash of some emotion in his face as their eyes connected and consciously lowered the tone of her voice before she added carefully, but firmly, 'If you were I wouldn't be here. I've already told you that if I thought you being around Jamie would harm him, I would build a fifty-foot-high wall to keep you out.

'I was close to my father,' she volunteered, not aware that her own expression softened as she spoke. 'But there were only the two of us.'

'Your mother died?'

'My mother walked out on us soon after I was born,' she revealed with a casualness that to Roman's watchful eyes seemed too contrived. As if she still carried the invisible scars of the rejection but would die before she'd show it. 'She didn't like being a mother because she felt it "crushed her vitality".'

He didn't need to see quotation marks painted in the air to know she was directly quoting her mother. They were words that should have had a crushing impact, but her expression was serene. True, there was a sadness in her smile, but there was no discernible resentment that he could detect.

He thought about the extensive file headed 'Marisa Rayner' that remained unopened on his laptop.

Why commission something and not make use of it? He had fully intended to but in the short intervening time between requesting an in-depth report on Marisa's life and it dropping into his email inbox something had changed.

He had been reluctant to admit it. He'd told himself that he was too busy to read it, that he wasn't in the right frame of mind to view it objectively, he was too angry or too tired... But his inventive powers had eventually deserted him and he was left with only the truth, which was that he still wanted to know all about her, but he wanted her to volunteer the information.

'She actually said that to you?'

'Gracious, no...' She flashed him a small smile, and in the semi-light her eyes made him think of pools of liquid gold.

'Well, I suppose she *might* have,' Marisa conceded, oblivious to his discomfort. 'But as I was two months old the last time we met in person, I don't really recall.'

Did the joking response hide a multitude of hurt, he wondered, or was she *really* as all right with being rejected as she sounded?

'Actually she wrote me a letter when she left, for me to read when Dad thought I was old enough.' It wasn't the letter that had hurt, it was what she had discovered when she'd wanted to find out more about her mother, when her seventeen-year-old self had wondered if perhaps they could be friends as adults.

When she had found her mother online she had discovered that the woman who'd felt unable to be her mother was now remarried and was the mother to three step-children as well as a child of her own, Marisa's half-sister.

No, they could never be friends.

She levelled her clear gaze on Roman's face and thought about the demons he would never reveal, let alone allow her near enough to help him move past. And she *wanted* to help him, she *wanted*… Shock filtered into her eyes as she stilled, and everything inside her seemed to stop as the truth hit her.

She loved Roman; she had when he'd proposed to her, but she had taken refuge from the truth, telling herself it was just physical because the reality was too painful to own—the fact that she'd had to walk away from the only man she had ever loved.

The man who would never forgive her for her double deception of being married and hiding the existence of his child from him. If he had ever loved her, she had surely killed that love stone dead years ago, and that was her punishment to bear.

'Are you all right?'

'Fine,' she lied, forcing a smile. 'I loved my father. And he loved me, but he left me in a desperate situation when he died. Without Rupert I really don't know what would have happened to me. But that's the way with addicts and Dad was a reckless gambler who walked the line between being legal and being a con man, although mostly he stayed on the right side of the law. He never really grew up, my mother deserted her own child, but nevertheless I am not like either of them. Who you are isn't all about DNA and you can't allow an accident of birth to define who you are.'

Roman closed his eyes, wishing he had her certainty and hoping that she never had that belief crushed, because he knew what that felt like. 'You really believe that, don't you?'

She nodded. 'Yes,' she said simply. 'I do.' She eased her back away from the sofa. 'Do you mind if I go to bed now? I'm pretty tired.'

He vaulted to his feet without a word. 'I'll see you tomorrow. I hope Jamie has an undisturbed night.' He turned away but then swung back almost immediately. 'I'd say whistle if you need anything but in this place I wouldn't hear you.' He picked up her mobile phone from where it lay on the coffee table and, flicking through it, he punched in a rapid series of numbers. 'So call me if there are any problems.'

'How did you know my phone pin?'

'Jamie's date of birth? You really should double protect.'

Outside the door he leaned against the wall and wished that protection against the hunger Marisa aroused in him were so readily available.

CHAPTER TEN

MARISA WAS IN her bedroom hanging her belongings in the cavernous walk-in wardrobe when she heard the knock. Tightening the belt on her robe, she hurried past Jamie, who was still in his pyjamas, bent over colouring books and crayons he had spread across the coffee table.

She took a deep breath and opened the door. Despite the mood-lowering sense of anticlimax when she saw a young woman in a neat uniform standing there, she kept her smile painted in place.

'*Buenos dias, señora.*'

'*Buenos dias.*'

'I am just asking if you would like to take your breakfast here or in the breakfast room with Señor Roman.'

'I'm hungry, Mum!'

'All right, big ears,' she tossed back. 'In here, if that is no problem.'

'And what would *señora* like?'

'Coffee, juice and toast, please. Oh, and some fruit would be lovely too.'

'Scrambled egg,' came Jamie's voice.

Marisa smiled at the girl. 'And scrambled egg.'

'*Sí, señora.*' She bobbed a little curtsy and walked away swiftly.

'Have you cleaned your teeth yet?'

'Yes,' he said with his hand over his mouth.

Marisa's lips twitched. 'Go clean them again, please. I can see you found the clothes I left on your bed but you did actually wash your face, didn't you?'

Jamie looked hurt. 'Of course I did.'

Squatting down to readjust the top that Jamie had put on back to front, she let it pass, putting a hand on the floor to stop herself losing her balance when there was a knock on the door. She had already opened the doors to the balcony where the table and chairs afforded a gorgeous view of the acres of green manicured lawn and the mountains beyond.

'Come in!' she yelled, then as the door opened she asked without turning around, 'Could you put it on the balcony, please? It's such a glorious morning.'

'Sí, señora.'

She almost lost her balance before finding her centre of gravity and rising rapidly to her feet. 'Roman!' Tall, effortlessly elegant and showing no after-effects from yesterday's emotional dramas, he made her heart pick up tempo. 'I thought you were the—'

'Maria.' His grin flashed, making her remember how easily he could charm her when he wanted to. 'An easy mistake to make. Many have commented on the likeness.'

Roman's lips twitched as she tightened the knot on her robe, but she couldn't add a few more inches to the length and it showed an amazing amount of her smooth shapely legs, which he thoroughly enjoyed looking at. He was able to observe her tousled, just-got-out-of-bed appearance without feeling tortured, because there was nothing to be tortured about. She was utterly gorgeous and he wanted her.

There were two options: he either did something about it or he didn't. Neither choice was going to have life-changing consequences. If he opted for the sex, he had no doubt it would be absolutely fantastic.

His sleepless night had not been a total waste. After ruminating for hours, he now knew he was seeing problems where there were just choices, and nothing, as he reminded himself again, was life-changing.

Jamie was life-changing, and now that he'd had the time to consider it objectively Roman realised that his son was not just life-changing, but life-enhancing.

Jamie's mother, on the other hand, well, that ship had sailed years ago. Roman had been a fool to propose to her, and, although at first she had taken a part of him with her that had left him feeling as though he had lost a limb, he had rebuilt his protective walls until they now formed an impenetrable barrier.

Even if he hadn't, it would take a very stupid man to allow a woman to do that to him twice, especially one who had already displayed a disturbing ability to wander around inside his head.

Marisa fought off a smile at his teasing and bit her quivering lip. 'Sure, you and Maria could be twins.' She sucked in a dismayed breath but the words were out before she could pull them back.

'I already have a twin. I believe you know him.'

And they were right back onto the subject that could never be a winner for her, but she squared her jaw. There were limits and she was getting tired of dissolving into an apologetic heap all the time. 'Not really. I've only ever seen him when he looks as if he is wrestling with a choice between the fire or the frying pan. I imagine he has his lighter moments.'

'Rio is considered in every way more upbeat than me. I am the deep thinker, apparently.' His grin did not reach his dark heavy-lidded eyes.

'Which is not saying very much.'

His sudden laugh dissolved the tension before it reached critical mass.

'So do you want this breakfast on the balcony?'

She nodded. 'Come along, Jamie.'

She ushered Jamie through the door to the balcony, following the tall figure who was positioning their breakfast on the wrought-iron table.

'I like it here,' Jamie declared.

'Do you, darling?'

'I'm glad he likes it. It'll be his one day or at least half of it will be. I imagine Rio's children will inherit the other half of the place.' Her eyes flew wide open and he laughed. 'You really haven't considered that, have you?'

Recovering from the shock, she rallied. 'Don't be stupid. I'm the woman who married a dying man for his money, ask anyone.' She heard the bitterness in her voice and winced. The scar on that particular wound was not as healed as she liked to think.

Forgetting that he had thought exactly that about her, he felt an urge to wipe the shadows from her face and berate the idiots who had put them there. 'Anyone that actually counts?'

Her burst of angry resentment fizzled away. 'Thanks for that. I know it's stupid to let it bother me but the story was doing the rounds when I first discovered I was pregnant and it was sort of a double whammy, though when it became public knowledge I was pregnant I morphed into a lonely brave widow overnight.'

She glanced towards Jamie, who was ignoring them and tucking into his breakfast, and she smiled. Seeing him wolf down food never failed to make her happy.

'He has a robust appetite.'

She nodded and said quietly, 'For so long he had no appetite at all and it seemed like he was fading away before my eyes.'

'You will, as well, if you don't eat. Anyway, I came to ask if you would like the guided tour in, say, an hour.'

'I would love to, but Jamie has been up since five.' At least it had given her the opportunity to finally enjoy the pleasures of the decadent bath.

'Which means you have been up since five too.'

She shrugged. 'Give it another hour and he'll be fading. He'll need a nap.'

She saw the disappointment on Roman's face and found herself suggesting, 'How about this afternoon instead?'

'That sounds like a good option but, in the meantime, how about I give the you the grown-up tour this morning? I'm sure we can cover more ground without Jamie.'

Marisa froze. She didn't want to be without Jamie. Jamie's presence was her shield, her protection against the feelings she didn't want Roman to pick up on, the ones she didn't want to feel.

If that made her a coward, she really didn't care.

'Sorry,' she said, adopting an unconvincing expression of regret as she leaned forward to snatch a piece of fruit off the breakfast tray. 'I couldn't possibly leave him.' She bit into a juicy peach and wiped the juice off her chin with a self-conscious grimace of apology.

'You could,' he said, while in his head he was tasting the sweetness of peach juice in her mouth and the resultant rise in his core temperature made him glad of the light breeze. 'Maria, who you've already met, would be more than happy to babysit. I'd say being the eldest of seven makes her more than qualified and I have personally witnessed her keep several feral brothers in line without breaking a sweat. She is truly a phenomenon.'

'She seems a bit wasted carrying trays, then.'

'She is off to train as a children's nurse next year.' He offered up the information smug in the knowledge that he had delivered a deal clincher. 'So…?'

'All right, I suppose so.' It wasn't exactly a gracious acceptance but he didn't seem to notice. After he had left she comforted herself with the fact that a tour couldn't take long, and she was making a fuss about nothing; it wasn't as if they were talking about a candlelit meal.

She was wrong; it did take a long, *very* long time.

The previous night she had not really taken on board the sheer vastness of the place or the number of people it seemed to employ. Aside from the private rooms, and the multiple banquet-size spaces and numerous bedroom suites, there were the domestic areas; not just the kitchen complex with its walk-in fridges and freezer and numerous ancillary rooms, but offices that housed the army of people involved in the running of several thousand acres of the estate, which boasted a bewildering diversity of industry from an organic vineyard to an area of productive forestry.

She would have been interested because Roman was a very well-informed guide, but he was still Roman and she had no Jamie to hide behind.

She had a suspicion that her fear, well founded, of revealing by a look, a gesture or a word the true depth of her feelings made her appear stiff, and her monosyllabic responses earned her more than a couple of puzzled looks.

But she could cope a lot better with his puzzled looks than with his pity—or he might even be angry? It was not a mystery she was in any hurry to solve, even though normally she relished a puzzle.

There was one thing that aroused her curiosity as they walked through the bewildering network of rooms and corridors. The staff they met, especially the ones that had known Roman as a child, displayed an obvious fondness for him, and Roman clearly felt the same, considering his relaxed manner with them.

There was respect and fondness on both sides and for someone who professed to hate this place he seemed to have a great deal of knowledge of its workings.

They had only explored a fraction of the buildings, she suspected, when he led her outside. The heat of the sun after the cool afforded by the thick stone walls hit her like a wall and she was grateful of the thin-strapped sundress she had chosen to wear. She was glad she had applied a liberal coating of suncream to her exposed flesh, but beside her Roman didn't appear to even notice the heat.

'You must need an army of gardeners.'

'Some, but they are not here today. There is a horticultural show on locally, so they have decamped en masse. The tennis courts are that way.'

She could make out some green through the screen of trees in the direction he pointed. She had left behind her idea that this would take half an hour tops when he mentioned visiting the olive groves that were only half a mile away, groves which apparently kept the estate supplied with their own olive oil all year-round.

She had rather tetchily pointed out that as no one lived here that couldn't be so difficult, at which point he had made her feel silly by explaining about all the families that lived on the estate as well as the satellite farms.

'Would you like to see the pool now?'

She dragged her eyes away from admiring his impossibly long eyelashes. 'No, that's fine. I'm sure you have other things to do. You've already been very kind with your time—' Her voice faded in the face of his unblinking stare.

'I am rarely kind, *mi vida*.' The slow, contemplative, wolflike smile that accompanied his drawled observation sent a shiver right down to her toes.

'I just meant—'

'This way...' He placed his hand between her shoulder blades, his eyes darkening as he felt the silky warmth of her suncreamed flesh.

His light touch carried an electrical charge that sent a convulsive shiver over which she had no control through Marisa's body, silencing the protest on the tip of her tongue.

'Are you cold?'

'No, I'm fine.' Shrugging off his touch would have been too revealing of her helpless reaction so she had no option but to endure the torture.

Her escape in the end didn't come in the form of a rehearsed ploy, but a natural spontaneous reaction to the sight of the huge outdoor pool.

Roman watched with a smile, contrasting her childlike enthusiasm with the image of serene elegance she projected in public. Right at that moment she looked just like a carefree teenager.

She balanced on the edge, taking it all in. It wasn't just the size; it was the way it was landscaped almost organically into its setting. Along one length was a series of arches housing stone benches and formal potted palms; the other length was landscaped with opulent-looking greenery interspersed with splashes of colour provided by exotic flowers. Beyond the waterfall that cascaded over artfully arranged rocks, there was a terracotta-roofed gazebo that sheltered low daybeds piled high with cushions.

This was one aspect of a billionaire lifestyle that she had no problems with! She kicked off her sandals and flexed her toes against the marble tiles swirled with pink that edged the pool. By contrast the pool itself looked as though it was scooped out of solid polished stone.

'Are those reeds?' she exclaimed, directing an enquiring look over her shoulder before she turned back to look at the greenery growing in the water.

'They provide a natural filter because there are no chemicals in the water.'

'I might camp here.' Her childish enthusiasm was contagious.

'You enjoy roughing it, then?'

She threw him a twinkling grin of reciprocal amusement that faded when she realised who she was with. This rapport would only ever be an illusion and there was far too much risk in lowering her guard around Roman.

'This is all pretty spectacular.'

Roman felt a sting of frustration as he sensed the restraint in her response, as if she was suddenly thinking twice about each syllable before she gave voice to an entire sentence.

Marisa blinked and closed her eyes as a sunbeam fractured on the water's surface, dazzling her.

There were some moments in life that were indelibly imprinted on your consciousness and this, he recognised, was one of them. He would never forget the image of Marisa, slim and supple, her body curved, poised like a dancer on the edge of the pool with her head thrown back, eyes closed, her face lifted to the sun.

'You look like a nymph. Is the water calling to you?'

She turned, shading her eyes before she turned back

to the pool. 'I wish I'd thought to wear my swimsuit,' she admitted, gazing deep into the inviting turquoise depths.

He walked towards her. 'You really don't need one.'

She shook her head then as comprehension dawned, and darted him a shocked look.

'You know you want to,' he taunted, sliding a finger under the top button of his shirt.

'You wouldn't,' Marisa gasped with a weak laugh, but she knew of course that he would.

Another button and then another followed. 'You don't have to watch,' he taunted.

Actually she did, and she stood there, throat dry, one hand pressed to her parted lips, unable to tear her eyes off the slow teasing reveal as each successive button slipped from its mooring. His shirt gaped a little more, revealing another tantalising section of golden chest and ridged washboard-flat belly.

'Roman...you... Someone might see!' Her voice was barely more than an agonised husky whisper.

'Would that be so terrible?'

'Don't. I—' She took a step backwards, then another, then his own cry of warning blended in with the splash as she hit the water backwards. Her own scream was lost beneath the surface as she sank like a stone, hitting the bottom before she popped back up like a cork only moments later. She spluttered, choking a little as her head broke the surface.

Once he saw she was all right Roman started to laugh.

Treading water, half the pool streaming down her face, Marisa dragged back the tails of her saturated hair from her face and directed her wrathful incredulous gaze at the heartless figure standing there, immaculate and dry, and roaring his head off.

'You think this is f...funny,' she choked. 'You...you...'

Her voice was suspended by another fit of coughing to the backing track of his laughter.

Recovering slightly, she hit at the surface of the water, angrily pounding it with both hands, which only made him laugh louder when her feeble efforts failed to direct much more than a drop on his tailored linen trousers.

Teeth gritted in determination, she flipped onto her back and beat at the water with her feet until she sank.

When she surfaced again he was still standing there, as dry as a bone, his hands thrust deep inside his pockets. 'Sorry,' he said, not looking the least bit sorry.

Marisa smiled and floated forward, her arm barely raising a ripple now as she slid gracefully through the water. His own smile died as he watched her progress, completely riveted. She was as innately elegant in the water as she was on land.

Marisa reached the side of the pool and began to tread water. 'I suppose I must have looked pretty funny,' she commented, tilting back her head to look at the tall figure at the poolside. She stretched up a hand, pushing the sagging strap of her sundress that was floating around her like a bell up along the curve of her arm. 'Give me a hand up?'

The moment he reached down, long brown fingers extended to catch her wrist to haul her out, she took a deep breath, and sank to the bottom, using her foot to springboard up out of the water. As she broke the surface her hand shot out and as she grabbed his extended wrist, she fell back into the water, holding on hard.

Caught by surprise, he seemed to hover on the edge for what seemed like an age before he lost his balance, though somehow he still managed to twist so that he hit the water in a creditably clean dive and emerged only a few feet away.

'You little—'

She saw the retribution shining in his eyes. 'No, Roman!' she exclaimed, holding out a hand and shaking her head.

He shot her a white grin and she felt her pounding heart respond to his devilish teasing. 'Yes... I think yes...'

With a squeal she turned and began to swim away. Even hampered by her clothes her body was sleek in the water and she was fast but not fast enough, because he overtook her in seconds.

He caught her calf and sank with her; she went down twisting and turning like an otter to free herself, looking like a mermaid as she struggled to escape his grip, her hair floating like pale fronds of exotic seaweed around her face.

When they broke the surface he had her around the waist, her back against his front as he pulled her in close.

'Surrender?' he said in her ear.

She went limp in his arms. 'Yes.'

The moment his grip relaxed she slithered away and swam a few strokes before she flipped over and suspended her hands, patting the water either side to keep herself afloat and laughing her triumph at him.

Roman, the water streaming off his brown face, his dark hair slicked back, didn't return her smile, the sudden intensity of his stare making her own smile flatten, the sparkle in her eyes fading as, heart thudding with a mixture of excitement and fear, she waited for him to cover the distance between them in a couple of powerful strokes.

When he stopped and lifted his head he was only a foot away.

'Roman.' Her lips moved but she couldn't hear her breathy whisper above the frantic thud of her heart.

Their glances caught and held.

Unable to think beyond the need pounding inside her, she watched Roman reach out to her, his fingers sliding over her wet hair as he cupped his hand around the back of her head.

There was no resistance in her as she floated into him, her face coming up to his, her nose grazing the side of his own. This no longer felt like a game; it felt urgent, the urgency inside her as strong as the need to draw in oxygen.

She didn't close her eyes even when his face blurred darkly through her half-closed lids and the hissing ebb and flow of their breaths mingled and became one.

Feeling the *rightness* of it, she tilted her head fractionally to one side to allow him access. He covered her mouth, her lips parting as the tip of his tongue traced a path along the plump lower curve before, with a groan, he plunged his tongue inside her mouth.

With an answering groan, her legs wrapping themselves around his waist to anchor herself up tight against his body, she kissed him back, matching his frantic hunger with her own. She could feel the heat of his body even through the layers of wet clothes as she pressed close, but still not close enough as the hunger that had exploded inside her took control.

The kiss was so all-consuming that she wasn't really conscious that they had sunk beneath the water until her lungs began to scream and in unison they kicked for the surface. They floated apart dragging air into their lungs, until he had enough to strike out for the side of the pool. Beside him Marisa matched him measured stroke for measured stroke.

He hauled himself out of the pool in one smooth fluid

motion, the ripple of the powerful muscles in his shoulders and back visible through the clinging fabric of his shirt.

She watched, waiting for the hand he stretched down, allowing him to pull her up as though she weighed nothing until she was standing beside him.

'Ro—' Her voice was lost in his mouth, the kiss fierce, and hungry.

She kissed him back without restraint, giving in to the craving that sang through her blood. Her arms were around his neck when he scooped her up and carried her to the gazebo and laid her down on the daybed, pushing some of the cushions to the floor to make space.

CHAPTER ELEVEN

SHE WAS OUT of the water but Marisa still felt as if she were floating as she lay there on the daybed, her heart pounding in heavy anticipation as she watched him begin to fight his way out of his saturated clothes.

His shirt fell first, and his damp skin gleamed gold in the sunlight. He was beautiful and she was mesmerised but, even so, there was still a tiny shred of sanity filtering into her overheated brain.

'Someone might see us...' she murmured, and felt a surge of relief when he ignored her and unzipped his trousers and tore himself loose. A moment later he was standing there naked, and the ache of longing inside was almost too much to bear. Every individual nerve ending was screaming, and a keening moan of need vibrated in her throat as she raised herself up on one elbow.

Eyes blazing, utterly wild, he fell down to his knees beside the daybed, pushing aside more of the cushions to frame her face with his big hands. Marisa's hands were on his body as the force of his kiss bent her backwards onto the bed. Her fingers glided over the hard ridges of muscle in his powerful shoulders and back and then moved lower, down his flat belly, then even lower, causing him to suck in a sharp breath when she cupped his hard, hot length in her hand.

'So hot, so smooth—'

Roman swore, knowing he was perilously close to losing control. He pulled back, sitting on his heels as he took her hands from his body and raised them above her head.

The wet sundress came away easily and landed with a soggy thud on the floor feet away. His burning glance was almost hot enough to evaporate the water on her skin as it roamed over the slim, supple curves of her body.

'I think you'll be more comfortable without this,' he rasped, pulling down one of the thin straps that supported the tiny lacy bra she wore over one smooth shoulder.

She blinked and sighed. 'I will be more comfortable with you inside me.'

His polished ebony eyes flamed at the throaty provocation and his hands were trembling as he applied himself to removing the last physical impediments to satisfying her wish.

It took him what felt like a century to peel off the bra. Wet, it had adhered slickly like a second skin to her body, the now transparent fabric outlining the puckering skin of her areolae and the thrusting prominence of her erect nipples.

When he had finally exposed her body to his hungry gaze his frustration gave way to ruthless desire.

'You are so beautiful!' he groaned, lowering his length onto the narrow bed beside her and watching her face as the first skin-to-skin contact drew a low feral cry from deep inside her chest.

He rolled her under him and, resting on his elbows, kissed her almost savagely while he nudged her legs apart with his knees.

Marisa could feel the heat engulfing her body, moist and waiting, when he slid into her in one slow, measured thrust.

A deep growl vibrated in his chest as she tightened around him, and he gritted his teeth, his blazing eyes devouring her flushed, aroused face as he began to move, increasing his speed and drawing a series of fractured cries of encouragement from her lips as the delicious pressure between them built.

When their climax came, for Marisa the release was so intense that she almost blacked out, the pleasure almost too sharp, too sweet, but she held on and slowly drifted back to earth, her head tucked into the angle of his jaw, her legs wrapped tightly around his waist.

As her sense of self slowly filtered back into her brain, the first strands of self-consciousness began to take control.

Suddenly feeling intensely vulnerable, she unwrapped her legs and rolled away to lie stiff and still by his side.

He had a forearm across his eyes and she had no idea what he was thinking. Then again, she told herself bitterly, why should he be thinking anything? It was only sex for him.

Roman felt her slide away from him with a sense of regret. Her warmth gone, he felt the coldness seep back into him even though it was thirty degrees in the shade. He fought the irrational urge to drag her back against him and feel her burrow into him, as he lay there trying to insulate himself from the emotional fallout of what had just happened between them.

There didn't have to be any fallout; he had to accept it was just sex, great sex but just sex. He could deal with that; it was the unwanted emotions that complicated things.

He felt the cushions beneath him shift as she quietly got up. He opened his eyes ignoring the feeling of *right-*

ness that had stubbornly lingered, despite his best efforts to ignore it.

He propped himself up on one elbow in time to catch a glimpse of her narrow back and the tight peachy curve of her bottom, the gentle swell emphasising the length of her long coltish legs. He felt his sated body stir with desire that pooled heavy in his groin as he watched her drag the wet sundress over her head and a moment later her slim curves were enveloped in the loose folds of material.

She picked up the bra, which now had a little tear in it, and her panties, and squeezed out the excess moisture. Shoving them into one of the big pockets in the skirt of her dress, she looked around for her sandals.

'What are you doing?'

Her gaze lifted but her eyes skittered away from his, the veneer of calm thin enough to reveal the delicate quivering muscles along her jaw, the blue-veined pulse throbbing against the transparent skin of her temple.

'Exactly what it looks like. I need to get back to Jamie.'

'You do know you use Jamie as an excuse to avoid any discussion you don't want to have?'

She sealed her lips and said nothing.

'So this is your plan, to pretend nothing has happened?' he asked, choosing to forget that barely a minute earlier that had been his own plan A.

'Jamie will always come first,' Marisa said, looking away as he swung his legs over the side of the low bed they had shared. The flash fire of desire she felt as his naked body was revealed in all its glory scared her; the complete lack of control she'd just displayed scared her.

And with good reason. She knew from experience that where Roman was concerned she had no pride whatsoever, that when he was in the equation need and desire overrode every moral and practical consideration.

She had finally achieved the safety and stability her life had always lacked. Roman was the antithesis of safe and stable; he was wild and unpredictable... If it had only been her own heart and pride she was gambling with she would've thrown caution to the wind, she would have followed her heart, her instincts.

But this wasn't just about what she wanted, what she *craved*. It couldn't be. She was a mother now, and it wasn't enough to tell her son that she loved him—after all, her own father had loved her. She was determined that Jamie would have the stability that she had always longed for growing up.

Roman was in their lives now, but for how long would that last, especially once he realised how she felt about him? The fact she hadn't blurted out her feelings for him during their recent lovemaking had been luck rather than any caution on her part. If she allowed it to happen again she might not be so lucky next time.

'Should I have a problem with Jamie coming first? I feel the same way,' Roman said.

You can talk the talk, Roman, but can you walk the walk? he thought broodingly. *If you know your son's best interests are best served by taking yourself out of his life, will you do the right thing—will you even recognise what the right thing is? Or will you be blinded by love and even blinder to the damage you inflict in its name?*

He turned his head sharply, his chest heaving with the effort of pushing away the mocking voice of self-doubt in his head as he countered the argument by admitting that he loved his son, but what he felt for Marisa was likely as much to do with the chemistry of dopamine levels in his brain as any deeper romantic connection.

'You...?' She stopped and then redirected her gaze over one of his powerful shoulders, staring off into the distance. 'Will you put some clothes on? I can't concentrate when you're...like that. Just put some clothes on,' she finished lamely.

Pushing free of the battle in his head, he grinned, eliciting an indignant outburst from her.

'Do not look so damned smug!'

His grin did not fade as he walked across to a wooden chest the other side of the daybed. Lifting the lid, he rifled through the folded contents and in moments brought out a pair of swimming shorts and a tee shirt.

'There are swimsuits in there,' she accused.

Pulling the tee shirt over his head, he paused to nod before smoothing down the fabric that clung to the dampness of his skin, moulding it to the corrugated muscles of his belly. 'Some.'

'Why didn't you mention it before?'

'You didn't really give me the chance, did you? You jumped in fully clothed.'

She didn't respond to this vastly modified version of events.

'Why did you marry Rupert?' he suddenly asked.

The shock of the question made Marisa freeze. 'You know why.'

'I know there's something you aren't telling me, because you wouldn't have the sense to marry for money.'

'Dad's debts were—' She stopped and gave a deep sigh, deciding to tell him everything. She was certain Rupert wouldn't have minded her telling the truth to the father of her child. 'Rupert knew he was dying when he asked me to marry him, Roman, and he had already lost his lover—the love of his life. You see, Rupert was gay. His partner was not out, because he'd been married with a family, and then he died very suddenly. Rupert couldn't even go to his funeral. So he had no one to be with him during his last illness. I think it broke Rupert's heart when his lover died, and his biggest fear was being alone when he died.'

'And so he wasn't,' Roman said softly.

She shook her head. 'No, because I agreed to be his wife, in name only.' Her eyes lifted and there were tears standing out in them. 'He really was a very lovely man. A kind, thoughtful person.'

'He would have made a good father.'

'*You* are Jamie's father.'

'Yes, I am, and...so I've been thinking about Jamie.' Not exclusively, he had to admit, because he had been mostly thinking about how his and Marisa's bodies and desires were so perfectly attuned. How much he wanted her.

At what point did wanting become dangerous?

'Oh?'

He stifled the stab of guilt he felt at what he was about to suggest. He knew he was exploiting her greatest weakness, which was Jamie.

She probably deserved better than he was about to offer.

There was an irony in the acknowledgment when you considered that, to him, for the last few years she had symbolised everything that was treacherous. She had highlighted his weakness, a weakness he hadn't known he had.

He nodded towards the pile of tumbled pillows. 'That was great, I hope you'll agree.'

'I assume you're not asking me for reassurance on your technique, Roman, or a score out of ten.'

'No, but neither am I suggesting marriage.'

Her eyes flew wide. 'I never thought you were,' she said faintly. 'Do you mind telling me what you *are* suggesting?'

'That we become a…team.'

'A team? Is there a uniform? Do we have a coach?'

He frowned at her flippancy. 'Team Jamie, I mean. Because we both want what is best for him—I think we have already established that.'

She nodded.

'What just happened—'

'Can't happen again,' she interjected swiftly.

He looked knowingly at her. 'But we both know that it will. Don't we?'

Her eyes slid from his.

'You are the best sex I have ever had, and we already have a son together so I don't think it would require any great sacrifices for us to work in partnership to ensure the best interests of our child. It will require a few adjustments, but we could divide our time between Spain and England, and I think exclusivity is an obvious—'

His ability to make the outrageous sound normal took Marisa's breath away but she finally managed to speak. 'Let me get this straight. You are offering me exclusive access to your body in exchange for letting you be part of Jamie's life?'

'A bit simplistic but essentially, yes. You have no family, no support network.'

'So you want to be my family, but you also want your freedom. You want to take me to bed but you don't want to take me on a date,' she charged angrily.

'You want to go on a date?'

'Right now I want…' Her eyes slid to the sensual line of his lips and instantly he moved in closer.

'You can have everything you want,' he promised throatily.

But not love, she thought sadly, *not love.*

'I want to be Jamie's dad.'

'I know, but… What if you meet someone else who—'

'I suggest we cross that bridge if we ever come to it.' He arched a brow. 'You're not saying no, so you're thinking about it.'

'Family is about love, not convenience, Roman.'

'I love Jamie.'

She swallowed. 'I know you do,' she admitted, standing there and letting him kiss her.

'We could make this work, Marisa.'

The words were whispered against her mouth.

'What do you say?' Another drugging, persuasive kiss.

'I don't know… We could maybe try…?' she murmured, unable to think straight.

The kiss swept her off her feet and they sank together back onto the cushions of the daybed.

CHAPTER TWELVE

IT HAD BEEN three weeks since they had made love by the pool and so far their unconventional arrangement meant that some of his clothes hung in Marisa's wardrobe and there were two toothbrushes in the bathroom.

Was it enough?

Not nearly but it was all she had.

Would she walk away from it? Did she even want to?

It seemed to Marisa that her life suddenly had a lot more questions than answers. There had been moments when her doubts had become so deafeningly loud that she felt as if her head were exploding, but then she saw Roman and Jamie together, a look, a laugh, a small hand enfolded in a strong one and the noise abated to a soft, bearable murmur of unease.

She glanced at her phone before she slid it back into her pocket. Roman had taken Jamie to visit the stables so that he could give the carrot he'd selected to the pony he had fallen in love with. She had expected them back some time ago, but had they already returned and she'd missed them?

If Jamie had fallen for the pony, he had fallen even harder for his father. Yesterday she had found him sitting alongside Roman in his study, cutely mirroring everything his father did. She decided to try there first before she checked out the stables.

The study was empty but, drawn to the crayon drawing on the desk that Roman had framed, she wandered in to take a closer look. As she picked it up, a smile curving her lips, she hit the corner of the desk and the open laptop wobbled and came to life.

She was about to close the lid when she saw what was on the screen and froze.

An hour later Roman was making his way along the hallway to his study when he saw Marisa coming out of it; she was still in the study when she heard Roman's footsteps in the hallway, her face a mask of grim determination.

'Where's Jamie?' she demanded.

'Were you looking for me?' Roman asked, looking past her through the open doorway she had just appeared through. He was still buzzing with what had just happened outside and he had an idea that he wanted to run past her. An image of the wistful look on Jamie's face as he'd watched two of Maria's brothers playing together appeared in his head. Would Marisa also see the logic in wanting to give Jamie a brother or sister?

Marisa said nothing, just turned and walked back into his office.

'Did you tell Jamie I'm his father?' he asked.

She shook her head and looked confused for a moment.

'Well, he knows.'

She frowned. 'No, that isn't possible.'

'I'm telling you, he knows—I heard one of Maria's brothers ask him if I was his dad and Jamie said yes... The thing is he sounded so casual, like it wasn't even a big deal.' He gave an incredulous laugh and dragged a hand through his hair. 'And we were worrying about when to tell him. I suppose kids hear more than you imagine, and…' His brow furrowed as he registered the tear stains on her pale cheeks, and his concern was immediate. 'What's wrong? Are you all right?'

Hands on her hips, she fixed him with an ice-cold stare. 'I said, where's Jamie?'

Right, so something *was* wrong, very wrong. Roman didn't need to be psychic to see that.

'He's playing with Maria's brothers, the two youngest. He was so thrilled when they invited him to play. It's fine—they can speak enough English to make themselves understood.'

'I need him to come back here now.'

'OK…' he said slowly. 'Maria said she'll fetch him back in time for lunch. Marisa, you should have seen his face when he was watching them play, before they invited him to join them; he looked so wistful. I always had Rio… Do you ever think Jamie's lonely?'

Marisa just stared at him. 'Did you hear what I said?'

'What's the hurry? He's safe and enjoying himself.'

'We are going home!'

His eyes narrowed and without his even moving a muscle his body language made a dramatic shift. When he spoke his voice was flat, his speech slow and deliberate. 'Are you going to tell me what's wrong?'

'Oh, I'm sure *you'll* tell *me*. After all, you already know everything about me, don't you, Roman?' She threw him a look of utter disdain and stalked stiff-backed across to his desk where his laptop lay open. 'I was looking for you when I bumped into the desk. The thing woke up…and can you imagine my surprise when I saw *my* name on the PDF file on-screen?'

As she spoke, a chill spread through his body. He knew before she'd reached the big reveal what had happened. *Dios*, the file was only there because he had intended to delete it and then… He couldn't even remember what had distracted him. The missed call from his mother, maybe—he still hadn't rung her back.

'This isn't what it looks like, Marisa.'

'Oh, you mean you didn't sit there and let me spill my guts to you about my dad's gambling and my mother finding me so lovable that she wiped me out of her life, while already knowing all about it?' Marisa's voice cracked and she had to take a deep breath before she could trust herself to go on. 'You let me open up to you, Roman, when all along you already knew every last tiny detail. There is stuff in that file that even *I* had forgotten.'

She stood there *willing* him to intervene, *willing* him to say something that would put her in the wrong. She so *wanted* to be wrong about this. But his stony expression and the sinking feeling in the pit of her stomach told her she wasn't.

He might not love her, but she had started to believe and respect the fact that he didn't pretend, that he was upfront, and all the time he'd been manipulating her emotions to get what he wanted. Frustration and fear settled over her like a dark fog. She had started to fool herself that they had something beyond the physical and Jamie, but she was wrong.

She had *wanted* to believe that *Team Jamie* was some sort of permanent solution, which only made her look completely sad and pathetic, she concluded.

It begged the question: how many nasty realities was she prepared to turn a blind eye to? Without warning an image of her dad's face floated into her head, his optimistic smile that he had fallen lucky, that he was onto a sure thing that would turn around their fortunes, even though she had been able to see the sadness in his eyes, because he didn't really believe it himself.

Her hunger for security and continuity and Roman's love was, she realised now, as strong as her poor dad's drive to be the big personality, the success story.

The memory of her first instinct when she had seen her name on the open file surfaced. She hadn't closed the laptop or her eyes—but she had really, really wanted to. Would she keep her eyes open the next time…and the next…or one day would she close them? Did she want to live her life with that same desperate fake optimism she had regularly seen in her dad's eyes? And how long would it be before Jamie could see all the lies too?

She squared her shoulders and unconsciously donned a quiet dignity as her eyes found his.

'Have you any idea how it makes me feel,' she said quietly, 'to know that all the time I was opening up to you, you knew? You knew about Dad's debts after he died, the men who threatened me when I couldn't pay the money back, and said I could make things easier on myself by being nice to some of their *friends*. Somehow sleeping my way out of debt didn't feel like such a great option to me. You know, that look on your face really is very convincing,' she admired nastily as the betrayal rising up inside her grabbed her in a vicious chokehold. 'You've got the horrified thing off really well.'

He shook his head, looking more shattered now than shocked, but she refused to be influenced by his superlative acting skills. She'd been fooled by him before.

'It's all there in black and white.' She pointed at the computer screen. 'My life has tabloid headlines written all over it, doesn't it? Maybe one of your Hollywood friends could make it into a movie?'

It took Roman several moments before he could trust

himself to speak, to control the images her shocking disclosures had stirred to lurid life in his head. Several more moments to move beyond the protective rage that made him feel nothing was more important than seeking revenge on the animals who had issued the vile threats to her. Ripping the world apart until he found them did not seem at all excessive to him.

A sordid world had touched Marisa but she had emerged untainted. She was, he decided as a surge of cleansing emotion supplanted his anger, the strongest person that he knew.

'I didn't know.' It sounded as pathetic a response as it felt, his brow furrowed as he registered his own outstretched hand. He saw her flinch away and let it fall, acknowledging the knife thrust of pain that her rejection inflicted on him.

Marisa's body was tense, every muscle quivering and taut. She had wanted so much to be able to reach out and be pulled into his body, to pretend that none of this had happened. There was still a shameful part of her that wished she had not confronted him.

'Do you know how all this makes me feel?'

Betrayed, she thought, ruthlessly pushing down the sob in her throat.

'Other than I don't want to be in the same room as you?'

She saw his nostrils flare as he inhaled sharply as if she had struck him, and told herself she didn't care. She wanted him to hurt, because he had hurt her; he had *betrayed* her trust.

'I've never told anyone about my mum and her *other* family either, not even Dad. He never knew that she had remarried, and that her social-media accounts are full of photos of her great, talented stepsons and her lovely daughter—my half-sister.

'Turns out, you see, that it wasn't motherhood she couldn't cut, it was *me*. And to escape me she ran all the way to America, where she has a lovely family she dotes on, bakes cakes for the church fetes and fundraisers for the local school. But, yet again, I'm only telling you what you already know—*aren't I?*'

'I am so sorry, Marisa,' Roman said, aching for her pain, seeing vividly the little girl who had lived with the worst possible rejection grow up only for it to happen all over again. 'If I had known—'

What, Roman? What would you have done?

Protected her!

The thing she needs protecting from is you! sneered the unrelenting voice of disdain in his head.

'Do not *dare* say that,' she hissed through clenched teeth. 'And don't dare to act as if this is all news to you. You already know everything about me, whether I've chosen to tell you or not.'

'I know you're the bravest, kindest, warmest, strongest person I know.'

And I love you, he thought desperately as the self-deception he had clung to like a lifeline finally slipped through his exhausted grip like wet rope. Maintaining that deception had been such a struggle, but letting it go came without relief because along with it went the protection it had afforded.

While he had been able to deflect and think only of chemistry, sex, passion—anything but love—he had been able to tell himself that this situation was manageable, desirable even.

People spent their lives looking for love, but he had spent his life avoiding it, knowing better than most the dangerous, destructive powers of living with such an all-consuming obsessive passion.

The sincerity in his voice as he'd listed her qualities had clearly only made her angrier than ever. She gave a shudder of disgust and held up her hand as he surged towards her, his hands outstretched. 'No!'

He stopped at her command, his hands falling to his sides once more, his face a mask of pain.

He saw the hurt, the pain, the utter rejection in her face and felt his heart sink. Was she right to hold him off? True, he hadn't done what she'd imagined, he'd never read that extended report on her, but he was capable of doing a lot worse, he knew that. He was never going to be a positive influence in her life or Jamie's.

How could he be? He was far too flawed. His father had not set out to hurt him, but the end result was the same and he was his father's son, wasn't he? It was a fact and a fate that he could not escape.

His father had crushed his mother with his love, instead of setting her free. The idea of inflicting that sort of pain on Marisa and their son was too painful for Roman to contemplate.

In one way at least he could prove that he was not his father's son, that he was better than that, or at the very least possessed some self-awareness of the damage he could do.

The cost...the price...would be high but the only way he could prove his love for Marisa and Jamie was to let them go.

It was something he knew he had to do before his selfish instincts, the ones that were screaming at him to keep them close, drowned out his better self.

'I'm sorry.'

It was subtle, almost imperceptible, but the change, the *something* in his manner brought a defensive stiffness to Marisa's attitude. She found herself bracing herself for something—though the *what* remained elusive.

'I think you're right, this isn't working,' he said.

She knew this, she'd been screaming for him to recognise this, so why did hearing him confirm what she already knew feel as though someone had just kicked her in the stomach?

'So what…?'

'If you want to go home I'm not going to stop you.'

She took a deep breath, and refused to flinch as his words and their meaning hit painfully home. She passed a hand across her eyes as she blinked away tears of anger and humiliation. This was one occasion when she didn't want to be proved right.

It didn't matter that she'd been planning to walk through the door anyway. It was, she discovered, an infinitely more humiliating thing entirely to have it held open for you as you went.

'I never needed your permission,' she flared back before, a moment later, her haughtiness morphed into bitterness. 'So you got bored with being a father after all.' It was as if he'd just decided the hassle was all too much trouble, easier by far to walk away. Only better still, he didn't have to because this was his home and she was the one walking away from him.

Something flashed in his dark eyes, but a moment later it was gone. His voice was flat and even as he said quietly, 'I'll make sure the jet is available.'

Pride was the only thing stopping her falling down as he walked away. The moment he vanished so did her defiance, but she was robbed of the release of tears because Jamie arrived smelling of the stables and demanding she come with him so he could show her the correct way to groom a horse.

* * *

The *castillo* had never felt this empty before.

Roman had locked himself in his study and sat looking at a decanter of brandy, although his glass remained
empty. He knew it wouldn't help because it would take
a lot more than alcohol to dull the pain, the emptiness
inside him.

The first time his mobile rang he ignored it. The second time he intended to do the same, then with a sudden
intake of breath he reached for the offending instrument.
What if it was Marisa and she needed him? It was amazing how many nightmare scenarios a man could imagine
in between grabbing a phone and ramming it to his ear.

'Roman, my, you are a difficult man to get hold of.'

His shoulders sagged. 'Mother.'

'So glad you recognise my voice after all this time
and, before you say it, I know I wasn't very welcoming the last time you saw me, but hospitals really do not
bring out the best in me. I wanted to tell you that I am
back home now after what I hope will be my last surgery. Everything went well and I'm planning to visit my
granddaughter shortly. I thought you could possibly join
me at the beach house? You have no idea how happy I
am that at least one of you is settled. I was always worried about Rio.'

'Why Rio?' Roman asked, pretending an interest he
didn't feel as he reached for the decanter and filled the
glass. It might not help but he was now working on the
theory that it could surely not make things any worse.

'I know I'm being silly, but he could just be so possessive as a child and, when he was angry, he had a way of
holding his head that occasionally made me think of...
But of course, he is nothing like your father.'

Roman placed the glass down with a bang that sloshed

the contents over the polished surface. 'Rio, like Father?'
He had to have misheard.

'I know… I know, so stupid of me. You are both your
own men, and you always were.'

'Rio?'

'Are you all right, Roman?'

'People used to say that *I* was like Father.'

His mother's merry laughter echoed down the line.
'What people?' she scoffed. 'Heavens, are you serious?
You?

'You are *nothing* like your father at all. In fact, you
are the total antithesis of him, which is why I never worried about you as much as I did Rio. You are moody and
emotional, and your father was a very cold and calcu-
lating man. Oh, he spoke a lot about love, but the truth
was he was incapable of feeling the emotion, because he
was all about control and revenge. The only thing you
inherited from your father was your head for business!
Roman, are you still there?'

'Yes, Mother, but I have to go now.'

Could it be true?

Was it possible that he was so afraid of becoming the
very thing he'd most despised and feared, he had created
a scenario that did not exist, and he had seen monsters
in him that were not there?

He picked up the framed drawing from the desk before
the spreading brandy reached it, and stared at the childish drawing, feeling as if his heart would burst.

He ached for Marisa.

He ached for their son too, yet his suffering was of
his own making. He'd thought he was being noble, doing
the right thing for them…but what if all he was actually
being was a coward?

He had sent them away! A sound of disgust was

wrenched from his throat. He was sitting here alone, being a martyr, when actually he was simply a fool—a coward and a fool.

A sense of calm settled over him as he brushed the mess off the desk with his forearm and placed the picture back carefully centre stage, which was where his family should be.

He reached for his phone to call his pilot.

'Santiago, I have a favour to ask.'

The 'staying cheerful' thing was taking its toll. Marisa already felt exhausted after a journey from hell to the private airport, during which Jamie had loudly demanded to take his pony and Roman, not necessarily in that order, back home with him.

All she wanted to do was curl up in a corner and cry, but crying was not a luxury that mums always had.

And now, just when she'd thought the worst was over, the flight, for some reason that was too technical for her to grasp, was delayed. At least they were delayed in luxury and the on-board staff were keeping Jamie amused playing games. She glanced towards her son, who was crying out, 'I win, I win,' after he had carefully counted out six on the dice.

'Excuse me.'

She turned to see the pilot standing beside her.

'Not more delay?' She sighed.

'Everything is moving along nicely,' he soothed. 'But there is an issue with some of the luggage. If you could just come outside for a moment?'

'Luggage?'

He shrugged and smiled. 'These officials can be persistent.'

Which told her nothing at all. She glanced over at Jamie.

'He'll be fine. I'll keep an eye on him myself.'

She recognised the sleek supercar before she even saw the driver.

'Hello, Marisa.'

She spun around, her blonde hair flying around her face. Brushing the shiny strands from her face gave her time to think, except of course she couldn't. Thoughts were firing off at wild tangents in her head, not making any sense, the processes of logic completely overwhelmed by the surge of raw emotion that blocked out everything else... There was just her heartbeat and the sensation of deep longing.

'I like your hair loose.' His caressing glance drifted over her pale hair before coming to rest on her face, his own settling into an expression that hinted at an aching loneliness inside him.

She cleared her throat and looked away, refusing to see things that were not there. She had to deal with the real world, not fantasies, which were lovely while they lasted but so, so painful when you woke up.

'What are you doing here, Roman?'

Her chin lifted as she added silently, *Besides compounding my misery.* She hadn't asked to fall in love but she had, and as she looked up at his perfectly gorgeous face she could not imagine a time when he did not make her ache with longing.

With a tiny groan she squeezed her eyes closed and begged huskily, 'Will you just go away and leave me in peace?'

'No.'

Her eyes opened in response to the thumb under her chin.

He was there standing right in front of her, his body

blocking out everything else, but then when he was around there was nothing else for her to see.

'Not yet.' His lips were warm as they moved across her own. 'Not ever,' he added on a throaty murmur as he kissed her again, this time with a ferocity that matched the possessive intent etched on his dark features.

Hands clenched at her sides, she fought against the surge of passion that made her want to cling to him, and with a small cry she stepped backwards, her pallor highlighted by the two patches of colour on her cheeks as she panted like someone who had just run a marathon.

'What is this all about, Roman? Because...' She glanced at the stationary jet, its metallic paint glinting in the sun. 'You arranged this delay, didn't you?'

'Yes. I needed to talk to you.'

She touched her lips. 'That wasn't talking.'

Roman sketched a smile that did not reach his dark eyes, which remained desperate and determined. 'Your mouth always distracts me. The *castillo* felt empty when you left.'

Empty, sterile, safe...*very* safe—just like his life. People called him reckless and a risk-taker when he pitted himself against an unclimbable peak, but he wasn't a risk-taker, he was a coward, he thought with a fresh surge of self-contempt. What he was about to do, now *that* was real risk-taking.

Giving something of himself.

The cost of moving on was high, but he needed to let her see him as he really was.

'Yes, I did order that dossier on you to be compiled, but I hadn't ever opened it. I had no idea what was in it until you told me.'

She planted her hands on her hips, an effect spoilt by the fact she had to brush away the tears that were trickling down her cheeks. 'You've driven all this way just to tell me that? You expect me to *believe* you?'

'No, but it happens to be true.' His chest lifted in a deep sigh. His future, his soul depended on him convincing her.

'I had every intention of deleting it from my computer, I really did.'

'Because you were not interested in my skeletons,' she said dryly.

'I'm interested in *everything* about you,' he said honestly. 'And I was very tempted to access that material, but I didn't because… I think I wanted you to tell me yourself, when you were ready.'

'Because you are *so* patient.'

He conceded her jab with a shrug. 'Maybe it was arrogant of me, but I wanted you to trust me.' His lips quirked in a bitter little smile. '*Dios*, this is not easy.'

'And flying away from you is?' she yelled back.

'Then don't go,' he pushed out fiercely through clenched teeth before continuing in the same driven tone. 'I wanted, I *needed* you to trust me enough to tell me. I genuinely had no idea about your mother and half-sister until you told me. For the record, it is not your fault, it is hers, and not having you in her life is definitely her loss. I am speaking here as someone who has lost you once and, while I am so glad Rupert was there to save you, I just wish it had been me instead, *mi vida*.'

She blinked and he took encouragement from the doubt that he saw creep into her golden eyes.

'I don't believe you.' But he didn't think she sounded completely sure and he pressed home the only advantage he had left.

'It is true. What is also true is that I love you. You are the only woman in the world I have ever said that to. The last time you threw it back in my face and walked away with a chunk of me that I've never got back.'

She took a step towards him, her eyes scanning his face. 'You love me...?'

'From that very first moment I saw you.'

She looked utterly shocked.

'I have always been afraid that if I let myself care about someone, allowed myself to fall in love, I would become just like him and destroy the very thing that I loved most.'

'Your father?'

He nodded. 'The anger, the rage inside me when you told me you were already married...it was...' He closed his eyes, the sinews in his neck standing out as he fought against the tidal wave of black memories. 'I walked away from my life, and I rebuilt those walls you knocked down around my heart, but I added a few more feet for good measure, as much to keep my anger in as to keep love out. I shouldn't be telling you this.'

'You *should* be telling me,' Marisa contradicted, stepping in and framing his face with loving hands and sharing a watery smile when he opened his eyes.

'You believe me.'

'I do.' She felt lighter for just saying it. 'I love you, Roman, so much it scares me, because loving you feels like I'm stepping into moving traffic with my eyes closed.' She gave a wild little laugh. 'They say the best cure for fears and secrets is fresh air. You can't keep everything in, and I can't any more,' she admitted.

'If it ever gets too heavy for you to bear, you need to share—you need to share with me. You really are incredible, you know.' Unable to resist the soft invitation of her lips, he kissed her with a tenderness bordering on reverence.

'You'll make me cry,' she warned thickly.

'If I ever hurt you, Marisa, it would kill me—' he groaned out fiercely.

'You are *nothing* like him,' she cut in fiercely. 'Do you hear me, Roman Bardales? Nothing! There is a massive difference between wanting to *protect* someone because you love them and wanting to *control* them because you don't know what love really is. You love our son and I know that you will always protect him. That makes me feel…safe. You make me feel safe.'

'Marisa.' He swallowed, his voice cracking with emotion as he stroked a finger down her smooth cheek.

'I want to be Superman for our son.'

'He doesn't need a superhero, he just needs a dad. He needs you.' Her lashes dipped over her eyes as she gazed at him through them. 'We both do, Roman.'

'You have me, you have had me from that moment in the rain when you looked up at me and the rest of the world went away.'

'You and Jamie are my entire world,' she whispered against his mouth.

He sighed in contentment. 'Let's go home.'

EPILOGUE

'WHY ARE WE HERE? I have a table at the restaurant booked for—' Roman turned his wrist, pushed up the cuff of the fine black cashmere sweater he wore over black jeans and glanced at the metal-banded watch '—half an hour ago.' He sighed. The famous Michelin-starred restaurant was the only thing that would normally have made the journey to this quiet south coast seaside town worthwhile.

When he had acquiesced to Marisa's surprise request to spend the weekend here he had assumed that the place had some special significance for her, maybe from childhood, but no, she seemed as unfamiliar with the place as he was.

The mystery remained but he was content to let it play out.

'I am not dressed for the beach.' He looked around at the empty stretch of sand lined with beach huts, but it did not surprise him it was empty; the wind was blowing up a positive sandstorm. 'Sand gets everywhere.'

'Don't be such a grouch,' she retorted. 'We are nearly there.' She was studying the brightly painted beach huts they were passing and was, he realised, counting under her breath. 'This is it!' she exclaimed.

He shook his head. He could see someone jogging along a deserted promenade and a dog walker who was a mere dot in the distance.

'You have bought me a beach hut?'

It was a joke, but then she went to knock on the door of the candy-striped wooden box they were standing beside.

'Marisa!'

She shook her head, suddenly looking nervous. 'You will thank me, I promise you,' she said, sounding as if she was trying to convince herself. She tapped on the door, which opened immediately.

A slim figure wearing large sunglasses and a loose hooded sweat top that concealed her hair stepped out, nodding at Marisa, who turned to him with a plea in her golden eyes.

'Just please go inside, Roman, and then you'll understand.'

He would have stepped inside a burning building if she had asked him, so this request did not require much thought. He ducked to go through the door and heard a key click in the lock behind him.

'I'll come back for you in half an hour!' Marisa yelled through the door.

As he had already seen through the disguise of the woman in the hoodie he was not surprised by the identity of the solo occupant of the beach hut, who was sitting on an unfolded deckchair.

The figure got to his feet. 'It would seem you are late.'

'If I'd known where I was going, I wouldn't be here at all,' Roman said, staring with distaste around the hut's interior, lit by a single bulb suspended from the ceiling. 'I am assuming that we are meant to sort out our differences in half an hour, and then emerge as friends?'

'That appears,' Rio agreed dryly, 'to be the general idea. Or I could even the scales and put you on the floor this time,' he added, rubbing his clean-shaven jaw.

'You could try,' Roman retorted.

The brothers stood staring at one another for a moment, then in unison they grinned and, stepping forward into one another, embraced.

'So who do you suppose had this cunning little idea?' Rio asked. 'Gwen or Marisa?'

'I think I know when they made contact, because a couple of weeks ago Marisa was looking *really* guilty.'

Rio nodded. 'Yes, that time frame works for my end too,' he admitted with a laugh. 'Well, are we going to tell them this little charade was not actually necessary, that we'd already met, shook hands and made up?'

'How about we leave them thinking they have knocked our stubborn heads together and saved the day?'

Rio grinned. 'Shall we throw a few things around too to make it look authentic?'

'What is this place anyway?'

'I think we might find our other halves bid for it in an online auction—but it could have been worse,' Rio said.

'How so?'

'They could be leaving us in here for an hour.'

Roman laughed. 'And in the meantime do you have those dates?' he asked, digging in a pocket for his phone.

'You spoke to Mum?'

Roman nodded. 'She is willing to come back to the *castillo* for the big day, as long as she can bring her significant other.'

'He really is all right, you know.'

'So long as he makes her happy,' Roman said simply.

'Wow, you really have changed your tune—is that Marisa's influence?'

Roman slung him a look. 'So the venue is sorted, it's just a matter of when suits us all.'

'The sooner the better, as far as I'm concerned…' Rio paused. 'Before Gwen starts showing.'

Roman's eyes widened. 'Congratulations… I don't suppose that this is a spring baby?'

'End of—' Rio stopped dead. *'You too?'*

Roman nodded, looking proud. 'Well, not me personally, but Marisa found out last week. Jamie is going to have a brother or sister, maybe both if we're really lucky.'

'Twins?' Rio released a low chuckle. 'This is going to be one hell of a wedding, brother, in a good way.'

'I have a feeling it's going to be one hell of a life, in the very best way,' Roman countered.

Not just a society wedding, but a *joint* wedding of the most eligible bachelors in Europe, held in the incredible setting of the Bardales estate.

The world's media only had one complaint: that they were not allowed inside. The rich and famous were invited and, so it was said, most of the locals for miles around too. They took comfort in the knowledge that someone would have smuggled in a phone, that *someone* would be tempted by a fat wedge of cash.

They would get their story.

What they did get was a snapshot made publicly available that showed both couples sitting on a bale of hay looking happy, and the world's media spent a full week furiously speculating on who was responsible for this naturalistic shot.

A week later, sprawled on the cushions of the daybed beside his wife, Roman watched Jamie swim-splashing in the new addition to the landscaping, a baby pool filled with inflatable toys, while he read aloud an article in the paper.

'"It seems that the truth is out: the wedding photo, it has been definitively decided, was taken by famous photographer Sir Robert Chambers, who is refusing to confirm the rumours, but a source close to him apparently says"—'

A protective hand on the gentle swell of her belly, Marisa broke into peels of musical laughter.

'Imagine,' Roman said, leaning over to remove her hand and kiss the small bump before he placed it back and covered the pale fingers with his own big hand. 'If our son has a talent worthy of such a towering artistic icon at only four.'

'Five next,' Marisa corrected with a grin.

'Five next, but imagine what he will be capable of by the time he is eighteen.'

'If he is anything like his father, he'll be breaking hearts, I would think.'

Roman caught her hand and pulled Marisa against him. 'There is only one heart I am interested in,' he husked, curving a possessive hand over the curve of her left breast, 'and I do not want to break it. I want to love it like I do every single part of you.' He placed a gentle kiss on her mouth.

'Well, soon there'll be a lot more of me to love than there was, so you'd better leave plenty of time,' she retorted against his warm lips.

'Time is not a problem. We have the rest of our lives.'

With a sigh Marisa allowed herself to be drawn into his arms and Roman held her tight. He never wanted to let her go.

He wasn't aware he had spoken aloud until Marisa whispered back, 'Don't even try to let me go, Bardales. I'm a keeper.'

* * * * *

HER
WEDDING NIGHT
NEGOTIATION

CHANTELLE SHAW

Her white blouse was buttoned up to her throat and her navy skirt fell to several inches below her knees. She wore her reddish-brown hair in a no-nonsense braid that hung between her shoulder blades and she could have passed for a nun—or Mary Poppins.

Her personality seemed to be as unexciting as her appearance, although Marco had been intrigued by the flush of rose-pink that had spread across her cheeks as she'd mumbled a greeting when James had introduced them. It had been a long time since he'd seen a woman blush. Marco had revised his opinion of Leah as plain at that point, acknowledging that she was actually very pretty, albeit not his type. He liked sexually confident women who understood that he wasn't interested in commitment and would never, ever offer them marriage. Once had been enough.

He glanced at his watch and cursed beneath his breath. In an hour it would be Nicky's bedtime and Marco had wanted to spend some time with his son. He already felt guilty that he'd been called away on an urgent business trip which had meant him leaving Nicky behind at Nancarrow Hall with the nanny for the past week.

Guilt played a big part in his relationship with Nicky, he acknowledged with a deep sigh. The psychotherapist who had been working with the little boy insisted that a five-year-old did not have the emotional capacity to blame Marco for the accident in which Nicky's mother had died. But Marco blamed himself. He had failed Nicky in the past, and he was failing him now because he could not seem to find a way to connect with his traumatised son.

Where the hell was James?

Marco saw Leah check her phone, and her shoulders slump. She looked a forlorn figure as she waited at the altar for her bridegroom, but he reminded himself it wasn't up to him to explain that James was not the Prince Charming she clearly believed he was.

His thoughts returned to his son. He'd bought a toy sports car—a model of his own Ferrari—for Nicky, and he was looking forward to watching him open the gift. Perhaps the little boy would give one of his rare smiles.

Marco refused to waste any more time waiting for the wedding rehearsal to begin and he stepped out of the recess into the main part of the chapel.

'Is there *still* no sign of the bridegroom?' The vicar smiled sympathetically at Leah.

'I can't imagine what has happened to James,' she said, checking her phone again. 'He was going to Padstow to pick up a few last-minute things for our honeymoon, but he promised he would be back by six-thirty for the wedding rehearsal.'

There was no message from her fiancé to explain why he was delayed, but Leah remembered how James had driven at a snail's pace along the narrow Cornish lanes on the way to Nancarrow Hall a week ago. He was certainly not a daredevil, and she reassured herself that if he'd had an accident the emergency services would have alerted his parents. It was more likely that he'd lost track of the time, which was not unusual.

James tended to daydream, and he was hopelessly disorganised. Sometimes Leah felt more like his nanny than his partner, and since she'd arrived at Nancarrow Hall and met his parents she'd realised that they were overlyprotective of James. She suspected that he had been cosseted his whole life. But he was amiable, and easy-going, and their relationship had none of the drama and tension that Leah remembered from her childhood, when her mother had lurched from one disastrous love affair to another.

They had only been dating for six months, but she'd pushed away her doubts that their courtship had not been long enough for her to be certain she wanted to spend the rest of her life with James Fletcher. He had been in a strange mood since they had arrived at his family's gothic mansion on the edge of Bodmin Moor, but surely it was natural that they were both experiencing pre-wedding nerves.

Leah's conscience pricked. She knew that she should have told James about the money she had been left by her grandmother. But she'd been worried that the stipulation in Grandma Grace's will that she must be married before she could claim her inheritance might complicate her relationship with James. She loved him. She *did*.

Leah refused to listen to the voice of her conscience, which warned her that she was rushing into marriage because she craved the kind of settled life that she'd never known during her chaotic childhood.

'I have an appointment with the Bishop later this evening,' the vicar said. 'We will have to start the rehearsal without James. Perhaps someone can stand in for him until he gets here?'

He surveyed the group of people assembled in the private chapel. It was a small wedding with only forty guests. Thirty-nine of them were friends and family of the groom.

Leah directed a questioning look at Amy, her best friend from university and bridesmaid. Amy was an old school friend of James and it was she who had introduced him to Leah at a party. Leah had been flattered by his attention. She considered herself no more than averagely attractive and she'd assumed that good-looking, public-school-educated James was out of her league.

She had been drawn to the sense of security he represented. Once they were married they planned to move out of London and buy a little cottage with roses growing around the front door, and in time they would have two children and a dog. Other women might yearn for riches, designer clothes and dazzling jewels, but Leah's dream was a family.

Amy gave a shrug as an awkward silence followed the vicar's request for a stand-in bridegroom.

'I'm sure there must be a good reason why James is late.' Davina, the ultra-efficient wedding planner spoke in an oddly thick voice, and she looked as though she had been crying.

'Ideally we need someone who doesn't have a prominent role in the wedding ceremony to act as the groom.'

'I'll take James's place.'

The deep voice laced with a sexy accent came from the back of the chapel.

Leah stiffened and felt a peculiar sensation, as if her stomach had swooped down to her toes. That voice could only belong to Marco De Valle, James's Italian half-brother. Earlier in the day she had watched a tall, dark-haired man climb out of a sleek silver sports car and inexplicably her stomach had done the same swooping thing it was doing now.

When the stranger had walked into the drawing room and James had introduced him Leah had felt overwhelmed by Marco's magnetism. His supreme self-assurance gave him a presence that made everything and everyone around him fade to grey. She had darted a glance at Marco's face before hastily dropping her gaze, feeling as flustered and tongue-tied as a teenager who had just met her celebrity idol. Her blood had pounded in her ears as she'd mumbled a greeting.

That brief look had revealed that the half-brothers bore no resemblance to each other. James, with his blond hair and clean-cut image, was boyishly handsome. He had done some modelling work and appeared on the front covers of several glossy magazines of the kind which featured articles about stately homes and Royal Ascot.

The kind of publication that might have a photo of Marco De Valle on its front cover would be magazines about extreme sports or how to survive if you were stranded in the Amazonian jungle, Leah thought wryly. There was something untamed about him, and she sensed that he lived by his own rules and did not care a jot what others thought of him.

That feeling had been reinforced when she'd watched him from her bedroom window, striding across the moors—an imposing figure with his black coat swirling in the wind and his hair blown back from his face.

James had told her that the jagged scar on Marco's face was the result of a terrible accident in which his wife had been killed, leaving his five-year-old son motherless. Poor Nicky. The little boy was clearly still disturbed by the tragedy, and he rarely spoke or smiled. It was obvious to Leah that, having lost his mother, he needed to be with his father as much as possible, but James had said that Marco often left Nicky at Nancarrow Hall while he went abroad.

Perhaps Marco's absences were unavoidable, but having grown up never feeling that she was her mother's main priority, Leah had felt her heart go out to Nicky. His big brown eyes reminded her poignantly of her little brother, who had died when he was not much older than Nicky. There was not a day when Leah did not think of Sammy, and spending time with Nicky during the past week, while James had been busy, had been bittersweet.

Her thoughts scattered now, as she watched Marco stroll down the aisle towards her, and she was dismayed when her pulse quickened in an unbidden response to him.

She noticed that his scar sliced down his cheek from just beneath his right eye to the corner of his mouth, making his top lip curl slightly and giving him a permanently cynical expression that was mirrored in his wintry grey eyes. On any other man the scar might have been regarded as a disfigurement, but it merely accentuated Marco's raw masculinity.

'Handsome' did not come close to describing his chiselled features: razor-sharp cheekbones and a square, determined jaw shaded with dark stubble. Above that sullen, sexy mouth was a strong nose rising to meet heavy dark brows. His hair was the same shade of almost black, overlong and dishevelled, as though he had just left a lover's bed after a night of passion.

Where that last thought had come from Leah had no idea, but the picture in her mind of Marco's naked body sprawled on satin sheets did nothing to help her already shaky composure.

She had never even seen a naked man before.

Other than on a no-holds-barred television dating show which, to Leah's mind, had been completely unromantic.

Marco moved with the silence and speed of a panther stalking its prey. Before Leah had time to collect her wits he was standing beside her. Her mouth dried as she forced herself to meet his sardonic gaze and she wondered if he heard her heart as it collided with her ribs. The jolt of awareness was unlike anything she'd ever felt before.

Not even for James. whispered her conscience, which seemed hell-bent on causing trouble.

'You don't have to do this,' she told Marco stiffly. 'I'm sure James will be here any minute now.'

'Your confidence in my brother is admirable,' he drawled, 'but James is as bad at time-keeping as he is at holding down a job.'

'It wasn't *his* fault he was sacked from the art gallery.' Leah sprang to her fiancé's defence. 'It was unfortunate that his alarm failed to go off and he overslept. He was only late for work a few times.'

'Well, I'm not prepared to wait any longer for him to show up.' Marco's gaze narrowed on Leah's flushed face. 'I understand you have only known my brother for a matter of months? If you'd like my advice, it is that you should postpone the wedding until you're certain that you are both ready for marriage.'

'I *don't* want your advice, thank you,' she snapped with icy politeness.

His grey eyes gleamed. 'The little mouse has a temper?' he said softly. 'Perhaps you are not as uninteresting as I thought when James introduced us.'

He ignored her furious gasp and turned to speak to the wedding planner.

'Reverend Tregarth is right. We should push on with the rehearsal without James. My housekeeper is planning to serve a buffet dinner this evening to allow the kitchen staff time to start preparing the wedding food for tomorrow.'

Leah saw Davina nod meekly. Marco had an air of authority and obviously expected other people to accept his leadership. But she was puzzled that he had spoken of *his* housekeeper. Surely the staff were employed by James's parents, whom she assumed were the owners of Nancarrow Hall? James had said that Marco lived mainly in Italy, where he headed De Valle Caffè—a world-famous coffee company and coffeehouse chain.

The wedding planner opened the folder she was holding, entitled *Fletcher/Ashbourne Wedding 21st July*. 'We'll start without James and I can fill him in on what he needs to know later. As all the guests are here, I'll ask everyone to stand in their correct places while we run through the order of service.'

The vicar stood on the chancel steps as Davina directed people to their places.

'The groom and best man will stand on the right side of the chapel. The bridesmaid and the bride's family will be on the left side. But it might be better if the groom's friends and relatives fill the pews on both sides of the nave,' the wedding planner said hurriedly, realising that Leah's side of the chapel would be empty apart from Amy. 'And the bride and groom will stand facing the minister.'

As Leah moved into place she glanced over her shoulder, hoping to see James rushing through the doorway. She noticed a satisfied expression on his mother's face and guessed that Olivia Fletcher would not be disappointed if James had changed his mind and called off the wedding. Olivia had more airs and graces than royalty, and had made it plain that she believed her youngest son was marrying beneath him.

'It's *such* a shame your mother is on an around-the-world cruise and won't be able to share your big day,' Olivia had said with fake sincerity when Leah had explained that her father was dead, and her mother wouldn't be attending the wedding.

Her mother being on a cruise had been a blatant but necessary lie. Leah shuddered at the idea of her mum staggering into the church and behaving outrageously, as Tori had done many times in the past. She had even turned up drunk to Leah's university graduation ceremony and ruined what should have been a proud day.

James had only met Tori once. Leah had invited him round early one Saturday morning, when her mum was usually still sober. The meeting had gone without incident, although Leah had quickly invented an excuse when James had suggested they all go to the pub for lunch.

During James's visit Leah had seen her mum almost as she'd remembered her from long ago: intelligent and articulate with a hint of the great beauty she had once had in her smile. But when she'd gone into the kitchen to make a cup of tea she had found a bottle of vodka that Tori had hidden in the cupboard under the sink. She hadn't had a chance to pour the vodka away, and she knew that Tori would have finished the bottle by that evening and visited the local supermarket to buy more.

Leah had felt too embarrassed to tell James about her mother's drink problem. She'd spent her childhood wishing that her mum was 'normal', like other parents. It hadn't been so bad when they'd lived abroad in a commune, with Tori's artist friends. But when Leah was twelve they had moved back to England.

She cringed at memories of her mum attending school functions drunk and talking too loudly, attracting attention. Once at a prize-giving ceremony Tori had flirted with the headmaster and then thrown up in the school hall in front of everyone. From then on Leah had never invited Tori to school events, but that hadn't stopped the other kids' taunts that her mum was 'an alky'.

After the wedding she would explain to James that her mum was what was termed a 'functioning alcoholic'. Somehow Tori managed to hold down her job as a book-keeper with a building firm, but her heavy drinking every weekend was destroying her health. Leah was sure James would be supportive of her intention to use some of her inheritance to pay for specialist treatment for her mum.

Where was he?

She started to turn her head towards the back of the chapel, hoping to see that James had arrived, but her gaze snagged on Marco's enigmatic grey eyes. She estimated that he must be three or four inches over six feet tall, as she had to angle her neck to look at him, and his chiselled features had a peculiar effect on her pulse. From where she was standing, she couldn't see his scar, and her breath caught in her throat as she studied the sculpted perfection of his bone structure. He was beautiful in a powerfully masculine way.

She could not stop staring at his face and he lifted one dark brow mockingly, as if he was aware that she was fascinated by him. Blushing hotly, Leah jerked her eyes towards the front of the chapel. She was trembling. *Not* because she was fiercely aware of Marco, she assured herself, but because she was angry at his arrogance when he had said he thought she was uninteresting.

She forced herself to concentrate when the vicar spoke.

'At the beginning of the ceremony the bride and groom will turn to face each other and hold hands.'

Reluctantly Leah turned towards Marco, and her heart gave a jolt when he reached for her hands. She was about to tell him that it wasn't necessary to practise *every* detail of the wedding, but before she could speak he wrapped his strong fingers around hers, enveloping her small hands in his much bigger ones.

She inhaled swiftly as a sensation like an electrical current shot through her fingers and up her arms. Marco's touch was warm and firm, and she sensed inherent strength in his grasp. She stared down at their linked hands and noted how his darkly tanned skin contrasted with her milky paleness. Her traitorous mind imagined his fingers skimming over her naked body and curving around her breasts.

Swallowing hard, Leah raised her eyes to Marco's chest, where the top few buttons of his sky-blue shirt were undone, revealing a vee of tanned skin and a sprinkling of black hair. He smelled of soap and spice: exotic notes of a bergamot and sandalwood cologne mixed with an indefinable scent that was raw male.

On the periphery of her mind she registered that the vicar was explaining how he would talk them through the ceremony rather than read through the entire wedding service word for word.

'You will want to save making your vows until the actual wedding, and to the right bridegroom,' he said, giving Leah a pointed look.

She felt guilty colour rise in her face. Had the vicar guessed that she was having inappropriate thoughts about the man who tomorrow would become her brother-in-law? How could her mind be so disloyal to James? Her reaction to Marco De Valle was inexplicable and inexcusable.

She tried to withdraw her hands from Marco's, but he tightened his fingers and stroked his thumb lightly back and forth over the pulse beating erratically in her wrist. Perhaps it was meant to be a soothing gesture, but it had the opposite effect, making Leah's heart pound so hard that she was surprised it wasn't visible beneath her shirt.

'After the declarations and the vows and the exchange of rings, the congregation will be seated while the bride, groom and witnesses accompany me into the vestry,' the vicar explained. 'Once the register has been signed, the newly married couple will return to stand at the altar rail, and I will invite the groom to kiss his bride.'

Leah's eyes jerked to Marco's face and she stared at his sensual mouth as he lowered his head towards her. Her heart lurched. He *wouldn't*! He *couldn't* mean to kiss her.

It must be shock that was keeping her feet welded to the floor. She did *not* want Marco to claim her mouth with his, she assured herself.

His dark head came closer and she felt the hard glitter in his eyes evoke a wild heat inside her. He filled her vision, and when her eyelashes swept down she could still see his chiselled features as though they were imprinted on her retinas.

The air around them seemed to tremble and Leah could hardly breathe. They stood like that—close, but not close enough—for what felt like a lifetime. But it could only have been a few seconds before the spell that Marco had cast on her was shattered.

'Sorry I'm late!'

The voice from the back of the chapel jolted Leah to her senses. Her eyes flew open and she drew a shuddering breath. Marco had already straightened up. Perhaps she'd only imagined that he had been on the brink of kissing her. His eyes were hooded, and she could not read his expression.

With a low cry she snatched her hands out of his and ran down the aisle. 'James, where have you been? Why didn't you answer your phone when I called you?'

'The battery died.' James's eyes sidled away from Leah's. 'You know how I always forget to charge it.'

She bit her lip. 'We had to start the rehearsal without you...your brother offered to take your place,' she explained, when Marco walked up to her and James.

Leah had previously sensed the coolness between the brothers, and now the temperature in the chapel seemed to drop by several degrees as the two men faced each other.

'I trust you will afford your bride the courtesy of turning up on time for your actual wedding tomorrow?' Marco said curtly.

'*You* are hardly the right person to give me advice on how to treat my bride,' James muttered. 'Your marriage lasted for just a year, and it's rumoured that your wife died trying to escape from you.'

Leah's eyes flew to Marco. She expected him to say something in his defence, but he stayed silent. His face might as well have been carved from the same unforgiving granite as the chapel walls, and his eyes were the dull, cold grey of a midwinter sky. The scar on his cheek was a stark white line ruining the perfection of his olive skin.

He was beautiful, and terrible, and Leah could not understand why he had such a devastating effect on her. She was shocked by her uncontrolled response to Marco. A knot of tension tightened in the pit of her stomach as she wondered if her mother had been overwhelmed by this same helpless fascination with a man every time she'd rushed headlong into a new relationship.

She was *not* going to make the same mistakes as her mother, Leah promised herself. Thank goodness she was marrying dear, *safe* James, she thought as she watched Marco stride out of the chapel.

CHAPTER TWO

THE REHEARSAL DINNER was already underway when Marco entered the orangery. A buffet was laid out on long tables and guests were helping themselves to food. He accepted a glass of wine from the butler, but he felt too wired to eat.

One reason for his lack of appetite was his increasing concern about his relationship with his son. It had been too much to hope that Nicky would be pleased to see him, he thought heavily. After the wedding rehearsal had finished he'd hurried back to the house so that he could see him, but even when he'd given the little boy his present Nicky had shown no emotion apart from the wariness in his eyes that felt like a knife through Marco's heart.

The truth, Marco acknowledged, was that he had felt awkward when he'd sat there on the nursery floor and sought to engage his son in pushing toy cars along a track. He did not remember his own father ever playing with *him* and he had no real idea how to be a good parent. Yes, he'd read numerous books on parenting, but none of them had offered advice on how to win the trust of a child who seemed afraid of his own father.

He raked his fingers through his hair as his thoughts turned to the other reason for his black mood. He must have suffered a temporary mental aberration in the church when he'd almost kissed the bride-to-be. Marco remembered Leah had looked as stunned as he had felt by the chemistry that had blazed between them.

He'd told himself that her air of innocence must be an illusion. It was inconceivable that she and James were not lovers, seeing as they were about to marry. However, according to his housekeeper, James and his fiancée were *not* sharing a bedroom at Nancarrow Hall.

Marco had sensed a vulnerability in Leah as he'd stood next to her in front of the altar. It was a place he had vowed never to stand again after his disastrous experience of holy matrimony. These wedding preparations were evoking bitter memories of Karin and reminding Marco of why he would never trust a woman again.

He glanced around the room and saw James standing at the bar with the wedding planner. They appeared to be having a casual conversation, but Marco curled his lip sardonically. Nothing that happened at Nancarrow Hall did not reach his ears. But what his half-brother got up to was none of his business, he reminded himself. It was not up to *him* to tell the bride of his suspicions about James.

Marco spotted Leah over by the window and shock ricocheted through him as he took in her transformation from dowdy and dull to absolutely stunning. He barely recognised her. She had changed her boring skirt and blouse for a cocktail dress in a pale apricot shade that emphasised the colour of her hair—which, now that it was not tied up, Marco saw was a riot of glorious red curls. She had drawn the front sections back with clips, but feathery strands had escaped and now framed her heart-shaped face. The strapless dress left her slender shoulders bare, and the skirt was made of layers of a wispy material that floated around her legs when she walked.

From where Marco was standing, on the other side of the orangery, he could not see the colour of her eyes, but he knew they were a startling vivid green. She was beautiful, he thought as he took a long sip of his wine, savouring the full-bodied Barolo on his tongue. Leah was a quintessential English rose, with creamy skin and hair the colour of burnished copper.

When he'd stood beside her in the private chapel he'd noticed that her face and arms were covered with tiny freckles, and his fingers had itched to unbutton her shirt and see if that dusting of gold continued lower. She was petite, and had a slender figure, but her breasts were surprisingly full and firm. Marco knew instinctively that they would fit perfectly into his palms.

He swore beneath his breath as he felt his body respond to the erotic images in his mind, but he could not tear his eyes from her. He knew that her mouth would fit his as if it had been designed purely for his pleasure. But thank God his sanity had prevailed and he'd resisted the temptation to kiss her in the chapel.

He watched Leah step outside onto the terrace and fought the urge to follow her. This strong attraction he felt for her was unsettling, and he was glad he was returning to Capri immediately after the wedding tomorrow. *Dio!* Desiring his soon-to-be sister-in-law was an unforeseen inconvenience.

He swung away from the window and frowned as he saw the nanny approaching him. Stacey was teetering on high heels, and her dress had a plunging neckline that left little to the imagination.

'Is Nicolo asleep?'

Marco had a relaxed attitude to his staff, and he had invited Stacey to join the party after Nicky had fallen asleep. His son did not like being left alone at night, and the nanny was supposed to stay with him in the nursery until he'd nodded off.

'He didn't seem tired, so I thought you wouldn't mind if he stayed up a little later than usual.'

Stacey stepped closer to him and ran her fingers through her blonde hair in an artful gesture that Marco found irritating.

'It's way past Nicky's bedtime,' he said tersely.

'It isn't fair to make him stay in his room when he can hear people enjoying themselves.'

Stacey sounded petulant, and Marco was in no doubt that she had wanted to join the party rather than sit in the nursery with a five-year-old. He sighed.

Nicky's previous nanny had left suddenly, to care for her elderly father. While they were staying at Nancarrow Hall he had arranged this temporary nanny through an agency. Unfortunately Stacey was more interested in flirting with him than looking after his son.

When he returned to Italy he planned to interview applicants personally, and find a suitable nanny for Nicky. With luck—and the promise of an exceptionally generous salary—he would be able to appoint someone who was prepared to stay for a few years and give his son some much needed stability.

'Where *is* Nicky?' he demanded, scanning the room.

'He must have gone outside. God, that kid!' Stacey muttered. 'I told him to stay inside.'

Marco was already walking swiftly over to the French doors. The sun was sinking behind the row of hawthorn trees that marked the boundary between the Nancarrow estate and the moor. He shaded his eyes against the golden rays as he stared across the wide expanse of lawn. An icy hand clutched his heart when he spotted a small figure with a mop of black curls down by the lake.

Nicky had climbed onto the wooden jetty where a rowboat was tied up. He was running to the far end of the jetty and peering into the water. Marco knew that the lake was deep, and well-stocked with carp and perch, and guessed that Nicky must be watching the fish.

'Nicky!'

It was unlikely that his voice would carry the length of the garden, Marco realised as he sprinted across the terrace and down the steps. Everything seemed to happen in slow motion. He watched his son lean over too far and topple into the water.

'*Madre di Dio!*'

He ran faster, his heart pounding with fear.

A figure in an apricot-coloured dress was some way in front of him, hurtling towards the lake. Leah. She kicked off her shoes and tore along the jetty. Without hesitating, she plunged into the water where Nicky had fallen in.

Marco imagined his son caught in the thick weeds that grew in the lake, choking for breath. How long would it take a child to drown?

His feet pounded on the wooden jetty and relief almost made his knees buckle as Leah surfaced, holding Nicky.

'It's all right, sweetheart, I've got you. Hold on tightly around my neck,' she instructed as she swam towards the jetty with the little boy clinging to her.

Marco knelt on the jetty and held out his hand to lift Nicky out of the water. 'Stand there and don't move,' he ordered.

Adrenalin was still surging through his blood and his voice was harsher than he'd intended. *Dio.* He had almost lost Nicky a year ago. Watching the little boy fall into the lake just now had made him sick with terror that he might lose the only person who mattered to him for good. Guilt stabbed him as his son's big brown eyes filled with tears.

'Don't you dare tell him off.'

Leah glared up at Marco. She was treading water, and

the gauzy material of her dress billowed around her, reminding him of a waterlily. He offered her his hand, and when she grabbed it he hauled her onto the jetty. Her hair had come loose and she raked her fingers through the waist-length curls.

'It wasn't Nicky's fault that he fell in. You shouldn't have allowed him to be unsupervised by the lake.'

'I *didn't* allow it,' Marco gritted. 'I believed Nicky was safely in bed. And he has been told many times that the lake is out of bounds unless he is with an adult.'

'Most children are fascinated by water.'

Marco felt Leah stiffen when he lifted his hand to her shoulder. Her skin felt like satin and his eyes were drawn to the pale slopes of her breasts that were rising and falling jerkily. He wondered if she was breathing hard simply after the exertion of swimming, but his instincts told him that she was as aware of him as he was of her.

'I was removing a leech from your shoulder,' he explained.

Her eyes widened. 'There are leeches in this lake? Ugh! Are there any more on me?'

'I can't see any.' Her soaking wet dress clung to her body and she looked like a beautiful water nymph.

'I can feel something,' she yelped, frantically pushing her fingers inside the top of her dress and pulling out a handful of weed. 'Oh, it's slimy…but at least it's not a leech.'

Nicky made a muffled noise that might almost have been a laugh. Marco froze. He had never heard his son laugh.

Leah crouched down beside the little boy. 'I think it would be a good idea for you to have some swimming lessons. But until you *can* swim will you promise not to go near the lake unless a grown-up is with you?'

Nicky nodded.

'He doesn't speak much,' Marco told Leah gruffly.

'I know.' She remained crouching beside Nicky and kept her gaze on his face. 'It's okay,' she said softly. 'I'm your friend. We've had lots of fun together while your *papà* has been away, haven't we?'

'Yes.'

Nicky's response was quiet but clear. Marco was surprised that his son had even spoken. Usually the little boy was withdrawn and silent with strangers, but Leah seemed to have established some kind of a rapport with Nicky in a way no one else had been able to.

She stood up and gave Marco a withering look that irritated him. 'I've spent quite a bit of time with Nicky while you were away. Your girlfriend often says she feels unwell, so I offered to look after him. I'm used to young children.' A small frown furrowed her brow. 'James had gone off to play golf every day. I didn't realise he was so keen on the game... But Nicky and I kept each other company.'

'Stacey is *not* my girlfriend. She is my son's nanny.'

Marco had heard the disapproval in Leah's voice and it increased his sense of guilt. She made him feel like a terrible parent, but he was already painfully aware of his failings. He did not know how to bond with his son, and he envied Leah because she had evidently won Nicky's trust.

He felt a punch in his chest when Nicky moved closer to her and gave one of his shy smiles.

Marco acknowledged that although he had come to hate his ex-wife, Karin *had* been his son's mother. Not a very good mother, from what he'd heard, but Nicky must miss her. The little boy needed someone in his life he could form a bond with. Marco had hoped that person would be him, but so far his attempts to build a relationship with the little boy had been unsuccessful.

He noticed that Nicky was shivering. Although it was a warm evening the lake would have been cold. Marco slipped off his jacket, intending to wrap it around his son, but Nicky shied away from him, so he thrust the jacket at Leah, who draped it around the little boy.

'Nicky shows many of the classic signs of post-traumatic stress. I know he lost his mother a year ago,' she said softly, 'have you sought any kind of help for him? It's much better to deal with psychological issues quickly, rather than hope the problem will simply go away.'

'I hardly think *you* are qualified to comment on my son's psychological state or offer advice about his upbringing,' Marco grated. He had a vague idea that Leah worked in an art gallery and it was there that she'd met his half-brother.

He felt defensive, because in truth he did not know how to help Nicky. The doctor at the hospital in Mexico, where Nicky had been treated after the accident, and the psychotherapist he'd found in Italy had both advised that Nicky needed time to process everything that had happened. But it had been a year and he was still suffering.

'As a matter of fact I have a degree in special educational needs and a post-graduate qualification in early years primary education. I teach children in the three-to-seven age group who have special needs.'

Leah's tone was frosty, but then she turned back to Nicky and smiled warmly at him.

'Let's get you back to the house and into the bath. Do you want your daddy to carry you or would you like to hold my hand?'

Nicky's eyes darted to Marco but he slipped his hand into Leah's. The rejection felt like another punch to Marco's chest and he shoved his hands into his pockets, avoiding Leah's gaze as they walked back along the jetty.

He'd tried everything he could think of to try to win his little boy's trust. But Nicky had been just a baby when Karin had disappeared with him. When Marco had finally been reunited with his son a year ago Nicky hadn't remembered his father.

Wet chiffon flapped around Leah's legs as she walked back across the lawn. Some of the party guests had come outside to see what was happening and she felt self-conscious as she climbed the steps up to the terrace and caught sight of her bedraggled reflection in the windows of the orangery.

She looked around for James but couldn't see him. When she walked into the house the horrified expression on James's mother's face when she caught sight of Leah was almost comical.

'Do try not to drip on the carpets,' Olivia said in a pained voice. 'Your dress must be ruined.'

'I'm sure it will be fine after a wash. Anyway, I'd rather have a ruined dress than for Nicky to have drowned,' Leah said pointedly.

She had expected Olivia to comfort her grandson after his ordeal of falling in the lake. Poor child. His grandmother seemed uninterested in him and his father was utterly heartless. She frowned as she remembered how Marco had snapped at the little boy.

Leah glanced over to where Marco was now talking to his son's very attractive nanny. Stacey was practically falling out of her low-cut dress. It was obvious that Marco had chosen the nanny for her physical attributes rather than her ability to care for a child, Leah though disgustedly.

He turned his head in her direction and she quickly averted her eyes from his hard stare. Nicky was led away by the housekeeper, a cheerful Cornishwoman named

Derwa, and Stacey and Marco continued their conversation for a few minutes before the nanny walked off.

Leah was desperate to go upstairs and change out of her wet dress. From the way that it was sticking to her body she knew it was very obvious that she wasn't wearing a bra, she realised, glancing down and seeing the outline of her nipples jutting beneath the wet silk.

Then she saw Marco walking towards her, and her feet seemed to be welded to the floor. He looked breathtaking in a black dinner suit and her stomach swooped when she noticed the shadow of dark chest hair beneath his white silk shirt.

It was unfair that he was so gorgeous, and very wrong for her to find him so attractive when she was about to marry his brother. Ashamed of her traitorous thoughts, and dismayed by her fierce awareness of Marco, she could not bring herself to meet his gaze when he halted in front of her.

'I apologise if my face repulses you,' he said in a grim voice.

Her eyes flew to his face and she shook her head when he ran his hand over the scar on his cheek. 'It doesn't repulse me.'

'Then why are you so reluctant to look at me?'

'I'm not.'

'Prove it. Look at me, Leah.'

His voice was like warm honey sliding over her. Surely she hadn't heard a hint of self-doubt in his tone? Marco De Valle was the most self-assured man she had ever met.

Leah huffed out a breath. 'You must know that with or without your scar you are very good-looking.'

Something flickered in his eyes. 'And you, *bella*, look as beautiful in your soaking wet dress as you did before your impromptu swim in the lake. Which leads me to say what I should have already said, and that is thank you for rescuing my son. If it hadn't been for your quick response Nicky could have drowned.'

'You would have saved him. I just happened to be closer to the lake when he fell in.'

Did that breathless voice belong to her? Hearing Marco say she was beautiful had clearly affected her vocal cords.

He smiled, and the tight band around Leah's lungs contracted even more. His scar made his smile a little lopsided, but no less sexy.

'And now I must go and run Nicky a bath,' he murmured.

'I thought the nanny had gone to do that.'

Marco's face hardened. 'I gave Stacey the option of terminating her contract voluntarily or being fired. She decided to leave Nancarrow Hall immediately. My son's welfare is paramount,' he insisted as Leah's eyes widened. 'I regret that circumstances meant I had to rely on an agency to appoint a temporary nanny for him instead of vetting someone properly myself. And, by the way, I feel the need to tell you he has regular consultations with a child psychologist who is trying to help him.'

'Don't blame yourself for Nicky's problems,' Leah said softly. 'Your wife's death must have been devastating. You need—'

'You have no idea what I need.'

Marco cut her off, his voice as cold as the arctic, and Leah told herself she must have imagined that his inflexible mouth had ever curved into the briefest of smiles.

She couldn't explain why tears welled in her eyes as he strode away. Maybe it was the haunted look on Marco's face at the mention of his wife—as if he hurt deep in his bones, in his soul.

Leah understood the pain of loss. Not so much for her

father, whom she remembered only vaguely, but because his death had been the beginning of her mother's self-destruction. And then there had been Sammy, her sweet, funny little half-brother, with his cherubic smile. She had adored him for the few precious years of his life.

She pictured the other little boy with big brown eyes, who reminded her of Sammy. Marco's son.

In her job, Leah had met many children who'd suffered emotional trauma following bereavement or the loss of a close family member. She knew from experience that Nicky was desperate for reassurance after losing his mother, and that the best person to give him the love and support he needed was his father.

But Nicky seemed wary of Marco, and it wasn't hard to understand why. Marco was an iceman. Leah grimaced as she remembered how he had been so cold towards Nicky when he'd pulled him out of the lake, instead of cuddling him and showing him the affection that the little boy clearly craved.

She wished she could help Nicky, but there was no time. Tomorrow evening she and her new husband would be on a plane, flying to the Seychelles for their honeymoon at a luxury spa hotel.

Thinking of James, she went in search of him and found him playing billiards in the games room. His face was flushed, and she guessed he'd had too much to drink.

'Whass happened to *you*?' he slurred when he saw her.

'Your nephew fell in the lake and I jumped in and pulled him out.'

'I hope the lord of the manor was impressed that you saved his kid.'

James picked up his glass and swallowed its contents. Leah wrinkled her nose at the smell of whisky and felt a familiar cramp of tension in the pit of her stomach—a throwback to her childhood, when her mum had started drinking heavily.

'Why did you call Marco the lord of the manor?'

'He owns this place.'

James laughed at Leah's obvious surprise.

'Marco inherited Nancarrow Hall from his father— my mother's first husband. Vincenzo De Valle bought the house when they married, but he died suddenly, leaving all his assets—including the coffee business in Italy and the Nancarrow estate here in Cornwall—to Marco, his son and heir. Marco was just a kid, so the house was held in trust and run by my mother. A couple of years later she married my father and I was born. Nancarrow Hall was our home. When Marco was eighteen he became the legal owner. He allows us to continue to live here, but he never lets me forget that I am reliant on his charity. Marco is the one with the money,' James said sulkily. 'You're marrying the wrong brother, sweetheart.'

'You are the man I want to marry,' Leah assured him softly.

She felt relieved that she had an explanation for why James had seemed so moody since they had come to Cornwall. He resented his older half-brother. Perhaps he also suspected that she found Marco attractive, she thought, with a mixture of guilt and shame. No other man unsettled her the way Marco De Valle did. Luckily he lived in Italy and she was unlikely to meet him very often, she reassured herself.

'Tomorrow is the start of our life together,' she murmured as she moved closer to James and pressed herself up against him. She tilted her face and parted her lips for his kiss, but he turned away from her.

'You're all wet,' he muttered. 'You had better go and get changed.'

'Why don't you come upstairs and help me take my dress off?' she asked. Tomorrow she would become James's wife, and it suddenly seemed ridiculous that he had never seen her naked.

He looked awkward. 'There'll be plenty of time for that sort of thing when we're on our honeymoon.'

Leah felt a flicker of foreboding at James's lack of enthusiasm. Asking him to come to her bedroom and undress her had been a big step in their relationship for her, and she was confused that he had rejected her. In less than twenty-four hours they would make a vow to honour each other with their bodies, but James seemed reluctant even to kiss her.

She looked over at the bar in the games room, where James's best man Philip had lined up several bottles of spirits.

'I want to have a few drinks on my last night of being single,' James told her.

It was only natural that he wanted to celebrate his last night as a bachelor. He wasn't having second thoughts about the wedding and neither was she, Leah told herself firmly. Marriage was all about compromise.

She smiled at him. 'Don't get too drunk. I'll see you in the church tomorrow.'

Her bedroom was in the newest wing of the house. Derwa had explained to her that the extension had been added in the eighteen-hundreds, but the original house, where the family's bedrooms were, dated back to the fourteenth century.

Leah headed straight into the en suite bathroom, peeled off her sodden dress and dropped it into the bath. It wouldn't be the end of the world if the dress was ruined, although she wished she hadn't spent so much money on it.

Amy had persuaded her to buy the striking apricot-coloured dress instead of the navy blue evening gown which, in Leah's opinion, would have been far more suitable. Her red hair meant that she tended to play safe with colours, and the apricot cocktail dress was strapless and showed off a daring amount of her cleavage—a far cry from her usual style. Leah was not daring, and she preferred clothes that allowed her to blend into the background.

She stepped into the shower cubicle, and as she shampooed her hair to wash away the smell of lake water she couldn't help feeling unsettled by James's response—or lack of it.

When they had started dating she had been grieving for her grandmother, who had died a few months earlier, and she hadn't felt ready for a sexual relationship. The truth about why she was still a virgin in her mid-twenties was rather more complicated than that, though, Leah acknowledged with a sigh. She'd dated a few guys at university, but when they had wanted to take things further than a kiss at the end of the evening she'd always broken up with them. It wasn't that she disliked the idea of sex, but finding someone she trusted enough to want to share that level of intimacy with was another matter. To her, passion suggested a loss of control.

In her mind, she heard her mother's voice. *'One day you'll know how it feels to fall wildly and crazily in love.'* But Leah had seen the way her mother's affairs had inevitably ended after just a few weeks or months, and the tears and drinking binges that had followed.

Leah did not want 'wild and crazy' in a relationship. She wanted steadiness and reliability and gentle affection. She'd been grateful that James hadn't tried to rush things. He had been sweet and patient, and it had been his suggestion to wait until their wedding night to consummate their relationship.

Perhaps that was the problem, she brooded. James seemed so on edge since they had been at Nancarrow Hall because he was frustrated, but he was clearly determined to honour his promise to wait until they were married before they had sex.

After her shower, Leah wrapped herself in a robe and returned to the bedroom. The rehearsal dinner would be finished by now, and there was no point in her going back downstairs. She left her hair to dry naturally rather than make any inexpert attempts to blow-dry it. Anyway, the hairdresser who had been booked to come to the Hall early in the morning planned to style her unruly curls in an elegant 'up-do'

She flicked through the TV channels but gave up when nothing caught her attention. There was a bottle of wine chilling in an ice bucket in her room. She sent Amy a text, asking if she wanted to join her for a pre-wedding drink.

Moments later, her bridesmaid texted back.

I'm with Philip in the boathouse!

She followed it with a thumbs-up emoji.

Amy had set her sights on the best man, and it was no surprise that the couple had got together. Leah envied her friend's uncomplicated attitude to relationships.

'Have you really never had casual sex?' Amy had once asked her.

Leah hadn't admitted that she'd never had *any* kind of sex.

She sighed. If Amy was with Philip it seemed likely that James had finished drinking. Perhaps he had gone to bed. Common sense suggested it would be a good idea for her to get an early night before the wedding too.

She opened a drawer and took out one of the oversized

T-shirts she usually slept in. Folded next to it was the daring black chemise that Amy had persuaded her to buy for her honeymoon. On impulse, Leah slipped the chemise over her head and stared at her reflection in the mirror.

It was amazing how a wisp of silk and lace made her look different. Sexier. Her red hair was the bane of her life and she kept it tied up most of the time. But now it tumbled around her shoulders and spilled over her breasts, which were inadequately covered by the flimsy nightwear. The silky chemise felt sensual against her skin and she noticed that her dark areolae were visible through the sheer lace cups.

She imagined olive-tanned hands cupping her breasts, strong fingers sliding the straps of the chemise down her arms, baring her to the gaze of grey eyes, which would be gleaming as he bent his head and closed his mouth around one taut nipple…

No! *Wrong man. Wrong fantasy.*

Leah pressed her hands against her hot face, but she could not banish the erotic images of Marco touching her body. She had *wanted* him to kiss her in the church, she admitted shamefully. It was as though he had awoken a desire that had lain dormant for all her adult life—until now.

CHAPTER THREE

WAS SHE HER mother's daughter after all?

Despair swept through Leah. As an adult, she looked at her mum's choices of unsuitable lovers—men who had been selfish and sometimes brutal—and wondered how Tori could have been so weak, following her heart and letting her actions be dictated by her sexual desires.

Leah had always been proud of her own common sense, but now she understood what her mum had meant about falling crazily. Not in love but in lust. Want, need.

She had never felt those things until she'd met Marco.

But she was about to marry James.

Why had she thought that marrying for security and safety would guarantee happiness?

Leah buried her face in her hands as she realised she had been fooling herself. Passion and desire were important elements in a loving relationship, but she didn't even know if she and James were sexually compatible. She bit her lip as she remembered how he had spurned her tentative advance earlier, when she'd invited him to her room.

She *must* make love with James tonight!

The realisation struck Leah like a thunderbolt. She could not make a solemn promise to spend the rest of her life with him while the huge question of whether they desired each other remained unanswered.

She was not by nature an impulsive person, but she didn't wait to consider more carefully if she was doing the right thing and tore out of her room before her nerve failed.

James's room was in the old part of the house. Leah had only been there once before, when she'd gone to look for him after he'd been late meeting her to go and play tennis. The butler had escorted her along a maze of passageways, but now she'd have to try to find the way on her own.

The lamps along the landings were dimmed at night, and twice she took a wrong turn. But she remembered that there had been a large Grecian urn on a table next to the door of James's room.

Leah halted in the corridor and wiped her damp palms down her chemise. Tension cramped in the pit of her stomach and she took a deep breath and tried to relax. This was the right thing to do, she assured herself. Once she had made love with James it would put an end to her doubts about their relationship and she was sure that her fascination with Marco would disappear.

Leah stepped into the room and closed the door behind her, shutting off the chink of light from the passageway. The darkness was impenetrable, but as her eyes adjusted she could make out a four-poster bed. Her heart was beating painfully hard. She hadn't expected to feel nervous about having sex for the first time—surely it was way overdue, she thought wryly. But what other reason could there be for her reluctance to put into practice what she had come here to do? Why did every thud of her heart urge her to retreat back to her room? James *was* the right man for her, she told herself.

Maybe if she told herself enough times she would be convinced.

She stiffened when she heard the mattress creak. 'Are you awake?' she whispered.

The muffled response could have been a snore or a sleepy grunt of surprise. Leah resolutely ignored the clamour of doubts in her head and climbed onto the bed.

'I know you must be surprised that I've come to your room, but I want you to make love to me.'

She crawled along the mattress and almost lost her nerve when her hands skimmed over hard thighs. She felt the outline of powerful muscles through the sheet. Moving higher, she discovered hip bones and a taut abdomen.

She leaned forward, bracing herself with her hands on either side of his head, so that her breasts were pressed against his chest. His face was shadowed, but Leah was glad of the concealing darkness as she bent her head and sought his mouth. She brushed her lips across his and instantly it felt as though a bolt of electricity had zapped right down to her toes.

Relief swept through her. There had been no need for her to doubt that sexual chemistry existed between them. Every nerve-ending in her body tingled with anticipation.

'Kiss me, *please*.' She whispered the words into his mouth.

He hesitated for a fraction of a second before he obeyed.

Leah's heart slammed against her ribs when he moved his lips over hers—gently at first, and then with an increasing passion that made her tremble with needs she did not fully understand, which evoked an ache low in her pelvis.

He was heat and fire and she melted, stretching her body out on top of his. Strong arms curved around her, trapping her against his powerful physique as he pushed his tongue inside her mouth. Leah had never experienced such an intensity of passion before. Her heart sang and her spirit soared as she matched him kiss for kiss, and he made a rough sound that was muffled against her lips.

The sheet was a barrier between their bodies. She gave

a moan of frustration that turned into a sigh of pleasure when he pushed his hand between them and spread his fingers possessively over one breast. Her nipple peaked and thrust against the lacy barrier of her chemise.

Everything was going to be all right. The flood of warmth between Leah's legs was proof that she was ready to give herself completely and exclusively to him.

'I want to have sex with you,' she said breathlessly. 'I don't want to be a virgin for a moment longer.'

'A virgin? *Madre di Dio!*'

Before she knew what was happening Leah found herself lifted by strong hands and dumped unceremoniously on the mattress. The bedside lamp was switched on and she blinked in the sudden bright light.

'*You!*' Incomprehension turned to shock, horror and finally toe-curling mortification as she stared at Marco. 'Where's J-James?' she stammered. 'Why are you sleeping in his room?'

'This is my bedroom. James's room is directly above mine on the third floor.' Marco leaned back against the headboard and narrowed his eyes on Leah's hot face.

She silently cursed her fair skin. But far worse than her tendency to blush easily were her navigational skills.

'*Oh, God!*'

This had to be the most humiliating moment of her life.

'Seriously? You're a virgin?'

Leah felt the heat on her face spread down her neck and across the upper slopes of her breasts so very revealed by the skimpy chemise. 'It's none of your business,' she choked.

'It would have been very much my business if you had seduced me into having sex with you.'

The hint of laughter in Marco's voice was unexpected. She hadn't known that he was capable of laughter, so grim and forbidding as he was. But the fact that *she* was the source of his amusement made Leah want to slap the mocking grin off his face.

'I wasn't trying to seduce *you*. I thought you were James. It was dark and I couldn't see you,' she said tautly when Marco raised one eyebrow. 'I went to the wrong room by mistake.' She jerked at the strap of her chemise which had slipped off her shoulder, pulling it back into place. 'I feel a complete idiot. Why didn't you stop me?'

'*Cara*, when I am woken by a woman begging me to have sex with her I rarely refuse.'

'It happens to you a lot, does it?' she snapped.

For some reason, the thought of Marco taking his pleasure with other women who were far more beautiful and sexually experienced than her evoked a sensation like a sharp knife shoved between Leah's ribs.

He wouldn't take his pleasure selfishly; he would give the utmost pleasure to his lovers. She had no idea how she was so certain of that, but her pulse accelerated when she looked at him and found he was studying her with eyes that gleamed bright and sharp, as if he could see inside her head.

'I enjoy sex as much as every other red-blooded male,' he said, folding his arms behind his head and drawing Leah's attention to the bunched muscles in his shoulders. Her gaze dropped to his broad chest, covered with crisp, dark hair that arrowed down his flat abdomen and disappeared beneath the sheet. It occurred to her that he might be naked, and her breath became trapped in her lungs.

'You must have guessed that I'd come to the wrong room and I believed you were James,' she muttered.

'No, *cara*, I assumed it was *me* you wanted to have sex with.'

If her face burned any hotter she would combust. 'Why

would I want to sleep with you when I'm about to marry your brother?'

'A good question,' Marco murmured with a hint of laughter in his voice again. 'Perhaps James doesn't excite you? That must be the case if you haven't allowed him to take you to bed yet.'

'It was a mutual agreement to wait until we were married,' Leah said stiffly.

'If you were *my* fiancée you would not want to wait—and I sure as hell wouldn't be able to keep my hands off you.'

The lazy amusement in Marco's tone had disappeared. He sat up straighter, so that the sheet slipped down dangerously low, and stared at her with an intensity that made her feel dizzy and weak—and, worse, tempted her to lean forward and cover his hard, sexy mouth with hers.

She knew the beauty of his kiss now. A little shiver ran through her as she remembered how his lips had moved over hers with bold assurance and devastating sensuality.

She should go. *Now.* Get out of his room and be thankful that he had stopped her before it was too late. But the common sense that she prided herself for possessing seemed to be taking a holiday.

She tilted her chin belligerently. 'I did not beg you for sex.'

'Yes, you did. And what's more you *knew* it was me you were kissing.'

Marco gave her a sardonic look as she shook her head wildly, so that her curls flew like red sparks around her shoulders.

'You might be a virgin, but you must have kissed James. You know what his mouth feels like beneath yours. You know his taste. And now you know mine,' he said harshly.

His words hovered in the air, challenging her to deny

them. Leah had thought he was a terrible man and now she knew just how lethal he was. If she lived to be one hundred she knew she would still see his face in her dreams. The perfection of his sculpted features, the darkness of his unshaved jaw, the tragedy of the scar that for some inexplicable reason made her want to weep.

'I believed I was kissing James.'

It was the truth, she insisted to herself. But her conscience reminded her that the kisses she'd shared with James had never blown her mind or made her tremble with desire the way she'd trembled when Marco had clamped her against his body and she'd felt the hard ridge of his arousal through the thin sheet.

It wasn't fair to compare the two men, she thought desperately. If she and James had become lovers before he had brought her to Nancarrow Hall she would not have developed a silly schoolgirl crush on his half-brother.

She waited for Marco to say something, but his silence filled the room and the oxygen was sucked from her lungs when he pinned her with his brooding stare. His eyes roamed over her, and to her horror she felt her nipples harden so that they pushed against the sheer lace cups of her chemise.

Galvanised by the molten gleam in his gaze, Leah scrambled across the mattress. 'I'm going to find James.'

Her conscience would not allow her to marry him tomorrow after the way she had responded to Marco tonight. Leah knew it was only fair that she admitted to James her reservations about their relationship.

'I made a genuine mistake when I came to your room,' she told Marco. 'I'd be grateful if you would forget that anything happened.'

'Nothing of any consequence *did* happen. Trust me, if

it had you would be begging to remain in my bed for the rest of the night,' he said lazily.

His arrogance took Leah's breath away, but before she could slide off the bed his hand shot out and he caught hold of her arm. This time when he spoke his voice was low and unexpectedly fierce.

'Take my advice and go back to your room. Don't visit James tonight.'

'I've already told you that I don't want your advice.' She jerked free from his grasp and ran over to the door.

'Leah.'

His husky accent turned her name into a caress. She paused with her hand on the doorknob and turned to face him, knowing it was a mistake—another mistake.

Marco shoved a hand through his thick hair. He was still sprawled on the bed, propped up on one elbow—indolent and far too sexy for his own good. He was a disaster waiting to happen, but he wouldn't be *her* disaster.

Leah thought again of all the men her mother had given her heart to, only to have her romantic dreams shattered time and time again. 'I'm not listening to you.' She clung to the doorknob as though it was a lifeline.

'You will be making a mistake if you marry James. Come here and let me prove it to you.'

For one terrible, shameful second she was tempted. 'You have no right to say such things,' she said huskily. 'Where is your loyalty to your brother?'

'Perhaps you should discuss *loyalty* with James.'

'What do you mean?'

Marco swore and raked his fingers through his hair again, as if he needed an outlet for his restless energy. 'It is not for me to comment on your relationship with your fiancé,' he said gruffly.

'Then don't.' Leah tore her gaze from his and opened

the door. 'I'm going to see James and nothing you say will stop me.'

A flight of stairs at the end of the corridor led to the third floor. Leah tore along the hallway and saw a Grecian urn on a table—a replica of the one outside Marco's room on the landing below. Light filtered beneath the door of James's bedroom and she guessed that he was still awake.

She knocked, but she was too agitated to wait for a response and flung the door open. 'We need to talk… *Oh!*'

Her words died on her lips and she stared in stunned disbelief at Davina the wedding planner, in bed with James.

'Leah! What the blazes are you doing here?' James demanded, while his companion dragged the sheet over her naked breasts.

'I'd like to ask Davina the same question,' Leah said, frozen in the doorway, too shocked to be able to think clearly. Her legs felt wobbly and she clutched the doorframe for support. 'I don't understand.'

But the situation was humiliatingly clear. James had rejected her because he'd planned to spend the night with Davina.

'I thought you loved me,' she whispered, feeling more of a fool than she had ever felt in her life.

James blew out a breath. 'The truth is that I was never in love with you, Leah.'

Marco shoved his hair off his brow with a hand that remarkably—for a man who never, *ever* allowed himself to be affected by a woman—was not entirely steady. He should have stopped Leah. But not from crawling all over him while she pleaded with him to make love to her.

His mouth dried at the memory of her nubile body stretched out on top of him.

He had been half asleep, and for a heart-stopping moment he'd thought that the erotic fantasy he'd been having about Leah had come true. She'd looked incredible, in a sexy black negligee that had framed her voluptuous breasts. His blood had heated as he'd anticipated stripping her so that he could trace his lips over her silken skin. But then she had gone and ruined it when she'd said that she was a virgin.

Dio. How was that even *possible*? She was the most responsive woman he'd ever put his mouth on—and there had been many, Marco acknowledged. He'd had his fair share of lovers before and after his marriage—but not during it. He happened to believe that marriage was a serious commitment, which was why he intended never to do it again. One cheating, lying ex-wife was enough.

A message flashed on his phone, advising him that the movement sensor alarm on the third floor had been activated. He thought of Leah, on her way to offer herself to James. Muttering a curse, Marco slid out of bed and pulled on his robe, wincing as the towelling brushed against his still uncomfortably hard erection.

He should have stopped her from running out of his room. All it would have taken was him tugging her back down onto the bed and kissing her until she made those little moans in the back of her throat that he'd found such a turn-on.

He could still taste her...honey and vanilla on his tongue. She'd insisted that she'd believed she was kissing James, but was that true?

He strode up the stairs and along the third floor landing, halting next to one of the ugly Grecian urns that his mother collected. Leah was standing in the open doorway to James's room, her hands gripping the frame. Marco sensed that if she let go her legs would buckle beneath her.

'I thought we were friends, Davina,' she said in a choked voice.

Marco felt no surprise that the wedding planner was in his brother's room. At the wedding rehearsal he had tried to suggest to Leah that she should postpone marriage until she'd had a chance to know James better, and this was why.

There was a sweetness about Leah that made Marco wish he could have saved her from the pain of disillusionment. But she would get over it with time, he thought. And if she had any sense she would learn that love was a lie put about by poets and dreamers.

He was about to return to his room, but Leah was speaking again, and Marco succumbed to curiosity and withdrew into an alcove in the passageway.

'James, if you have never loved me, why did you ask me to marry you?'

'Your inheritance,' James muttered. 'I owe a lot of money to some people who are likely to get nasty if I don't repay them soon. I borrowed heavily, to invest in a business deal that promised amazing returns, but then the goldmine in Africa flooded and I lost my investment. I can't ask my parents for help because my father advised me against the deal.'

Marco rolled his eyes. It wasn't the first time James had sunk money into a get rich quick scheme that had failed. He'd bailed his half-brother out many times in the past and refused to do so again.

'How on earth did you find out about my inheritance?'

Leah sounded shocked, and it struck Marco as odd that she had tried to keep something like that a secret from her future husband.

'Amy mentioned it that night she introduced us at her party. She was drunk, and she told me that you had been left millions of pounds by a relative, but couldn't claim the money until you were married. To be honest, you seemed like the perfect answer to my problems.'

'I don't think I ever told Amy the exact amount of my inheritance, but it isn't millions. How disappointed you would have been after you had gone to all the trouble of pretending to be in love with me.' Leah's voice trembled. 'All you wanted was my money. That's despicable.'

'Don't act so righteous.' James sounded sulky and defensive. 'You're not in love with me, either. Amy said you were desperate to get your hands on your inheritance. That's why you were so eager to marry me, isn't it? We were both willing to use each other.'

Leah did not deny James's accusation.

Marco frowned. He'd been feeling sympathy for her—even a degree of guilt. If he had given his half-brother the loan he'd asked for James would not have tried to trick Leah into marriage. But now it sounded as though Leah had a strong incentive of her own, he thought as he made his way back to his bedroom.

He paused outside the nursery and opened the door, entering the room quietly. Nicky preferred to sleep with a nightlight, and the soft glow from the lamp danced across his black curls. His impossibly long eyelashes fanned on his cheeks.

Marco's heart clenched. He would never forget the first time he'd held his son in his arms. His marriage had already been strained, but he had been instantly smitten with his baby boy and had vowed to do everything he could to create a happy family life for his son.

When Karin had disappeared with Nicky the pain Marco had felt was indescribable. It had been more than three years before he'd seen his son again, in Mexico, where Karin had been living with her lover, a low-life crook. Who knew what kind of life Nicky had led for those crucial years of his early development? The little boy had never spoken about what had happened to him, and Marco felt powerless to connect with this son who regarded him as a stranger.

He leaned over to tuck the bedcovers around Nicky, curious when he saw a piece of paper sticking out from beneath his pillow. Marco carefully slid the paper out and stared at the childish drawing of a person with long, curly hair drawn with an orange crayon. There was no doubt that the picture was meant to be of Leah, and the smaller black-haired figure holding her hand was Nicky's attempt to draw himself.

Marco turned the paper over, wondering if his son had drawn him, but the other side was blank.

As he slipped the drawing back under Nicky's pillow and returned to his own room he recalled the trusting expression on the little boy's face when he'd clutched Leah's hand after she had fished him out of the lake. It was nearly midnight, but he felt too wired to sleep.

Pulling back the curtains, he glanced up at the moon, suspended like a silver disc in the inky sky. He was puzzled when he saw a figure by the gate which led from the garden onto Bodmin Moor. She was silhouetted in the moonlight, but even from a distance Marco recognised Leah. He watched her walk a little way onto the moor and then hesitate where the path forked before turning in the direction of Hawk's Tor.

What the hell was she doing out on the moors at night?

Leah was not his responsibility, he reminded himself, but he knew how easy it was to become lost in such a remote place. He swore as he pulled on jeans and a sweater then strode out of his room.

As a boy, Marco had spent many hours walking on the moors after his father's death, but his absence from the house had mostly gone unnoticed. His mother had been widowed for just a year before she'd married Gordon Fletcher. Ten months later she'd given birth to James and Marco had been sent away to school. Olivia had paid little attention to her eldest son when he'd come home for the holidays.

Marco had always felt an outsider at Nancarrow Hall, and as soon as he'd become an adult he'd settled in Capri and made Villa Rosa, the house owned by three generations of the De Valle family before, his permanent home.

But he knew from those lonely hikes across the moors that the weather could change quickly, even in summer. He exited the house and garden, following the route he'd seen Leah take. A breeze had blown up, sending clouds scudding across the sky so that every now and then the moonlight was obliterated.

Earlier, Marco had called one of his security personnel, and within the hour had received confirmation of Leah's academic and professional qualifications. Her experience in teaching children with special needs, and the bond she seemed to have formed with Nicky, meant that Leah might be the one person who could help his little boy.

CHAPTER FOUR

THIS COULDN'T BE the shortcut to the village. Leah peered through the darkness, hoping to see a light in a cottage window or some other sign of civilisation. But there was nothing apart from the outline of a stunted tree which had been bent and twisted by the wind that whipped across the moors.

She'd fled Nancarrow Hall because she hadn't been able to bear to stay after she'd been so humiliated. She never wanted to see James again after his betrayal. But although she was bitterly angry with him, she was also furious with herself too, for making such an error of judgement. She had seen in James what she had wanted to see, Leah acknowledged. Her longing for security had made her ignore her doubts about their relationship.

As for Marco...

A shudder of embarrassment ran through her when she remembered her inexpert attempt to seduce him, believing he was James. It was all immaterial now, she thought grimly. She had accidentally gone to Marco's room, but it had been no accident that the wedding planner had been in bed with James.

A sob rose in her throat, but she brushed her tears away. Crying wouldn't help a situation that had gone from bad to disastrous.

After she had discovered James's duplicity she'd rushed back to her bedroom. Her phone had been ringing, and Gloria, her mum's neighbour in London, had explained that Tori had collapsed in the street and been taken by ambulance to hospital.

'I think your mum had been drinking again,' Gloria had said gently. 'She was upset and kept asking where you were.'

'Thanks for letting me know,' Leah had said.

She'd felt a mixture of shame at Tori's behaviour and guilt that she hadn't been around to help her. She'd known she needed to return to London immediately, but couldn't ask James to drive her. So she'd left a note for Amy and left.

But she must have taken the wrong path to the village and now she was lost on the moors. Leah looked back over her shoulder and felt a ripple of fear when she could not see the Hall. She had walked further than she'd realised. The moon had disappeared and the darkness was thick around her.

That eerie noise was just the wind, she told herself. She froze when she heard another indistinguishable sound that seemed to be getting closer. Someone or something was following her. An animal, perhaps? But what sort of animal?

Her heart was thudding as she felt in her jacket pocket for her phone. The *no signal* icon flashed at the top of the screen. She switched on the phone's torch and gasped when she saw a huge figure coming towards her. This night from hell was rapidly turning into a nightmare! Leah's emotions were already in a fragile state and her imagination took over from her common sense.

'What do you want? Get away from me!' She started to

run but stumbled on the uneven ground. The harsh, panting noise was her own breaths, she realised. 'Leave me alone!'

'Leah!'

The voice was shockingly familiar. She held up her phone so that the torchlight flickered over Marco's chiselled features and revealed the scar carved into his cheek.

'Oh, it's you.' She released a shaky breath as her fear evaporated. But her heartrate accelerated when he came closer and she caught the drift of his spicy cologne. 'I thought...' She shook her head. 'Your housekeeper told me there are legends about evil spirits and other strange phenomena who roam the moors.'

'Did you think I was the Beast of Bodmin?' Marco asked drily, running his hand over his scar.

'I don't know what I thought.' Leah couldn't hold back a sob. Reaction to the night's events was hitting her hard and she buried her face in her hands.

'What are you doing, wandering around the moors in the dark?'

'I was trying to get to the village, and from there to the station at Bodmin.'

'At midnight?'

'I couldn't remain at the house and see the pitying expressions on everyone's faces tomorrow. Did you know that James and Davina are lovers? I suppose you did as you warned me not to go to James's room,' she said dully. 'Apparently they started an affair in London soon after I hired Davina to organise the wedding. For the past week James has been meeting Davina in secret at a hotel in Padstow, instead of playing golf, as he told me. And tonight I found them in bed together.'

Her voice cracked.

'The wedding is off, in case you were wondering. Davina has just found out she is pregnant. That's why she looked so upset at the wedding rehearsal. James says he is going to stand by her.'

Marco tugged her hands away from her face and stared at her, his eyes glittering hard and bright. 'You have been crying.' He sounded surprised.

'What did you expect?'

Leah had not been able to hold back her tears. She was hurt that James had lied and her pride was dented. In addition, with the wedding called off she would not be able to claim her inheritance, and now worrying about her mum made her feel as if she was balanced on an emotional tightrope.

'I feel such a fool for believing that James was in love with me. I thought he was different to other men I'd dated, and he didn't put pressure on me to go to bed with him.'

'*Cara*, if he didn't want sex with you it was because his interests lay elsewhere,' Marco said bluntly.

'Sex is not the most important part of a relationship,' she argued. 'There's love and trust.' She gave another sob. 'I trusted James.'

'But you didn't desire him or you would have wanted to sleep with him.'

Leah bit her lip. Marco's assessment was too close to the truth. She *hadn't* felt a burning desire to have sex with James—or any other man. Well, one other man, she thought shamefully, remembering how her body had ached for fulfilment when she'd stretched out on top of Marco and felt the hard proof of his arousal.

On a subconscious level she *had* realised that he wasn't James, she acknowledged. Marco was the man of her fantasies—but she wasn't about to admit to the effect he had on her.

He towered above her, darkly beautiful in black jeans and a matching fine wool sweater. He was inherently dangerous to her peace of mind and he evoked a longing in her that no other man had ever done.

For too long Leah had supressed her sensuality, but now it blazed, needy and desperate. She swayed towards him and her tongue darted across her lips, issuing an unconscious invitation.

He stared at her mouth and there was something primitive about the stark hunger in his gaze. She wished he would haul her against his muscular body and carry her away into the darkness. Out here on the ancient moors they were simply a man and a woman drawn together by a desire as old as mankind.

She could feel the urgent beat of her pulse, the sharp pull of her nipples and the flood of molten warmth between her legs. She heard the unevenness of his breath and felt the tension that emanated from him. A shaft of moonlight revealed his skin stretched tightly over his razor-edged cheekbones.

He slowly lowered his head and she held her breath, waiting, wanting…

Abruptly he stepped back from her and shoved a hand through his hair. 'I'll show you the way to the village.'

He took her holdall from her nerveless fingers and walked off in the opposite direction to the one she had taken when she'd left the house.

Reality kicked in, bringing memories of the phone call she had received from her mum's neighbour. 'I need to catch the train to London,' she said as she hurried after Marco.

'You're too late. The last one has already left. But you can stay at the pub tonight.'

She struggled to keep pace with his long strides and was out of breath by the time they reached the village. There were no lights on at the Sailor's Arms. The sign hanging on the post creaked. 'Of course the pub is closed now,' Leah muttered, feeling sick at the thought of returning to Nancarrow Hall and having to face James tomorrow.

Marco slipped his phone into his jeans pocket. 'I sent a message to the landlord asking him to prepare a room for you.'

'Won't he mind that it's so late?'

'I own the pub,' Marco said drily. 'The whole village belongs to the Nancarrow estate.'

He led Leah round to the back door of the pub and ushered her into the tiny bar.

'This is Bill.' He introduced the man who had walked through from another room.

The landlord took Leah's holdall. 'I'll carry your bag upstairs, Miss Ashbourne. Come up when you're ready and I'll show you to your room.'

Marco moved towards the door. 'Try to get some sleep,' he advised. 'I'll come back in the morning. I have a proposition that I want to discuss with you.'

Leah's imagination went into overdrive. Those moments on the moors when Marco had looked at her with hunger in his eyes, as though he wanted to devour her, burned bright in her memory.

'What sort of proposition?'

He laughed softly and his grey eyes gleamed with amusement and something else…an intentness that made Leah supremely conscious of her femininity.

'Not the sexual kind,' he drawled. 'I'm afraid you will have to play out those fantasies with someone else. I don't take wide-eyed virgins to bed.'

She ground her teeth as Marco's grin widened. 'You really are the most arrogant beast,' she snapped.

Her insides squirmed. How could he know that she'd had erotic fantasies about him? Was her fascination with him so obvious? Leah wished that the trapdoor in the pub floor would open so that she could leap into the black void below.

Marco lifted a hand to his face and traced the line of his scar. 'It's true. A beast *is* what I am.'

There was no laughter in his voice now, just a grimness that hurt Leah although she could not explain why.

He caught hold of her chin and tilted her face up to his. 'You would do well to remember that, Beauty.'

She stared into his eyes—not cold as an arctic sky, but gleaming like molten silver, glinting with promise and a wicked intent that made her tremble.

'Tell me the truth,' he said softly. 'Did you know that you had come to my bedroom instead of James's?'

Leah bit her lip. She was innately truthful, but she did not dare admit to Marco that *he* was the man she had been thinking about when she'd left her room.

'I was confused,' she muttered.

He gave a harsh laugh. 'You proved when you kissed me that you have passion and fire. How could you have contemplated a passionless marriage?'

'I didn't know that I could feel such strong desire,' she whispered, 'until…'

Marco's eyes glittered. 'Until?' he prompted.

'Until I came to your room and…and kissed you.' The damning words left her lips on a sigh.

Her heart leapt when his head swooped down and he claimed her mouth with devastating authority. She was impatient for his kiss and pressed herself against him, tipping her head back, softening her lips and parting them beneath his.

He tasted divine, and the spicy tang of his aftershave mixed with the almost imperceptible scent of male pheromones was more intoxicating than any drug. Flames swept through her body, setting every nerve-ending alight. Marco was demolishing her barriers with terrifying ease, and she felt unmoored, scared of the firestorm he had unleashed inside her and yet compelled to burn in the conflagration.

He muttered something in Italian against her lips as he slid his hand along her jaw, commanding her with a flick of his tongue to open her mouth and allow him access. But then—shockingly—he wrenched his mouth from hers and captured her wrists, pulling her arms down from where she had wound them around his neck.

Leah stared at him in confusion which quickly turned to embarrassment with the realisation that the panting breaths she could hear were *hers*, not his. He set her away from him and she knew she must have imagined there was a look of regret in his grey gaze.

'Sweet dreams, *bella*,' he said, in that mocking way of his that made her hate him and hate herself more. Because she could not resist him and he knew it.

Surprisingly, Leah slept soundly. The kindly landlord had brought a mug of hot milk to her room the night before, explaining that he'd added a tot of Irish malt to help her sleep. It must have worked.

When she opened her eyes, sunlight was poking in through the gap in the curtains. It looked as though it would be a perfect day for a wedding.

She felt a pang of regret for the dream that she now realised would have quickly turned sour. James hadn't loved her, and in her heart she knew she had not been in love with him. But she had imagined herself to be in love with him precisely because he did *not* arouse strong emotions in her, and she had felt in control.

Her reaction to Marco was far more worrying. She certainly wasn't in love with him. She didn't even *like* him.

But when he'd found her on the moors she had wanted to surrender to him.

Dear heaven!

Where had *that* thought come from?

Leah covered her burning face with her hands. What had happened to her determination to listen to her head, not her heart—or in this case her hormones? What she felt for Marco was lust—wild and unrestrained lust. It had taken over her body with its insistent demands, and she was suddenly terribly afraid that she was like her mum after all.

Her phone rang, and she gave a small sigh when she saw Tori's name on the screen.

'Mum, how *are* you? Are you still at the hospital?'

'The doctor in A&E said I could be discharged once I'd sobered up. Gloria came and drove me home.' Tori was crying so hard that it was difficult for Leah to understand her. 'Oh, Leah, I've made such a mess of my life. Last night I just wanted to drink until I forgot everything.'

'What did you want to forget?' Leah asked gently.

'The money...' came the almost incoherent reply.

'What money?'

'The money I took from work.'

Foreboding slithered down Leah's spine. 'Mum! Stop crying and tell me what you've done.'

'It started two Christmases ago,' Tori said dully. 'Remember you saw that lovely coat in the shop on the high street? You said it was too expensive, but I wanted to buy it for you. You're a good girl, Leah, and you deserved a nice Christmas present. But I couldn't afford it.'

Leah loved the grey wool coat with its exorbitant price tag. 'You told me you'd bought that coat in a pre-Christmas sale.'

'I paid full price for it. I wanted to see you happy, darling. I know I've been a useless mother to you. It was easy to borrow a few hundred pounds from the company. Chris Hodge is a good builder, but he knows nothing about finance and accounts. I made up a couple of fake invoices and paid the money into my own bank account.'

'God! Mum, that's fraud.'

'I planned to pay back what I'd taken. But then I fell behind with the rent and there were other bills. When Sammy's grave was vandalised I felt like I'd lost my precious little boy all over again.' Tori wept harder. 'I took a couple of thousand pounds from the company to pay for a new headstone. Every time I made up a false invoice I promised myself that I'd put back all the money I'd taken. But last week the auditors did a cash-flow report and discovered what I'd been doing.'

Leah slid out of bed and crossed to the window to pull back the curtains. Scattered clouds raced across the blue sky, sending shadows dancing over the moors. In the distance a bird of prey hovered perfectly still before it swooped towards the ground. She wished she was a bird, soaring free in the sky.

'What will happen now that your theft has come to light?'

'Chris has been very good about it. That's the worst of it—knowing that I've betrayed our friendship. He's given me to the end of the month to repay all the money, and he's going to allow me to resign rather than be sacked.' Tori's voice trembled. 'But if I don't put the money back he will call the police. Leah, I could go to prison. I know I've done wrong, but I can't bear the idea of being locked up. I wish I wasn't here any more. I want to be with Sammy.'

'*Don't* talk like that, Mum.' Leah pinched the bridge of her nose and forced back her own tears. 'Everything will be okay.'

She had some savings, and she might be able to get a bank loan—although she would need to find a job quickly. Her teaching contract at a special educational needs school in London had finished at the end of the summer term, and she'd intended to wait until after the wedding before looking for a new placement.

'How much money do you owe?'

'It's about...well, just over thirty thousand pounds.'

'*Thirty* thousand?' Leah felt sick. There was no way she could raise that amount—certainly not at short notice.

'Leah, I'm sorry...'

Tori sounded like a small child, and in many ways their roles *had* been reversed, Leah thought. She'd always had to be the responsible one and take care of her mother. That was why Grandma Grace had left Tori, her only daughter, out of her will and bequeathed her money to her granddaughter.

'I'll think of something, Mum. Try not to worry,' Leah murmured before she ended the call.

She had no idea what she was going to do, though, and frustration surged through her when she remembered her grandmother's last will and testament.

I give to my only granddaughter, Leah Rose Ash-bourne, the sum of five hundred thousand pounds.

Half a million pounds was more than enough to save Tori from a possible prison sentence and cover the cost of private treatment for her alcohol addiction. Leah had also hoped to buy a flat for her mum, so that she could make a fresh start. But the stipulation in Grandma Grace's will was a major stumbling block and there seemed no way around it.

The money is only to be made available on the date of my granddaughter's marriage.

Of course her grandmother had been entitled to dispose of her assets as she'd seen fit. And Grandma Grace had held the quaint belief that every woman needed a good and supportive husband.

Perhaps it was because her grandparents had enjoyed a happy marriage for nearly sixty years before her grandad had died, followed two years later by her gran, Leah mused. Tears filled her eyes. She missed her grandparents. When she was a child, she'd loved going to stay with them. But those visits had been rare events because Tori hadn't got on with her parents and they had disapproved of her unconventional lifestyle.

Thinking of her mum pulled Leah's mind back to the present. Standing around and moping would not solve anything, she told herself firmly. It sounded like the plot of a Victorian novel—but she needed to find herself a husband.

Marco checked the ground-floor reception rooms but there was no sign of Nicky. He raked his fingers through his hair, feeling guilty that he'd been on his phone dealing with an urgent issue at De Valle Caffè instead of having breakfast with his son.

'He refused to eat anything,' the housekeeper had reported. 'I only went into the pantry for a minute, and when I came back to the kitchen he'd gone. The back door is locked, so he can't have gone outside.'

Derwa had rested her hands on her hips.

'Mr Marco, what shall I do with the wedding food that has already been prepared? It seems a terrible shame to throw it away.'

'What about offering it to the local care home? I'm sure

the elderly residents there would enjoy smoked salmon blinis.'

As Marco strode up the stairs he told himself that Nicky could not have disappeared altogether. But the boy was not in the playroom, or his bedroom. He continued his search, feeling ever more frantic as he walked from the old part of the house into the newer wing, where the guest bedrooms were located.

It was early in the morning and no one else was up yet. He felt no sympathy when he thought of James having to explain to the guests the reason why the wedding had been cancelled.

The door to Leah's room was open and he gave a sigh of relief when he saw Nicky sitting on the bed.

'Hey, there you are.' Marco crouched down so that he was at eye level with his son. 'We're going back to Capri today.' He frowned as Nicky shook his head. 'Don't you want to go home?' The little boy said nothing, and Marco sighed. 'Come on, it's time to go.'

'Leah.'

Shock jolted through Marco. He felt as though his heart was being squeezed in a vice when he saw the little boy's unhappy face. Nicky had not cried since the accident. It was as if his emotions had been frozen since he had lost his mother. But now he had asked for Leah.

Marco automatically ran his hand over the scar on his cheek. He hated Karin for depriving him of his son for the first three years of his life, but he wished he had been able to save her for the little boy's sake.

He gently wiped Nicky's tears away. 'Would you like Leah to come to Capri with us?'

There was nothing he would not do for his son, Marco thought when Nicky nodded. Somehow he must persuade Leah to accompany them to Italy.

When he'd walked back across the moors to Nancarrow Hall after he had kissed her the previous night, he'd realised that he had to have her. And with her wedding plans in ruins, he had seen no reason to deny himself. A brief affair with her, on his terms, would suit him.

He visited London regularly for work, and he had planned to lease an apartment in the capital and establish her there as his mistress. Undoubtedly the chemistry between them would burn out after a few weeks, or months at most, and he would move on. Their white-hot attraction couldn't last. In his experience it never did.

But now the situation had changed, and he wanted Leah to help his son. That meant he must ignore his inconvenient hunger for her.

Denial was meant to be good for the soul, Marco reminded himself a short while later, after he had left Nicky in the kitchen with the housekeeper, making pancakes.

He drove the short distance to the village. His pilot was preparing his jet, ready for their flight to Naples later on, and Marco was determined that Leah would be on the plane with them.

'Miss Ashbourne is still in her room,' the landlord told him when he entered the pub. 'She asked for some coffee but didn't want breakfast.'

The Sailor's Arms dated back to the thirteenth century and had once been the meeting place of a local smuggling gang. Marco ducked his head to avoid the low ceiling beams as he climbed the stairs. He knocked on the door at the end of a narrow corridor and Leah opened it almost immediately. She was even paler than usual, and her eyes were the slate-green of a stormy sea. Tears clung to her copper-coloured eyelashes.

'I was just about to leave,' she said flatly, hooking her

fingers under the strap of the holdall hanging from her shoulder. 'There's a train to London at nine-forty.'

Marco braced his hands on either side of the door frame. 'Had you forgotten that there is something I want to discuss with you?'

'I hadn't forgotten, but I'm not interested in your proposition.'

'That's not the impression you gave me last night, *bella*.'

He was fascinated by the flush of rose-pink that stained her face. Before she could stop him he stepped across the threshold, so that she had no option but to back into the room. Her obvious distress puzzled him. When he'd overheard the conversation between Leah and James last night it had not occurred to Marco that she might be emotionally invested in his half-brother. He was surprised by how much he disliked the idea.

'How do you know you're not interested when I haven't explained what I want from you yet?'

Without giving her time to speak, he pressed on.

'I am offering you a job as my son's private teacher. When I tried sending Nicky to school he became deeply upset, and I was advised to keep him at home until he had recovered from the distress of losing his mother. But I'm concerned that he will fall behind in his education. I want you to stay at my home in Capri so that you can work with Nicky every day. I know you have experience of teaching traumatised children and I know you have formed a bond with my son.'

Leah shook her head. 'I can't help Nicky. I'm sorry.' Every vestige of colour had drained from her face and she looked tense and unhappy.

Marco was frustrated by her flat refusal. 'But Nicky likes and trusts you. I've checked your qualifications and your employment record and I believe you are the best person to help him.' He exhaled heavily when she continued to shake her head. 'I will pay you generously.'

Instead of replying she turned away from him and walked across the room to stare out of the window. Marco let his eyes roam over her, admiring the way her jeans moulded her pert derriere. She had restrained her hair in a braid again, and he longed to untie it and sink his hands into her riotous curls while he covered her mouth with his.

He swore beneath his breath as he felt his body's predictable response to his erotic thoughts. Somehow he would have to ignore this desire for Leah.

'There is nothing I will not do for my son,' he said deeply. 'Name your price.'

She swung round to face him and hugged her arms around her slender body. Marco had the odd sense that she was trying to stop herself from falling apart.

'My price is marriage. Marry me before the end of the month and I will do my best to help Nicky.'

CHAPTER FIVE

'I'M FLATTERED,' MARCO said drily. 'Have you fallen in love with me? Is that why you are so eager to be my wife?'

'Of course I'm not in love with you.' Leah had been aiming for the same mocking tone Marco had used but her voice emerged annoyingly husky.

His brows rose. 'Then I assume your urgency to get me to the altar is so that you can claim your inheritance?'

She stared at him. 'Does the whole world know about my inheritance?'

'When you left my room last night you set off a movement sensor linked to the burglar alarm system. I followed you so that I could reset the sensor and I overheard you talking to James.'

'So you are aware of the stipulation in my grandmother's will that I must be married before I can access the money she bequeathed to me?'

Leah couldn't believe what she had done. She must have lost her mind to demand that Marco marry her in return for her helping his little boy. But she was desperate to keep her mum out of prison.

He had offered to pay her well if she went to Capri to work as Nicky's teacher, and she had briefly considered accepting the job and asking him for an advance on her salary. But she needed thirty thousand pounds immediately, so that Tori could return the money she had stolen.

It was unlikely Marco would be sympathetic if she revealed that her mother was a thief and had a drink problem. Leah remembered the shame she had felt as a teenager, when a teacher at school had asked if her mum was an alcoholic and gently suggested involving social services. Out of loyalty she had refused to betray Tori, and she would not do so to Marco now.

She forced herself to meet his enigmatic gaze. He was her only hope of claiming her inheritance. She did not have prospective husbands queuing outside her front door, she thought wryly. Besides, she had become fond of his son. She felt sorry for Nicky and wanted to help him.

'What I am suggesting is a temporary marriage while I work with Nicky to try and build his confidence.'

Her heart missed a beat as Marco strode towards her. He dominated the small bedroom, but it was not just his size and impressive physique that made Leah feel that the walls were closing in around her.

His charcoal-grey suit was undoubtedly bespoke. The elegant jacket was undone to reveal a navy blue silk shirt stretched across his broad chest. He wasn't wearing a tie, and the top few buttons of his shirt were open so that she could see a vee of olive-tanned skin and a sprinkling of black chest hair.

He halted in front of her—too close for her peace of mind. The exotic scent of his aftershave sent a coil of heat through her and she despaired of herself when she felt her nipples tingle. She crossed her arms tighter over her chest, to hide the betraying signs of her awareness of him.

'You admit the reason you want to marry me is money?'

He spoke in a lazy drawl, but his eyes were coldly contemptuous and Leah realised that he was furious.

'*My* money, not yours,' she said quickly. 'I know you are wealthy but I'm not a gold-digger. And it wouldn't be a real marriage.'

'In what way would it not be real?'

'Well, we wouldn't…sleep together.' Her voice faltered when his dark brows drew together.

'Perhaps you would like me to be neutered?'

There was no humour in his wolf-like smile. And his low, dark laugh sent a quiver through Leah. She realised then how much danger she was in. Not from Marco, but from her body's instinctive response to his potency.

'What makes you think I would agree to a sterile marriage with a virgin bride?'

She bit her lip. 'I've explained that it wouldn't be a proper marriage and I realise you will want to take a mistress.' Leah could not understand why she so disliked the idea of him sleeping with another woman.

'How very understanding of you, *cara*.'

The bite in his voice made her flinch.

'But if I decide to accept your proposition it will be on *my* terms, not yours, and I will have certain expectations. Number one being that you *will* share my bed.'

Leah hated the way her body responded to Marco's silky voice, but she could not control the spike of heat that centred deep in her pelvis as shockingly erotic images filled her mind of his naked limbs entwined with hers.

She swallowed. 'Are you saying you would force me to have sex with you?'

His jaw hardened, and there was no mistaking the furious glitter in his eyes. 'I have never forced a woman to do anything against her will. I find the idea abhorrent and frankly I'm insulted by your suggestion. I know you want me, *bella*. You proved it when you came to my room last night and crawled all over me.'

'You know I made a mistake when I came to your room,' she said hotly.

'I know you are a liar—to yourself as well as to me.'

He drew back his cuff and glanced at his watch. Leah couldn't help noticing the black hair on his wrist, that curled around the gold watchstrap. She imagined those darkly tanned hands touching her body, those long fingers dipping between her thighs and moving higher, seeking her feminine warmth...

'I gather from your silence that marriage to me has lost its appeal now you know what it will entail?' Marco said drily. His eyes narrowed on her flushed face before he swung round and walked back across the room. 'The train to London leaves in fifteen minutes. I'll give you a lift to the station.'

'What about Nicky?' Leah said sharply. 'I'm sure I can help him.'

Her heart softened when she thought of the little boy who reminded her so much of Sammy. Thankfully Nicky did not suffer from a rare degenerative disease, as her brother had, but there was a vulnerability about Marco's motherless son that tugged on Leah's emotions. All children needed a mother's love.

She sighed when she thought of her own mother. Tori hadn't been a conventional parent, but Leah had never doubted that her mum loved her.

Marco shrugged. 'I'll find another teacher for him.'

He had reached the door and started to open it.

'Wait.' She could hear her heart pounding in her ears, drowning out the voice of caution. 'I'll be a proper wife to you.'

He turned around slowly and pinned her with his searing gaze. Leah did not understand the reason for the simmering fury in his eyes.

'Clarify that statement,' he bit out.

Common sense told her that she should retract her damning words before the hole she was digging for herself got even deeper. But something stronger than reason and the sensible rules she had lived by all her life compelled her to lift her chin and meet his gaze.

'I'll have sex with you...if I have to.'

Marco closed the door and leaned back against it, crossing his arms over his formidable chest. 'How enticing,' he said sarcastically. 'You make it sound as if you will be doing me a favour, but the reverse is true. Initiating a virgin is tedious, or so I've heard. Especially if that virgin is metaphorically clutching at her pearls and feigning distaste of carnal pleasures.'

'Why, you arrogant...' Words failed Leah.

Humiliation scorched her cheeks. So Marco thought that having sex with her would be tedious? Never had she wished more fervently that she was as sexually confident and experienced as most of her friends. She was sorely tempted to tell him to go to hell. But if he walked away now she would never see him again.

It was that thought above any other that made her lift her chin and meet his hard stare. 'What do you want from me?' She felt near to tears and painfully out of her depth, but she refused to show any sign of weakness in front of him.

'Not to be a sacrificial lamb, that's for sure,' he drawled. 'You will have to try harder to persuade me that it would be a good idea to marry you.'

So he hadn't ruled out marriage. Hope flickered inside her. 'How?' she asked.

'I suggest you think of something fast. I'm growing bored.'

Once again Leah sensed that he was angry, although she still did not understand why. When he had kissed her last night, before he'd left her at the pub, she had felt sure he desired her. And now she had agreed to make their marriage real. But maybe he needed to be convinced that she would keep her word and sleep with him.

The reality of what she had done caused her nerve to falter. Was she *really* prepared to lose her virginity to a man who held all the aces up his sleeve?

Then Leah thought of her mum crying on the phone and knew that she had no choice. If Tori was charged with theft from her employer there was every chance she would be given a custodial sentence. She was already emotionally fragile, and prison would destroy her.

'Goddamn you...'

Anger surged as hot as molten lava through Leah's veins. She'd always prided herself on being calm and level-headed, but she was *furious* at the situation she was in. She would rather walk over hot coals than marry Marco. He was everything she disliked in a man—arrogant and cock-sure, certain that he was irresistible to women. She seethed at the memory of how he had called her uninteresting. It would give her great pleasure to make him eat his words.

Casting aside caution, she gripped the hem of her sweat-shirt and pulled it over her head. 'There. Does that per-suade you?'

'Not particularly.'

His facial muscles did not even move when he lowered his gaze to her plain white bra. To her chagrin, he yawned.

Leah had to admit that her underwear was functional, rather than decorative. But Marco's lack of even a flicker of excitement acted like a red rag to a bull, goading her to elicit a response from him.

Reaching behind her back, she unclipped her bra and

tugged the straps down her arms. The bra slipped to the floor leaving her breasts bare. Her skin felt cool after the warmth of her sweatshirt. It was for *that* reason that her nipples had hardened, she told herself.

The old, sensible Leah was appalled by what she had done, but this new, fiery Leah, who she did not recognise as herself, rested her hands on her hips and tilted her chin belligerently.

Marco did not look bored now.

Leah's heart clattered against her ribcage as he stared at her naked breasts with an intentness in his gaze that sent a shiver over her skin.

'*Sei squisito.*'

His voice was deeper than Leah had ever heard it. Something moved within her—heat and flame and an ache that was so strong it hurt. She knew that *squisito* meant exquisite, and the hungry gleam in his eyes evoked a fierce need inside her.

'Untie your hair,' he growled.

His husky demand rolled through her and, although the sensible Leah despaired at her inability to disobey him, she quickly unravelled her long plait and tugged her fingers through her curls. The feel of her silky hair on her naked shoulders was deliciously sensuous. She was aware of her feminine strength and her weakness for him—only for him.

Her pulse accelerated when Marco covered the space between them in two strides. 'Are you satisfied now?' she asked him sweetly, with a bravado she hadn't known she possessed.

'If you think I will be satisfied by an incomplete striptease you have a lot to learn, *cara.*'

To her surprise, he bent down and picked up her bra and sweatshirt from the floor.

'Get dressed,' he said curtly. '*Dio*, you must want your inheritance very badly if you are willing to give away your virginity so inconsequentially. Do you want to tell me why you need the money?'

Leah shook her head. Something in Marco's rough tone made tears prick her eyes, and for a second she was tempted to confide in him. But why should she trust him? If she told him about the money her mum had taken he might decide that he did not want the daughter of a thief to teach his son—and he might refuse to marry her.

'You can relax,' he said drily, perhaps guessing that she was so tense she might snap. 'For now, all I want from you is your professional expertise and your commitment to help my son. I assume you have your passport with you?'

When she nodded, he continued.

'I had planned to take Nicky to New York in a couple of weeks, to visit my cousin and her children, but I'll bring the trip forward and we'll fly to America immediately. We can marry twenty-four hours after obtaining a marriage licence there. My lawyer will draw up a pre-nuptial agreement, which you will sign, stating that you will not be entitled to receive any financial provision from me when we divorce.'

Elation swept through Leah. He was handing her a lifeline which would save her mum from prison. But could she really marry a man who was almost a stranger and who aroused feelings in her that she did not understand?

'I've told you that I don't want your money,' she said huskily. 'Once I have a marriage certificate I will be able to claim my inheritance.'

Marco gave her a cynical look. 'The contract will also set out all the additional terms of our marriage—specifically that you will live in Capri for a year and work to the best of your ability to help my son overcome his trauma.'

'A year?' Leah could not hide her dismay. 'I was thinking of a couple of months... I really do want to help Nicky,' she said quickly, when Marco frowned, 'but I can't put my life on hold for a *year*.'

He captured her chin in his lean fingers and brought her gaze up to meet his. 'Nicky has formed an attachment to you and he needs stability. My son's welfare and happiness are all I care about. Not the games we play and not you. I strongly advise you never to forget those facts.'

Leah held his gaze before shifting away from him and touching her jaw where Marco's fingers had been. Marco looked so grim and forbidding that her heart sank.

'My God, I've made a deal with the devil,' she whispered as the enormity of what she had done sank in.

His eyes gleamed as cold and hard as polished steel. 'I told you what I am, Beauty. You should have heeded my warning. It's too late to back out now.'

He must be out of his mind! Marco tightened his hands on the steering wheel as he drove away from the pub. He could not believe that Leah had demanded he marry her before she would help Nicky—and that he had agreed! He was incensed that she had in essence blackmailed him and then told him that she did not want a real marriage.

But he had called her bluff when he'd insisted that he would want her to be his wife in every sense. He'd expected her to back down from her marriage demand then. And when she'd primly agreed to sleep with him, making her reluctance obvious, and even worse suggested that he might *force* her to have sex, his temper had skyrocketed.

He'd wanted to teach her a lesson, but what had happened next had tested his self-control to the limit.

Marco swore as he remembered how Leah had taken off her bra to reveal pale breasts tipped with rosy nipples.

She was beautiful, and he had been fiercely tempted to kiss the sweet curves of her body before tumbling her down onto the bed.

But he had reminded himself that she was out of bounds. He hoped only that Leah would bring Nicky out of his shell and help him come to terms with the loss of his mother.

Marco frowned as he thought of Karin. When the car she had been driving had crashed and burst into flames he'd had to choose between pulling his son or his ex-wife out of the wreckage first. Nicky had been his priority and Karin had died.

He could not give Nicky back his mother, but he had promised the little boy that Leah would come to Capri with them. And if accepting her marriage deal was the only way he could make his son happy he would go through with it, Marco vowed grimly.

In Central Park, two days later, Marco stood a little away from Leah and watched her rub sun lotion onto Nicky's arms. New York was in the grip of a heatwave, and the bright sunshine had encouraged the turtles in the park out of the water to bask on the rocks—much to the little boy's evident delight. He hadn't stopped smiling since they had arrived at the pond.

'Look, Nicky, there's another one.' Leah pointed to the water. 'Do you think your *papà* would like to see the turtles too?' She looked over her shoulder and beckoned to Marco.

He stiffened when he saw Nicky's smile disappear. The wary expression on the little boy's face made his heart clench. It was clear that his son preferred to be with Leah—he had hardly left her side since they had boarded the plane for their flight to America.

At least she genuinely seemed to care about Nicky, and

for that reason Marco had organised the necessary paperwork and booked a wedding officiant to marry them tomorrow.

His phone rang and he answered it when he saw his PA's name on the screen. Thinking about work stopped him thinking about his failure as a father.

During his conversation he was aware of Leah glaring at him before she turned away and knelt beside Nicky. Minutes later Marco finished the call. He wished he could just stroll over to the pond and crouch down beside his son, so they could watch the turtles together. It would be the most natural thing for a father to do. But he did not know how to connect with Nicky. He envied Leah's natural affinity with the child—the way she ruffled his hair and slipped her arm around his shoulders to gently draw him away from the water's edge.

It was obvious that she was good with children—which must be important in her job as a special needs teacher. But Marco was curious. He had sensed a sadness in her sometimes when she was with Nicky. Perhaps she had hoped to have children of her own when she'd planned to marry James. He frowned as he remembered his half-brother's accusation that Leah had only wanted to marry him so that she could claim her inheritance.

Clearly the money was important to her. Why else would she have issued her outrageous marriage demand to him? Marco brooded. But he had spent a good deal of time with her since they had arrived in New York and she did not strike him as someone who was obsessed with money or impressed by it.

Her motives were of no interest to him, he reminded himself. All he cared about was the connection she had formed with his son.

Against his will, his gaze was drawn again to Leah.

Her outfit today was a shapeless dress in an unbecoming beige colour. The previous day she'd worn a navy blue skirt with a hemline way below her knees and, as always, had had her hair scraped back from her face and tied in a schoolgirlish braid.

But her unexciting clothes did not disguise her natural beauty. She would look stunning in a dress that made the most of her gorgeous figure, and breathtaking without any clothes on at all.

Marco expelled a ragged breath. Usually when he was interested in a woman he slept with her, and then his fascination tended to fade quickly. Perhaps the fact that Leah was off-limits served to increase his interest. He'd never had to deny himself before, he acknowledged wryly. Money and power were aphrodisiacs to many women and the truth was that he'd become jaded.

Leah looked over at him again. 'Nicky would like to go in a rowboat. Is there somewhere to hire one?'

Marco pointed to a building across the park and the three of them walked along the path to a restaurant which offered boats for hire. Leah put a lifejacket on Nicky, and helped him into the boat, but she shook her head when Marco climbed in and held out his hand to help her aboard.

'I'll stay here and keep in the shade, under the trees. I forgot to bring a hat, and I feel as though I've had too much sun,' she said.

It was true that her nose and cheeks were pink. Marco guessed that Leah's fair skin would burn easily, but he couldn't help thinking that she had made the excuse so that he would be able to take Nicky in the boat without her.

He looked at his son. 'Okay, are you ready?'

He half expected that Nicky would refuse to go without Leah, but after hesitating for a moment he nodded.

As Marco rowed across the lake he looked around at the

other families who were having fun on the water and felt an ache in his heart. Nicky had never had the support of both his parents because Karin had disappeared with him when he was only a few months old. Now his mother was dead.

An inquest had confirmed that Karin had died from the impact of the crash, before the car had caught fire. There was nothing he could have done to save her, Marco knew.

He studied Nicky's grave little face and sighed. If Leah had come in the boat Nicky would be enjoying himself. Marco was annoyed that she had forced him into a situation where he was alone with his son. He had no problem chairing a meeting of the company's directors, or negotiating a deal in a boardroom, but he was struggling to think of something to say to a five-year-old.

'Look, Nicky, there's a heron.' He pointed to the tall grey bird standing on the bank. The bird spread its wings and took off, soaring gracefully into the sky.

'Herons are big,' Nicky said in his soft voice. There was a rapt expression on his face as he watched the bird fly to the opposite side of the lake. 'How can they fly, *Papà*?'

Marco searched his mind for facts about the heron's biology. 'Well, you can see that they have very wide wings, and they use the strong muscles in their bodies to flap those wings. And their long beaks allow them to catch fish to eat.'

'There's another heron!' Nicky pointed to a white bird in the reeds.

'I think that one is an egret.'

'You know lots of things, *Papà*.'

Nicky fixed his big brown eyes on Marco and for once he did not look wary.

'We could buy a book and learn some more about herons and other birds if you like.'

His heart contracted when his son gave a tentative

smile. It was the most response he'd ever had from the little boy, and it gave him hope that he would be able to start rebuilding a relationship with Nicky, with Leah's help.

But he still resented her marriage demand, and he resented even more the inconvenient desire she aroused in him. Marco was determined not to forget that marrying Leah was a business deal.

CHAPTER SIX

THE HOTEL'S PENTHOUSE suite had stunning views of New York. Central Park looked like a green oasis amid the iconic skyscrapers, and in the distance the Hudson River glinted like a silver ribbon. It had been a relief to Leah to step into the air-conditioned building and escape the heat outside.

Nicky had been tired after their trip to the park, and Leah had settled him in front of the TV in his bedroom to watch cartoons for half an hour.

She returned to the lounge, where Marco was sitting on the sofa, working on his laptop. As always, the impact of his stunning good-looks made her catch her breath, and the coward in her wanted to retreat to her own bedroom. But she forced herself to ignore her awareness of him while she discussed his son.

'Nicky enjoyed going in the boat with you.'

'Good.' Marco glanced at her briefly before turning his attention back to his screen.

Leah frowned. 'But you need to try harder with him.' She did not understand Marco's attitude. 'For half the time we were at the park you were on your phone.'

'I am the head of a multi-billion-dollar company and I'm rarely off duty. Nicky was having a good time watching the turtles with you.'

She marched across the room and shut the lid of his laptop. 'That poor little boy has lost his mother, and you are so distant with him. Nicky acts like you're a stranger rather than his father.'

'That is because until a year ago I *was* a stranger to him.' Marco's hard features showed no expression. 'I was divorced from Nicky's mother and I did not see my son for three years.'

'Why didn't you visit him?' Leah could not hide her shock.

Something flickered on his face but disappeared before she could try to guess his thoughts.

'It was…difficult.'

His phone rang yet again. Did he sleep with it clamped to his ear? she wondered.

'I suppose you were too busy with your work schedule to have time to spare.'

Marco's eyes glinted with anger, but Leah was too angry to care. She walked across the room while he answered his phone.

She remembered how Sammy's father Jez, who had been her stepfather for a couple of years, had cleared off after her half-brother had been diagnosed with an incurable brain condition. As the disease had progressed Sammy had needed round-the-clock care, and she had helped her mother as much as possible. It had been a difficult and ultimately tragic time, and it had been after Sammy had died, that Tori had started drinking heavily.

Leah stood in front of the huge windows that overlooked the park. This hotel was reputedly the most expensive place to stay in New York, but the luxurious surroundings meant nothing to a little boy who needed love.

Nicky must have been only a baby when his parents had divorced, and he would have been too young to remember Marco. He must have felt desperately alone when his mother had died and he'd been reunited with a father he did not know, who was cold and unfeeling.

She knew it would be very easy for her to become emotionally attached to Nicky. But she must not, she reminded herself. Her marriage to Marco was to be a temporary arrangement, and thankfully there was no danger of her emotions being involved with him.

The hairs on the back of her neck prickled and she turned her head and found he was standing beside her.

'I wish you wouldn't creep up on me,' she said crossly, feeling herself blush.

The spicy scent of his aftershave assailed her senses and her breath caught in her throat as her eyes clashed with his enigmatic grey gaze.

One dark brow lifted. 'I wonder if jet-lag has made you irritable? These shadows suggest a lack of sleep,' he murmured, tracing his finger lightly over the purple smudges beneath her eyes.

Leah swallowed. He was invading her personal space, but she couldn't bring herself to move away from him. She felt the betraying tightening of her nipples and hated how her body responded to Marco's potent masculinity.

'That was my aunt on the phone. She is in New York, visiting her daughter and grandchildren, and is on her way here to the hotel to collect Nicky. They are all going to the zoo this afternoon and Nicky has been invited to sleep over with my cousin's children tonight.'

'I'll go with him if your cousin won't mind me staying at her home,' Leah offered.

'That won't be necessary. Nicky met Chiara and her family when we stayed at my aunt's house in Tuscany a couple of months ago. He likes the children, and it will be better if he is not at our wedding tomorrow. I've decided not to tell him that we are getting married—at least for now. He is too young to understand.'

Leah nodded. It made sense not to risk confusing or upsetting a little boy who had been through so much.

'But before my aunt arrives you'll need to put this on.'

Her heart missed a beat when Marco took a small box out of his pocket and opened it to reveal an exquisite ring. The stunning green centre stone was surrounded by a circle of diamonds that sparkled in the sunlight.

'The gemstone is a tourmaline,' he explained. 'My aunt is a die-hard romantic and she will think I chose the ring to complement the colour of your eyes.'

'Is this really necessary?' Leah asked, stiffening when he reached for her hand. 'I assumed that our marriage would be secret. After all, it will end once we've both had what we want from it.'

'Thanks to social media, secrets tend not to stay secret for long,' Marco said sardonically. 'I am a well-known figure in Italy and the paparazzi take a great interest in my private life. It will be better to make a public announcement of our marriage rather than have a nosy journalist expose it in the newspapers and start digging around for a scandal.' His brows rose. 'Do you have any dark secrets I should know about?'

Leah bit her lip, worried at the idea of a reporter finding out about the money her mum had stolen. 'Do *you* have secrets?' she countered.

She could not decipher the expression that flickered on Marco's face. 'I prefer not to have my personal life used as tabloid fodder. If we attempt to keep our marriage a secret people will wonder what we are hiding. Obviously Nicky does not read newspapers, so he won't find out. And I have already told my mother and James that we are getting married.'

Leah gave him a startled look. 'What did they say? I can't imagine Olivia was pleased. She made it plain that she believed I wasn't good enough for James, and I imagine she feels the same way about me marrying you.'

'My mother has never taken much interest in what I do,' Marco said drily. 'James offered his congratulations and said that he intends to marry Davina before their baby is born.'

'I see.'

Leah felt a flicker of envy for the wedding planner, who would now have the security and family that *she* had dreamed of. But then she reminded herself that neither she nor James would have been happy if they had married.

She pulled her thoughts back to the present and watched Marco slide the ring onto her finger. It fitted perfectly, as if it was meant to be there. For no reason that made sense tears pricked Leah's eyes. Of course he had not *really* chosen the ring because the tourmaline matched her eyes. He had probably ordered any ring from the jeweller without specifying a style or gemstone.

She sighed. It had seemed a simple idea to marry him so that she could claim her inheritance, but the reality was proving to be far more complicated.

'You will need to act like an adoring fiancée in front of my aunt. She won't understand that we are marrying for convenience and it will be simpler to allow her to believe that we are in love,' he drawled, in that cynical way of his.

'I'm not that good an actress,' Leah muttered.

'Then I suggest you learn—fast. When our marriage becomes public knowledge the board members and shareholders of De Valle Caffè will be interested because I am the CEO of the company. It is another good reason why there must not be a whiff of scandal about our relationship.'

'How am I supposed to pretend that I adore you when I don't even *like* you?' Leah asked curtly.

Marco laughed. 'You gave a very good impression of liking me when you came to my room in the middle of the night and kissed me.'

Her cheeks reddened. 'Do you *have* to remind me of a night I'd rather forget?'

'I wish I could forget it too, but I can't.'

His voice had roughened. Leah's eyes flew to his face and she felt her heart kick in her chest when she saw that his jaw was tense and his skin was drawn tightly over his sharp cheekbones.

She licked suddenly dry lips and Marco gave a low groan as his gaze focused on her mouth. He lowered his head towards her.

'What are you doing?' she whispered, mesmerised by the predatory gleam in his eyes.

'I want to kiss you, *cara*. And I think you want me to—don't you?'

'It's not a good idea…' Her protest sounded unconvincing. If only her brain would work, she might remember *why* she should ignore the tumultuous desire coursing through her body.

'It's a terrible idea,' he agreed thickly. 'But you are a madness I can't seem to control.'

His lips were so close to hers that she felt his warm breath on her skin. And Leah offered no resistance when he brushed his mouth over hers. She wanted his kiss, and she could not fight her longing any more.

She opened her mouth beneath his, and her breath left her on a soft sigh of pleasure when he ran the tip of his tongue over her lips, exploring their shape. He moved his hand to cradle the back of her head while he continued to kiss her with a sensual expertise that made her shake as starbursts of pleasure exploded inside her.

It was impossible to control the thunder of her heart.

Desire swept like molten lava through her veins. With a low moan she pressed her body against his and surrendered to his sorcery. She did not have the willpower to deny him when it meant denying herself what she wanted: his lips possessing hers, his strong arms around her, drawing her against the solid expanse of his chest. She opened her mouth at the demanding flick of his tongue, and as her eyelashes swept down he filled her senses.

Marco's skin felt warm to her touch as she ran her fingertips over his muscular arms with their fine covering of silky black hair. She dipped her tongue into his mouth and he tasted like heaven. The evocative smell of his cologne filled her lungs and she heard his ragged breaths echoing hers as she was lost to the hungry demands of his kiss...

'You look suitably ravished, *cara*. My aunt will certainly believe we can't keep our hands off each other.'

Marco forced himself to speak in a casual tone to hide how shaken he was by his reaction to Leah. *Dio*, it had been a mistake to kiss her, but he'd been unable to stop himself.

He felt a stab of remorse when she gave him a dazed look. Her pupils were dilated and ringed with irises of dark green—the exact colour of the tourmaline in the ring. He silently cursed his crazy impulse the previous day, when he'd left Leah with Nicky at the hotel for an hour to shop for an engagement ring even though it would have been simpler to phone a jeweller and order a standard diamond solitaire.

A knock on the door brought him to his senses and he raked his hand through his hair as he walked out to the hallway and opened the door of the penthouse.

His aunt was tiny in stature and comfortably plump. Her hair had turned white overnight when his uncle Federico had died, and this visual sign of the grief that Marco had shared still gave him a pang.

She greeted him effusively and chatted in voluble Italian while he ushered her into the lounge.

'Tia Benedetta, this is Leah,' Marco said when his aunt finally paused to take a breath. 'My fiancée and soon-to-be wife.'

Benedetta was stunned into silence for thirty seconds before she started to offer her congratulations in Italian.

'Leah is English,' Marco interrupted his aunt.

'Please forgive me. I should have guessed from your fair colouring that you are not Italian,' Benedetta said, speaking in English.

Leah smiled. 'Actually, I learned to speak Italian as a child when I lived in Italy and I'm fairly fluent.'

That was news to Marco. What other secrets did Leah have? he wondered.

He slid his arm around her waist and gave her a warning squeeze when he felt her stiffen. 'Are you going to show Tia Benedetta your ring, *tesoro*?' he said softly.

'Of course, *darling*,' she replied, in a saccharine-sweet voice that caused his lips to twitch.

The first time he had met Leah at Nancarrow Hall he'd thought she was docile and, in truth, rather boring. He should have realised that her red hair was an indication of a hot temper.

He was conscious of the firm swell of her breast pressed against the side of his chest, and he was more fascinated than he should be by the jerky motion of the pulse beating at the base of her neck. Her body fitted against his perfectly, but he tried to ignore his awareness of that as she held out her left hand to show off the glittering ring on her finger.

Benedetta threw her hands in the air and a tear ran down her lined face. 'I am crying with joy, Marco. You deserve to be happy after your sadness when Karin—'

Marco frowned.

'Your engagement is wonderful news,' his aunt said hurriedly. 'What does Nicolo think?'

'We're not going to tell him just yet. It will be better to wait until he feels more settled.'

Benedetta nodded. 'You must all come and visit me soon. I have a farmhouse in Tuscany,' she told Leah. 'Marco brought Nicolo to stay recently and he loved feeding the chickens. Where in Italy did you live?'

'In Tuscany, as a matter of fact. In a place called Calana.'

'Ah, I know it. I believe that Calana is a medieval town which was saved from developers by a group of artists who formed a commune. Are your parents artists?'

'My father died when I was very young. My mother was a painter, but she stopped painting after...' an odd expression flickered across Leah's face '...after we moved back to England.'

Marco wondered what she had been about to say. He was curious to know more about Leah's past.

But just then Nicky ran into the lounge and gave one of his quick smiles when he saw Benedetta. While the older woman made a fuss of the little boy, Marco went to pack him an overnight bag.

'Are you going to give your *papà* a hug?' Benedetta asked Nicky when they were ready to leave.

Marco wanted to scoop his son into his arms and press his face against his dark curls. He ached to hold Nicky close, but he was afraid of rushing things. There had been a breakthrough while they were in the rowboat, but there was still a long way to go before the little boy accepted him.

He forced a brisk laugh as he opened the door. 'Nicky is too grown up for that kind of thing. Have a good time at the zoo, *piccolo*.'

He watched his aunt and his son step into the lift. The

doors closed and Nicky's face, dominated by those huge brown eyes, disappeared. Marco felt a hollow sensation in his chest. What if something happened to Nicky and he never came back?

He had a flashback to the agony he'd felt when Karin had disappeared with his baby son. His shock and anger had given way to raw pain as time had passed, and he'd been very aware that he was missing the important milestones of Nicky's life: his first steps, his first tooth, his first words.

Why was he letting Nicky out of his sight now?

Marco tried to control his fear. He was strongly tempted to take the other lift down to the ground floor, grab hold of his son and never let him go. But Nicky had been excited about the trip to the zoo and he would be disappointed if he wasn't allowed to go.

Marco wondered if Karin had made him out to be a monster to his son, and that was why Nicky was wary of him.

Rage at his ex-wife stirred rancid and bitter in the pit of his stomach. But still, despite what Karin had done, he felt guilt that he had been unable to save her.

'I can't *believe* you just told your aunt that Nicky is too grown up for you to hug him,' Leah muttered when she followed Marco into the sitting room in the penthouse. 'He's *five,* for goodness' sake.'

'I know my son's age,' Marco said curtly. 'I was only two years older than him when I went to boarding school.'

She stared at him. 'Your parents sent you away to school when you were *seven*?'

Perhaps having to be independent when he was so young explained why Marco seemed so self-contained.

'My father had died suddenly of an undiagnosed heart condition. When my mother married her second husband

and James was born she was busy with her new family. It was easier for everyone if I was away at school most of the time.'

Leah pictured Marco, not much older than Nicky, being sent away from home while his mother doted on a new baby.

'I was two when my dad died and I don't really remember him,' she said softly. 'But you were old enough to have had a relationship with your father. You must have missed him.'

He shrugged. 'I used to pretend that he was on a business trip. My father travelled a lot for work, and I told myself that he would come back the next week, the next month…'

Something in his voice told Leah that he had never stopped waiting for his father to come home. She felt sympathetic that he had lost his dad at such a young age, but she was also puzzled.

'I don't understand why you made no effort to see Nicky after you and your wife split up. You must have realised from your own childhood experiences how important it was for him to have regular contact with his father.'

Marco walked over to the bar and poured himself a drink. 'My ex-wife moved to Mexico with Nicky after the divorce.'

Leah guessed from his harsh tone that he wanted her to drop the conversation, but she persisted. 'Is Mexico where the accident happened and your wife died? I intend to encourage Nicky to talk about what he remembers, and it would be helpful if you could tell me what happened.'

For a moment she thought Marco wasn't going to answer. He took a long sip of his drink and walked over to the window, standing facing away from her so that she had a view of his austere profile.

'Karin took Nicky out in her car. She lost control and the car came off the road. It must have rolled over several times,' he said tautly. 'When I arrived a few minutes after the accident I could smell petrol. I managed to pull Nicky out of the wreckage, but the car exploded while Karin was trapped inside. Mercifully she was almost certainly already dead before it happened.'

He ran his finger over the scar on his cheek.

'I was hit by a shard of glass when the windscreen shattered in the explosion. The cut went down to the bone. If it had been an inch higher I would have lost my eye.'

'My God! No wonder Nicky was traumatised,' Leah said, shaken by what Marco had told her.

'He was hospitalised with concussion, but thankfully he was otherwise physically unhurt.'

She frowned. 'So you were there in Mexico when the accident happened? I thought you didn't have any contact with Nicky?'

'It was his birthday, and Karin had allowed me to visit.' Marco swung round and scowled at Leah. 'Nicky was semi-conscious when I pulled him out of the car. I doubt he remembers anything about the accident. I see no point in you dragging up the past with him. He needs to move forward and your job is to build his self-confidence.'

He swallowed the rest of his drink and slammed his glass down on the table before he strode out of the lounge. Moments later Leah heard the thud of his bedroom door being closed with barely restrained force.

CHAPTER SEVEN

MARCO HAD GIVEN Leah some insight into the terrible events of his ex-wife's death, although she sensed that he had not told her everything. Knowing Nicky had lived abroad with his mother had also given her a better understanding of why he did not have a close relationship with his son.

Perhaps he resented the change of lifestyle that being the single parent of a young child entailed?

She dismissed the idea. Marco must love Nicky. He had agreed to marry her so that she could help the little boy.

She wondered whether it had been him or his wife who had wanted a divorce. Maybe he'd still had feelings for Karin and was struggling to come to terms with her death.

She heard his phone ring and saw that he'd left it on the coffee table. The ringtone stopped, but seconds later it started again. It was probably a work-related call, she guessed. De Valle Caffè was a global business, and as CEO Marco was obviously heavily involved in running the company.

But she wondered if he used his work commitments as a form of escape from emotions he did not want to face in the same way that her mum masked her pain with alcohol. When she had first met Marco she'd thought he was cold and unfeeling, but now she was sure that wasn't true.

He cared for Nicky, but he seemed to find it difficult to show his feelings.

His phone was still ringing.

The call must be important.

Leah's heart lurched at the sudden thought that it might be Benedetta, trying to contact Marco because something had happened to Nicky.

Grabbing the phone, she sped down the hallway and knocked on his door. He did not respond, and she opened the door and stepped into the room just as he strolled out of the en suite bathroom. A towel was draped low on his hips and droplets of water clung to his chest hair. He'd obviously just taken a shower.

His brows rose as Leah stared at him. 'You seem to be making a habit of entering my bedroom without an invitation,' he murmured.

She couldn't drag her gaze from Marco's almost naked body. Heat swept through her, spreading from her pink cheeks over her breasts and down to the molten place between her legs. His rampant masculinity made her feel weak as she moved her gaze over his broad chest, following the arrowing of dark hair that disappeared beneath the towel.

As he walked towards her she noticed the powerful thigh muscles that she'd felt beneath her when she'd stretched out on top of him on that fated night at Nancarrow Hall. Her blush deepened as she recalled vividly the hardness of him pressing against her stomach...

Belatedly, she remembered his phone in her hand, which had now gone silent. 'Someone was ringing you,' she mumbled, holding the phone out to him. 'I thought the call might be urgent.'

'Thanks.' He glanced at the screen before dropping the phone onto the bed. 'Was there anything else?'

The gleam in his eyes told Leah that he had noticed her gaze flick towards the big bed.

'I…um… I've decided to go out for a while.'

'Shopping?'

She shook her head. 'I thought I'd do some sightseeing as I've never been to New York before. I hate shopping,' she added with feeling.

'It wasn't a suggestion,' Marco said drily. 'We are going shopping. You need a new wardrobe. When we go to Capri there will be numerous social functions which you will attend with me as my wife. You'll need suitable clothes.'

She was irritated by his superior tone. 'What's wrong with my clothes?' Her dress was smart and unfussy and, more importantly, it didn't attract attention.

'You need to ask when you are wearing a beige *sack*?'

'It's a tunic dress and the colour is ecru…or maybe taupe.'

'I don't care what it's called. It's coming off.' Marco grinned when she gasped. 'Not right now—although I won't object if you want to take it off.' He moved his hands to the edge of the towel around his waist.

'What are you doing?' she squeaked.

'I'm about to get dressed.'

His husky laughter followed her as she fled from his room.

'I'll be done in a couple of minutes. Wait for me.'

No way! Leah thought as she grabbed her handbag on her way out of the penthouse.

The lift whisked her down to the foyer, but when she emerged from the hotel and blinked in the bright sunlight a man appeared at her side.

'Please come this way, Miss Ashbourne. My name is Aaron and I work for Mr De Valle.'

A sleek, black car had pulled up next to the kerb and the man opened the rear door.

'If you'd like to get into the car Marco will join you in a couple of minutes.'

Leah found herself politely but firmly bundled onto the passenger seat, and when she looked to the front of the car the chauffeur smiled at her in the rearview mirror.

'Good afternoon, ma'am.'

Escape was impossible, she realised when she saw Aaron standing on the pavement in front of the car door. She wouldn't be able to open the door on the other side of the car because of the steady stream of traffic on the road.

Minutes later Aaron held the door open and Marco slid in beside her.

'Do you always get your own way?' she snapped.

'Always, *cara*.'

Amusement gleamed in his grey eyes as she shifted further along the seat away from him.

'Is Aaron your PA?'

'He's one of my security team.'

'You have a *bodyguard*?'

Leah supposed she shouldn't feel shocked. Out of curiosity she had checked Marco's profile on the internet. There was very little information about his private life, but she'd discovered that he was one of the wealthiest men in Europe. He had only been a boy when he'd inherited his father's coffee empire, and the company had been run by another member of the De Valle family until Marco had turned twenty-one and became executive chairman.

He had been a very young man when he'd had so much responsibility thrust upon him, and from what he'd told her of his childhood it was not surprising that he'd learned to be self-reliant from an early age. Perhaps that was another reason why he kept an emotional distance from his son.

Leah sighed as her eyes were drawn involuntarily back to Marco. He'd swapped the jeans and black polo he'd worn to the park for a light grey suit and white silk shirt. She noticed that his hair was still damp from his shower.

She noticed way too much about him, she thought ruefully, tearing her gaze from the sexy black stubble on his jaw.

'We're on Fifth Avenue,' he told her as the car crawled along in the queue of traffic. 'Over there is the Empire State Building. But there won't be time for you to do much sightseeing as we'll be flying to Italy straight after our wedding.'

Her heart missed at beat at the prospect of marrying him and her doubts must have shown on her face.

'Are you having second thoughts?'

Too many to count! But she wasn't going to admit it to him.

'I haven't changed my mind,' she told him firmly.

He put his hand inside his jacket and withdrew a document which he unfolded and handed to her. 'My lawyer has sent the marriage contract. Read through it and, if you are happy with it, sign it.'

'What if I'm not happy with it?' She bit her lip, thinking that she should ask a solicitor of her own to check the details of the contract before she signed her life away.

'Without your signature there will be no marriage,' Marco said implacably.

Grimacing, she focused her attention on the document. It stated that she would live in Capri exclusively as Marco's wife for one year and accompany him to social and business functions in support of his position as CEO of De Valle Caffè. She would fulfil the role of his son's teacher and to the best of her ability help Nicky overcome the problems caused by the trauma he had suffered. She would not be entitled to receive any money as part of a divorce settlement when the marriage ended.

'I told you I don't want your money.' She felt embarrassed that he might still suspect she was a fortune-hunter.

'So you did. But I married my first wife without a prenup and I have no intention of repeating the mistake,' he said sardonically as he handed Leah a pen.

She was startled by the bitterness in his voice, and glanced at his hard features before taking a deep breath and signing her name at the bottom of the document.

The car came to a halt outside an iconic designer store and the chauffeur jumped out and opened the door. Marco slid his hand beneath Leah's elbow and escorted her into the shop. She was glad of his presence beside her as she looked around at mannequins draped in beautiful clothes that she knew, even without seeing their price tags, would be way beyond her budget.

'I don't know where to start,' she muttered. 'None of these clothes will suit me. They're too colourful and too...' she searched for the right word '...noticeable.'

'You don't like to be noticed?'

She touched her hair. 'This makes me stand out too much as it is. That's why I prefer to wear neutral colours.'

'I will *not* have a wife who wears beige,' Marco growled as he steered her towards a private area at the back of the store, where an impossibly elegant woman was waiting for them.

'Mr De Valle, Miss Ashbourne, may I offer my congratulations on your engagement? My name is Julia and I am a personal stylist. It will be my pleasure to help you choose a trousseau,' the woman told Leah.

Twenty minutes later Leah had stripped down to her knickers and had wrapped a robe around her while the stylist rifled through the racks of dresses that had been brought into the changing room.

'This one will be perfect for formal evening wear.' Julia held up a full-length ruby-red velvet gown.

'I can't wear red with my hair,' Leah protested.

'You'll be surprised. Your complexion can take strong colours.'

Against her better judgement Leah stepped into the dress and the stylist ran the zip up her spine. It had narrow shoulder straps and a plunging neckline. Clever boning in the bodice pushed her breasts high without the need for a bra. The clingy velvet moulded her figure like a second skin. There were shoes to match the dress, and the four-inch stilettos had the effect of making her hips sway when she walked.

She certainly wouldn't blend into the background in this dress, she thought wryly as she studied her reflection in the mirror.

'What did I tell you?' Julia said in a satisfied voice. 'But it's not my opinion that counts.'

She pulled back a curtain and indicated for Leah to step forward into the viewing area before she allowed the curtain to fall back.

Marco was sprawled on one of the plush sofas with his long legs stretched out in front of him. He looked every inch the high-octane billionaire tycoon, with a hefty dose of sexual magnetism thrown in for good measure. As was inevitable, he was talking on his phone, but when he saw Leah he finished the call and sat up straight. The flare of heat in his eyes scorched her from across the room and a familiar weakness invaded her limbs.

She ran her hand down the velvet dress. 'I don't think...' she began uncertainly.

'*Dio*, you look incredible.'

His rough voice caused the tiny hairs on her body to stand on end, and the possessive gleam in his eyes evoked an ache of longing in the pit of her stomach.

'You should not try to hide your beauty with unflattering clothes, *cara*. In that dress you will be the centre of attention.'

That was what Leah was afraid of. At school she had been a misfit ginger-haired kid whose mum was a drunk, and she had done everything possible to avoid attracting the bullies' attention.

'Why are you shaking your head? Don't you believe me?' Marco stood up and prowled towards her like a jungle cat intent on capturing its prey. 'See, *bella*?' he murmured as he placed his hand on her shoulder and turned her to face the mirror. 'You are gorgeous.'

She stared at the mirror, but it was the naked desire stamped on his face rather than the dress that arrested her attention. She'd never had the confidence to wear clothes that flattered her figure, and she'd always downplayed her looks because she wanted to avoid attention from men. But Marco made her feel beautiful, and she noticed now how the fitted bodice of the dress made her waist seem tiny and her breasts more voluptuous.

Her eyes met his intent gaze in the mirror and heat coiled through her, centring in her feminine core.

The stylist put her head round the curtain. 'I have many more outfits for you to try on…'

But Leah had caught sight of the eye-watering figure on the price tag. Even when she converted it from US dollars to British pounds it was extortionate. Her credit card would have to take the hit. At least she would be able to pay it off when she received her inheritance.

'I'll just take this dress,' she told Julia, thinking there

must be other shops in Manhattan which stocked clothes that did not cost the earth.

'My fiancée will need more than one dress,' Marco assured the stylist, who looked much happier as she disappeared back into the changing room. 'I expect you to choose daywear and evening gowns,' he told Leah. 'And I suggest you buy some new lingerie. Your bra looks as though it's a remnant from your schooldays.'

He took no notice of her angry gasp as he opened his wallet, removed a credit card and offered it to her.

'When you have finished here, the chauffeur will drive you to your appointment at a beauty salon. I have decided to follow your suggestion that I need to spend more time with Nicky, and I have called Benedetta to tell her that I'll meet them at the zoo.'

Leah shook her head, refusing to take the card. 'I won't allow you to buy me clothes. I don't want anything from you.'

'Other than my name next to yours on a marriage certificate?' he said drily.

'We both want something from our marriage,' she reminded him.

He continued to hold out the credit card, so she plucked it from his fingers and slid it into the top pocket of his jacket.

'We made a deal and that's as far as our relationship goes.' She ignored the dangerous gleam in Marco's eyes. 'You can't buy my clothes and you definitely can't buy *me*.'

A violent thunderstorm kept Leah awake for much of the night. Despite the air-conditioning in her room, the electrically charged atmosphere felt oppressive. She sat up in bed to watch the dramatic lightning that forked across a purple sky. In literature, storms were often a portent of disaster, and she could not shrug off the sense of foreboding that marrying Marco would change her fundamentally.

But of course her life was about to change. She was going to live in Capri, and she was to start structured lessons with Nicky. He was a dear little boy, and she'd found that being with him helped to ease her sadness about Sammy's death.

The prospect of her public role as Marco's wife was more daunting. Wearing designer dresses would not turn her into a sophisticated socialite, Leah thought ruefully. Besides, she had only bought a couple of new outfits, which she'd paid for herself.

She fell asleep at last and was woken by the sound of someone knocking on her bedroom door. Her heart gave an annoying flip, as it always did whenever she thought of Marco. But after she'd hastily pulled on a robe and opened the door she was greeted by a waiter who wheeled a trolley into her room. The aroma of coffee from the cafetière assailed her, and she lifted a lid to reveal a dish of freshly baked croissants.

A single white rose lay on the trolley. Leah picked it up and tears blurred her eyes as she inhaled the flower's heady fragrance. Was the rose a peace offering from Marco? She hadn't seen him since they'd argued the previous day, when he'd left her to continue shopping. If she'd been a millionaire, she would have loved to buy *all* the beautiful clothes she'd tried on. Instead she'd chosen only a few key pieces—what the personal stylist had called a 'capsule wardrobe'. The bill had been more than she had ever spent on clothes in her life and she'd winced when she'd handed over her credit card.

Her appointment at a hair and beauty salon had been more enjoyable than she'd expected. Her hair had looked amazingly glossy after the stylist had cut a few inches off the length and tamed her curls by adding some choppy layers. She'd even felt a flutter of excitement at the prospect of having dinner with Marco, but he'd sent her a text saying that after his trip to the zoo with Nicky he'd met up with a friend and did not know what time he would be back.

He hadn't returned to the penthouse by the time she'd gone to bed and she had tried not to think about the possibility that he was spending the night with a woman. She knew from the few kisses they had shared that he was an intensely passionate man. He had assured her that their marriage would be in name only, and she doubted he would remain celibate for a year.

With a faint sigh Leah placed the rose back on the trolley. As she pressed the plunger on the cafetière she noticed the *With Compliments* card.

Idiot, she berated herself. The hotel's wedding planner must have arranged for the rose to be delivered with her breakfast.

But there was nothing romantic about her wedding to Marco. It was a pragmatic arrangement and she couldn't think why she had wasted money on a dress to be married in.

She felt too on edge to manage more than a couple of bites of croissant. The marriage ceremony was to take place there in the penthouse, and the wedding officiant had been booked for ten-thirty. Leah filled the time by taking a luxurious bubble bath. After she'd dried herself, she smoothed jasmine-scented body lotion onto her skin. Her imagination ran riot as she pictured Marco kissing her neck before trailing his lips down to her breasts…

Cursing her inexplicable fascination with Marco, who was the absolute opposite of *safe*, she spun away from the mirror and forced her mind from the dangerous path it seemed intent on following.

Although her dress wasn't a bridal gown, it was made of white silk, with lace detailing on the bodice, and had narrow shoulder straps and a short skirt. With it she wore high-heeled satin shoes. She left her hair loose and clipped back the sides with diamante slides. On impulse, she broke off the long stem of the white rose on her breakfast tray and tucked the flower into her hair.

Her heart was thumping when she walked into the lounge. The floor-to-ceiling windows ran the length of the room, to make the most of the stunning view over Manhattan, clearly visible now that the storm had passed, leaving a cloudless blue sky, but it wasn't the view that captivated Leah.

Marco must have heard her, although her footsteps had seemed to make no sound on the plush carpet. He turned away from the window and her eyes roamed over his dark suit, crisp white shirt and silver-grey tie. His thick hair was more groomed than usual, and the sexy stubble on his jaw had been trimmed. The scar running down his cheek gave him a piratical look, and the ache inside Leah expanded until the air was forced from her lungs in a ragged sigh.

'*Tesoro.*'

His voice was dark and rich like bittersweet chocolate. As he strode towards her he subjected her to a scorching appraisal; from the silky curls tumbling around her shoulders to the swell of her breasts visible above the neckline of her dress. Finally he moved his eyes down the length of her slender legs to her pretty but impractical stiletto heels.

When he looked up again Leah glimpsed an indefinable expression in his eyes, and oddly she found herself wishing this was real—that they were in love and about to promise themselves to each other for eternity.

He captured her hand and lifted it to his mouth, brushing his lips across her fingers. 'You take my breath away,' he murmured.

A bolt of electricity shot through her fingers and up her arm, and she recalled that she had experienced the same fierce awareness of Marco when he'd stood in for James at the wedding rehearsal. Had it been only a few days ago? It felt like a lifetime since she had fled from Nancarrow Hall.

But this wasn't real, she reminded herself. The admiration in Marco's eyes, just like the tenderness in his voice, was there to convince other people that their relationship was genuine.

'Come and meet my friends,' he said, slipping his arm around her waist and drawing her forward.

Leah had only had eyes for him. But now she realised that they were not alone as a dark-haired man and an ice-cool blonde woman stood up from the sofa.

Marco introduced the couple. 'This is Paolo Bonucci and his wife Ashlyn. They live in Connecticut and flew down to New York this morning to be witnesses at our wedding.'

'It's good to meet you, Leah,' Paolo greeted her. 'I've been friends with Marco since we were at school together, but he still throws up surprises. Ashlyn and I couldn't believe it when he called us yesterday and said he was getting married again. We thought after Karin...' His voice trailed away.

Beneath his friendly tone Leah detected unease, and she saw the quick glance that passed between Paolo and his wife.

'As soon as I met Leah I knew I wanted to marry her,' Marco said smoothly. 'Neither of us could wait—could we *cara*?'

He met her startled gaze with an urbane smile. If he ever wanted a change of career he could star on Broadway, she thought wryly. Why, he almost had *her* convinced that she was the love of his life, instead of a woman who had used his traumatised young son to emotionally blackmail him into marriage.

'We are both very happy for you.' Ashlyn smiled warmly at Leah. 'Your dress is beautiful, and I'd give anything for Titian hair like yours.'

The wedding officiant arrived, and everything felt surreal to Leah as she and Marco stood in front of her at the window, with the Manhattan skyscrapers providing a stunning backdrop.

The civil ceremony was surprisingly brief. Marco said his vows, and the slight huskiness of his voice sent a quiver through her, but she knew the words meant nothing to him and the promises he made were meaningless.

And then it was her turn. Her heart leapt into her throat when the officiant spoke to her.

'Leah, will you take Marco to be your wedded husband, to share your life with him, to love, support and comfort him whatever the future may bring?'

Leah's voice was trapped in her throat. In her mind she was a child again and she heard Grandma Grace's voice. *'Nothing good ever comes from a lie.'* But if she did not marry to claim her inheritance and replace the money her mother had stolen there was a strong chance that Tori would be sent to prison.

She could not let that happen.

Leah's eyes were drawn involuntarily to Marco's chiselled features and she took a deep breath. 'I will.'

No emotion showed in his cool stare, and when the marriage officiant announced that they were man and wife he bent his head and brushed his lips over Leah's in a perfunctory kiss.

Afterwards, they went with Paolo and Ashlyn to an

exclusive restaurant for a champagne brunch. Paolo explained to her that he ran his family's banking business, but that when he was younger he had been a fashion photographer and had met Ashlyn, who had then been a model.

'I was glad to give up modelling and the lifestyle associated with it,' Ashlyn admitted when she and Leah slipped away to the restroom. 'Now, I feel I should apologise for my husband's lack of tact earlier, when he mentioned Marco's first wife. We both knew her. In fact Karin was a friend of mine in our modelling days, but she was much more sociable and loved to party. It was me who introduced her to Marco.' Ashlyn hesitated. 'I suppose he *has* told you about Karin?'

'A little,' Leah murmured.

But all she really knew was that Marco and his wife had divorced a few years before her untimely death, and she was curious to learn more.

'Marco doesn't like to talk about what happened. He was devastated when Karin went off the way she did—'

Ashlyn broke off as a group of teenage girls entered the restroom, talking and giggling loudly. Leah felt frustrated as she followed the American woman back to the table to join the men and knew there would be no further opportunity to discover more about Nicky's mother.

She felt unsettled by Ashlyn's revelation that Marco had been devastated by the break-up with his wife. She couldn't imagine him *devastated*. He was so enigmatic and guarded in his emotions. Was that because he'd been hurt in the past and had vowed never to risk his heart again?

Leah stared at the gold wedding band on her finger. Her heart missed a beat when Marco leaned across the table and covered her hand with his.

'I see you decided to wear the rose. I'm glad you like it,' he said quietly.

'Was it from you?' She touched the white rose in her hair, and a feeling she could not explain unfurled inside her when he smiled. She tried to remind herself that the rose, like the tourmaline engagement ring, were just props to make their marriage seem believable.

'Your eyes are the colour of the ocean and just as mysterious. What are you thinking, I wonder?' he asked.

The deep melody of his voice felt like a caress over her ultra-sensitive nerve-endings. She couldn't admit to herself, let alone to Marco, that she was jealous of the ghost of his first wife.

'I'm thinking of practicalities,' she told him coolly. 'I need to send a copy of the marriage certificate to the solicitors who are executors of my grandmother's will as soon as possible, so that they will release my inheritance.'

His withdrew his hand and leaned back in his chair, his eyes narrowing on her face. 'How very sensible of you,' he drawled. 'It would not do for either of us to forget the reasons for our marriage.'

CHAPTER EIGHT

IT WAS LATE afternoon when the De Valle private jet took off from Teterboro Airport in New Jersey en route to Italy. Nicky fell asleep almost as soon as they were in the air. He was worn out from his trip to the zoo the previous day and the sleepover—during which, according to Marco's cousin Chiara, none of the children had got much sleep.

Marco carried the little boy into the smaller of the two bedrooms at the rear of the plane and covered him with a blanket before returning to the main cabin, where Leah was sitting on one of the cream leather sofas.

She had slipped off her shoes and tucked her feet beneath her. He paused in the doorway and studied her. The sharp tug of desire in his groin made him catch his breath. His virgin bride was still wearing the sexy dress she'd married him in. Her mix of innocence and sensuality filled Marco with a restlessness which promised that the flight to Naples would be hellishly frustrating.

With any other woman he would have suggested making use of the plane's master bedroom to create their own in-flight entertainment. But he had vowed that he would resist the chemistry which had simmered between them when they'd been in New York. Presumably Leah had remained a virgin into her twenties because she was looking for something in a relationship—something that he was damned sure *he* couldn't give her, Marco brooded.

It did not help that he was certain she wanted him too. The hungry looks she darted at him when she thought he wouldn't notice would tempt a saint—and he was far from saintly, he acknowledged with a grimace. He had spent the previous evening alone in a bar, and hadn't dared return to the hotel until late, when he'd been sure she had gone to bed.

Leah shifted position, causing her dress to ride up her leg and expose a smooth, toned thigh. Marco imagined pushing the dress up to her waist and slipping his hand into her panties... He cursed silently when his arousal was instant and uncomfortably hard. *Dio*, she made him feel like a teenager with a surfeit of hormones.

He sat down on the sofa opposite her, fascinated by the soft pink stain that ran under her skin as she quickly averted her gaze from him. The stewardess came and served him his customary whisky and soda before retreating to the staff cabin at the front of the plane.

He stretched his long legs out in front of him and took a sip of his drink. 'You have gone to extreme lengths to claim your inheritance,' he murmured. 'What are you planning to do with the money?'

Emotion flickered across Leah's face but was gone before Marco could decipher it.

'I want to buy a house. It's impossible to get on the housing ladder without a decent deposit. My teaching salary isn't huge, and by the time I've paid rent and bills it's hard to save much each month.' She gave a faintly wistful smile. 'I'd like a house with roses growing around the front door.'

'I would have thought you would be more concerned about the location of a property and the number of bedrooms?'

'I don't mind about those things. When I was child I used to look at pictures of houses like that in magazines and pretend that I lived there.'

'You told my aunt that you spent some of your childhood in Italy and can speak the language?'

'Yes.'

Marco felt curious at her reluctance to talk about her childhood. 'You sound as though you did not like living away from England?'

She sighed. 'I had a nomadic childhood.'

'Tell me more,' he said softly when she fell silent.

'Why?'

'Because you are my wife and we are going to spend a year together. I'd like to get to know you better, *cara*.'

It was the truth, Marco realised. Leah intrigued him more than any woman had ever done.

She looked away from him and Marco sensed that trust was an issue for her—as it was for him, he acknowledged.

After a few moments she gave another sigh. 'When my dad died, I think my mum must have struggled with depression—although I was far too young at the time to realise it. Maybe she wanted to get away from her memories of him, but for whatever reason we moved constantly around Europe, staying with other artists for a few months before moving on to the next place. Eventually we settled at the commune in Tuscany. But even then we didn't have a proper home. The commune members all shared various spaces for sleeping and eating. Eventually we moved back to England and I went to the local comprehensive school, but I found it hard to fit in,' she said ruefully.

Marco pictured Leah as a little girl who longed to call one place home. His own childhood had been very different—structured around term time as a boarder at prep school and then a top English public school. In the holidays he'd stayed at Nancarrow Hall, or with his father's relatives in Capri. But, like Leah, he had wanted to feel a sense of belonging.

Her desire to buy a house that she could call home was understandable, but he couldn't shake off the idea that she was not being completely honest about why she was so desperate for her inheritance.

'Why did you and your mother return to England?'

'My brother was very ill.'

She drew her legs up and hugged her knees. Marco noticed that her toenails were painted a bright coral colour that he found surprising, considering her penchant for all things beige.

'Sammy was two when he was diagnosed with a degenerative neurological disorder which meant that he gradually lost the ability to walk, talk and feed himself. His father—my stepdad—didn't stick around for long, and then there was just me and mum to look after Sammy.'

Marco heard the bite in Leah's voice and guessed she was making a point. She believed he had not tried to keep in contact with Nicky. It wasn't true, he thought bitterly. He had employed private detectives to search for his ex-wife and his son, but Karin had changed her surname in a deliberate ploy to hide Nicky from him.

What a fool he had been, Marco thought savagely, to believe she'd had a change of heart and become willing to allow him to share custody of his son. He'd immediately gone to Mexico to meet Karin, but she had dashed his hopes.

In his mind he heard her sharp voice.

'You can take Nicky to Italy, but you'll have to pay. I'll let you have him for ten million dollars.'

Marco forced his mind away from painful memories as Leah spoke again.

'We moved back to England so that Sammy could receive specialist care, but children with the illness he suffered from rarely live to be teenagers, and he died when he was six.' Her face softened. 'Despite all his problems he was a happy, delightful little boy, and his smile lit up the room.'

'It must have been a difficult time for you and your mother.' Marco knew his words were inadequate. He understood the pain of loss, but at least he had been reunited with his son. 'You had a huge amount of responsibility put upon you when most girls of your age would have been experimenting with make-up and boyfriends.'

Leah gave a rueful smile. 'Yes, I was too busy helping with Sammy and trying to take care of Mum to have time for the normal teenage stuff. I felt older than other people of my age, and I suppose that created a distance between me and my peers.'

'I can understand that,' Marco murmured. 'From the age of seven I knew my destiny was to be CEO of De Valle Caffè—the company my great-grandfather had started, which my grandfather and father had built into a hugely successful brand. When other boys at school were flunking their exams and going out drinking I was studying hard and hoping I could live up to the expectations of my family.'

She nodded. 'I think my brother's illness gave me a different perspective on life. I was thirteen when he died. I decided that I wanted to teach, and Sammy was my inspiration to qualify as a special educational needs teacher.'

Marco's eyes met Leah's and they fell silent in a moment of shared empathy. They'd both had to grow up quickly.

'How is your mother now?' he asked. 'Has she been able to come to terms with the tragedies in her life?'

He wondered why Leah suddenly seemed tense, and knew the rapport between them had disappeared.

'Mum has *never* got over losing Sammy. I'll never give up on her, though,' she said in a low voice.

There was a mystery there, Marco brooded, but Leah clearly was not going to explain.

She picked up a magazine from the coffee table and flicked through it. He opened his laptop and tried to concentrate on a financial report, but his awareness of Leah was an unwelcome distraction.

Some time later Marco looked up from his screen and saw that she had fallen asleep. His eyes were drawn to the steady rise and fall of her breasts, framed by the white lace dress. Her cheek was resting on her hand and her lips were slightly parted. She looked as pure as driven snow, and yet at the same time incredibly sexy, with her vibrant hair spilling in silky curls around her shoulders.

Cursing beneath his breath, he stood up and lifted her into his arms. She stirred, but did not wake as he carried her to the double bedroom and laid her on the bed.

He knew the sensible thing to do would be to leave her to sleep and return to the main cabin, to continue working. But right now 'sensible' had never seemed less inviting.

Marco ran his hand around the back of his neck and felt a knot of tension. He'd hardly slept last night—although it had been the knowledge that he was alone in the penthouse with Leah rather than the thunderstorm which had kept him awake. The different time zones between the US and Europe meant that they would land in Naples at around eight o'clock tomorrow morning, and he knew he should try and get some sleep.

It was not the wedding night he would have planned, he mused as he kicked off his shoes and lay down next to his virgin bride. He'd never planned to marry again. Leah had forced his hand, and he had been angry. But he had discovered a vulnerability about her as well as a strong will, he thought ruefully, remembering her refusal to allow him to buy her clothes.

The unsettling thought struck him that he *liked* her—which he had not anticipated.

'There's Villa Rosa up ahead.'

Marco pointed towards an enormous pink-walled house standing on a rocky headland. The undisguised pleasure in his voice captured Leah's attention. Since they had boarded the helicopter in Naples, for the short flight to Capri, he had visibly relaxed.

Her breath snagged in her throat as his mouth curved in a crooked smile. His eyes were hidden behind designer shades. Dark stubble covered his jaw, and he looked utterly gorgeous in a pale denim shirt open at the throat, so that she could see a vee of olive-gold skin and a sprinkling of black chest hair.

She cast her mind back to earlier that morning, when she'd woken from a deep sleep and found herself in the bedroom of his plane which had still been heading to Italy. Her heart had jolted when she'd turned her head on the pillow and discovered Marco lying next to her. A blanket had covered both of them. He had been awake, and there had been a speculative gleam in his eyes when she'd peeped beneath the blanket and seen her relief that they were both fully clothed.

'You fell asleep and I thought you would be more comfortable on the bed,' he had explained. 'I was tired so I joined you, because Nicky was asleep in the other bedroom.'

Leah had felt herself blush as she'd recalled her erotic

dream, in which her hands had been roaming over Marco's body.

'I hope you stayed on your side of the mattress,' she'd muttered, not liking the wicked glint in his eyes.

'*I* did—but you cuddled up to *me* and it was difficult to resist you.'

She'd stared at him in horror. 'Are you saying that we…?'

'*Dio*, what do you take me for?' he'd growled, the amusement disappearing from his eyes. 'Your virtue remains safe.' He'd sprung up from the bed and scowled. 'If I had made love to you I guarantee you would *not* have slept through the experience. When I have sex with a woman I make sure that she is a willing participant—not comatose,' he said bitingly.

But now Marco was clearly in a better mood, and it was easy to understand why as the helicopter flew over the azure sea, sparkling like a precious jewel in the bright sunshine.

'Those rock formations coming out of the sea are called *faraglioni*,' he told her as they flew above three enormous limestone stacks. 'Behind us on the mainland you can see Mount Vesuvius—which is still an active volcano, although it hasn't erupted for many years.'

Minutes later the helicopter landed in the grounds of Villa Rosa and Leah climbed out after Marco. There was a tense moment when they both turned to help Nicky. The little boy hesitated, his eyes on his father, but he put his hand in Leah's.

Marco gave a shrug, but she noticed a nerve flicker in his cheek. If only he had scooped Nicky into his arms and swung him down from the helicopter, she thought. She did not understand why he kept his son at an emotional and physical distance.

They walked through a lush green garden, bejewelled with colourful plants and flowers: purple lavender, shocking pink bougainvillea and vibrant orange lantana. Marco led the way around to the front of the villa, where a steep driveway descended to the road. In every direction there was a panoramic view of the sea and Leah thought it must be the most beautiful place on earth.

'There are roses growing around the front door,' she said with a faint sigh.

Indeed, white roses clambered over the pink walls and framed the entrance, exuding a delicate fragrance that filled the porch.

'My great-grandfather commissioned the villa to be built here on the site of a Roman palace,' Marco explained as he ushered her through the door. 'He named the house after his wife and had the walls painted pink in her honour.'

The interior of the villa was a sumptuous mix of classic and modern décor, with cool marble floors and vaulted ceilings. Tall windows allowed light to flood in and framed spectacular views of the Bay of Naples. Through a set of French doors Leah saw an infinity pool and a sunbathing terrace, tennis courts and another large garden filled with flowers.

'You have a lovely home,' she murmured, glancing around an elegant but relaxing lounge, which was furnished with big, comfortable-looking sofas. Brightly coloured cushions and rugs added interest to the room, and on a low table was a framed photo of Nicky which must have been taken recently.

Next to it was a photograph of a beautiful woman. The picture was a professional shot and the woman staring directly into the camera was evidently a model. She was stunningly attractive, with long golden hair and slanting brown eyes.

'My ex-wife,' Marco said when he saw Leah staring at the photo. He picked it up and held it out to his son. 'Your *mamma* was pretty and kind and she loved you very much, Nicky,' he said softly.

Was Marco still in love with his first wife?

Leah could not explain why her stomach dipped. According to Ashlyn Bonucci he had been devastated when Karin had left him, which suggested that he hadn't wanted his marriage to end.

They climbed a sweeping staircase and Nicky ran ahead into his toy-filled bedroom. Further along the corridor Marco opened a door and ushered Leah into an airy room decorated in soft blue tones.

'This is your room. If you want anything press the bell and one of the household staff will come.' He paused on his way out of the door. 'I will be hosting a dinner party this evening. It was arranged a few weeks ago—before I knew that I would be blackmailed into marriage,' he said drily. 'But it will be a useful introduction for you to my social circle. I suggest you wear the red velvet gown.'

When Marco had stepped into the corridor and closed the door behind him, Leah gave in to a childish urge and poked her tongue out at him. Obviously she was relieved that he did not expect her to share his bedroom, she told herself.

Remembering his instruction about what she should wear to dinner she realised she didn't have a choice. It would have to be the velvet dress because she had ignored his order to buy multiple outfits suitable for her role as his wife.

Suddenly her legs felt wobbly and she sank down onto the bed. *She'd done it!* She had met the stipulation in her grandmother's will and emailed the executors a copy of her marriage certificate. Her inheritance had immediately been paid into her bank account, and she'd transferred thirty thousand pounds to the boss of the building firm her mum had taken the money from.

Tori was safe from prosecution and—vitally—had agreed that she needed professional help to overcome her alcoholism.

When Leah had been in Cornwall she'd visited a rehabilitation clinic which had excellent reviews. The Haven offered an intensive therapy program at a residential facility, followed by ongoing support to help its patients live their lives free from addictive substances. The fees were significant, but Leah had told Tori that a legal loophole had allowed her to claim her inheritance without marrying. The lie was better than admitting that she had negotiated a marriage deal with a man she hardly knew.

She inspected her bedroom and discovered a charming en suite bathroom. Her faithful holdall had been brought to her room, and she unzipped it and unpacked the few clothes she'd taken to New York. A door next to the bathroom led into a walk-in wardrobe, and her jaw dropped when she discovered racks of clothes there in her size. There were outfits for daytime and evening, as well as exquisite lingerie and nightgowns.

Leah recognised the dresses were the same ones she'd tried on at the shop on Fifth Avenue. But *she* hadn't bought them. The only explanation was that Marco had given his credit card to the personal stylist and paid for the clothes.

Her temper was simmering as she opened yet another door, expecting to see more storage space. Instead she found herself in an adjoining bedroom. It was a much bigger room than hers, and the colour scheme was an opulent mix of black, gold and rich burgundy. At one end of the room stood an enormous bed with a leather headboard. Her heart missed a beat when she saw a large mirror on the ceiling above the bed. Clearly the master bedroom had been designed for seduction and sex.

'You should be careful, *cara*. If you persist in barging into my bedroom I might think that you want our marriage to be real after all,' Marco drawled. 'Do you like my mirror?'

She swung her startled gaze away from the bed and saw him sprawled in a black leather armchair. Heat swept through her and burned hottest in her feminine core as she pictured them lying on those black satin sheets, their naked bodies reflected in the mirror above them.

She frantically tried to dismiss the erotic images in her mind and make her temper flare in response to his arrogance.

'I'm not here for...for what you're thinking,' she choked. 'I didn't realise that my room is connected to yours. I want an explanation for those clothes in the wardrobe.'

Marco stood up in a lithe movement and crossed the room with long strides, halting in front of her before she had time to retreat back through the door into the safety of her own room. The spicy scent of his cologne teased her senses, but she refused to be overwhelmed by his potent masculinity.

'Well?' she demanded.

'I have explained to you that people will expect my wife to wear haute couture,' he said, sounding bored. 'Think of the clothes as your uniform while you are married to me.'

'I'll pay back every penny of what they cost out of my inheritance.'

Leah bit her lip, aware that without Marco she would not have the means to do so—or to help her mum.

'I can't tell you how relieved I am to finally be able to claim the money my grandmother left me. I'm grateful for what you have done for me. I intend to keep to my side of our deal, and I'll start working on lesson plans for Nicky straight away.'

Marco gave her a brooding look. 'There is a room next to the playroom which you can use as a classroom. Give me a list of anything you need—books and so on—and I will arrange for them to be delivered.'

He moved back across the room, and Leah released a breath which she hadn't realised until then that she'd been holding.

'I intend to hire a nanny for Nicky,' he said. At her look of surprise he went on smoothly, 'Your role is to be his teacher. I don't expect you to care for Nicky all the time. For one thing you will have duties to fulfil as my wife—being my social hostess and accompanying me to business functions,' he explained drily when she frowned. 'However, I'll have to ask you to look after Nicky until I have found a suitable nanny.'

She nodded. 'Of course. But what about you? It doesn't sound like you plan to spend much time with him.'

A shadow flickered across Marco's face. 'Nicky will respond better to a nanny. You have seen how he shies away from me,' he said grimly.

'That's because you're a stranger to him.' Leah could not hide her frustration. 'You and I both know what it was like to lose a parent when we were children. Put yourself in Nicky's shoes. His world was destroyed when he lost his mother. He was thrown into a new life in a strange country with *you*—the father he doesn't know. You've asked me to help Nicky overcome his problems. I'm beginning to think that *you* are the biggest problem.'

She should not have blamed Marco, Leah thought, much later that night. His stern features hadn't revealed a glimmer of emotion when she'd suggested that he was to blame for his strained relationship with Nicky, but she'd sensed that he had been hurt.

He was an impossible man to understand.

She hadn't spoken to him for the rest of the day. Exploring the villa and its grounds had taken up the morning, and Nicky had nodded enthusiastically when she'd suggested swimming in the pool after lunch. She knew he couldn't swim, and one of the staff had found a pair of inflatable armbands for the little boy to wear.

Leah hadn't packed swimwear when she'd left Nancarrow Hall in a hurry. But in her wardrobe she had discovered a selection of gorgeous bikinis. They were much skimpier than anything she would have chosen, and she had felt self-conscious when she'd realised that Marco's study overlooked the pool and he might have been watching her and Nicky through the window.

He had come into Nicky's bedroom as she was reading him a bedtime story that evening. She'd left him to say goodnight to the little boy and gone to her room to change for the dinner party. Now, butterflies danced in her stomach as she applied more make-up than usual and bundled her hair into a reasonably neat chignon before stepping into the red velvet gown.

When she walked into the drawing room Marco said nothing for several long seconds while his eyes roamed over her. He looked stunning in a dinner suit and black silk shirt, and Leah's heart thudded as he strolled towards her, holding a rose with a short stem in his fingers.

'Sei bellissima,' he said, tucking the rose into her hair. 'But you are nervous,' he murmured when he stroked his thumb over her bottom lip and felt a betraying quiver.

'This is not my world,' she whispered.

The grandeur of the villa, the discreet but obvious signs

of huge wealth, even the designer dress she was wearing, made her feel like an imposter.

'It is for the next year.' Marco lifted her hand and pressed his lips against the gold wedding band beside the tourmaline ring on her finger. His eyes glinted. 'You made your bed and now you must lie in it, *cara*.'

In fact the dinner party was not the ordeal Leah had dreaded. If any of Marco's guests were surprised when he introduced her as his wife, they were far too well-mannered to comment. It helped that she was able to chat to them in Italian, and during the evening she had felt her confidence grow.

There had been a moment when she'd glanced across the table and found Marco watching her. She'd imagined what it would be like if their marriage was real. Would they both be impatient for the party to end so that they could spend the rest of the night making love in that decadent bedroom with the mirror above the bed?

Now it was almost midnight, and Marco and the household staff had retired for the night. But Leah's body clock hadn't adapted to the different time zone and she could not sleep. She slid out of bed and knelt on the window seat. The night was clear, and a full moon dappled the sea with its silvery gleam.

Suddenly a cry that sounded like an animal in pain rent the air. It was a chilling noise, and Leah's blood froze when it came again, raw and agonised, from the other side of the connecting door. Could Marco be ill?

Biting her lip, she stood by the door and listened. He was shouting in a harsh voice that grew louder and more urgent.

'*Karin! Come back!*'

CHAPTER NINE

'IT'S JUST A DREAM. Wake up, Marco!'

A hand on his shoulder…shaking him. A soft voice… Leah's voice.

Marco opened his eyes and saw her pretty face close to his as she leaned over the bed. He realised that she had switched on the bedside lamp. He shoved his hair off his brow with an unsteady hand. His mind was still trapped in the nightmare of Karin driving away with his son.

'Nicky…'

'I looked in on Nicky about half an hour ago. He's fast asleep. Lucky him. My internal clock can't work out if it's day or night and I'm wide awake.'

Leah spoke in a light voice and Marco realised that she was trying to distract his thoughts from the dream.

He sat upright and met her concerned gaze. Her green eyes were deep enough to drown in, and he wanted to lose himself in her and forget the images in his head, the fear that he could still taste in his mouth.

'Do you want a drink?' She picked up the glass of water from the bedside table and held it to his lips.

The simple, caring gesture shocked him. Tenderness had not been a feature of his childhood—his mother had married his father for money and had dutifully produced the next De Valle heir. The only time Marco had received anything like affection had been at boarding school, when the matron there had been briskly sympathetic after he'd broken his collarbone playing rugby.

When he'd met Karin, sex had lured him into believing that physical intimacy was love—but he'd quickly realised his mistake.

He leaned back against the headboard and watched Leah set the glass back down. As she perched on the edge of the bed her blue satin negligee rode up to reveal her slim thighs. Marco was wide awake now, and his hunger for her was a ravenous beast.

'I'm guessing your nightmare was about the accident,' she murmured. 'Would it help to talk about it?'

'I don't want to *talk*.'

He watched her eyes widen with the awareness that had simmered between them all evening. When she'd looked at him during dinner the naked longing in her eyes had made him instantly hard. If they had been alone he would have been tempted to sweep away the china and glass so that he could make love to her on the polished mahogany dining table.

A pink stain ran under her skin and the pulse at the base of her throat jerked erratically. 'I should go,' she said in a low voice.

But she remained sitting there on his bed as he leaned towards her. She flicked her tongue over her lips and Marco's gut clenched. Her skin was the colour of pale cream, dusted with tiny golden freckles. He wanted to taste each one.

Out in the hallway the clock struck midnight. The witching hour—and he was bewitched.

She shivered when he ran his finger over the narrow strap of her nightgown. 'Pretty,' he growled as he slid the strap a little way down her arm and brushed his lips over her bare shoulder.

'Marco...' she whispered, with uncertainty in her voice and something else that made his need darker and more dangerous.

'You came to my room, *cara*.'

'I heard you call out. You sounded—' Leah broke off.

Marco guessed it had been bad. His throat felt raw and he remembered that in the dream he had been shouting. Snatches of the nightmare returned. The car with Nicky inside. Smoke and flames as he fought to open the door and save his son.

'I thought there might be something I could do to help you.'

Leah's voice pulled him from the darkness of his thoughts.

'There is.'

He leaned even closer to her and sank his hands into her glorious hair. And then he did what he had wanted to do for ever, it seemed. He kissed her.

Her soft sigh filled his mouth and the sweet taste of her made him groan. He fell back against the pillows, pulling her down with him, his lips not leaving hers for a second. Her riotous curls cascaded around them like a fragrant curtain and he wound his fingers through the silky strands, angling her head so that he could kiss her again and again.

And she let him. More than let him, Marco thought, aware of an odd feeling inside him when she parted her lips beneath his. He told himself the feeling was satisfaction that he finally had her where he wanted her—in his bed.

He rolled her onto her back and stretched out next to her, propping himself up on one elbow. Her breasts rose and fell jerkily, and a flush of sexual warmth spread down her neck and décolletage.

'Tell me what you want,' he commanded. 'For me to kiss you here?' He pressed his lips to the little hollow behind her ear and heard her draw a shaky breath. 'Or here?' He trailed kisses down her cheek to the corner of her mouth.

'Yes.'

The simple honesty of her surrender stormed through him and Marco reminded himself that this was about sex—nothing more. He traced his mouth over the slopes of her breasts to the lacy edge of her negligee and untied the ribbon that held the front together. Slowly he pushed the satin aside and bared the breasts that he'd fantasised about far too often. He exhaled heavily as he studied the perfect roundness of her pale breasts tipped with rosy nipples.

'Ah, beauty…' He hardly recognised his own voice, so thick was it—so slurred with desire, as if he'd been drugged.

He had never wanted any woman as desperately as he wanted Leah. The realisation set an alarm bell ringing in his mind, but he could not resist the siren song of her body, and he liked it too much when a shiver ran through her as he cupped one creamy mound in his palm and bent his head to draw the stiff peak at its centre into his mouth.

The low moan she made tore through him. Surely his virgin bride could not be *such* an innocent? But he sensed that this was all new for her, and felt something worryingly like possessiveness surge through him.

If he was a better man he would send her back through the connecting door and advise her to keep it locked from now on. But the scent of her teased his senses: a delicate floral perfume mixed with the earthy sweetness of her feminine arousal. His body felt taut with need, but Leah needed careful handling and he was determined not to rush her.

Leah sucked in a breath. She was shaking, and every inch of her body felt too hot, too needy. Marco's hands were everywhere—cupping her breasts, then sliding down over her stomach and thighs. She had not even been aware of him removing her negligee. His fingertips traced patterns over her skin and every caress made the fire inside her burn hotter.

When he flicked his thumb-pad across the hard peak of one nipple, and then its twin, she twisted her hips restlessly, wanting to be even closer to him, desperate for him to assuage the ache deep in her pelvis.

'Touch me.'

The rasp of his voice made the trembling in her limbs worse. She placed her hands on his chest and felt the uneven thud of his heart. He was all muscle and sinew, darkly tanned skin and whorls of black chest hair that arrowed over his taut abdomen and disappeared beneath the sheet draped low over his hips.

The idea that he might be naked beneath the sheet made her heart thud harder. But her thoughts scattered when he slipped his hand between her thighs and stroked his finger over the lace panel of her knickers. An age-old instinct took over and she arched against his hand, needing more, needing—

'Oh...' A shudder ran through her as he pushed her panties aside so that he had access to the molten heart of her femininity. The wetness between her legs betrayed her. She could no longer deny that she desired him, and she caught her breath as he stroked his finger up and down her opening before he parted her and slid in deep.

It felt different from when she touched herself. It was shockingly intimate and utterly addictive as he began to move his hand in a rhythmic motion: pressing forward, withdrawing, pressing, withdrawing... Ripples tightened across her belly as pleasure built inside her. She closed her eyes, her entire being focused on the slide of his finger.

He rubbed his thumb-pad against the hard nub of her core and she shattered. It was indescribable—starbursts of glorious sensation so intense that it almost hurt. She'd read about mind-blowing orgasms, but this was so much more than she'd imagined—emotionally as well as physically.

She felt closer to Marco than she'd ever felt to any other human being, and gave a sigh of protest when he rolled away from her.

'I'm not going far, *cara*.'

His voice was indulgent, and the satisfaction Leah heard in his tone evoked a faint unease when he murmured, 'I assume you want *me* to take care of protection?'

Her eyes flew open and she stared at their reflection in the mirror above the bed. She did not recognise that wanton woman with her wild red hair spread across the pillows, naked apart from the strip of blue lace between her legs that had not been any barrier to Marco's bold caresses.

How had she got here?

A memory pushed through the fog of sexual delight. In her mind she heard Marco shouting a name. *Karin*.

He was opening the bedside drawer and taking out a packet of condoms. The cold reality of the situation doused Leah like a shower of ice. She had been compelled by Marco's haunting cries to rush into his room and wake him from his nightmare. When he'd kissed her she'd gone up in flames. But she was not the woman he wanted.

'*No!*' She jerked upright and grabbed her negligee, dragging it inelegantly over her head.

'No?' Marco's eyes narrowed until they were gleaming slits of polished steel, but he did not move towards her or try to prevent her from scrambling across the bed away from him. 'That's not the message you gave me a few minutes ago.'

'I won't be a substitute for your first wife.'

He stiffened and jerked his head back, shock and another indefinable emotion chasing across his stern features.

Silence stretched between them, simmering with tension.

'You called out for Karin in your dream,' Leah muttered.

While Marco had been kissing her, had he been thinking of his beautiful wife, whose photograph he kept in every room of his home?

'I'm not her.'

He laughed then, but it was an oddly harsh sound that held no humour. 'No. You are certainly *not* her.'

She caught her lower lip between her teeth as she tied the ribbon at the front of her negligee with hands that visibly trembled. She felt vulnerable and exposed—humiliated when she thought of how he'd watched her in the throes of orgasm.

With a muffled cry she went to stand up, but he caught hold of her arm and tugged her back down onto the bed.

'Leah. You are the only woman I want right now.' Marco feathered his fingertips along her collarbone. 'You feel the attraction between us as much as I do,' he murmured in a molten honey voice as he held his thumb over the pulse thudding at the base of her throat. 'This fire is not going to burn out any time soon.'

But all fires died when there was nothing to feed the flames, Leah thought. The spark of desire Marco felt for her would not last long.

He bent his dark head and she felt the silken brush of his hair on her skin as he pressed his lips against the side of her neck. 'You want to give yourself to me, beauty.'

So confident. So sure of himself—and of her. But she wasn't gullible, as her mother had been too often with lovers who had promised everything and given nothing.

'No,' she said firmly, pulling away from him and sliding off the bed. 'Sex isn't part of our deal.'

She sped into her own room as if the hounds of hell were snapping at her heels. As she shut the door she heard Marco's lazy drawl.

'It will be, *cara*. A year is a long time to fight the raging desire we both feel.'

The sound of the helicopter flying over Villa Rosa sent Leah's stomach into a nose-dive. She had learned from the housekeeper, Assumpta, that Marco was coming home today. It would have been nice if he'd phoned her and told her of his plans, she thought with a grimace. But he hadn't been in contact for the past week, since he'd left Capri to go on a business trip.

She had dreaded facing him at breakfast the morning after she'd gone into his room. Memories of how he had seduced her with his addictive kisses and pleasured her with his wickedly inventive hands had made her shudder with shame. But the butterflies in her stomach had been for nothing.

Signor De Valle had left in the helicopter very early, Assumpta had explained.

Now, Leah collected up the number cards she had been using to test Nicky's numeracy skills. 'That's enough sums for today. I think your *papà* has arrived. Are you looking forward to seeing him?'

Nicky nodded, and his shy smile tugged on her heart.

Every afternoon they went to the pool, so that she could teach him to swim. Supporting his little body while he kicked his legs reminded her of being in the hydrotherapy pool with her brother. Sammy had loved those sessions with the physiotherapist, but as his illness had progressed he'd become too weak to swim.

Being with Nicky was helping to mend the hole that had ripped open Leah's heart when Sammy had died. But her role in Nicky's life was not permanent, and it was important that he developed a trusting relationship with his father. Sadly that was impossible when Marco was never around.

'Let's go and see if Assumpta has your lunch ready,' she said to the little boy. 'Maybe your *papà* will come swimming this afternoon?'

He would if *she* had anything to do with it, she vowed a short while later, as she tried to ignore the frantic thud of her heart and knocked on the study door.

At his curt command she stepped into the room. Marco was on his phone, of course. He looked over at her and the predatory hunger in his eyes was shockingly exciting. Heat flared in her belly and she felt a betraying blush spread over her cheeks.

He finished the call and leaned back in his chair. 'Don't hover as if you're planning to scamper out of the door like a frightened rabbit. I'm not going to bite you,' he drawled.

She ground her teeth as she sat down on the chair in front of his desk. 'I'm here to discuss your son,' Leah said stiffly. 'And to show you this.'

She pushed a piece of paper on which Nicky had drawn a picture of his father across the desk.

A nerve flickered in Marco's cheek as he stared at the childish representation of himself. In the picture, the jagged line running down his face was obviously meant to be his scar. Nicky had scribbled it in red crayon over the paper.

'I asked him if the red was meant to be blood and he became upset,' Leah said quietly.

'What does it mean? Why did Nicky draw this?'

'I don't know. I'm not a psychotherapist.' She leaned

across the desk and held Marco's gaze. 'But I know Nicky needs to spend more time with you. I am convinced that his problems are linked to his relationship, or lack of one, with *you*. He needs you to be more involved with him.'

Leah gave a sigh of frustration when Marco stood up abruptly and strode over to the window.

She stared at his stiff back. 'Don't you *want* to be closer to Nicky?'

'Of course I do,' he said, in an agonised voice that tugged at Leah's heart.

He spun round and glared at her, and she was startled by the raw emotion on his face. His skin was drawn tight over his cheekbones and his scar was a livid white mark standing out against his olive complexion.

'I don't know how to be a good father.'

'You had a good relationship with your own father, didn't you?' she probed gently.

'I didn't spend much time with him, to be honest. He worked away for weeks at a time, and when he came back to Nancarrow Hall he was mainly interested in talking to me about the business. He used to joke that he was training me early to take his place.' Marco shrugged. 'Perhaps he had a premonition that he would die young.'

Leah remembered Marco had told her that after his father had died and his mother had remarried he had been sent away to school.

'Who ran the company until you were old enough to be CEO?' she asked.

'Tia Benedetta's late husband—Tio Federico.' Marco's face softened 'He was a good, kind man and he treated me like the son he never had.'

'*You* have a son.' Leah was too agitated to remain sitting, and she jumped up and walked around the desk. 'I implore you to make time for Nicky. You are the only parent he has and you must be the hands-on father he is so desperate for—starting from now.'

'You don't understand.' A nerve jumped in his cheek. 'When Nicky was inside the wreckage after the accident I could smell petrol. I was scared the car would catch fire before I could save him.' Marco swallowed convulsively. 'Finally I managed to get the door open. Nicky was wearing a seat belt, but he was limp and grey and I believed he was dead.'

Leah's heart clenched. The horror of the accident had left Marco traumatised as well as Nicky, she realised. But Marco's way of dealing with his emotions was to ignore them.

'Are you afraid to love your son because you can't bear the idea of losing him to another accident or a serious illness?' she said softly.

His jaw clenched. 'How the hell can you know that?'

'When my brother died it hurt so much I never wanted to love anyone again. But none of us can live our lives in fear of what might happen in the future. Nicky needs to know that you love him.'

'I don't think he likes me.' Marco ran his fingers through his hair until it stood on end.

'He doesn't *know* you.' Leah put her hand on Marco's arm. 'Take some time off work, turn off your laptop and phone and give fatherhood a chance.'

His eyes locked with hers, and Leah felt as though her heart was being squeezed when he said gruffly, 'I need you to help me.'

'I will. We made a deal, remember?' she said lightly, trying to ease the tension.

He gave her a speculative look. 'I am hardly likely to forget, *cara*.'

This was a different Marco. He was allowing her to

see the man behind the mask and revealing that he was vulnerable—at least where his son was concerned. When she had believed him to be cold and heartless it had been easier to tell herself that her awareness of him was a purely physical response, Leah thought ruefully. But now she had discovered that he was a complex man and her feelings for him were complicated.

She suddenly wished that they had met in the normal way and been attracted to each other without the marriage negotiation which was a barrier between them. Instead she was his wife in name only. Which was what she wanted—wasn't it?

CHAPTER TEN

FOR THE FIRST few days he did not go to his office in Naples, Marco felt cut adrift from the life he'd known since he was twenty-one. The responsibility of heading the family company, which had been entrusted to him, had dominated his waking hours for the past fourteen years, and he was the first to admit that he wasn't good at delegating.

But he was doing it—and slowly he was starting to see the rewards.

That first afternoon when he'd joined Leah and Nicky in the pool had been strained. His son had been wary of him, reinforcing Marco's conviction that he wasn't a natural father. He'd felt a fool, frankly, standing in the shallow end of the pool while he tried to coax Nicky to leave Leah's side.

'Talk to him about what?' he'd muttered, when she had suggested he tried to have a conversation with the little boy.

'Tell him about the things you used to do when you were his age,' she advised. 'Use your imagination.'

At the time his imagination had had him visualising untying the strings of her halter-neck bikini and peeling the gold triangles of material away from her breasts. Silently cursing his out-of-control libido, he'd searched his mind for something to say to his son.

'When I was a boy I lived in England, in that big old house where you fell in the lake.'

It hadn't been the best start, Marco admitted, recalling how he'd scolded Nicky then. He remembered that Leah had been furious with him as she'd sprung to his son's defence.

'My *papà* used to take me out on that lake in a boat,' he'd told Nicky.

Memories had surfaced of times when he and his father had gone fishing together. Happy memories that he'd forgotten, or maybe buried inside him when his father had died so suddenly. And Marco had realised that he had a lot to tell his son about Vincenzo De Valle—Nicky's grandfather.

Two weeks had passed since then, and there had been a huge improvement in Marco's relationship with Nicky. The little boy no longer shied away from him, and he seemed more relaxed when they were together—which was often.

Marco had discovered a world of train sets, toy cars and Nicky's favourite books. Goals had been erected on the lawn so they could play football, and daily sessions in the pool meant that Nicky could now swim without water wings.

Things were good—but they would be even better if Marco wasn't so sexually frustrated that he was climbing the walls.

He glanced over his shoulder to the stern of the motor cruiser, where Leah was sitting with Nicky. The little boy loved going on the boat, and they were returning from a trip to visit the famous Blue Grotto. As they sped over the waves the breeze blew Leah's red curls around her face and she laughed and caught her hair in her hand, winding it up and securing it with a clip on top of her head.

She became more beautiful every day, Marco mused.

Her skin had gained a light tan, and he now knew that the golden freckles on her nose and cheeks were also sprinkled over her breasts.

That night she'd come to his room to wake him from his nightmare was constantly in his mind. Her gorgeous body had been so responsive to his caresses, and her soft cries as she'd climaxed beneath his hand had fuelled his desire. He hadn't trusted himself to be near her and had left the villa early the next morning, having requested his PA to reschedule a business trip to Germany and make it start immediately.

Since he had returned to the villa the connecting door between his room and Leah's had remained closed. Marco had spent sleepless nights, his body aching with frustration.

He knew Leah was aware of the sexual chemistry between them—it was almost tangible. And if she hadn't been a virgin he might have tried to seduce her into his bed. But her innocence held him back. She deserved more than he could give her, and he sensed that for Leah desire would be inextricably linked with deeper emotions—like love.

In every other respect she was proving to be an ideal wife. She had accompanied him to dinner parties given by his friends in Capri and Positano, and looked stunning dressed in designer gowns. But Marco preferred her as she was now, wearing frayed denim shorts that revealed her toned thighs and a tight-fitting T-shirt that moulded her firm breasts.

No bra, he noted, his gaze lingering on the outline of her nipples.

Desire corkscrewed through him and he tore his gaze from her and concentrated on driving the boat.

It was not long before they reached the private beach

belonging to Villa Rosa, and after he'd secured the boat with a rope tied to a mooring post he jumped onto the jetty and turned to help Leah and Nicky disembark. The little boy ran ahead of them up the steep driveway.

'Nicky, wait!' Marco called as a delivery truck rumbled past on its way to the house. He glanced at Leah. 'I've left my sunglasses on the boat. You go on with Nicky while I run back for them.'

He jogged down the driveway and was almost at the bottom of the incline when he heard Leah scream.

'Marco, look out!'

Glancing over his shoulder, he saw the truck hurtling towards him. He realised in seconds, as it gained momentum, that the driver must have turned the vehicle at the top of the hill and parked, but couldn't have applied the handbrake properly. The driver was not behind the wheel, and the truck was almost upon Marco.

With nowhere else to go, he leapt over the wall and swore as he half fell, half scrambled down the rocky cliff before landing on a ledge. From above him he heard a crash, and guessed that the truck must have hit the wall.

His arms were covered in scratches from the brambles, and no doubt he would find bruises on his body, but he'd been lucky. If Leah hadn't alerted him the truck would have ploughed into him.

He hauled himself back up the cliff and hooked a leg over the wall to climb over it.

'Papà! Papà!'

Marco turned his head towards the house and saw Nicky, chased by Leah, running down the driveway. The little boy was sobbing hysterically.

'Papà!'

His son's distress tore at Marco's heart. Nicky had not

cried since the accident, but now tears poured down his cheeks.

'Nicky, it's okay,' he said huskily, hunkering down and wrapping his arms around his son's quivering body.

Nicky stared at him. 'You went away and another man came,' he choked through his tears.

'Do you mean at the hospital? I was there with you, Nicky. But maybe I looked different,' Marco said slowly, as he began to comprehend why his son seemed afraid of him.

He glanced at Leah.

'After the accident I had to leave Nicky in the children's ward while my cheek was stitched up. My face was covered in bandages for days, but it never occurred to me that Nicky might have thought I was a stranger. I must have looked terrifying to a child. It would have been another trauma on top of everything else he'd been through.'

Marco touched his scar and grimaced when he discovered the blood on his face.

'You've got a nasty cut above your eyebrow,' Leah told him.

Nicky was still crying, and Marco put his hands on his son's shoulders. 'It wasn't another man at the hospital, it was *me*, Nicky. My face looks different, but I am still your *papà*.'

Marco swallowed hard. He did not find it easy to reveal his emotions, but Leah had been right when she'd said Nicky needed to know that his father cared about him.

'You are my son and I love you,' he said softly. 'I will always love you, and everything is going to be okay.'

This time when he drew Nicky towards him the little boy wriggled closer. Marco pressed his face against his son's dark curls and felt tears burn his eyes. He looked at the smashed wall and the crumpled front end of the truck and knew he might have been killed if the truck had hit him.

Life was infinitely precious. He could never regain those first years of his son's life that he'd missed, but thanks to Leah he had a lifetime with Nicky ahead of him.

'I think we need ice-cream,' he said gruffly as he stood up and lifted Nicky into his arms.

He looked at Leah and saw a tear slide down her cheek. Her emotional response evoked an odd tug in his chest. Seeing her with his son for the past weeks had been a revelation. She was compassionate, and her beauty was much more than skin-deep.

It was becoming harder and harder to remember that she had blackmailed him into marriage. The situation between them couldn't continue. He was going out of his mind with wanting her.

'Thank you,' he said quietly as they walked back to the house.

She shook her head. 'I didn't do anything.'

'You saved my life. I didn't hear the truck because its engine wasn't running. More importantly, you have shown me how to connect with my son.'

'You've won Nicky's trust by spending time with him. You're a good father, Marco.'

Her smile stole his breath, and he felt a tug beneath his breastbone so intense that he pressed his hand against his chest.

'A couple of bruised ribs,' he lied when she looked concerned. He looked at his watch. 'The nanny will be arriving soon. I employed Silvana when I first brought Nicky to Capri, and since her father has passed away she is happy to come back to Villa Rosa. Silvana will take care of Nicky while we go to Rome.'

'We?'

She stared at him and he saw a mutinous expression replace her smile. They had reached the house, and Nicky ran inside. Leah stood in the entrance, framed by the profusion of white roses that clambered around the front door. Once again Marco pressed his palm to his chest and felt the erratic thud of his heart.

'Assumpta has told me that you are going away for the weekend. I wondered when you were going to mention it,' she said pointedly. 'But I'm not coming with you.'

'The annual charity ball sponsored by De Valle Caffè is the most prestigious event in the company's calendar, and it attracts the support of businesses and celebrities from all over Europe. You are the new wife of the CEO and it will look odd to the board members and shareholders if you are not with me. If there is any hint of a scandal the paparazzi will hound us, and negative publicity could harm the company.' Marco ignored the glitter in Leah's green eyes. 'In fact, I think we should practise showing a united front to the cameras.'

'Practise how?' she said suspiciously.

'Like this.'

He lowered his head until his lips were centimetres from hers and watched her green eyes darken to the colour of a stormy sea. Something held him back from claiming her mouth.

A memory slid into his mind of that time when she had suggested he might force her to sleep with him. She'd dented his pride then, and now he needed to be sure she was caught in the same web of desire that held him prisoner.

'Marco...'

The husky plea in her voice shattered his control and he brushed his mouth over hers gently, taking his time to savour her soft sigh of surrender. Only then did he coax her lips apart with the tip of his tongue.

She tasted like nectar, and the heady fragrance of her

perfume mingled with the scent of the roses and teased his senses. Passion exploded between them as he deepened the kiss until she melted against him and her lips clung to his.

The sound of someone shouting made him reluctantly lift his head, and he glanced up and saw the delivery driver running around the corner of the house.

Leah's face was flushed, and Marco ran his knuckles over her peachy skin. 'That wasn't bad,' he drawled, deliberately teasing her to stop himself from throwing her over his shoulder, caveman-style, and carrying her to his bed. 'But you'll need more practice at kissing if you're going to convince the public that you are besotted with your husband.'

He laid his finger across her lips. He could see from the furious glint in her eyes that an angry retort was about to burst forth. She sank her teeth into his finger and he cursed.

'Wildcat. Be ready to leave in an hour.'

Hunger was a vicious beast, clawing in his gut.

'And know this: bite me again and you'll have to be prepared for the consequences, beauty.'

The party was the most spectacular event Leah had ever attended and then some. It was held in the ballroom of the most exclusive hotel in Rome, and the great and the good of the Eternal City had gathered there beneath glittering chandeliers to drink champagne and feast on exquisite canapés.

An auction had raised a phenomenal amount of money for various charities, and Marco had given a moving speech about the work of a charity for homeless children which was close to his heart.

Leah's gaze had been riveted on him as he'd stood there on the podium. He looked breathtaking, in a black dinner suit that moulded his muscular frame. But she wasn't the only woman to be fantasising about loosening his bow tie and ripping open the buttons on his white silk shirt, she'd realised, when she'd noticed the admiring looks that practically every female in the room sent him.

But he was hers—in public, at least.

She was shocked by the fierce possessiveness she felt. He'd told her that they must act like happy newlyweds and she had thrown herself into the role, offering no resistance when he slipped his arm around her waist and held her close against his side as they strolled around the room and mingled with the other guests.

While a buffet was being served in another room the hotel staff cleared the ballroom of the tables where people had sat for the auction. Soon the band struck up, and Marco swept Leah into his arms and led her onto the dance floor.

'You have never looked more beautiful than you do tonight,' he murmured, his warm breath stirring the tendrils of curls that framed her face.

She wore the front of her hair up and had left the back loose. The white rose that Marco had given her was tucked into her hair. Her heart missed a beat when he wound a long curl around his finger. She wanted to say something flippant in response to his compliment, but the gleam in his eyes as he looked intently at her made her feel beautiful.

Her strapless sea-green silk evening gown felt sensuous against her skin as Marco whirled her around the ballroom. The diamond earrings dangling from her earlobes and the diamonds at her throat must be worth a fortune. She had protested about wearing them when he'd presented the jewellery to her after she'd emerged from her bedroom in the penthouse suite of the hotel where they were staying for the weekend.

'Humour me, hmm?' he'd drawled as he'd fastened the

clasp of the necklace and pressed his lips to the side of her throat.

A quiver had run through her and she'd accepted that trying to resist him was futile.

She wanted to make love with him. It was as simple and uncomplicated as that.

When she'd watched that delivery truck roll down the driveway and realised that Marco was unaware of the danger he was in she had been terrified. In those horrifying moments her thoughts had clarified into a stark truth. She could no longer deny her desire for him.

Tonight's glamorous party was *his* world, not hers, but their hunger for each other made them equal.

She did not fool herself that he loved her—which was what her mother had done every time she'd begun another affair. And Leah assured herself that she had more sense than to lose her heart to Marco. But she liked him, and she felt safe with him. Not safe in the way her passionless relationship with James had made her feel. Marco had shown her that her difficult childhood had made her strong and that she could handle a sexual relationship with him. That sometimes being in control was about knowing when to let go.

The tempo of the music changed to a slow number and Marco pulled her close, so that she felt the hard ridge of his arousal nudge her thigh. He smelled divine: of spicy cologne and another indefinable scent that was excitingly *male*. With a faint sigh she rested her head on his chest and heard the powerful thud of his heart. He brushed his lips over her shoulder, sending a shiver of reaction through her.

She realised that he'd been flirting with her all evening, taking every opportunity to caress her with a hand stroking her bare back or his mouth brushing over her cheek.

He was clearly intent on seducing her. But instead of pulling away from him she pressed her pelvis against his and heard him groan.

'You are driving me insane,' he said thickly. 'How much longer are you going to make me wait, *cara mia*?'

Fire licked through her. 'Well, I suppose we should stay here in the ballroom until the party ends at midnight as you are the host...'

'Like hell we should.'

He stopped dancing and clamped her to his side as he strode towards the exit.

'Won't you be missed?' she murmured when he ushered her into a lift.

'I don't give a damn.'

He leaned back against the lift wall and pulled her towards him, one hand splaying over her bottom, the other tugging at his bow tie. His urgency heightened her anticipation and her pulse quickened when the door opened directly into the penthouse suite.

She'd expected Marco to lead her straight to the master bedroom, and butterflies had taken up residence in her stomach. But he strode across the sitting room and opened the sliding glass doors that led out onto the balcony. Rome was spread out before them, a blaze of lights against an inky sky.

Leah followed him over to where he stood beside the balcony rail.

'Why did you want your inheritance so badly?' he asked. 'Was it really to get on the property ladder, as you told me?'

His curiosity took her by surprise. She bit her lip. 'Does it matter why?'

'You must have had plans for how to spend the money if you were prepared to marry a virtual stranger to get your hands on it,' he said harshly. 'But everything I've learned about you indicates that you are not money-driven.'

He gently captured her chin between his lean fingers and tilted her face up so that her gaze collided with his.

'Leah, do you trust me?'

Her breath left her on a long sigh as she realised that she did. Trust did not come easily to her, but Marco had been devastatingly honest when he'd confided that he did not know how to be a father to his son.

'I needed the money for my mother. I've done my best to look after her for most of my life,' she admitted.

Marco said nothing and his eyes did not leave her face.

'Mum is…an alcoholic. She's always liked a drink, but after my brother died she started drinking heavily.'

Leah tensed, expecting Marco to be disgusted or judgemental—which were the reactions she'd had in the past if she ever spoke about her mum's reliance on alcohol.

'It must have been difficult when you were growing up—having to be responsible for a parent when she should have been the one taking care of you,' he suggested.

She nodded. 'I felt helpless. I didn't want anyone at school to know that my mum was different to other mothers, or that a normal weekend for me was to find Mum passed out on the bathroom floor. I used to get up early to take the empty vodka bottles to the bottle bank so that no one would see me.'

Leah sighed.

'Despite everything I know Mum loves me—and I love her. She is all I have. The inheritance money is paying for her to be treated at a private clinic.' She gave Marco a faint smile. 'Mum is halfway through the programme and she's doing well.'

'*Dio!* Why didn't you just borrow the amount you needed to pay for your mother's treatment?'

She gave him a wry look. 'Would *you* have agreed to give me a loan? Especially as I had no way of paying it back? And my mother had other problems which needed to be resolved quickly.'

Leah's voice faltered, but she realised that Marco was waiting patiently for her to continue, and she felt a sense of relief in unburdening herself of the worry she'd felt that her mum could go to prison.

'Mum stole some money from the company she worked for and I needed to repay it before the police got involved.'

He swore softly. 'So you negotiated a marriage deal with a man you barely knew?'

'I didn't know what else I could do. You were my only hope of helping my mother.'

Marco nodded. 'But we are no longer strangers.'

The expression in his eyes made Leah's heart lurch. 'Do you want to make our marriage real?' she whispered.

'What I want from you, *cara*, is your honesty.'

CHAPTER ELEVEN

'I WANT TO have sex with you. Is that honest enough?'

Leah followed Marco into his bedroom and watched him shrug off his jacket and unfasten the top few buttons on his shirt.

'Prove it.'

He sat on the bed and leaned back against the head-board, folding his arms behind his head. His eyes gleamed as he raked them over her like a sultan inspecting his favourite concubine.

Once she might have turned tail and fled. But she wasn't that person any more. She knew what she wanted and she was prepared to fight for it.

With sudden insight Leah understood that Marco needed to be sure she was coming to him willingly. Her heart contracted.

'If you don't make love to me tonight, I think I'll go out of my mind,' she said huskily.

'I've spent the evening fantasising about you wearing those diamonds and nothing else,' he growled.

His voice had roughened, and Leah felt a thrill of feminine triumph when she realised that he wasn't as relaxed as he wanted her to think.

'I'll fulfil your fantasies if you promise to fulfil mine.'

His sexy smile set her pulse racing. 'Be careful what you wish for, beauty.'

She ran her tongue over her dry lips. The time for talking was over.

Reaching behind her, she ran the zip of her dress down her spine. The green silk fell away from her breasts and slipped down her body to pool at her feet.

Marco sat upright and his breath hissed between his teeth.

Carefully she stepped away from the dress and kicked off her stilettos. The only remaining item of clothing was her black lace knickers. She hesitated for a second, and then hooked her fingers into the top and pulled them down.

Leah's nerve faltered when she was finally naked in front of Marco and feeling self-conscious of her body's imperfections.

'Look at me,' he commanded softly.

She obeyed, and her heart started to pound. Desire was stamped on his face and his eyes glittered beneath heavy lids. He stood up and came towards her, running his fingers over the diamonds nestling between her breasts.

'*Bellissima...*' he murmured, but she had an idea that he wasn't referring to the necklace.

He took the rose from her hair and trailed it down her cheek. The flower's heady perfume filled her senses and the petals felt like gossamer against her throat and breasts as he held the stem between his fingers and traced patterns on her body with the rose. He moved his hand lower, sweeping the flower over her stomach and thighs.

She did not know what to expect when he suddenly dropped to his knees and splayed his hands possessively over her hips.

'*Oh...*' Her breath hitched when his tongue licked along her inner thigh. 'I don't think...'

'Much better not to think.' He glanced up at her face and smiled wickedly. 'Hold on to my shoulders.'

And then his dark head was at the junction between her legs as he put his mouth on her and drove every thought from her head. Shock ricocheted through her when he pressed forward and ran his tongue over her moist opening.

He couldn't mean to…

But he did.

Heat swept through her veins as his intimate caresses grew bolder and the fire inside her became an inferno. It was too much and not enough. Pleasure bordering on something so needy and intense that it almost hurt. And the ache, the terrible yearning, built to a crescendo as Marco closed his lips around the tight nub of her core and sucked.

Leah cried out something incomprehensible as she climaxed against his mouth. Ripples contracted and released deep in her core.

Her legs buckled and he stood up and swept her into his arms. He strode over to the bed and laid her down on satin sheets that felt cool against her passion-flushed skin. She propped herself up on her elbows, wondering how she could feel so uninhibited at being naked, with her legs splayed open and the scent of her arousal in the air.

'You have too many clothes on,' she told Marco.

He shoved his thick hair off his brow with a hand that Leah fancied was a little unsteady.

'Another of my fantasies is for you to undress me,' he muttered.

Moving to kneel on the bed, she undid his shirt and pushed it off his shoulders. His muscles rippled beneath her fingers as she explored his powerful biceps and then placed her hands on his chest and felt the uneven thud of his heart. Following the dark hair on his flat abdomen to the waistband of his trousers, she freed the button and hesitated for a fraction of a second before running the zip down.

Her knuckles brushed against the hard length of him, making him swear softly.

'Witch… I'm enjoying this too much. And I don't want to risk disgracing myself or disappointing you,' he said gruffly as he pushed her hands away and finished undressing himself.

Her mouth dried and her eyes widened as he pulled off his boxers and his erection sprang free, proud and thick.

Marco gave a low laugh. 'Keep staring at me like that, *cara*, and this will be over embarrassingly quickly.'

'You're beautiful.' She blurted the words out and blushed, mortified that she sounded so gauche.

But his body was incredible: a broad, bronzed chest, an impressive six-pack, a taut torso and lean hips. Her gaze was drawn inexorably to his arousal, and she felt a melting sensation between her legs as she tried to imagine what it would be like to have that thick length inside her.

She stretched out her hand and touched him, startled to feel solid steel beneath satin skin when she skimmed her fingertips over his shaft.

'*Dio*…' he growled. 'You're killing me.'

She watched him roll on a condom. A nerve flickered in his jaw and she sensed the restraint he was imposing on himself.

'Are you sure, Leah?'

She was still kneeling on the bed, and instead of answering him she cupped his face in her hands and covered his mouth with hers.

At first he allowed her to control the kiss, but passion swiftly spiralled out of control and he eased her down so that she was lying on her back and he was positioned over her.

'Bend your knees.'

His molten honey voice quelled the faint jangle of her nerves. She caught her breath as he feathered kisses over her breasts before he sucked on one nipple and then the other, until she was aware of nothing but fire and need and a powerful womanly urgency for him to possess her.

She brought her legs up so that her pelvis was flush against his. Marco pressed forward and she felt his swollen tip rub against her opening. His hand slipped between their bodies, so that he could guide himself into her slick heat. Slowly, surely, he eased inside her and paused, his brow resting against hers as she twisted her hips and her internal muscles stretched to accommodate him.

'Am I hurting you?'

'No.'

There was no pain—just a delicious heaviness in her pelvis and a sense of completeness. She gave an experimental wriggle and heard Marco exhale a ragged breath.

'It feels good,' she whispered.

'This is just the beginning, *cara*.'

He claimed her lips again, and there was an unexpected tenderness in his kiss that tied her heart in knots. And then he moved, effecting a deep thrust that drove the air from her lungs as he filled her. And then there was only him inside her, around her, his male scent intoxicating her, his breath mingling with hers.

He set a rhythm that was impossible to resist. Every thrust of his steely hardness created a wonderful friction in her molten core. Leah dug her fingers into his shoulders and hung on tight as the storm inside her built and grew ever stronger.

Marco slid his hands beneath her bottom and lifted her, angling her so that his relentless strokes, in and out, felt that much more intense. She looked at his face and wondered anew at the stark beauty of his features. The dull flush on his cheekbones and the silver gleam in his eyes told her that this was good for him too. Although 'good' did not come near to describing the exquisite sensations rolling through her, wave after wave, so that it was impossible to control her thundering heart.

It couldn't last.

She arched her hips to meet the bold thrust of his and he held her there, poised on the edge of an unknown place that she was desperate to reach. *So* desperate. Her breath came in harsh pants, as if she'd run a marathon, and her body trembled and shook.

'Now!' he said thickly, before he covered her mouth with his.

Her sharp cry was lost in his kiss as something inside her snapped, and the drenching, sweet pleasure of her orgasm was so intense that she wondered how she could possibly survive it.

Impossibly, it wasn't over.

Marco muttered something in Italian that might have been a curse or a prayer, increasing his pace with a new urgency that made her realise how much he'd had himself under control—until now. He thrust the deepest yet and threw his head back, his harsh groan reverberating through Leah as she climaxed again, swift and sharp this time, while he collapsed on top of her and pressed his lips to her neck.

For a long time afterwards he lay lax on top of her, and she relished his weight pressing her into the mattress. There was a sense of security in the arms holding her, in his fingers playing idly with her hair. She pressed her face against his shoulder and hoped he wasn't aware of the tears that trickled from the corners of her eyes.

He had made her first time amazing. The physical experience of making love with Marco had been mind-blowing. But she hadn't expected it to make such an impact on her heart. In those moments when they had soared together to the stratosphere it had seemed as though her soul and his were joined, just as their bodies were entwined.

But she would not get carried away with a romantic fantasy, Leah promised herself.

When she pushed against his chest he rolled off her and murmured something about dealing with the condom, before walking into the en suite bathroom.

Perhaps it was a cue for her to leave? She didn't want to appear clingy.

Swinging her legs over the side of the bed, she spied her expensive ball gown lying in a crumpled heap on the floor and, more damning still, the knickers that she'd discarded along with her inhibitions.

Swallowing the lump in her throat, she scooped up her clothes and hurried over to the door.

'Leaving so soon, *cara*?' Marco drawled.

Leah spun round to face him and her heart missed a beat at the oddly gentle tone in his voice.

'I told you…we've only just begun.'

'I haven't done this before. I don't know the protocol after having sex with a lover.'

Leah sounded defensive, and her green eyes were too bright. The faint tremor of her mouth smote Marco like an arrow in the centre of his chest and he rubbed his hand over the area above his breastbone.

'We are not lovers. I am your husband and you are my wife,' he said mildly. She was as edgy as a colt and he didn't want to spook her.

It was odd how much he liked calling her his wife. He would have sworn he did not have a possessive bone in his body. He told himself that this proprietorial feeling was because Leah was the only virgin he'd ever taken to bed. But he could not dismiss his satisfaction that she was *his*.

'I don't know what's supposed to happen next,' she muttered.

'Come with me and I'll show you.'

He held out his hand and refused to question why his heart leapt when, after hesitating for a moment, she put her fingers in his. He led her into the bathroom, where he'd already started to fill the circular bath. The hotel had provided an array of toiletries, and he added a liberal amount of scented bubble bath to the water.

Leah was clutching her dress as if it was a security blanket. He placed in on a chair and wound her long hair up, using the diamante clip she'd worn for the evening to secure her curls on top of her head.

'I've never shared a bath.'

Leah looked at him uncertainly when he climbed into the tub, scooped her off her feet and deposited her in the water. He turned on the jets and felt his heart clench when she let out a deep sigh as she slid down so that her shoulders were beneath the bubbles.

'This is heavenly.'

'It is a night of firsts, *cara*.'

Marco was fascinated yet again by the rosy colour that ran under her skin. She looked very young, with stray curls clinging to her flushed cheeks and her eyes enormous in her heart-shaped face. He felt fiercely protective and possessive and a host of other emotions he did not care to examine.

'I hope you were not disappointed with your first sexual experience.'

Her mouth curved in a rueful smile. 'You know I wasn't. It was wonderful.'

Dio! Marco was shaken by this unexpected emotional response to Leah. He tore his gaze from her lovely face and lifted the bottle of champagne from the ice bucket.

'Next time it will be easier for you.'

'Is there going to be a next time?'

'Would you like there to be?' He found he was holding his breath as he waited for her reply.

'Yes.'

He popped the cork and poured the champagne, handing her a glass. 'I propose a toast, Signora De Valle. To a fresh start.'

Her smile became impish. 'Mind where you put your foot, Signor De Valle.'

Marco put his glass down carefully on the side of the bath, not entirely surprised to find that his hand was shaking.

'Come here.'

He read the excitement in her eyes as she set her glass down and shifted across to him. She gave a gasp when he lifted her onto his lap and his arousal pressed against her bottom. Her mouth met his, and he loved her eagerness as she returned kiss for kiss. He gave himself up to a passion that had never been as intense with other women as it was with Leah.

This fire could not last, he assured himself, perplexed by the pang he felt at the certainty that it would burn itself out. Nothing good lasted for ever.

He rose out of the bath, taking her with him, and wrapped her in a fluffy towel before briskly drying himself. When he carried her through to the bedroom and laid her on the bed she sat up and gave him a shy smile.

'I have another fantasy...'

His breath hissed between his teeth as she moved down his body, her silky curls brushing over his abdomen and thighs as she put her mouth on his sex.

'*Madre di Dio!*'

'I'm sorry.' She lifted her head and her uncertain expression undid him utterly. 'Am I doing it wrong?'

'It's perfect,' he said hoarsely, tangling his fingers in her hair as she bent her head once more and licked along his throbbing shaft. '*You* are perfect.'

The still functioning part of Marco's brain acknowledged that he'd made a good decision to insist that their marriage contract was for a year. He'd done it because it would not look good to the company's shareholders if he broke up with his bride too soon after the wedding. But as his body shook, and he fought for control when Leah closed her mouth around the swollen tip of his manhood, a year did not seem nearly long enough with a wife who was more fascinating with every new discovery he made about her.

It had been a night such as he'd never experienced before, and Marco had made sure that Leah was as sated as he by the time they fell into an exhausted sleep.

He woke first the next morning, and propped himself up on his elbow while he watched her sleep. She was more beautiful that anything he'd ever seen, with her riotous hair spread over the pillows and her creamy breasts bearing faint red marks from his beard.

Marco pushed to the back of his mind the thought that he was behaving like a man who, if not lovesick, was dangerously close to it.

Leah opened her eyes and gave him the sweetest smile, and he assured himself that the tangled knot in his gut was simply desire. He had wanted her for a long time and now, finally, she was beneath him, her legs spread wide and her hips lifting to meet his. He tested her with his finger and found her wet and ready for him.

He reminded himself that this was all new to her and silently cursed his thoughtlessness. 'Do you feel sore?'

'No. I want you.'

She urged him down onto her, and with a groan he sank between her thighs and drove his shaft deep into her welcoming heat.

They finally made it out of bed late in the morning, and enjoyed a leisurely brunch in a charming café at the top of the Spanish Steps, with wonderful views over the city.

Rome in the middle of summer was thronged with tourists. 'We'll come back and I'll take you sightseeing,' Marco promised, when Leah told him that this was her first trip to the city.

He knew she was as keen as him to return to Capri to be with Nicky.

The days following their return to Villa Rosa stretched into weeks, but Marco barely noticed. His relationship with his son continued to flourish as Nicky's self-confidence grew and the trauma of the accident gradually faded for both of them.

Marco slipped into a routine in which he left early in the helicopter for his office in Naples most days, but returned to the villa by mid-afternoon. Leah taught Nicky in the morning, and the three of them spent the rest of the day swimming in the pool or at the beach, or strolling around the winding, narrow streets of Capri.

Nicky loved to ride in the chair lift to the top of Monte Solaro, the highest point on the island, but Leah preferred the less hair-raising charm of La Piazzeta, the lively square in the centre of Capri which was a wonderful place to enjoy a slice of *torta caprese*, the island's famous chocolate and almond cake.

'This is heavenly,' she said as she and Marco sat in a café one lazy afternoon.

They were spending the afternoon without Nicky as he'd gone with Silvana the nanny to a birthday party for Silvana's niece's young son.

Leah popped the last forkful of cake into her mouth. 'I'll have to watch my figure if I carry on eating so much of this wonderful food.'

'You have a gorgeous body,' Marco assured her. He leaned across the table and wiped a smear of chocolate off her lip with his thumb. 'It's a novelty to be with a woman who enjoys food. Eating is a sensual pleasure...like making love.'

He held Leah's gaze as he lifted his thumb to his mouth and licked the chocolate from it.

Her eyes widened and rosy colour stained her cheeks. 'Marco! Someone might hear you.'

He laughed huskily. 'How can you still blush like a virgin after what we did last night?'

His arousal was instantly rock-hard as he pictured Leah, bent over the side of the bath while his hands had roamed over her as he'd taken her.

She gave him an innocent look. 'Maybe we should go back to the villa so that you can remind me of what we did?'

Stifling a groan, he paid the bill and slid his arm around her waist, urging her to walk faster across the *piazza*.

'Something tells me you're in a hurry,' she murmured, her eyes alight with teasing laughter and an excitement that made Marco's heart race.

'I am very hungry, *cara mia*.'

It occurred to him that if anyone had told him a few months ago that he'd happily delegate work so that he could leave the office early and rush home to be with his teasing minx of a wife he would not have believed it. The company had dominated his life for more than a decade, but now he had discovered that the simple enjoyment of kicking a football around the garden with Nicky or spending a long night in bed with his wife meant more to him than pulling off a brilliant business deal.

As for Leah—her passionate and sensual nature had been a revelation. But it was more than just great sex, Marco acknowledged. He liked being with her. She had been reserved when he'd first met her, but trust had grown between them and she'd lowered her guard and let him see that she was witty, with a dry sense of humour and a kindness that he would miss when the storm she evoked in him finally blew itself out.

But his desire for her showed no sign of abating yet, and he'd decided to stop wondering when it would happen and instead enjoy the lingering days of summer with her before winter and cold reality arrived.

As they hurried through the front door of Villa Rosa Marco paused to pick a white rose, which he tucked into Leah's hair.

'I can walk,' she protested when he scooped her into his arms and carried her up the stairs.

'Not fast enough,' he growled, shouldering open the door to the master bedroom, which they now shared.

He rid them both of their clothes before they fell onto the bed, mouths fused together, his hands curving possessively over her breasts.

'See what you do to me?'

He lay on his back beside her and his gaze met hers in the mirror above the bed. Their reflection showed Leah's slim yet curvaceous body, her pale skin an erotic contrast against the black silk sheets, her nipples red where he'd sucked them. His erection was thick and hard, and he groaned when she ran her fingers over the sensitive tip.

'I prefer action to looking,' she said, with one of those smiles of hers that did strange things to his insides.

And then she rose up and straddled his hips, leaning forward so that her nipples brushed across his chest while he guided his shaft between her soft thighs. She took him deep inside her and he watched their reflection as she rode him, her red hair spilling around her shoulders. She tipped her head back and her eyes were as dark as a stormy sea when they reached the plateau simultaneously and tumbled together into the abyss.

Much later, Marco padded out of the bathroom, rubbing a towel over his wet hair after his shower, and found Leah sitting on the bed wearing his shirt.

How did she look so goddamned sexy in a shirt that was much too big for her? he wondered, admiring her toned thighs where the edge of the shirt finished. It was safe to say that she wouldn't be wearing it for long.

He forced himself to concentrate when she spoke.

'Silvana called to say that Nicky is having a great time at the birthday party. It's good for him to spend time with children of his own age. Your Aunt Benedetta will see a big change in him when she brings her grandchildren to stay, and Nicky will love playing with Dario, Aria and Giovani.' She hesitated, then said, 'Nicky is doing so well—I think he'll be ready to start school when the new term begins. He won't need me to give him lessons any more, and I've been thinking I should start to look for a teaching job in England.'

Marco felt the unpleasant sensation of his stomach dropping like a stone.

'I did not bring you to Capri only as Nicky's teacher,'

he said. 'You signed a contract stating that you will be my wife for a year. If we were to divorce earlier it would give an impression of instability in my personal life—which, as CEO of the company, I want to avoid.'

She looked away from him. 'Is that the only reason you want our marriage to continue?'

He shrugged. 'For Nicky's sake too. The psychotherapist says it's important to maintain a sense of continuity so that he feels secure.'

'I wouldn't drop out of his life. I'd come back to Capri to visit him. But I have a career. My inheritance money won't last long, and I need to work.'

Marco raked a hand through his hair. 'With regard to the divorce... As the contract stands you will not receive a settlement, but I am going to instruct my lawyer to alter it so that you will be awarded one million pounds at the end of our marriage.'

Leah stared at him. 'A million pounds?'

'It will allow you to buy a house in London and pay for your mother to continue her treatment.'

'What exactly are you paying me a million pounds *for*?' she asked, in a sharp voice with an underlying note that Marco could not decipher. 'Sex? Do I earn a certain amount per night?'

'Don't forget the days,' he growled. 'You are always eager for sex first thing in the morning.'

His jaw hardened as colour flooded her face. He was stunned that she seemed to be throwing his offer back in his face.

'I thought you'd be pleased that you won't have to worry about money in the future.'

'Oh, I'm *thrilled* that you think I'm a prostitute.'

'*Dio*—I don't think that. I made the offer as a sign that I...'

'That you what?' Her eyes flashed dangerously.

Marco unconsciously rubbed his hand over the ache in his chest. He didn't know what to say. He cared about what happened to her and he wanted to make her life easier—frankly, it did not sound like a bed of roses. But he sensed that Leah wanted a different answer from him.

'I made the offer as a token of my respect for you.'

She scrambled off the bed and marched over to the connecting door between her room and his.

'You know where you can put your million pounds! I don't want your money, and you have a funny way of showing your respect!'

She stepped into the other bedroom and Marco heard a tremor in her voice when she spoke again.

'I'll stay for as long as Nicky needs me, but then I demand you set me free.'

The slam of the door had a ring of finality to it.

CHAPTER TWELVE

THE STAND-OFF HAD so far lasted for four days and nights, and Leah was determined she would not be the one to break it. She was bitterly hurt by Marco's offer to pay her at the end of their marriage. It wasn't only the implied insult in his belief that she would accept the money—it was his admission that the reason he wanted her to remain his wife for a year was to keep his shareholders happy.

She'd thought that they had grown closer these past weeks. The attraction between them was stronger than ever, but she'd believed there was friendship too.

She had mentioned looking for a job in England partly to test the waters and see if she'd imagined that he felt something for her. Marco had not lost his air of self-containment, but she'd hoped that he liked her a little and even felt some degree of affection for her.

Clearly, he did not.

And perhaps he wasn't a slave to their passion the way she was. Every night she tossed restlessly in her bed and stared at the connecting door between their rooms, willing him to walk in and sweep her into his arms. She missed his body on hers...she missed waking in the morning with him beside her. She missed him so much it was agony, she thought miserably.

To add to the difficult situation, his aunt had arrived

with her three grandchildren. There was no time during the day for her and Marco to be alone, and they were both putting on an act of being happily married in front of Benedetta. Even the joy of hearing Nicky chattering confidently to the other children was bittersweet when she could not share it with Marco.

Leah walked into the lounge and her heart gave a flip at the sight of him in jeans and a black T-shirt that clung to his muscular chest. His hair was ruffled, as if he'd been running his fingers through it, and she told herself she was imagining that the grooves on either side of his mouth might be caused by the same strain that she was feeling. He was sitting on the sofa with Nicky perched on his knee, and the three other children were grouped around him.

The little girl, Aria, held out a photo to Marco. 'Who is that lady? She's pretty.'

'That's Nicky's *mamma*, who is sadly no longer with us. She was very pretty and kind and talented. She hoped to be a great actress, and I'm sure she would have been. She loved Nicky very much.'

Leah felt as though an arrow had pierced her heart, hearing the huskiness in Marco's voice. It should not matter to her if his heart belonged to Karin, she told herself. But the burn of jealousy in the pit of her stomach mocked her belief that she was in control of her feelings.

The truth made her tremble. She had fallen in love with Marco. And this time she knew it was real. The mild affection she'd felt for James had never threatened her determination to stay in charge of her emotions. What she felt for Marco was terrifying and utterly uncontrollable.

She swallowed when she discovered that he was watching her, and turned away from his speculative gaze, afraid that he might see the truth in her eyes. Her heart was as fragile as spun glass and he could easily shatter it.

'Benedetta said you wanted to see me about something,' she said stiffly.

'Tio Marco, can we tell Leah about the surprise?' Aria looked excited. 'You are having a special lunch in the summerhouse for your anniversary.' She sighed theatrically. '*We* are not allowed to come.'

'You children are going to have a barbecue by the pool.' Marco stood up and walked over to Leah.

Her brows lifted. 'Anniversary?'

'We have been married for two months, *cara*. Surely you have remembered?'

He smiled and brushed his mouth over hers in a tantalisingly brief kiss. For his aunt's benefit, Leah told herself as Benedetta appeared.

'How could I forget?' she murmured.

Her stupid heart was thumping when he took her arm and led her out of the villa, and she was glad she was wearing a blue silk dress that she knew Marco particularly liked.

'I suppose Benedetta arranged this?' she said, as he ushered her inside the pretty summerhouse set in a quiet corner of the garden. The table was set with cutlery and glasses on a snowy white cloth, and an arrangement of heavenly scented roses made a stunning centrepiece.

'No—I did.' He drew out a chair for her. 'We need to talk, but we'll eat first.'

He could not possibly be *nervous*, she thought as he poured her a glass of wine before filling his own glass.

There was a selection of delicious-looking dishes on a trolley, ready for them to serve themselves. Leah took some salad leaves and prawns, but her stomach was tied in a knot and she only ate a few mouthfuls.

'I'm sorry I upset you,' he said, putting his wine glass down. 'It was not my intention.'

'Maybe I overreacted,' she murmured, trying to dismiss the hurt she'd felt. His apology meant a lot, and she wanted their relationship to return to how it had been. 'But I'm not interested in your money, Marco.'

'I know that, *cara*.' He trapped her gaze. 'Over the past two months we have become friends, I hope?'

She nodded, not trusting herself to speak. She longed for them to be much more than friends. And this was not the stony-faced stranger of the past few days. This was *her* Marco—the man who had taken her to the pinnacle of pleasure countless times, always tempering his passion with a tenderness that had wrapped around her heart.

Guilt assailed her that she had misjudged him. 'I'm sorry I suggested that you were trying to pay me for being married to you.'

He reached across the table and linked his fingers with hers. 'Our talk of divorce made me realise that it is not what I want.'

'Oh?' Her breath was trapped in her lungs. 'You...you *don't* want us to divorce after a year?'

'No.' He stroked his thumb pad over the pulse that was thudding like crazy in her wrist. 'It makes more sense for our marriage to become a permanent arrangement.'

'It makes more sense?' she parroted, ice replacing the warmth in her veins. 'How, exactly?'

'I never planned to marry again.'

Leah remembered how his voice gentled whenever he spoke of Nicky's mother and felt a stab of jealousy. 'But I blackmailed you into it?' she said flatly. 'The truth is I would have helped Nicky even if you had refused to marry me. I was shocked when you agreed.'

'I was, and am, willing to do anything for my son.' Marco lifted her hand to his mouth and pressed his lips against her fingers. 'You have enabled me to build a relationship with him, and I've seen the affection you have for him. I want you to be Nicky's mother. Hear me out,' he said, when she tensed. 'We like each other, and we get on well. We can be parents to Nicky. He adores you, and we can give him the family we both longed for when *we* were growing up.'

Leah bit her lip. Pride demanded she must not let him see that his words felt like a hammer-blow to her heart.

'I'd have no objection if you wanted to work,' Marco continued. 'You do an important job and you would easily find a teaching post for children with special needs in Naples. But at some point you might want to have a child. It would be nice for Nicky to have a little brother or sister.'

Listening to him was like refined torture, Leah thought bleakly. She *would* like children some day. It was her cherished hope that she would meet the 'right man' and settle down to have the family life she'd craved during her own chaotic childhood. Now Marco was dangling that dream in front of her, but instead of a pot of gold at the end of the rainbow, it was an empty bucket.

She eased her hand out of his. 'What about affairs?'

He frowned. 'I am fairly liberal-minded, but not about infidelity. You will be mine exclusively.'

His eyes glittered, and Leah despised herself for feeling thrilled that he sounded so very Italian and so very possessive.

'I meant you. Would you have mistresses? Presumably you'd be discreet, so that the paparazzi and your company's shareholders didn't find out?'

'You have my word that I'll be a faithful husband. I will commit fully to you and Nicky and the children I hope we'll create between us.' He leaned back in his chair and gave one of his sexy smiles that ripped the breath from her lungs. 'Seriously, *cara*,' he murmured in a softly teasing voice that, if it hadn't already been broken, would have shattered her heart into a thousand pieces. 'I'm a good catch. Say yes and we can spend the afternoon in bed.' His eyes gleamed like molten silver. 'I've missed you, beauty.'

It was terrible how tempted she was. Marco was offering her everything she'd ever wanted except for one thing. He did not love her.

'I need to think about it.' The chair legs scraped over the stone floor as she jerked to her feet. 'It's a big decision and I need time to consider my options.'

He stood up and walked around the table. She thought she sensed a new tension in him, but maybe it was her imagination. It would be so easy to fall into his arms, his bed, his charmed life in Capri that could be her life too. But there would always be something missing. His heart would never be hers.

He was so close that she could smell his evocative male scent: spicy cologne mixed with something that was uniquely *him*. She held out her hand as if to ward him off when he lowered his head. If he kissed her she would be lost.

'I need to be sure I make the right decision—for you, me and Nicky.'

Something flickered in his eyes, but he dropped his arm and did not try to stop her when she hurried out of the summerhouse.

Leah walked through the gardens and sat on a bench in a secluded corner, but she did not notice the colourful flowers or hear the birdsong. Her heart was thumping as if she'd run a marathon and her breath came in short gasps.

Since her argument with Marco four days ago she had longed for them to make up. But now she realised that they could never go back to their old relationship. Either she agreed to their marriage being permanent or she would have to leave. Both choices would break her heart.

Torn by indecision, she eventually returned to the villa and found her feet drawn to Marco's study. The faint tang of his aftershave hung in the air and her stomach muscles contracted. She stood by the window, which overlooked the pool, and watched him with Benedetta and the children. The sound of childish voices and laughter taunted her as she imagined having a family of her own—Nicky playing with his younger siblings, Marco cradling their newborn baby in his arms. The dream was hers to take, and she ached with longing.

But what would happen if the chemistry fizzled out and he no longer desired her?

Would she become bitter and resentful, knowing that he would never love her as she loved him?

She had spent her life feeling second-best to her mum's alcohol addiction. Her mum loved her, but she loved alcohol more.

Choking back a sob, she turned away from the window. Her gaze fell on the photo of Marco's first wife that he kept on his desk. Karin had been so beautiful. Her ghost was everywhere in the villa, and the many pictures of her were a constant reminder to Leah of everything *she* lacked.

The designer dresses she wore to parties gave her a veneer of gloss and sophistication, but she was just an ordinary woman who had foolishly fallen in love with an extraordinarily handsome and attractive man. She had tried once or twice to ask Marco about Karin, but he had retreated behind barriers that Leah understood now she would never breach.

She sagged against the desk, tears filling her eyes at the thought of saying goodbye to him and to Nicky. Marco had been right when he'd guessed that she had formed a strong bond with his son.

Glancing out of the window again, she saw Nicky playing happily with his father. In a few months he would probably have forgotten her. The kindest thing to do was to leave now, with no emotional goodbyes and no risk of Marco persuading her to stay, Leah thought as she hurried up to her room.

It did not take her long to shove a few clothes into her holdall and grab her passport. Writing a note to Marco took longer, but she kept it brief.

When she went back downstairs, the maid was taking delivery of a huge bouquet of roses. Dozens of exquisite pink and white blooms tied with pink ribbon. Perhaps Marco had ordered them for his aunt's birthday tomorrow.

The florist's van was parked outside, and Leah stepped out of the house and spoke to the driver.

'Si, signora,' he said, not hiding his curiosity. 'I can take you to the ferry port.'

Marco had left the children watching a film in the TV room. They were worn out after an afternoon in the pool. His heart had swelled as he'd watched Nicky playing and heard him chattering and laughing with his cousins. The change in his son was incredible, and it was mostly down to Leah.

He strolled across the entrance hall and discovered the bouquet of flowers he'd ordered for her on the table. His mouth curved upwards as he imagined her pleasure when he presented her with the roses. Pleasing Leah and making her happy was surprisingly addictive.

Picking up the bouquet, he ran upstairs and opened the door to her room, surprised to feel his heart thumping. She had asked for time to consider his suggestion that they tear up the contract which stated they would divorce after a year. He'd given her a couple of hours. Surely she would have an answer for him by now?

In truth, he'd hoped for a more enthusiastic response

from her when he'd told her his idea during lunch. He had known she wouldn't be impressed if he mentioned the wealthy lifestyle that would be hers if she remained as his wife. Leah was the most unmaterialistic person he'd ever met. Instead he'd played his ace—her love for Nicky.

Her room was empty. He had already checked the living rooms downstairs—the only place left to look for her was his bedroom. Was she waiting for him to make love to her there?

Desire jack-knifed through him as he visualised her naked body reflected in the mirror above the bed. He pushed open the connecting door and his anticipation turned to disappointment when he saw she wasn't there.

The ominous sight of a folded piece of paper made his stomach swoop. Jaw tense, he strode across the room and snatched it up from the dressing table. Leah's neat handwriting covered three lines on the paper.

Three goddamned lines—that was all he was worth!

His temper simmered, but in the pit of his stomach he felt sick with dread as he read the note.

Marco,
I appreciate your offer, but your reason for making our marriage permanent is not good enough for me to agree.
It's best if I go now, before Nicky becomes too attached to me.
Be happy.
Leah

The words 'be happy' mocked him. How the hell was he supposed to *be happy* when the only person other than his son who made him happier than he'd been in his entire life had disappeared, leaving behind a pithy note that might as well have been a coded message for all that he understood it.

Dio, he had asked Leah to be his wife for ever and he'd promised her his fidelity. What more did she want? If those things were not enough to persuade her to stay married to him…he would have to set her free.

He sank down onto the edge of the bed, feeling the sickness in his gut intensifying to a raw agony that he'd felt only once before.

He would never forget the day he'd gone to the house in Rome that he'd bought for Karin—on top of the multi-million-pound divorce settlement he'd agreed to give her. He hadn't resented paying for it, so that Nicky would have comfort and security, but Karin had gone. She had disappeared with his baby.

Initially Marco had been terrified that they'd been kidnapped. But the police had confirmed that Karin had emptied her bank account, and a neighbour had stated that she'd told him she was moving abroad.

Losing contact with his son had felt like a bereavement, and there had been times when his grief had been overwhelming. His gutted feeling now, finding Leah had gone, was an inexplicable emotional response. He didn't believe in romantic fantasy, and he had no idea why he felt as though his heart had been ripped out of his chest.

A shattering idea pushed into Marco's mind and crystallised into a certainty that stunned him. There was only one real reason why he wanted Leah to be his wife. But instead of being honest with her he'd asked her to stay in their marriage for Nicky.

The truth was that he wanted so much more. He groaned and pressed his hand against his breastbone, where the pain was savage.

CHAPTER THIRTEEN

THE MIST WAS a thick blanket over Bodmin Moor, and the rain which had been fairly light when Leah had left the village lashed her face, driven by a vicious wind that felt no pity for anyone unwise enough to walk out on the moors without a coat. She had not taken account of the autumn storms that blew in off the sea around the Cornish coast.

When she had boarded a plane bound for the UK a week ago it had been warm and sunny in Naples. Now Leah doubted she would ever feel warm again. Or that the sun would ever shine.

The sullen sky reflected her mood as she bowed her head against the relentless wind and huddled into the woollen wrap that the landlady at the Sailor's Arms had lent her.

'Be careful up on the moor,' she'd warned. 'It's easy to lose your way.'

Nancarrow Hall rose out of the mist, grim and forbidding. *Like its owner*, Leah thought. At least that had been her first opinion of Marco. But that had been before she'd realised that he'd buried his heart with his first wife.

Grief took a terrible toll. Look at her mum after Sammy had died.

If anything good had come from her crazy decision to force Marco into marriage, it was the fact that Tori was stronger and more positive than Leah had ever known her to be. She did not suppose that her mother was completely free from her reliance on alcohol. There was no magic pill that would cure that kind of dependency. But ongoing therapy was helping Tori come to terms with the past.

Leah now understood the desperation to escape the pain of a broken heart. For the first two days after she'd arrived in England she'd shut herself in her flat, crawled under the duvet and cried a river of tears. She understood the temptation to anaesthetise agony with drink or drugs. But she hadn't. She'd discovered a steeliness in herself that would not allow her to wallow in self-pity or rush back to Capri and accept Marco's flawed idea of marriage.

She deserved to be loved. And she had to believe that one day she'd meet someone who would give her his heart.

If only she could rescue her own bruised heart from a life sentence as Marco De Valle's prisoner…

She brushed her hand over her wet face and told herself it was rain, not tears, running down her cheeks. Pulling the wrap tighter around her, she began to walk back towards the village. The sound of footsteps behind her made her glance over her shoulder, and her heart stopped as a figure strode out of the mist.

'*Madre di Dio!*'

Marco's expression was thunderous as he scowled at her, his eyes gleaming like tensile steel.

'Why are you standing out in the rain looking like a waif and stray from a historical melodrama? Do you see yourself as Cathy and me as Heathcliff?' he asked sardonically. 'Perhaps you have come to haunt me?' His mouth tugged into a crooked smile that did not warm his cold, cold eyes and he touched his scarred face. 'God knows I'm an ugly enough brute to play Heathcliff.'

'You are not a brute—and you are certainly not ugly,' Leah snapped.

She was still reeling from his materialising in front of her when she'd believed she would never see him again. His mockery had stirred her temper. She felt alive for the first time since she'd left Villa Rosa—but that was the effect Marco had on her, she thought bleakly.

'It's not *me* who haunts you,' she said in a low voice.

'What does that mean?'

She shook her head. 'What are you doing here? Is Nicky with you?'

'He has stayed in Capri with my aunt. As to why I am here...' Marco shrugged. 'You are in Cornwall so of course I followed you.' While Leah was still trying to assimilate this astounding statement, he murmured, 'I have just come back to the house after visiting your mother at The Haven.'

'What? How did you know...?'

'I first looked for you at your flat in London. Obviously you were not there. But your neighbour—Gloria, I think she said her name was—told me that your mother was having treatment at a private clinic in Cornwall. You told me your mother has an alcohol dependency, and my housekeeper remembered that you had asked her for directions to The Haven earlier in the summer.'

'Quite the sleuth, aren't you?' Leah muttered.

'I was surprised that you hadn't told your mother you are married to me. She offered us her congratulations, by the way.'

She gasped. 'You had no right to tell her. I didn't want Mum to know that I'd had to marry a stranger so that I could claim my inheritance and pay for her treatment.'

'I assured her that we had married for conventional reasons.'

'Wanting me to be a mother to your son is not a conventional reason—nor a good enough reason for us to stay married.' Leah couldn't disguise the raw emotion in her voice.

Marco stared at her. 'Why did you rush away like that, without a word?'

'Didn't you see my note?'

He swore and shoved his wet hair off his brow. It was only then that Leah realised how heavy the rain had become. Marco's jacket was plastered to his body, and her curls were flattened against her head.

'What is the only reason you would agree to stay married to me?' he asked.

'The fact that you don't know says everything,' she said thickly.

'I think I do know. You have fallen in love with me—haven't you, *cara?*'

Heat scorched her face. 'I don't have to stand here and listen to you. It's over between us.' She swung away from him, and would have tripped on a grass tussock had his arm not shot out to steady her.

'Like hell it is,' he growled. 'You are my wife and I want you back.'

'Why?' Leah tried to pull her arm free, but he tightened his grasp. 'You don't want me!' she cried.

'*This* is what I want, beauty.'

He hauled her against him, one hand in her hair, the other caressing her jaw as he bent his head and covered her mouth with his own. He kissed her with a barely controlled passion that fired Leah's blood and made her heart sing. If this was the last time that she was to be in his arms she wanted to leave her mark on him, so that every time he kissed another woman he would remember *her* mouth softening beneath his and would taste *her* on his lips.

She tipped her head back to allow him better access to her mouth and wound her arms around his neck. He groaned and pulled her hard against him, so that her breasts were crushed against his chest and she could feel his powerful thigh muscles through the thin skirt that was clinging to her legs.

His hand on her jaw gentled and he stroked his finger down her cheek, brushing away the raindrops and the tears.

'This is what I want, Leah,' he said roughly, when he lifted his head at last. He stared down at her, his eyes glittering beneath heavy lids. 'Your fire, your beauty, your unique mix of innocence and sensuality that drives me crazy with wanting you. *Always.*'

'But what you are offering is not enough for me.' She stepped away from him and it was the hardest thing she had ever done. 'You have my heart, Marco.' She could no longer deny her love. 'But I don't have yours because it belongs to your first wife. I know you are still in love with Karin.'

He jerked his head back as if she'd slapped him. 'I didn't love her. I *hated* her.'

'Don't lie.' She dashed her hand over her eyes. 'You keep pictures of her in every room at your house in Capri. She was so beautiful... I can't compete, but I won't be an afterthought in your life, always knowing I'm second-best. I can never replace Karin.'

'No, you damn well *can't*!'

Marco was staring at her, and the dangerous look in his eyes made Leah shrink from him.

He frowned and held out his hand. 'Come,' he said tersely. 'Before we both drown.'

She put her hand in his because she did not have the willpower to walk away from him. She was weak, she told herself as he led her through the gate on the boundary of Nancarrow Hall and across the garden.

As they neared the house she hesitated. 'I can't see your mother and stepfather looking like this.'

'They're not here. They're staying in Northumberland to be near James and Davina and the baby, when it arrives in a few months.' He gave her a wry look. 'My brother was always my mother's favoured son. The house has been shut up since they left and the central heating has packed up,' he explained when they entered the chilly sitting room.

The embers of a fire were in the grate and he rebuilt it with logs and kindling. He struck a match, and soon yellow flames were dancing.

Leah drew nearer to the fire while Marco disappeared. He returned minutes later, wearing dry clothes, and handed her a towel and one of his shirts.

'Get out of your wet things and maybe you won't look so goddamned fragile,' he muttered, in a rough tone that curled around her foolish heart.

Ignoring his sardonic look, she stepped behind a big winged armchair while she stripped off her sodden skirt and top and put on his shirt, fastening the buttons. When she returned to the fire he had brought a tray with steaming cups of coffee. She wrapped her cold hands around the warm mug and stared at the flames, conscious of the erratic thud of her heart.

Marco did not join her on the sofa. Instead he leaned against the stone fireplace. He looked devastatingly handsome in faded jeans and a grey wool sweater, his damp hair curling at his nape. Leah stared at his bare feet and wondered how she was ever going to get over him.

'I met Karin soon after my uncle died,' he said sombrely. 'Federico had been like father to me and I missed him badly. Karin was beautiful, and vivacious, and I was lonely.' He gave a harsh laugh. 'It's strange how you can have a full social life and plenty of friends but still feel alone.'

Leah nodded but did not speak, afraid to interrupt Marco now that he was finally opening up.

When it's too late, she thought, biting her lip.

'Soon after we started our affair Karin told me she was pregnant. I wanted my child so I married her. But cracks had already appeared in our relationship,' he said.

Leah gave him a startled look.

'De Valle Caffè was going through a difficult period and I often worked eighteen-hour days. Karin was bored, and after Nicky was born she left him with the nanny much of the time while she went out with her friends.'

He paused to stoke the fire until it blazed.

'She had ambitions to be an actress, and when Nicky was a few months old she started sleeping with a film producer. We decided to divorce, and I agreed to her extortionate settlement in return for shared custody of our son. A week after I'd paid her the money she disappeared and took Nicky with her.'

His jaw clenched.

'I employed private detectives to find her. The trail led to Mexico, where her lover came from, but they were never found. I'd given up hope of seeing my son again when Karin contacted me four years later and said I could visit Nicky.'

Leah put her coffee cup down and waited tensely for Marco to continue.

'They were living on a rundown ranch,' he said. 'Her lover had turned out not to be a hotshot film producer after all, and Karin had spent all her divorce settlement. She told me that I could have custody of Nicky, and take him to live in Italy, but only if I paid her ten million dollars.'

He grimaced when Leah gasped.

'I was incensed that Karin was prepared to sell Nicky to me.' Marco stared at the fire and when he spoke again his voice was strained. 'I lost my temper and told her I was going to fight her for custody of my son and she could rot in hell. I refused to give her any more money.'

He raked his hand through his hair.

'I went outside and walked around the ranch while I tried to bring my temper under control. When I returned to the house I discovered that Karin had driven away with Nicky. I couldn't bear to lose him again. I jumped into my car, praying I would be able to catch up with her so we could have a reasonable discussion about Nicky's future.'

A haunted look crossed his face.

'I drove round a sharp bend and saw Karin's car on its roof at the side of the road. She must have taken the corner too fast. There was a strong smell of fuel...' He swallowed. 'All I could think of was getting Nicky out of the car before it caught fire. I didn't make it back in time for Karin.'

'Marco!' Leah jumped up and went over to him, her soft heart aching at the agony in his eyes. 'You were not to blame.'

'I know—but I didn't know it then. It was only later that an inquest confirmed that Karin had died on impact. I hated Karin for depriving me of my son, but she was Nicky's mother and I still wish I'd been able to save her.'

Leah touched the scar on his cheek. 'You risked your life to save Nicky from that burning car.'

He captured her hand and linked his fingers through hers. 'I keep those pictures of Karin to show Nicky. I tell him that his mother was wonderful and she loved him. He must never know that she was willing to give him up for money.'

His eyes narrowed and Leah attempted to ease her hand out of his.

'I had no intention of marrying a second time. Yes, I wanted to take you to bed, but I had no need of a wife—especially one who seemed as money-orientated as my ex.'

'No wonder you were so furious when I proposed a marriage deal,' Leah mumbled.

'But I quickly realised that you are kind and caring, and you established a connection with my son that I had been unable to do.'

'You were right when you guessed that I love Nicky,' she said in a choked voice. 'But even for him I can't accept a loveless marriage.'

'I didn't want to fall in love with you.'

Marco slid his hand beneath her chin and gently forced her to look at him. The expression blazing in his eyes robbed her of her breath.

'I don't have much experience of love,' he said huskily.

Leah's heart shattered into a thousand pieces.

'Even when I suggested making our marriage permanent I was arrogant enough to believe that you were no threat to my barren heart. But then you left.'

'I had to,' she whispered. 'You offered me everything except the one thing I truly wanted. Living with you, knowing that you would never love me, seemed worse than leaving and hoping that I'd get over you.' Her mouth crumpled.

'Ah, Leah, my love,' Marco said quietly. 'When I read your note I realised what a fool I had been. I'd kidded myself that I was in control of my feelings, but you had gone, and the truth hit me. I wanted you to be my wife for ever because I will love you for eternity.'

He brushed away her tears with fingers that shook, and Leah's heart turned over when she saw that his eyelashes were damp.

'You have my heart and my soul, *tesoro mia*. All I ask

in return is that you promise to love me and stay with me for the rest of time.'

'I will,' she said simply.

'Why are you crying, *amore*? I intend to spend every day of my life making you happy.'

'I *am* happy. But I'm scared this won't last.'

Marco nodded, and there was a wealth of understanding in his tender expression. 'It will. We have it all, my angel. Passion, friendship, trust and love. Always love.'

He drew her down onto the rug and they undressed each other with trembling hands. When he took possession of her mouth there was such beauty and promise in his kiss that the last of Leah's doubts disappeared. And when he made love to her it felt new and wondrous, because there was honesty in every caress and love beyond measure.

'*Tu sei la mia amata rosa,*' Marco whispered as he held her against his heart. 'You are my beloved rose. *Ti amo.*'

EPILOGUE

'IT WAS A lovely christening,' Leah said as she climbed out of the helicopter and Marco slid his arm around her waist, walking with her across the garden at Villa Rosa. 'James and Davina looked so proud of baby Sophie—and your mother is obviously smitten with her new granddaughter.'

Marco nodded. 'And Nicky seemed to enjoy spending time with his English relatives. It was James's idea to have the baby christened in Nancarrow Hall's chapel.' He looked down at Leah and his tender smile stole her breath. 'I'm glad we went to Cornwall to meet the newest addition to the family, but it's good to be home.'

Home. It had a wonderful sound, Leah thought as they strolled into the villa. It was early summer and the roses around the front door were starting to open, filling the warm air with their exquisite perfume.

'*Papà*, you promised we could go swimming!' Nicky ran up to his father, his big brown eyes shining. 'And Mamma too.' The little boy grinned at Leah. 'Will my baby brother like swimming when he's born?'

'I'm sure he will,' she said softly. 'When he's big enough you will be able to teach him.'

'Cool. He can have my armbands, because I don't need them any more.' Nicky tore up the stairs and paused to hang over the bannister. 'I'm going to get my swim-shorts. Hurry *up*, Mamma and *Papà*.'

'I don't know where our eldest son gets his energy from,' Marco murmured.

'Our younger son is pretty energetic too.' Leah captured her husband's hand and held it against the swell of her stomach. 'Can you feel him moving?'

Marco's features softened as he spread his fingers over her bump and the baby kicked. They both smiled at this sign of the new life they had created.

Tesoro...' he said huskily, before claiming her mouth in a lingering kiss. 'In a couple of months we will be a family of four.'

'I can't wait for Matteo to arrive.'

'Have I told you how happy you make me?'

'Many times.' She linked her arms around Marco's neck as he scooped her up and held her against his chest, as though she and the child that she carried were infinitely precious. 'You make me the happiest woman in the world. I love you.'

His grey eyes gleamed. 'And I love you.'

* * * * *

MILLS & BOON

Coming next month

ITALY'S MOST SCANDALOUS VIRGIN
Carol Marinelli

Dante's want for her was perpetual, a lit fuse he was constantly stamping out, but it was getting harder and harder to keep it up. His breathing was ragged; there was a shift in the air and he desperately fought to throw petrol on the row, for his resistance was fast fading. 'What did you think, Mia, that we were going to walk into the church together? A family united? Don't make me laugh...'

No one was laughing.

'Take your tea and go to bed.' Dante dismissed her with an angry wave of his hand, but even as he did so he halted, for it was not his place to send her to bed. 'I didn't mean that. Do what you will. I will leave.'

'It's fine. I'm going up.' She retrieved the tray.

'We leave tomorrow at eleven,' he said again as they headed through to the entrance.

'Yes.'

She turned then and gave him a tight smile, and saw his black eyes meet hers, and there was that look again between them, the one they had shared at the dining table. It was a look that she dared not decipher.

His lips, which were usually plump and red, the only splash of colour in his black and white features, were for once pale. There was a muscle leaping in his cheek, and she was almost sure it was pure contempt, except her body was misreading it as something else.

She had always been aware of his potent sexuality, but now Mia was suddenly aware of her own.

Conscious that she was naked beneath the gown, her breasts felt full and heavy, aware of the lust that danced inappropriately in the air between them. The prison gates were parting further and she was terrified to step out. 'Goodnight,' she croaked, and climbed the stairs, almost tipping the tray and only able to breathe when she heard the door slam.

Tea forgotten, she lay on the bed, frantic and unsettled. So much for the Ice Queen! She was burning for him in a way she had never known until she'd met Dante.

Mia had thought for a long time that there was something wrong with her, something missing in her make-up, for she'd had little to no interest in sex. Even back at school she would listen in on her peers, quietly bemused by their obsessive talking about boys and the things they did that to Mia sounded filthy. Her mother's awkward talk about the facts of life had left Mia revolted. The *fact of Mia's life*: it was something she didn't want! There was no reason she could find. There had been no trauma, nothing she could pin it to. Just for her, those feelings simply did not exist. Mia had tried to ignite the absent fire and had been on a couple of dates, but had found she couldn't even tolerate kisses, and tongues positively revolted her. She couldn't bear to consider anything else.

And while this marriage had given her a unique chance to heal from the appalling disaster that had befallen her family, the deeper truth was that it had given her a chance to hide from something she perhaps ought to address.

A no-sex marriage had felt like a blessing when she and Rafael had agreed to it.

Yet the ink had barely dried on the contract when she had found out that though those feelings might be buried deep, they were there after all.

Mia had been just a few days into the pretend position of Rafael's PA, and the carefully engineered rumours had just started to fly, when Dante Romano had walked in. A mere moment with him had helped her understand all she had been missing, for with just a look she found herself reacting in a way she never had before.

His dark eyes had transfixed her, the deep growl of his voice had elicited a shiver low in her stomach, and even his scent, as it reached her, went straight to form a perfect memory. When Dante had asked who she was, his voice and his presence had alerted, startled and awoken her. So much so that she had half expected him to snap his fingers like a genie right before her scalding face.

Three wishes?
You.
You.
You.

Continue reading
ITALY'S MOST SCANDALOUS VIRGIN
Carol Marinelli

Available next month
www.millsandboon.co.uk

COMING SOON!

We really hope you enjoyed reading this book.
If you're looking for more romance, be sure to
head to the shops when new books are
available on

Thursday 9th July

To see which titles are coming soon, please visit

millsandboon.co.uk/nextmonth

MILLS & BOON

LET'S TALK
Romance

For exclusive extracts, competitions
and special offers, find us online:

 facebook.com/millsandboon

 @MillsandBoon

@MillsandBoonUK

Get in touch on 01413 063232

For all the latest titles coming soon, visit
millsandboon.co.uk/nextmonth

JOIN US ON SOCIAL MEDIA!

Stay up to date with our latest releases, author
news and gossip, special offers and discounts, and
all the behind-the-scenes action
from Mills & Boon...

 millsandboon

 millsandboonuk

 millsandboon

It might just be true love...

MILLS & BOON
HEROES
At Your Service

Experience all the excitement of a gripping thriller, with an intense romance at its heart. Resourceful, true-to-life women and strong, fearless men face danger and desire - a killer combination!

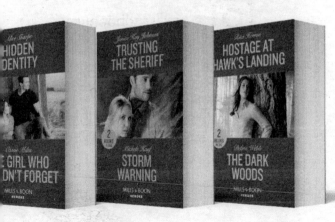

Eight Heroes stories published every month, find them all at:

millsandboon.co.uk

MILLS & BOON

Desire

Indulge in secrets and scandal, intense drama and plenty of sizzling hot action with powerful and passionate heroes who have it all: wealth, status, good looks… everything but the right woman.